CN01507007

About the Author

Gill was born in Reading but moved to Fareham where she now lives.

Having always been a 'reader', she particularly enjoyed stories with dark themes. After joining a creative writing group in 2001 she began writing short stories, most of which reflected the 'dark theme leaning'. She was encouraged when she was lucky enough to win some writing competitions and have stories appear in Writers magazines.

She based one of her short stories on a childhood memory. Whilst lying awake at night in her parents' house, she used to wonder and worry about the weird sounds she often heard through her bedroom window. She believed they were the plaintive voices of children that were lost and crying for their parents. Later she realised it was just the wailing of the foxes that lived at the bottom of the garden.

This memory proved a base for a tale, but the story took on a life of its own and propagated. The characters needed to tell their story and a novel called 'Diamonds are for Never', the first of a trilogy, was born. It outlines Reading police's efforts to eradicate paedophiles from civilised society. 'Rubies on the Moon' is the final book in the trilogy.

Books in the series:

Diamond are for Never
Opals in the Sky
Rubies on the Moon

Rubies
ON THE
Moon

Gill Wallbanks

Copyright © 2020 Gill Wallbanks

Gill Wallbanks has asserted her right under the Copyright, Designs and Patents Act, 1988 to be identified as the author of this work.

This book is sold subject to the condition that it shall not, by way of trade or otherwise, be lent, resold, hired out, or otherwise circulated without the publisher's prior consent in any form of binding, cover other than that in which it is published and without similar condition including this condition being imposed on the subject purchaser.

All the characters in this publication are fictional and any resemblance to real persons, living or dead is purely coincidental.

ISBN 979-8-6348539-4-9

Book design by The Art of Communication   www.book-design.co.uk
First published in the UK 2020

Dedication

Brian, where ever you are.

Acknowledgements

My thanks to June Hampson who encouraged my interest in writing, and taught me the skills of putting pen to paper. Thanks also to the members of the Café Writers Society and The Porchester Writers Circle for their help and support during the writing of this book.

I particularly want to acknowledge Christine Hammacott of the Art of Communication for her great design suggestions for the covers and layout. Also express my thanks for her helpful suggestions to my questions, therefore allowing me to achieve my aims of publishing my trilogy of books.

Last but not least, my husband Bob for often having to finish cooking dinner because I needed to write a few more lines.

Prologue

I slice the knife across her throat. She stands for a few seconds, her arms outstretching like a ballerina's, her legs then give way and she elegantly collapses, slowly dropping to the floor. Before the blood can spurt, I lean over and press a compress over the wound. Experience has shown that this calms the surge and subsequently the blood seeps out in manageable flowing droplets. I straighten up and watch as the eyes, wide with surprise that conveniently allows me to see the pupils expand as death claims her. It only took a minute and twelve seconds.

Despite the cold rain spluttering in my face as the wind swirls and buffets all in its way, I don't allow the foul weather to spoil my enjoyment. I gaze at her, stretched out so stylishly across the damp ground, unaware of the storm; looking serene, arms extended as though crucified; legs crossed, resembling a virgin refusing to give in to a lover's plea for satisfaction. Her cobalt eyes are now half-open, perhaps surprised at what has happened. Maybe shock that I, her best friend, her confidant, her gentle lover, had done what I had done. She had trusted me completely and had come to me without question or disquiet. Perhaps my normal garb had reassured her…foolish girl!

The early autumn storm is slowly clearing. The suffocating atmosphere of the day now replaced by a fresh ambience. I breathe in deeply. The smell of freshly fallen leaves and wet grass is pleasant, reminding me of my childhood, when I remembered summers and early autumns as always being sunny and warm. If it had rained or been chilly, then convenient memories and time have wiped that unpleasantness away.

An owl is hooting his lonesome protest at the weather, or maybe disappointment because the squall has forced his potential supper to run for cover. His noisy remonstration, easily heard above the wind, would have ensured that the sharp ears belonging to his prospective meal had made that tiny delectation wary and nervous, and consequently tucked itself safely away in its cosy den.

I return my thoughts to my treasure. I savour the dark red line, almost black in the half-light, across her throat; as decorative as a delicate necklace of dark rubies strung closely together. I take a deep breath, and I bend and gently touch the cut to see if it has stopped weeping. In this new position, I notice her lips are slightly parted as though waiting for my kiss; and know her words of protest never emerged; instead they'd slipped noiselessly through that neat gash of her slender throat.

You see, I keep my weapon lethally sharp, as though honed to perfection in the roaring fires of the underworld. It's pragmatic, because a neat cut will kill more efficiently and with less mess than a clumsy slash, and that halts any noisy, annoying screams. It's not that I'm sadistic, on the contrary, after all, a razor-sharp edged weapon prevents any unnecessary suffering on their part. It's almost instantaneous for them. I don't call them victims, rather my customers or my clients. Yes, client, umm, sounds… professional.

I open my holdall and take out my plastic apron and gloves. I'm efficient and leave nothing to chance,

This is my third prize, well in this area, not counting the other clients in my previous neighbourhood, and the original patrons from my beloved hometown. It's all so exciting, and

2

I've got another customer…oops, sorry…client, lined up in the pipeline.

I don't think of them as prey either, more a trophy. Yes, that's an apt description. I'm so clever with words.

Bending closer, I stroke her face. Her skin's already cold, but not due to death, her life left her only a few moments ago, but the sudden late summer squall had been unseasonably cold, and the lashing rain cooled her quickly. I cut a lock of her mousy hair and place it in the pocket on the side of my wallet. It will join the other three curls in my secret place. I ease open her clenched hand, the left one, and my darling, proficient weapon takes less than three minutes to cut it away. I place my trophy in a thick plastic bag, carefully wrapping it so that none of the blood touches even my plastic apron donned for hygiene and security. I push the prize into my large, specially designed pocket inside my coat. I do so love my organisational skills.

I pick up her body, so light, even her relaxed pose of death does not prove a problem, stand, and walk to the crypt. No hurry; no-one is around on a night such as this. The unexpected and inclement weather has helped. Easing open the unlocked door, I shuffle carefully in the dim light to the pre-opened tomb, placing her on top of the mouldering body. Two for one! Cut price burial! I pull back the heavy stone lid to reseal the coffin and excite myself trying to imagine if she was still alive, how she would feel with the light totally extinguished, and knowing she would lie in the infernal blackness forever.

I exit the crypt, my job done. Someone emerges from the shadows thrown by the swaying trees. She was probably watching my escapade. I knew she'd show up, impatient for pay-back for securing the 'client'. She grins. *God, I hate that look*.

"I've done my job," she smirks. "Now it's time for my reward."

I nod and walk away, calling over my shoulder so I do

not have to look at her for any length of time. "Soon." It's all I can bring myself to say to this evil person. I only suffer her because she has uses…for now!

A week later

Jason wasn't so sure of his position now. The man held his hand firmly so there was no chance of running away. It was cold, and he had only put on a thin jumper as it had been warm during the day, but now the goose bumps on his arm felt huge. Glancing up at the full moon, he thought the man in the moon was smirking and the boy was even more ill at ease.

He had come willingly, the promises of a new life being the great attraction. No more beatings from his father; no more school with the nuns pinching his arm when he couldn't read the difficult words in books. Although nine years old, the almost dormant habit of sucking his thumb took over. The comforting custom, knocked out of him years previously by painful clumps around the head or sharp kicks on the shins, always returned when stressed. Not that Jason understood that word or its meaning, but his subconscious did. Gradually the pain had won, and despite the great longing of a consoling thumb, he had publicly stopped the habit, although in the comfort and privacy of his bedroom, head under the bedcovers, he had satisfied his longing for some minute consolation in his life.

"You never mentioned you're leaving to anyone?" the man asked for the third time.

Jason shook his head, but the man needed verbal confirmation.

"Well?"

"No, sir. Promise. Never said nufffink to nobody."

"Good boy."

"Is it far now?" Jason was tired. It was late and his eyes felt heavy. He thought about his bed and wished he was snuggled up in it. His father rarely disturbed him in bed, too busy drinking the whisky.

"Here we are, my son. We're here."

He knocked on the old-fashioned door; it reminded Jason of a door you'd see in a horror film, although when opened quickly by a woman there was none of the creaking, squeaking or groaning that normally accompanied the film version. Jason didn't like the look of her. Long, straight hair, black as the raven's wing he'd found in the back garden, and dark eyes that bored a hole into his brain. His stomach turned and he knew he shouldn't have come.

"I don't like her," he whispered.

"You'll be fine, Jason. I'll look after you," the man lied.

PART 1
The Reunion

Chapter 1

Detective Constable Luke Steiner hurried over to talk to Police Constable Tom Carter. His colleague, DC Meena Mesbah, joined PC Simon Leadbetter, who had arrived first at the crime scene and had made the telephone call for assistance back to the police station. PC Leadbetter was standing next to the jogger who had discovered the body of a child. Their faces were an identical shade, the pasty white of a cheap envelope, clearly indicating someone about to faint.

DS Dan Blake, checking his team was making the necessary enquiries, turned back to contemplate the crime scene. With instant re-call, he visualised the details of what he had seen when he'd previously examined the area before the SOCOs with their cameras and equipment had politely but firmly asked him to step outside the crime scene tape so they could complete their work. Mulling over in his mind the things of possible lesser importance, he dismissed them for immediate consideration, but tucked them away to the back of his mind. He then stored away other facts he considered more pertinent in the filing cabinet situated at the front of his mind for retrieval and contemplation when he needed to analyse what he had seen. Carefully considering the circumstances, his eyes swept the scene, and he analysed what was missing, what was present, and would be germane to the investigation.

Digging his hands deep into his overcoat pockets, as his concentration deepened, two furrows appeared between his eyebrows. He knew his colleagues nicknamed this contemplation the 'Diamond Brain Coma' but they rarely interrupted his deliberations.

Patiently waiting until Dr MacDeath, the police's moniker for Dr Macfarlane, the police pathologist, finished his notes and examination before he felt able to enquire as to whether the doctor had formed any early conclusions. The pathologist's reply after three 'humphs' was curt, his pitying look at such ignorance clearly signalling that *obviously* he'd know more when he'd performed the post-mortem. The doctor, well known to Dan and very likeable despite his gruff manner, had a way of making any questioner sound idiotic. Dan, well used to the doctor's far from bedside manner, grinned as the man shuffled away in his cover-all.

Dan was keen to view the site again; he called it his 'one-time-look'. Although there were photographs to examine later, he always found that the image ironed onto his brain during his first examination was the most revealing.

The sight of the young boy's body discovered by the jogger was heart breaking. Dan was an experienced officer, but it didn't matter how many times he saw a murder victim, especially a child, it was difficult to stomach, and he felt sick that there were people in this world that could perform such gross acts. What made it worse was the fact that four years ago he'd been involved in a police investigation working to prevent a nationwide paedophile gang kidnapping children. Dan had no proof that today's events had anything to do with that episode, and normally he made no decisions unless he had solid facts, but for some bizarre reason, he had an awful premonition something very similarly nasty was going down again. The taste of déjà vu was bitter in his mouth for the second time in the course of an hour. Once again, he silently renewed his vow to himself to rid the world of nonces, by whatever means it took, by the letter of the law, or not, if that ensured success.

Dan had just returned after secondment to another force in the Midlands where he had worked for the past three years on an undercover investigation. Returning this very morning to his normal haunt at the Reading Police station where the welcome he'd received had cheered him immensely. Not realising until he had walked through the station door exactly how much he'd missed his Reading mates, and how pleased he was to return to his friends and colleagues. Recalling the morning greetings from his friends, he shook his head with disbelief. With the crime scene laid out so starkly before his eyes, he couldn't believe that things could change so quickly in a matter of hours.

"Bloody hell, by all that's holy, it's the ginger giant," exclaimed DC Luke Steiner. Dropping his half-eaten bacon butty onto his desk, he stood up, wiped his hands down his jeans, and thrust his right one forward in greeting. "How long have you been back? Thought you were up north on undercover."

"Hi, mate, long time, no see." DS Dan Blake pumped the hand that Luke offered. "Finished the operation two weeks ago. Good result. Just had annual leave and now I'm back ready to lead in my usual efficient manner that I'm sure you've all missed."

Luke chuckled. "Yeah, if you say so, boss. Anyway, it's good to have you back. You've come just at the right time. The late heat wave seems to have put the criminals off the track. Things haven't been so quiet for weeks. You can put up your size twelves and relax for a change."

Dan shrugged. "Well it's pouring cats and dogs at the moment so let's hope the dodgy weather doesn't alter things. My desk still?" he asked, hanging his lightweight coat over the back of the chair.

"Sure, why not. Adam, the mad Irishman's been using

it since the change round of rooms, but he's on a course in London, or so he says. Not back for a couple of days. Big skive if you ask me. Fancy a coffee?"

At that moment, a door opened, and a policewoman entered. Dan stared at the attractive vision.

"The beautiful DC Meena Mesbah. My God, you look more stunning every time I see you, or is that considered a sexual harassment type remark?" Before she could answer, he continued, "Did you miss me?" He grinned, his obvious admiration for the woman painting his face, but knowing his companion well enough to know she wouldn't be offended by his words.

Her dusky complexion coloured to a rose pink.

"Boss," she said. "Good to see you. Didn't know you were back. Anyway, I'm not offended by a compliment and…umm, no, didn't miss you at all." She returned his grin.

"Bet you did, and I know you lot couldn't manage without me. Right, coffee, let's get our priorities right. The kettle still playing up?" Dan said.

"Kettles are banned. Fire hazard. We've had a new drinks dispenser installed, but the drinks bear no resemblance whatsoever to the labels," said Meena. "As this is your first day back, I'll get you a coffee. After today, remember women's lib and equality, you'll be getting your own."

As she left the room, Dan admired her trim figure and turning to Luke, said,

"Ooh, things haven't changed then. She's as feisty as ever."

The phone rang and as Luke picked it up, he put his hand over the mouthpiece and whispered, "You're not kidding. She gets more aggressive every day. She calls it assertive but then a woman would." Putting the phone to his ear, he said, "DC Luke Steiner, how can I help?"

Dan watched as the mirth drained away from Luke's

face and his complexion turned ashen. The young copper nodded to Dan to pick up the extension phone, and his insides tightened with discomfort as the hysterical voice on the other end described his findings. Luke nodded as though the caller could see his affirmations and hastily scribbled the essential details as he listened.

"OK Simon, hang fire, we'll be there in about fifteen minutes. Are you with any other officers?" Luke was relieved to hear that the young officer was with PC Tom Carter, an older and very experienced police officer.

As the two officers simultaneously replaced the receivers, DC Mesbah walked in bearing three cups in a moulded polystyrene tray containing the promised coffee.

"Grab your coat, Meena, we'll gulp down the coffee as we go," said Dan. "I'm only back five minutes and the dire times are returning. I hope I'm not the bringer of bad luck. We've been here before."

"What's going down?" she asked, pulling a coat from the back of her chair. "Things have been really quiet these last couple of weeks."

"Young boy's body has been found in the Warren in Caversham," said Luke as he opened the door for Dan and Meena to pass through. "Apparently a jogger stopped for a pee off the road and found the body. Called 999. Tom Carter and Simon Leadbetter were the nearest patrol car and responded. Soon as they saw the situation, they called for backup. That was Simon calling in. Not experienced with this sort of situation, used to his comfy desk job. Sounded pretty hysterical."

"Doesn't matter how many times you see a child's body, even experience doesn't improve the situation and help your reaction. We taking your car, Luke?" said Dan.

"Yeah, over here."

As the three officers hurried to Luke's car situated in the corner of the car park, he updated Dan with the likelihood of the murdered lad's identity. A Jason Stone had been reported missing a few weeks ago. He had run away from home a few times, and they suspected this was the case because there had been no sign of him, and he would normally return after a few days. Now with a child's body turning up, and from Simon's brief description of the boy given over the phone, it appeared they had been terribly wrong about him eventually coming home.

"Whilst we're driving, you going to phone and update the guv?"

"Sure," said Dan. As he phoned his boss, the feeling of déjà vu again washed over him, and the wave was churning with impending unpleasantness.

DI Roy Cole, the Detective Inspector and the officer to whom Dan reported, was known affectionately as 'Coley' behind his back. A small man, foxy face, totally lacking a sense of humour and although the team might not like him, every police officer in his squad at the station had a great respect for his experience and knowledge. If a crook or an honest man crossed DI Cole and he glanced your way, the razor-sharp look had the metaphorical capability of slicing off your scalp. Hardened criminals were known to shake in their shoes if they irritated this Detective Inspector.

As they drove out of the police car park, the traffic in front of them was heavy, and Luke was obliged to switch on the siren in order for them to make reasonable progress until they reached the Caversham Bridge which spanned the river Thames. Across the bridge, due to restoration, the traffic was down to single lane either side, and consequently Luke, forced to weave through the traffic, had to manoeuvre down the narrow middle of the road. This initially attracted shaking fists and rude signs until the signallers realised it was a police car when they spotted the blue flashing light on the roof and heard the siren.

Once clear of the bridge, and swinging left and up the hill, the road to the area known as the Warren was clear, and it only took a few more minutes to arrive at the crime scene.

Drawing alongside the area of activity already taped off with blue and white crime-scene ribbon, a white van pulled up behind them and three people quickly exited the vehicle and hastily started to don white over suits.

"Jeez, that's never Dr MacDeath," said Dan, referring to the pathologist. "Thought he'd have retired long time since."

"He's not that old," reprimanded Meena, well known by her male colleagues for keeping them 'in check'.

"Luke, you talk to Tom. Meena, question Simon and the chap in shorts and tee shirt. Assume he's the jogger. I want to view the scene before the SOCOs get started and boot me out."

Dan wandered over to the crime scene, the cheerful arrival back to the police station and the friendly greetings already forgotten. Again, a feeling of being here before invaded his body, and he didn't like the feeling of impending disaster one bit.

Chapter 2

Lilly Taylor poured herself a large white wine. Glancing at her watch she realised it was only five o'clock; rather early for alcohol, but she shrugged her shoulders and downed the drink anyway, and promptly poured herself another one. She knew she was drinking too much lately, but couldn't seem to stop, and the thought hit her that maybe she wasn't just a heavy drinker now, but was on the verge of being an alcoholic, probably due to dire loneliness since she had broken up with John. It didn't take long to finish off the second glass either.

"Tomorrow, I'll cut down tomorrow," she promised herself. Placing the empty glass on her coffee table, she hurried to the bathroom for a shower. Catching a glance of herself in the hall mirror as she wandered past, she knew tomorrow wouldn't be too soon. Alcohol contains 'empty' calories and although Lilly was aware when made up and wearing tight-fitting, sexy clothes, many men found her attractive, the weight was slowly beginning to pile on. As she undressed to shower, she glanced down and consciously pulled in her stomach.

"OK, tomorrow I said," she emphasised to the long mirror on the bathroom door that showed a reflection of a young woman that was no more or less attractive than the one in the previous mirror. "Look, I'm tense. I just need a drink to steady myself. This date tonight is with a really dishy guy and I want to appear cool, in control."

As she showered and washed her hair, the face of her date floated through her mind. The guy was probably ten years older than her, but mid-thirties men were still considered attractive whereas she was twenty-six next week, and the only one in her gang of friends who wasn't attached in some way. Samantha and Jen were married, both with two kids; Di and Tania were living with blokes, and even Patsy who was gay, fat and promiscuous, currently had an adoring partner. Without being vain, Lilly knew she was just as attractive as her friends, but never seemed to meet the right person. So, she couldn't believe her luck the previous night when this total dish in the nightclub was downright attentive, and then slobbering all over her in the most delightful manner.

He was well over six feet, had thick black hair swept back in what Lilly considered a gangster style, and when he smiled his teeth were to die for. He bought her drinks all night and was an absolute gentleman when he escorted her home. Lilly couldn't remember the last time she'd been treated so courteously.

The blokes she normally met had definite rules. If they bought you one drink, that entitled them, as far as they were concerned, to a quick grope. If they bought you two, that definitely entitled them to a quick shag, and any more drinks meant oral sex all night.

She took extra time in blow-drying her hair and then applying her make-up. Knowing what to wear proved a problem as she didn't know his preference in how he liked his women to look. She didn't want to look tarty, but equally didn't want to look old fashioned. Hurrying in the kitchen to top up her glass again, she remembered the dress she'd bought about a month ago and had stuffed to the back of her jam-packed wardrobe because the right occasion to wear it hadn't materialised.

As she looked at herself in the black crepe number, she knew it was just right; short so it showed off her long legs which were her best feature, and although it had a round neck, it wasn't so low that her tits were hanging out. She had a feeling in her water he wasn't a tits man. The finished article looking back at her in the mirror was OK, and Lilly was thrilled with the result, and knew she'd be a hit.

Her doorbell rang at precisely seven o'clock and she grabbed the money he had given her to pay for the taxi that he'd previously arranged to come and pick her up. She'd never had a date where the guy had sent a taxi, and the feeling that this was the start of something exciting in her life spiralled through her body.

On opening the door, she was surprised the driver was a woman. Her shoulder-length, black hair made her face long and horse-like and Lilly didn't like the glitter in her eyes. If the driver had been a man and he'd worn that expression, Lilly wouldn't have got into his cab, but a woman, despite her looks, was safe.

"Taxi for Miss Taylor?" the woman smiled, and Lilly felt re-assured.

Lilly closed the door of her apartment and slipped her key into her purse, not realising this was the last time she would see her home.

Chapter 3

The taxi driver occasionally glanced surreptitiously into the mirror to watch her passenger. The woman, obviously excited about her date, twice checked her make-up in a small handbag mirror, and licked her lips constantly. Yvette Van Looy couldn't decide if she was trying to make them look sexy with moisture or was nervous. Despite strict orders not to engage her in conversation, she couldn't resist saying, "You look well turned out this evening. Going somewhere nice?"

The passenger's kohl-outlined eyes met Yvette's in the mirror as she answered.

"Hopefully. My date hasn't told me yet where we're going, but no doubt it will be somewhere pleasant."

"Hope you don't think I'm being rude or forward, but you look really smart and have obviously made an effort. I bet he must be really dishy."

"Yes, he is, I've got to admit."

Yvette couldn't refrain from adding, "Let me guess. The proverbial tall, dark and handsome prince." Knowing full well that she was correct, she almost sniggered as she added, "Bet I'm right."

The woman laughed, excitement and pleasure colouring her reply. "You're dead right. Must admit, I haven't been out with someone so attractive for ages." Taking a deep breath, she added. "And he has good manners. Not like a lot of the slobs you meet nowadays, just after one thing and treat you like dirt."

"That's really good to hear. Not that I'm young like you, but when I was your age young men mainly behaved themselves and treated you like a lady. Nowadays, all you read in the papers or hear on the news is about stabbings, hooligans attacking elderly people and such like. It's terrible; don't know what's happening in this day and age."

Yvette actually couldn't care less what the slobs did, and if they got rid of old dodderers that was fine by her, but tonight she felt mischievous and was determined to bring out the passenger. Knowing the woman's fate, she was purposely acting the friendly taxi driver. In fact, she and the passenger's prospective 'date' had gone to the Hades nightclub with the sole purpose of Yvette spotting a potential victim, although her accomplice liked to call them his 'clients'. It was the girls sitting on their own, a drink in front of them and none of the ugly, spotty youths asking them to dance that made the choice obvious. As she drove, she recalled the evening when she'd spotted Lilly.

Glancing around the room illuminated by only a glittering ceiling globe, she had identified her potential immediately. She was probably at least ten years older than the average age of the female audience. She was smoking, frequently sipping her wine, and looking around the room in desperation for some male to ask her to dance or at least engage her in some chat-up type conversation. Yvette's co-conspirator liked them good looking even if they were desperate for company and this punter looked acceptable. Although her blond hair was bleached, it had obviously been done professionally and the chin-length cut of her hair was fairly modern. Her skirt, pulled well above her knees, showed off her long, shapely legs and Yvette knew she would be very suitable. Digging Matthew, his 'name' for these occasions, with her elbow, she looked in the direction of the woman, tilting her head to show him whom she had recognised as being a perfect candidate. His gaze followed her eyes' direction, and she whispered to him,

"The blond in the short black skirt."

Matthew sorted her out from the medley of eager young females hanging round the edge of the small dance space.

"She with anyone? Maybe waiting for someone, she keeps looking round," he asked, not certain his quarry was available.

"Believe me; she's just waiting for some-one like you. I can tell them a mile off. That's what you use me for, isn't it, my eye for the lonely, desperate, and vulnerable."

"You going to talk to her first, sus the situation?"

"No need, believe me, she's bursting for a chat-up."

Matthew looked at Yvette, not liking what he saw either in appearance or in character, but he had to admit she had the knack of spotting potential game.

"Well, you've been very successful so far I've got to admit. Give it five more minutes and if no-one joins her, I'll wander on over. What's she drinking?"

"White wine as far as I can see."

"OK, you watch her while I get her a glass. I'll be back in a sec."

When Matthew returned with the bait, Yvette just grinned, lifted her shoulders as though to say, "I'm right again." Watching as he wandered slowly over, she could barely suppress laughing aloud as he leaned over the woman, offering her the wine. Her eyes had opened in amazement at her change of circumstances, and then opened even wider in disbelief when she clocked the handsome dish in front of her.

Lilly's voice snapped her back to the present

"We've come a long way. How much longer?"

Yvette swung the car into the path that led to the house.

"We're here now and don't be misled by the appearance of the house, it's fabulous inside. You're going to have a great time, I'm sure."

Before Lilly could ask the driver how she knew about the furnishings of the house, the front door opened and a smiling Matthew emerged, hurrying down the short garden path, and opening the door of the car.

"Lilly, darling, at last. Come on in, we've got a wonderful evening ahead of us." He kissed her hand and any misapprehension Lily might have felt floated away like gossamer feathers in a breeze.

Yvette smirked as the door closed, and the country garden descended into darkness. She turned the car around and drove away, satisfied she had done another good job, and that her reward would soon be forth coming.

Chapter 4

Despite darkness having fallen, the night was still warm as Dan, Luke and Meena walked away from the secured crime scene. The SOCOs had just left, and uniformed officers were spread out in pertinent positions to keep out the nosey press and public. Word of the murder of a young boy had spread like wildfire, and already the news hounds were gathering, albeit at a distance, but the clamour of their conversation carried, bouncing along to the officers' ears.

"OK, I don't want any word or comment to these guys," Dan told his two colleagues. "They've already been told they will have an official statement from DI Cole or DCI Jacobs tomorrow."

"Doesn't stop their persistence though," Meena said, casting a dirty look down the road which she would have like to believe would have the strength to silence their lack of sensitivity.

"No, afraid not," answered Dan. "Right, you two get back to the station. I'm off with DI Cole to Jason Stone's parents. Christ, this is not going to be easy. The awful thing is we can't say a hundred percent that it's Jason until they've identified the body. This part of the job is definitely the worst".

Luke and Meena nodded their agreement.

"I'll walk back with you. Coley's apparently parked

next to your car, Luke," said Dan, referring to his boss. "I'll feel happier if I get the facts in writing as soon as. When we've left the Stone's household I'll be back to the station. Luckily for us, our transport's parked away from the press."

"Yes, but we'll still have to run the gauntlet. There's no other way out of here," said Luke.

"Actually, there is," said Meena. "If we follow the road to the end, turn left, we'll miss the crowds. Then we drive through the new housing estate and eventually you get onto the road that passes by the end of the Warren."

"Ok, you can guide me as we go." Luke turned to Dan as Meena hurried ahead. "I had a date tonight. Second time I've blown her out. Guess romance is definitely out of the question."

"Policeman's lot, mate. Anyone I know?" At the shake of Luke's head, he added. "Heard you were still getting it on with that Rock Star, Flash something or other. What happened there?"

"You're kidding. Lowly policeman, famous star. She's forever jetting all over the world. Fat chance."

"Yeah, I know the feeling."

"What happened to you and the dark-haired girl you fancied. The one that found the nonce's body parts. Then..."

"Lucy." Dan shrugged, and didn't continue.

Luke suddenly recalled that during that episode Dan's best friend Alex had been killed, stepping in front of him to protect him as he was being attacked by a cornered paedophile. Dan had also been injured, but the real damage was the grief and guilt he'd suffered from his friend's death. Deciding it was prudent to change the subject, Luke said, "Looks like a long night. Wonder if the lovely Meena'd see her way clear to picking up three coffees from the All-nighter on the corner of Broad Street."

"Don't be stupid, mate, miracles don't happen that often. She's definitely getting too assertive."

"I heard that," Meena's voice echoed back to them.

"You're right, no chance."

The two men looked at each other and grinned, and Luke was pleased the uneasy moment had passed despite their forced banter.

As they left the scene, all three of them could feel the depression spreading over them like a heavy blanket.

Chapter 5

Her job done; Yvette hoped her associate, she didn't consider him a friend, would remember that it was now his turn to cater for *her* needs. He had been successful in the past, and she appreciated in his situation he had to be more cautious than her. Although his status gave him protection, it also made him vulnerable after all the publicity of priests, teachers and child minders and such-like taking advantage of their position and abusing children.

"Bloody news media have a lot to account for," she muttered. A likeness of her face had been plastered all over national newspapers and the television news programmes many months ago, but she wasn't concerned now, and she walked about quite freely. The public's memory was short, and the cops had other things on their minds for her face to be at the front of their thoughts.

She drove quickly home and on entering her flat, walked straight to the kitchen, and poured a large red wine from a bottle she'd previously uncorked, giving it time to breathe. Flopping into an armchair, feet up on a stool, she mulled over recent events and how the past had developed, and she was where she was now…in league with this useful but arrogant Matthew Nielson as he liked to call himself when on the prowl.

Recalling how her enjoyment had been fulfilled with the

previous 'prize' that he had presented to her, and how, after the 'award ceremony' as she called it, she'd felt ecstatic and high as she made her way home. Crossing Reading Bridge on the way to her flat, she had stopped, ignoring the double yellow lines, got out of the car and gazed down into the river. The full moon shone into the blackness, broken into infinite diamond shapes as the Thames flowed towards London, but she'd soon stopped thinking about the view, remembering how her mind had wandered into the contemplations that always took over whenever the opportunity arose. Deciding nothing was to be gained by mulling over past events, she'd driven home.

As she sipped her wine tonight, her meditations wandered down the same path. Four years ago, the damn cops had broken up Operation Hobbledehoy in which she'd been involved. The intention was to abduct kids on a nationwide basis, but an Irish bastard police officer called Adam Kennedy had infiltrated the organisation and along with Detective Bastard Sergeant Dan Blake had foiled the plan. She and the leader of the cell of which she was a member, Gerry Tomas, had escaped, but many others within the cell had been apprehended. Not that she cared a jot about them as long as they kept their mouths shut and she was safe.

Her mind continued to swirl with memories. Two years ago, she and Tomas had kidnapped three children as bait and had used them to capture Adam Kennedy. They had done this on their own initiative, both feeling painful retribution was necessary. Unfortunately, the top leaders of cells who had also avoided capture had warned everyone to lay low, but she and Tomas were determined to punish Kennedy for his part in the operation's downfall and therefore deprive them of the pleasure they had anticipated.

With the kids safely kidnapped and hidden in their cellar, she and Gerry had then been ordered to appear before a panel of three Cell Leaders who had chastised them for letting this undercover cop infiltrate and fool them before the operation. Without meaning to, she'd slipped up by mentioning the missing kids and the old fogies had guessed their plans. Stupid buggers had threatened them. Eventually their attitude had driven her to distraction and in a fit of uncontrollable anger she had slit their throats. She giggled to herself as she recalled their stunned faces as death came calling. They were old men and hadn't stood a chance when she had exploded with fury like a volcano erupting in full throttle.

She and Gerry Tomas had escaped but it meant they had to move on to yet another hiding place.

Her thoughts returned to the three little bastards. Unfortunately, one of the kids was smart and streetwise, and had attacked her with a knife, allowing the other two girls to escape. Then the fuzz had discovered Kennedy and so he too had escaped their planned retribution.

Things went from bad to worse and sometime later other members of the old gang discovered their new hiding place and had killed Gerry. She'd been lucky and had been out of the house at the time of their visit. She'd returned in time to see them entering the hideout and had fled. She was on her own now, not counting the stupid Nielson, but he was just a stop gap till she got herself organised and the good times returned.

She finished the wine, walked to the kitchen and topped up the glass again. Returning to her comfy armchair, she continued with her musings. Not that she cared a toss what had happened to Tomas, the fool had asked for whatever had happened to him.

Even now, she hadn't given up hope of some dire retribution against Blake and Kennedy. She was still determined to make Kennedy pay, and had plans how to do just that. Kennedy had two young girls, twins of about three or four…ideal for her needs. Yvette knew that the worse punishment for him would be if something happened to his children, and a plan was forming in her mind. Dan Blake had recently returned to the area and didn't appear to have any family so he would be punished directly. That would be equally enjoyable.

Having been cautious, head down for well over a year, she now felt herself safe. Previous associates not concerned about the murders of 'the three old gits', had pointed her in the direction of Matthew when she'd contacted them. Discussing plans together, they had reached a mutually beneficial decision. She would seek out women for his pleasure and he would seek out children for her. The operation was working out just fine, but she hadn't forgotten her promise to herself to take revenge on Adam Kennedy and Dan Blake.

The time for laying low was almost over, and her forming plans were about to fall into place. Meanwhile, that still didn't stop her getting enjoyment from the kids that Matthew so cleverly provided. When Matthew had outgrown his use, she'd drop him, put her plans into place, and make the two cops pay! There was still time.

She got unsteadily to her feet, deciding she might as well finish the wine. The good times were returning, she just knew!

Chapter 6

Dan glanced at the clock and was surprised to see it was nine thirty. He leaned back in his chair, hit the 'print' button on his computer, and waited for the hard copies to spew from the printer. He'd eventually got back to the station at eight fifteen. Depression spread over him as he recalled the awful hour he and the guv had spent at the Stone's house.

It had been a long, sad day. The SOCOs had finished their work, and the lad's body had been taken away for the post-mortem examination. The whole incident had thrown a miasma of dejection over the station, and the silence hanging over the room was like a black rain cloud on a depressing winter evening.

Glancing round the large room, Dan noticed Luke and Meena typing, presumably finishing up their reports. Normally a great deal of banter would be taking place, but no-one was talking. The large get-together in the incident room had been the same, no repartee or playful backstabbing. A child's murder didn't allow for that.

Dan grabbed the pages from the printer, stacked them neatly, and slipped them in a Perspex folder. Tossing it in his in-tray, he was just about to ask the other two companions in the room how they were progressing, and tell them it was late and they ought to be heading home, when the double doors swung open, and a distinctly Irish voice announced,

"Your feckin' heart throb is back, not too much feckin' cheering, please."

It was as though the sun had suddenly appeared, and all three of them stood up to greet Adam Kennedy.

"Hey, hey, you Irish bastard," greeted Dan.

"Adam, a sight for sore eyes," said Meena, a grin spreading across a face that hadn't smiled since the fateful telephone call that morning.

Luke just stood, put his hands on his hips and said, "The Pope's right-hand man has just arrived in time. It's late, before anyone says another word, how about we rush to the pub on the corner, down our sorrows which this Celtic native can pay for."

Adam threw his brief case onto an empty desk near the door, clapped his hands and said,

"That's the first sensible remark I've heard in two weeks. Follow me, fans, the first two rounds are doubles and on me."

Within two minutes, the three previously despondent police officers had donned their coats and followed their wholeheartedly missed colleague through the door, down the stairs and into the street. The drizzle from the skies didn't dampen their enthusiasm, and as they pushed open the door to the pub, their spirits were soaring.

When eventually they sat in the corner, the three men drinking Guinness and Meena drinking a large, white wine, the whole world felt as though it was back on course.

"No doubt you've heard about the young lad's murder," said Dan to Adam after he had downed half his drink. At Adam's nod of affirmation, he added, "As sad as that is, we've worked hard, we'll work even harder over the next few weeks, but tonight we're all together again after the hell of the last few years, so tonight we celebrate. No more long faces, that's for tomorrow." He finished his Guinness, handed his glass to Adam, belched quietly and said, "You said two rounds, and doubles, so get 'em in.

I'll get the third."

"I'll get the fourth," added Luke, downing his as fast as possible.

"Oh no," groaned Meena, knowing this was going to be a disaster.

At closing time, she pushed Dan and Adam into one taxi, giving the driver both addresses as they were incapable of sensible conversation, and helping Luke into another with her as he was just as bad. She didn't know his address, and he refused to tell her, but drunkenly saying he'd kip on her sofa.

"Ok", she reluctantly agreed, "But if you're sick on my furniture or carpet, you're a dead man."

As he slumped back in the taxi's seat, he assured her in slurring words of his undying love and would marry her soon. She just raised her eyebrows and shook her head in exasperation as she looked at the grinning taxi driver's eyes in the mirror.

Chapter 7

Lilly Taylor couldn't believe her luck. As Matthew showed her into the living room, she had gasped with amazement. The furnishings were out of this world. The room's overall decor was pale golden beige, with an accent colour of deep cherry red that was picked out by huge cushions lying on the four-seater sofa, two armchairs and a round plush rug in front of the fire place, in which huge logs glowed, perfecting the look of opulence and comfort. The aroma from the burning wood had a scent that Lilly couldn't place, perhaps pine, but anyway it somehow put the finishing touches to the impeccable room. She compared it to her squat, grotty flat furnished with cheap flat-pack, and knew that if the rest of the house was as beautifully decorated, then she was in the company of a rich man with wonderful taste.

"Champagne suit, my dear?" Matthew asked, raising a tall flute with his right hand and a green bottle in his left. "It's Don Perignon, only the best for a lovely lady such as you."

Lilly tried not to simper, but the pleasure of the evening was making her feel heady before she'd even had the proffered drink. Nodding as coolly as she could manage, she accepted the glass, noticing how he glanced at her hand and was pleased that she'd made the effort to go to the beauticians and have pearl-pink false nails stuck over her stubby, bitten ones.

Normally not a great lover of champagne, Lilly accepted the bubbly tipple as though this sort of drink was quite usual. Matthew filled his own glass, raised it to his lips, staring into Lilly's eyes with a definite 'come-on' look that caused her stomach to jump with excitement.

"Here's to a wonderful evening with my beautiful companion," he whispered, the sexy implication colouring his voice stimulated a thrill between the tops of her legs. She knew then that if he tried to seduce her, she would never be able to refuse such a handsome lover.

Lilly lost count of the glasses of champagne that she drank and felt her head starting to swim. Not having eaten a morsel since lunchtime, assuming his invitation would include a posh dinner some-where, she felt hungry and delightfully drunk.

Initially, Matthew had sat on the end of the sofa, but with each glass, he moved closer. On opening the second bottle, Lilly was sure that she had drunk most of the first one, and the handsome prospective lover was sidling up closer and closer to her side. He slipped one arm around her shoulder and the other one on her leg, inches away from the bottom of her skirt. By the time she had downed the glass, his left hand was gently caressing her left breast, and his right hand was under her skirt, his fingers gently stroking the crutch of her lacy panties bought specifically for this date. She moaned in ecstasy, and when he pushed her rigid legs wider apart, they turned to jelly and spread ready for his embrace.

The mood suddenly changed as he withdrew his stroking hands, stood up and roughly pushed her skirt to her waist, ripping off her panties, and leaving her lying naked from the waist down with her legs spread ready for his entry. When nothing happened, she began to feel mortified by this position. Glancing up at him, with his eyes riveted on the black hair at the top of her legs, she squirmed, feeling self-conscious and she slid her legs together. She went to adjust her skirt and sit up, but he pushed her back down.

"Not a natural blond then Lilly," he said quietly, the sinister tone lacing his voice was disturbing. Lilly felt as though a spider with ice-cold feet was running up her back. He then ordered, "Don't close your legs, I've got something for your disgusting lady hole."

He pushed her legs open again, and when he withdrew a knife from his pocket, pressed the handle and a long, thin blade sprung from it, Lilly fainted.

On waking, the last and worst day of her life began and the pain she suffered made her glad when the blackness of death swallowed her up.

Chapter 8

Meena shook Luke hard as he lay slumped on the sofa, the cover she'd thrown over him the night before now fallen in a heap on the floor. He was still in his working clothes, and despite telling him in no uncertain terms he had to get up, and get to work, his eyes remained firmly closed. Eventually she managed to rouse him enough for an incomprehensible mumble to emerge and his eyes half open.

"Luke, you must wake up. It's almost eight o'clock and we're going to be late." When he peered up at her, she continued. "I'm going. It's your fault if you're late, but I'm not going to be. I've put a coffee on the coffee table next to you. There's a clean towel in the bathroom. Have a quick shower and get your arse into gear pronto. I'm off, see you at work."

Luke heard the front door slam. He groaned as the pneumatic drill pounding in his head continued to pulverise his brain.

"Fucking hangover," he muttered. On opening his eyes fully, he spotted the drink on the table on his left. Heaving himself up, he slurped the drink in one go, burped, and fell back down.

The irritating ringing of the telephone eventually disturbed him. He felt around and located the mobile in his pocket. He winced as he answered it and a sharp, female voice snapped, "You up? I'm almost at work. What excuse am I going to give for you being late?"

Luke glanced at his watch and the resultant shock of seeing the time caused him to sit bolt upright.

"Have you showered yet?" the persistent nagger continued.

"Yeah, yeah, I've just got out of the shower."

"Well hurry."

As the harridan ended the call, Luke groaned and rolled off the sofa. Staggering to the bathroom, he hurried into the shower and swore loudly as a gush of cold water hit him.

"Fucking hell," he yelled. He adjusted the water temperature and let the deluge flood over his head and body until he felt the hammers in his head start to subside, and the feeling of being almost human began to emerge.

Forced to wear yesterday's clothes didn't help but Luke knew he didn't have time to go home for fresh ones. About to leave the house, he realised he couldn't possibly have driven here in the state in which he'd been, and his car was still at work.

"Jesus H Christ, where's my phone? I'm gonna have to get a bloody taxi."

Luke bounded up the stairs to the office praying to a god he definitely should have prayed to more often that DI Cole wasn't around. Cautiously opening the swing doors, he was relieved to see everyone working quietly at their desks and the DI wasn't in the vicinity.

As he quietly tiptoed past Meena's desk he smiled weakly as she glared at him. Dan didn't appear to be in the room, and he slipped into his desk chair.

Switching on his computer, he took a deep breath, hoping he didn't look as scruffy as he felt, and no-one else in the room could hear the herd of elephants trampling through his head.

A heavy hand on his shoulder caused him to jump.

"Feckin' light weight you are," his Irish ex-boss quietly commented as he passed.

Luke nodded, knowing Adam's capacity for drink was famous throughout the office, and far outweighed his abilities. He silently vowed to keep off the Guinness followed by whisky chasers next time, and not compete with Adam and the red headed giant.

An hour later, having just completed some outstanding reports, Dan put his head round the door and announced the scheduled meeting would be in Incident Room 2 in five minutes.

Walking out through the door to the meeting at the same time as Meena, he whispered, "Thanks for putting me up last night."

She nodded, and then added, "Christ, your snoring must have woken the neighbourhood, it kept me awake even from my bedroom."

"It was my cold, not the drink, I only had two."

"Jesus, you're joking. Yeah, two hundred more like it."

Opening the door to the Incident room to let her enter, he chuckled and whispered. "You've just said Christ and Jesus and you're not even a Christian."

"I get my bad habits from these dodgy cops I mix with."

Despite his headache, Luke watched her walk away, admiring the slim shape.

Chapter 9

Emma Bradbury peered into her dressing table mirror to check the result of half an hour applying her make-up. She had outlined her green eyes in navy-blue eyeliner, and then applied jet-black mascara to eyelashes which Heidi Roberts, her best mate from school and college, had permed to perfection and hadn't charged her because she was broke. Until Heidi had attended the Hair and Beauty course at the local Technical College, Emma hadn't realised you could perm eyelashes and that the result was stunning. Blessed with naturally long lashes, they now swept up over her eyelids so much so that she looked as though she was wearing false ones. She'd thought about getting the latest product where false ones are individually stuck to your own and last a couple of weeks, but they cost about forty quid, and at the moment she was broke. Still the perm job looked OK. Emma straightened up, opened her eyes really wide, surveying the end-product.

"Not bad if I say so myself."

She brushed her long, dark inverted hair until she could see it gleaming in the mirror. Turning away from her image, she strolled to her wardrobe and rummaged through the untidy jumble for something good to wear that would show off her slim figure. At five feet ten inches tall, Emma looked glamorous in most things. After discarding eight *'aggie'* dresses that she'd had for months, she knew if she was to look good for her date, and with the shops closed thus ensuring that a bit of shoplifting for new gear was out of the question, the sizeable wardrobe next door might be the only answer.

Slipping on her dressing gown, she peered out of her bedroom to make sure her sister wasn't lurking, and slid along the landing, gluing her ear to the closed bedroom door to ensure she wouldn't barge in on Louise. Silence. Emma eased open the door and the dark room confirmed that Lou wasn't present. Gliding in quickly, she manoeuvred the door closed behind her and hurried to her sister's wardrobe. The sound of East Enders on the TV penetrating through the bedroom floor from the living room below assured her that her sister, a soap fan, would be ensconced in front of the tele and wouldn't return until the programme finished.

Opening the wardrobe, Emma couldn't help wondering about the difference between the layout of the clothes hanging before her to her own dishevelled closet. Lou's clothes, hanging neatly on hangers, started with light coloured ones on the right side, through to coloured ones on the centre part and then dark and black clothes on the left. Emma guiltily glanced round the bedroom and noticed the immaculately made bed with decorated pillows that matched the bedcover. Three dolls dressed in knitted dresses leaned on the pillows with pale pink cheeks, wide-open staring blue eyes and eyelashes equal to Emma's. The whole room was like a palace. Emma suffered a microsecond of guilt when she thought about her own slobbish bedroom. Shrugging her shoulders to dismiss her thoughts, the girl returned to the task. She didn't envy Lou's stack of clothes because her sister worked hard, earned good money and didn't have to exist on a student's pittance and the meagre earnings from a weekend job.

Finding what she wanted, a pale purple, clingy number that Lou had bought the week before and not yet worn, Emma yanked it off its hanger and re-arranged the clothes so as the missing article wouldn't be obvious. Then realising her eagle-eyed, meticulous sister would notice the empty hanger, she snatched that from the rail.

Carefully opening the door, she could still hear the London accents from the programme and knew she was safe to hurry undiscovered back to her bedroom.

"Lucky sis is as tall and skinny as me," she muttered as she pulled the dress over her head and smoothed it down over her body. The result was stunning, and Emma didn't have one iota of conscience as she slipped on her long black coat, not needed for this time of year but necessary to cover the purple ensemble. Hurrying to the stairs, and then creeping down as quietly and carefully as possible to avoid the inevitable creaking that always seemed to happen when attempting to sneak out unnoticed from the house. Unfortunately, her mother was leaving the kitchen holding two mugs of steaming tea and smiled at her youngest daughter.

"Nice make-up, luv," she said. "Do you need that long, thick coat? It's still quite warm. Anyway, don't be late."

"Mum, I'm not a baby."

"Emma, you're just seventeen. I wasn't allowed out after eleven at your age, so I want you in by eleven thirty. Plus, you've got college tomorrow and you're not that good at getting up."

"OK, mum, don't nag," Emma said, opening the front door before her mother asked what she was wearing, where she was going and with whom, which were her normal set of questions. It was too late.

"What you wearing tonight, Em? That nice white dress you got from the market?"

"Umm…no, one I borrowed from Heidi and before you ask, I'm going to the Hanging Man pub and meeting Heidi and Jose there. We're not drinking. It's a karaoke night. See you, Mum, won't be late, promise." Emma slammed the door before any more questions came her way. She felt a stab of conscience because she had lied but comforted herself with the thought that if found out, it would be as bad being lynched for one lie as for three.

Glancing at her watch and realising she had only ten minutes before the bus came, she attempted to run in her very high, strappy shoes. By the time she hobbled to the bus stop, she was out of breath and her feet were killing her.

"Bugger," she muttered after waiting a further five minutes, glancing continuously at her watch as though that would miraculously make the bus appear.

An old man in his mobility scooter came whizzing past her and almost ran her down.

She was just about to yell at him to be careful when two six-foot lads scooted up to the bus stop. They both stopped on seeing Emma, the one just behind bowling full pelt into the first one.

"If it isn't the glamorous Emma Bradbury," said the dark-haired one of the two. "Where you sneaking off to then, beautiful?"

"None of your business, Charlie Walsh. Anyway, what were you and Harry doing legging it down the road like that. A cat scare you or sommink?"

"Nah," said Harry, patting his long fair hair into place, a habit that earned him the nickname of Hairdressing Harry by his classmates. "Nuffink to do so we was just giving the old geezer in the scooter a scare by chasing him. Christ, you should see him go, almost bloody Mach one I reckon."

"That's really horrible, you two bastards," said Emma and standing on her toes as best she could, she slapped Charlie round the face. Harry looked shocked and then laughed as his friend's eyes opened in amazement, but the mirth was gone as quickly as it came when Emma clocked him round the face as well.

"Fucking hell, girl," said Charlie, rubbing his cheek, "What was that for?"

"That's for being a horrible bully, chasing that poor old man."

A voice from the bus that had pulled up unnoticed by any of them asked if Emma was all right, not being harassed by these two louts?

"You're joking, mate," said Harry, also rubbing his cheek. "This little fire-brand don't need no help."

Emma got on the bus but before she gave the driver her fare, she turned to the two boys.

"If I ever see you doing that again, you damn bullies, I'll report you to the bizzies. Now sod off home before you go chasing after a poor old woman 'cos that'd probably be all you'd dare do."

As the door of the bus closed, she heard Charlie shout, "Love you, Em, you little hell-raiser."

"Christ," said the driver as he took her fare, "Bet no-one crosses you."

Emma just looked at him, and as her look skimmed like a meat-cleaver over his cropped hair, he knew he was right. He grinned at the situation and then the irony as the young girl teetered down the moving bus, ridiculously high heels not helping her staggering gait. He noticed she never bothered to look out of the window at the two boys left behind who were giving her the finger, brave now she was out of reach and they were out of harm's way.

Emma plonked herself down as near to the exit door as possible and gazed at her reflection in the opposite window. Her stomach clenched with excitement as she thought about her date. The tall dark handsome stranger that she'd often fantasized about but never thought she'd actually ever meet. She'd met him in the Prada Nightclub and although he was a lot older than her, he had charmed her with his good manners, exciting conversation and charisma that oozed from his every pore. So different from the boys she'd known at school or that she came across at college. Wondering if this was going to forecast a change in her life, she enjoyed the feelings of excitement that spiralled through her young body.

Chapter 10

"OK, so what have we got?" Dan Blake looked around the incident room full of solemn police officers. Often, despite the gravity of an incident, spirits were high and even serious suggestions would result in some banter from the rest of the team. Today there was no repartee. A child's murder left no room for jokes of any kind.

"Jason Stone, brutally murdered. I want to hear we're close to catching the bastard who did this horrific thing. Meena, what've you got?"

"The pathologists report says he was tortured, and then strangled," said Meena Mesbah, reading from the paperwork she was holding. "You don't think this could be connected in any way with Operation Centaur?"

"Why would you think that?" said Dan, hoping in his deepest heart that this was not the case.

Almost four years ago, a large nationwide police operation had successfully foiled well organised cells of paedophiles from abducting children. Undercover Officers had penetrated various cells, thus saving many children from terrible fates. Dan had been the first line contact for undercover officer, DS Adam Kennedy who was involved in this investigation and had almost lost his life while penetrating the organisation. Although two of the leaders of the local cell, Gerry Tomas and Yvette Van Looy had not been apprehended at that time, a body later discovered in a house was identified by its DNA to be that of Tomas's.

Then just three months later, DNA taken from a body found in the River Thames matched DNA found at the murder scene of three elderly men. Evidence uncovered by police suggested that Yvette Van Looy had been present, and probably responsible for their murders. As the genetic material at that crime scene matched the genetic material of the body in the river, and there was a strong resemblance to the female predator despite the body being bloated, that hopefully meant she was also dead. Dan, however, still had feelings that this incident was not the end of the affair. He knew the pool of nonces was bottomless. Normally he worked only with facts and evidence, and this belief was merely intuition, but the feeling at times would wiggle through his thoughts like a persistent worm, refusing to go away.

Meena's voice brought him out of his musing. "Nothing concrete, but we haven't had a child's murder in this town since we brought that operation to a close, thank God. It's just I associate Gerry Tomas and Van Looy with anything as evil as child murder, and I have this niggly feeling we didn't completely get to the bottom of that investigation…I can't tell you why." She shrugged. "I know we should go by facts, evidence, motive, but…" Her voice tailed away, and she shrugged again with her misgivings.

Dan didn't reveal that he had the same instinct, and merely replied, "Something happen while I was away that makes you suspicious?" At the shake of her head, he continued. "Nothing will be discounted, but I think we need to stick to the facts, weigh the evidence, look for motivation until we have proof of who's involved."

"But at the moment we don't appear to have much evidence," added Luke Steiner. "House to house enquiries both around the area where the lad lives, and the area where his body was found, haven't turned up anything. Was he caught on any surveillance camera anywhere? Who was dealing with investigating that side of things?"

"I was," said a woman police officer, Mel Stubbs. "I've just obtained the films this morning and as we speak I've got WPCs French and Smith checking through them while I'm here to see if he was caught anywhere on camera. We know the lad left home at 1800 hours when it was still light. He was going to choir-practice…umm, that started at 1815, but never turned up. I'm not impressed with the father, rather bully type person. The mother seems a bit weak and obviously nervous of the husband. She says some of the boy's clothes are missing, but the father blustered and then got angry, saying there was no need for the boy to have run away."

"Did *he* have an alibi the time his lad went missing?"

"Well his wife confirmed he was at home with her, but as I've just said, she's scared of him. Their alibis are being verified."

"The nervous wife, I suppose she'd say anything he wanted."

Mel nodded and added, "Don't think we've really got enough to bring him in at the moment, but I think he should be kept on the radar."

"OK." Dan turned to Luke Steiner. "Luke, how did you get on talking to the Priest at St Anne's Catholic Church who was taking the choir practice? Father…" Dan checked his notes. "Father Bryan…umm, Bryan Futcher."

"Nothing. He said Jason often missed choir practice so when he didn't turn up, he wasn't unduly concerned. He had an alibi; the seven kids who were at choir practice. I've listed their names and checked with a couple of the parents who had driven their kids to the church, and they confirmed Father Bryan was at the church when they arrived and still there at the end, and had been with the kids all the time."

"I know this is newsworthy, and I don't want to be swayed by the press's need for news and sales, so discounting all the media hype about catholic priests, what's your take on him?"

"Seemed like a good bloke. Mind you, and this is probably me just being a suspicious sod…"

"Or a Police Officer using his intuition," said Dan.

Luke nodded. "Yeah, maybe. But I just got the impression his answers were very pat."

"Like he'd rehearsed them or what?"

"Yes, nail on the head. Like he'd rehearsed them. My experience has shown people, especially the innocent, not used to being interviewed by the police are often nervous, ill at ease. We know the bad guys are normally prepared and suave bastards, alibis at the ready." Luke leaned back in his chair, biting his lip as he thought through his explanation. "This one, I dunno, too prepared, bit glib."

"Yes, but remember he's a priest," said Mel, whose reputation for being argumentative and not the happiest person in the police station was well known. She was also a staunch Catholic. She snapped, "He's used to talking to people. Dealing with difficult situations, and difficult people."

"Steady up, Mel," said Luke, holding up his hands against her outburst, "I'm not anti-priests. I know most of them are the good guys, and all we hear in the media is about the odd balls. I'm just reporting what I saw."

"Yes, but you didn't see anything, you've just…"

"Hold on, Mel," said Dan, intervening before a lot of time wasting went on with Mel's feelings obviously running high and leading them off the subject. "As Luke said, he's just reporting what he thinks we ought to know. He might not have any evidence, but his instincts also count sometimes. This isn't a priest bashing session so get off your high horse."

Mel opened her mouth to retort, but Dan, usually easy going, glared at her and her mouth shut tight. He turned back to Luke. "OK, we keep him in mind. Anything else?"

"The sweep of the area produced nothing revealing."

"DNA?"

Luke shook his head. "But the doc did get some black fibres from the lad's clenched hands. Maybe clutching at someone's clothes while being strangled. They haven't been identified yet. Makes it difficult when there is nothing to compare them with…yet. As I said, forensics are still trying to classify them. Dr MacDeath reckons he'd not been dead that long, forty-eight hours at the most."

Dan glanced round, asking if there was anything else relevant. Noting the shaking of heads, he said, "Right, if there's nothing else to report, we'll wind this up. I want the house–to-house kept up. Widen the search area to all houses along the route he would have taken to the church. We need to find out how far he got before he left that route. Mel, the cameras might help us there. Let me know straight away if anything turns up. OK, keep asking, keep pushing; someone must have seen him at some point along the route. Also, I want more interviews with the parents. Push to see if the lad had ever mentioned anything to them that might help. Interview the mother on her own."

As the police officers left the room, the conversation was hushed. Dan knew the team was keen, not lacking in enthusiasm, but their spirits were low about this awful event. If they were going to solve this murder, he was going to have to keep them focused and moving forward, not despondent because of the apparent lack of progress. It was early days, and Dan had every hope they would solve the incident earlier rather than later, but realistically he knew they had a long haul in front of them.

Chapter 11

The three boys were standing in the shadow behind the church sharing a cigarette that Alfie Smith had filched from the packet his dad had foolishly left on the coffee table. If the truth was known, none of the boys actually enjoyed the sensation of sucking the smoke down into their lungs but confessing this would mean a great loss of face, and the probability of losing two friends because no-one wanted to be mates with a 'wuss'.

Joey Pritchard, known as Ginge due to his flaming hair, after taking a deep drag and trying to appear cool, passed the nearly finished cigarette to George Dexter. He was controlling the urge to gag and cough that was rapidly making its way from his chest up to his throat like a waterspout.

George, older than his two nine-year-old companions by two years and definitely the coolest in terms of street cred, took a deep drag and then blew the smoke into the air with the nonchalance of a fifty a day smoker. Alfie and Joey, eyes large with admiration, watched as he took the last drag and flicked the cigarette away using his thumb and forefinger.

Checking his watch, George said, "We still got over five minutes. I don't wanna go in till start time or Father Bryan'll make us put out the prayer books ready for Sunday."

The others nodded their agreement and Alfie walked to the corner and peered round to make sure no-one was around to check on their skiving before choir practice. All the boys and their parents knew that if they arrived in time, then the lads were expected to help with small jobs like putting out the prayer book or other chores that needed doing.

"Terrible about Jase, innit," said Ginge walking to his friend. "Dad wouldn't let me watch the news about him, but I put me glass to the bedroom floor, and heard them say that he'd been raped."

He looked at Alfie who raised his eyebrows but didn't say the thing he was hoping he would say. Both boys then looked at George who, being the eldest and the leader of the gang, consequently didn't have to worry about his lack of knowledge or losing face. He pondered a few seconds, then screwed up his face in thought before he said, "How can you rape a boy?" When both of his companions just shrugged, which was normally how they expressed their lack of knowledge about most subjects, he continued, "I can understand how a tart gets raped. Men just put their willies in the wee holes they got, but men haven't got holes, so how does that work out?"

Again, Alfie and Ginge shrugged, their shoulders reaching up so high they were in line with their eyes, both not willing to admit their absolute ignorance in this particular area and both praying George would enlighten them somehow.

"Just can't work it out." George stood, staring into space.

"I miss 'im," said Ginge, returning to the topic of his friend's death.

"Yeah, I do too," said Alfie. "Just can't believe he's dead. Wonder what it's like being dead? Wonder if it hurts?"

"Well it must hurt if you go to hell," said Ginge. "All that burning and fings. And I don't think he went to confession very often."

"My dad says hell, Jesus, God and that Heaven stuff's all a load of bollocks," contributed Alfie.

"Christ, he'll definitely go to hell then. He never comes to church do 'e?"

"Nah, he's not catholic. He's nuffink. My mum says he's a friggin' heathen."

"I've got it," said George, interrupting their stimulating conversation."

"What?"

"Raped. I bet they puts their willies up their bums." George looked from one to another, delight painting his face as the brainwork finally paid off.

"Course not, you dick-head," said Ginge, pleased with his bravery for actually daring to argue with George. "Your bum just ent that big."

Before the size of bums and their capacity could be discussed further, Alfie gasped, "Christ, we're late, let's leg it."

The three boys 'legged' it towards the church door.

"Anyway, I saw Jase the night he got killed. I saw who he was with. I told me dad but he just said to stay out of it, not get involved," whispered Alfie to his two companions as they hurried through the church door and into the body of the church, where Father Bryan stood with his hands on his hips, frowning at the late-comers.

Chapter 12

I carry Lilly into the crypt to join her sisters in death. I always pre-plan the necessary moves by leaving the crypt door unlocked just beforehand and removing the lid from one of the coffins not overly used by me thus far.

My other three prizes are safely entrenched with previous dead companions. I gently place Lilly, my fourth client, onto the decaying body of a member of the wealthy DeWit family who owned the tomb. Luckily for me, the local family has died out, and the crypt isn't now in use, which proved extremely handy to dispose of the remaining body-parts after I've taken my token. From Lilly I had removed her right hand to keep the symmetry going. I almost have a set: a left and right foot, and now the same in hands. Think the next pieces will be breasts. Yes, breasts… although they're nasty things.

Just as I place her on Mr Julian DeWit, deceased in 1973, I realise I haven't taken a lock of her hair. How remiss of me, I'm usually so organised, so precise with that sort of thing. It's not like me at all, and I feel very annoyed with myself. I plan all my moves before I meet with my clients because bad planning results in mistakes, and that means chances of being caught rise dramatically.

Taking my knife, I lean in and snip a lock of Lilly's bleach blond hair, careful not to look at the mouldering body beneath her. I find that sort of thing rather distasteful. I also hold my breath because although poor Julian has been dead many a year, not only does he smell musty there is also a lingering, underlying smell of decay which I also abhor. Although I'm not a wimpy person, there is a limit to the sort of thing one can stand.

To complete my eventual body, I still have to get two legs, two arms, a torso and a head, but I'm running out of space in these tombs. I'll have to give that some thought.

He felt the itch suddenly burst into life along the base of his spine. Before long he knew the itch would escalate into an urge, then burn through his body and the deep craving for inflicting power over a woman would explode like a super nova, blasting out of control.

He forced himself to relax and controlled his impulses by thinking about his old haunts and the secrets hidden in his old lock-up. Maybe a visit in the near future would salve the hunger until a fresh client arrived on the scene.

The man replaced the heavy lid, taking particular care to make sure it was exactly in position. He could hear the rain hitting the crypt's rooftop and knew he must get home before it poured down as forecast. Locking the door, he whistled cheerfully as he hurried away, looking forward to his nightly hot chocolate drink and looking through his stamp collection.

Chapter 13

On his way to work, despite the sharp cutting wind unusual for the season that had decided to pick up through the night, and hadn't diminished one bit by 7 am, Dan was sweating. Taking off his suit jacket, he slung it over his shoulder. He wanted to get into the station and put in an hour's work before the mad world decided every man and his dog would phone in, disrupting his thoughts and planning.

Glancing at his watch, he decided he had just enough time to swing into the small corner shop near the police station. He had run out of coffee and milk, and this was the third morning running he had left for work without so much as a comforting drink soothing his stomach.

He gave a nod and a 'Morning' to Ahmed, the owner who was staffing the till by the front door, and whose large nose was deep into his newspaper as punters were few and far between this early in the morning, Dan hurried down the centre aisle, towards the coffee shelf. Grabbing a jar of Nescafé, he headed towards the fridge around the corner. As he did so, he almost collided with a woman hurrying in the opposite direction.

The meeting caused both parties to gasp and stare. Dan recovered first. "Lucy Hamilton. Thought you'd gone to the moon."

She smiled, and he recalled that despite the investigation

he had been leading almost four years ago when he'd been initially suspicious of her involvement, he'd eventually found her attractive; both then and now by the way his stomach jolted with pleasure. Dressed in a black trouser suit with a white blouse, she looked striking.

She interrupted his thoughts. "DS Blake… or is it Chief Constable Blake? If you thought I'd gone to the moon, I guess it's because despite returning to this area some weeks ago, I happen to know you haven't bothered to check up on your friend Sara, thus discovering I'm still living."

"Two things, not chief constable and never will be. Also, I have text Sara a couple of times. She seems to be doing OK."

"She's doing really well considering what's she's been through. Mind you, something's happened that's cheered her up considerably."

"And that is…?"

"No way am I giving it away. When *you go and see her*, you'll find out then, but not from me."

"Fair enough. I promise you she's high on my list of 'must dos' as soon as I get two spare minutes'. I'm not making excuses…well, I am, but they're genuine."

She nodded. "OK, you're excused, temporarily. Even a five-minute visit would be appreciated."

He nodded in return. "Promise. How's that dog of yours, Higgins is it?"

"Trying to change the subject, eh?" She smiled, happy to talk about her beloved pet. "He's great. Still a fair-weather runner though."

"And your mate…umm…Freddy?"

Laughing out loud, she continued, "As daft and obnoxious on occasions as ever. Pete lives with him now, so he keeps him somewhat under control. They pop in regularly to check up on Sara too." She took a deep breath. "Ok, must get on." She lifted the wire-shopping basket. "Right, better pay for these, I suppose. Just on the way to school."

Dan leaned towards the upright fridge on his right and picked out a pint of semi-skimmed. "Been without a hot drink for three days now. Just popped in for coffee and milk before I hit the desk, and all the madness of the human race. I'll escort you to the till, madam, unless you're planning on doing a runner, and not pay for the goods, and that means I'll have to arrest you."

"I was, but now I've bumped into a giant Mr. Plod, I wouldn't dare."

Lucy was tall for a woman, 5'9", but compared to Dan's broad shoulders and 6'5" of height, she looked positively petite.

After paying her bill, she said, "'Bye, Dan. Maybe see you soon."

"Sure, take care." He waited until she had turned and taken two steps away before he summoned up the courage to say. "Maybe see you when I see Sara?"

Looking back over her shoulder, she said, "Maybe."

Seeing Lucy Hamilton again had stoked up memories of when his best friend Alex, had stood in front of him and taken the killer knife blow that was aimed at him. Alex had died in his arms, and now, nearly four years later, the hurt feeling wrapping itself round his heart like a tourniquet was just as painful. Alex had saved him twice and died on the second attempt. Dan had not contacted Sara since his return from the Midlands except by two texts, and if he were honest with himself, he had avoided seeing her.

Yeah, I've been busy. That's no excuse, you coward. Get your arse round and see how she's doing. Bugger your conscience. She doesn't blame you for Alex's death, she's told you that.

Dan straightened his shoulders. *Christ, we've been friends for over twenty years and I'm being a spineless, fucking wuss!*

Lucy's thoughts were quite different. She had a secret that didn't make relationships easy. She was still, after almost eighteen years, still in a police protection programme. Her mother had murdered her father and brothers. Although only 9 years old, it had been her testimony that had closed the case and put her mother away for a life sentence.

Lucy had been placed in witness protection, and then given "another life" after the trial. She had spent her existence from that point in avoiding attention, especially from the press or anyone that might spill the beans on her history. Her mother's family were vindictive and had vowed to hunt her down, however long it took, and wherever she hid.

When a teenager, she'd changed her appearance, dying her natural chestnut hair much darker and wearing coloured contact lenses. Keeping up a fitness regime had changed her from a chubby child into a tall, slender fit woman. Ever afraid of discovery and trusting no-one, and although during her involvement in DC Blake's investigation, if she were honest with herself, she had begun to find him attractive, she'd kept him at a distance. She knew then, and now, that being involved with a police officer was not wise; they had all the resources necessary to investigate someone's past. Knowing that she was stupid acting like this, she couldn't break the obsessive behaviour even though she was innocent and had nothing to hide.

Glancing back over her shoulder and seeing him at the till paying for his groceries, she noted his big frame and the red hair that always stuck up at crazy angles. She wished her life could be different, not forever looking behind her, suspicious of people's intentions, as she certainly had been towards him during his investigation. *Right. New Year's Resolution. I'm going to stop being suspicious of everyone's motive and start trusting people.*

After leaving the corner shop, Dan watched her walk down the road, get into her car, and drive away. He remembered she was a schoolteacher and guessed she was on the way to work. Hurrying to his car, he drove in the opposite direction.

Unaware of the coincidence, that after the meeting Lucy had reflected on her past, he found himself doing the same.

Like Lucy, he'd also had a past that he kept to himself. As a child, just a year after his mother had drowned whilst his family had been on holiday in Cornwall, he had been abducted by paedophiles. Although his mother's tragic death had been a terrible shock to him and his family, it was the abduction that had shaped his path in life. His friends Alex and Sara, both teenagers at the time, had rescued him. They had remained in touch and friends all their life until Alex's murder.

Although he'd studied physics and maths at University, he was determined to join the police and hunt down 'nonces' and clear them off the street. The investigation four years ago had gone a long way towards achieving his goal, but he knew the pool of predators was deep, and his work would never finish.

As Dan drove into a parking space behind the police station and switched off the engine, he paused for a time. He knew Lucy had been right, he'd returned from work in the Midlands a few weeks ago and neglected to check up on Sara.

I'll phone tonight and make a date. If Lucy's there too, that'll add to the pleasure.

He whistled cheerfully as he hurried to his office.

Chapter 14

Emma looked at her watch. One-minute past eight and Matthew had said he would pick her up dead on eight outside the Library, promising he wouldn't be late after she had told him she never waited for any date that never turned up on time.

Right, I given him an extra minute 'cos the traffic's bad an' that's more'n I usually do… then I'm off.

She looked up and down the road, realising if she hurried, she'd just catch the bus that would drop her off outside the Lotus Flower restaurant where she knew Heidi and Jose would be. She'd told her mum she'd be seeing them in the pub, but there had been a massive punch up the last time the girls had been there, and they decided it wasn't for them anymore. They'd decided that the 'Eat all you can for a tenner' offer on at the local chinky restaurant was a better deal. Emma remembered over-hearing them saying they would meet outside at quarter to eight, so she'd just make it, even if they had gone in and started their meal.

As she waited for a taxi to pass that was gliding slowly down the road, she was surprised when it drew up by her. The nearside window came down and a woman's voice said,

"Taxi for Emma Bradbury ordered by Matthew Nielson."

Emma bent down to peer in at the woman, wanting to

make sure everything was kosher. She definitely wouldn't get into a drive-by taxi with a man driving, whatever assurances he gave her after knowing about all the murdered prostitutes in Suffolk many years ago that she'd seen recently on a television documentary, but the woman's smiling face re-assured her.

"Actually, Matt's a mate of mine," said the woman, "but he couldn't get here by eight. He phoned me. I own this taxi business; said he'd been caught up at work and was running late. He's dashed home to have a shower and paid me, or will pay me when we get there, to come and pick you up. You OK with that? I've got his number if you'd like to confirm this."

"Where're we going then?" Emma felt fairly confident, but a mate of hers had been fooled by a similar situation a couple of weeks ago, and word had it there was a guy going round pretending to be a taxi driver, and picking up girls and driving them into the country-side and raping them. Emma didn't intend to have any of that milarky.

"Loddon House, just at the back of Coley Park. Built years ago, before the council estate was ever there. Matt inherited his mum and dad's house. It's smashing. Been there to a couple of parties. You won't believe the furniture, out of this world. Anyway, phone him if you want to be sure. He phoned me in particular because he thought you'd feel safer with a woman."

Emma fingered the knife in her right pocket and the pepper spray in her left and felt safe.

"OK, it's fine." She clambered into the back of the taxi. As the driver pulled away, Emma pulled out her mobile and text Heidi, briefly explaining she'd been picked up by taxi and the name of the house in Coley Park.

Can't be too sure, whatever she says.

Travelling through the town, the taxi drove along the by-pass and then up onto the top of Castle Street, and Emma felt relieved that they were going in the correct direction.

"I envy you," chatted the woman, glancing in her rear-view mirror. "Tell you what, if I was twenty years younger, I'd be after Matt. He's a real dish."

"You known him long?"

"Known him since we were kids. My mum used to work for his mum as her cleaner. Lovely family. When my dad died, I was ten, and Mrs Nielson was smashing to my mum. We were really hard up, so Mrs N. used to buy a huge joint of meat for the weekend meal, hardly use any of it, and give the rest to mum. Used to feed me and my twin sister for practically the whole week."

They continued to chat for some minutes and when they turned into an unmade-up road, lined with big trees, and no streetlamps, Emma realised she hadn't been paying attention to where they were actually going. Beginning to feel slightly anxious, she felt better when the driver, whose name she noted was Yvonne de Borg from the identity card hanging from the front mirror, swung the taxi right through some open, double gates and into the drive, said, "Well, Emma, finally here. Hope you have a great evening."

The front door opened, and Matthew walked out, a towel draped over his shoulder as though he'd just finished drying after a shower. However, his hair was dry and looking cool in a swept back style, and he was looking just as dishy as when he'd chatted her up in the nightclub, so she knew she *was* going to have a great evening. Opening the taxi door, he kissed her on the cheek as she alighted from the car.

"Sorry about not being there to pick you up as promised Emma, but hopefully Yvonne's explained to you."

Emma nodded and as she watched him hand the fare through the window to the driver, her stomach lurched with excitement. He led her by the hand to the front door and ushered her in.

"Come through to the living room. I'll get you a drink. What would you like, whiskey, wine?" Before Emma could answer, he laughed and said, "I know what a young beauty like you would fancy. How about a champagne cocktail, I make a really mean one?"

Emma had never even heard of a champagne cocktail but didn't like to show her ignorance.

"Yeah, sounds good."

She watched as he mixed the champagne and brandy in a cut glass jug that sparkled from the lamp on the coffee table that contained a variety of drinks. She was impressed as he wet the top of the glass in a pitcher of water, then dipped the rim of the glass into a bowl that appeared to contain sugar, giving it a really classy appearance. He poured the mixture into the glass and offered it to her.

"My party piece. Impressed?" He grinned at her, and once again her stomach flipped with excitement and she experienced a thousand butterflies flying madly round her insides. He was such a dish with dark hair that were a contrast to his blue eyes fringed with lashes that outdid Emma's own, even with the extra length the perm bestowed.

"I'm impressed. Hope it tastes as good as it looks." She then silently cursed because she didn't intend to give away the fact that she hadn't drunk such a flash drink before. She wanted to be cool, and although not often daunted by people, his age, experience and obvious sophistication made her feel young and inadequate.

"Sit on the sofa and sip your drink, I'll just finish drying the hair. Two ticks. Relax and enjoy yourself and when I return, we'll have a great evening."

As he left, Emma turned and inspected the large room. The sofa was dark brown leather and contrasted oddly with the two modern orange chairs either side of it. The coffee table was glass topped and the legs were chrome. She glanced round the whole room, noting that it seemed a mishmash of obviously expensive furniture, but it just looked as though the whole lot had been thrown carelessly together and the end result was an untidy looking mess. Emma was studying Art and Design at Sixth Form College and her artistic flair was not impressed by this furnishing combination. The taxi driver obviously didn't have any taste as she had made a point of saying the place and furnishings were fab.

Taking one sip of the drink, and although the taste was very more-ish, Emma, not normally a big drinker, was careful never to ever drink anything at the nightclubs she frequented if offered by young men in case they'd contaminated it with the 'date-rape' drug. However, she knew enough to know this drink was 'blow-your-head-off' liquor. Glancing round the room, she noticed a half-dead plant by the window and decided it needed the refreshment more than she did. She'd only sat back down for a few seconds when she heard Matthew's footsteps as he came down the stairs. As he walked into the room, his broad grin removed any doubt about his intentions, he seemed an OK guy.

"Enjoy the drink?" he asked, pushing the sleeves up to his elbows of his very expensive looking sweater. Her college course gave her a great deal of knowledge about materials and Emma reckoned it was cashmere, its smooth appearance giving the fabric a sheen that only comes with the goat's wool. At her enthusiastic nod, he continued, "Fancy another one?"

"No thanks, it was wonderful, but very strong. I'd be staggering if I had two."

"Don't worry about the staggering. I'll give you a lift home and escort you to your door." With that, he took her glass and topped it up.

Smiling sweetly, she took back the glass, but had no intentions of drinking the lethal combination. She was no pushover so when he turned his back to pour his drink, she put her glass on the coffee table at the end of the sofa. He sipped his drink, peering over the top of his glass, definitely giving her the 'come-on' look, and for the first time since entering the house, Emma felt slightly concerned and was glad she'd text Heidi with her whereabouts. She saw him glance at her glass and although he smiled at her, she couldn't read his mind and was glad that she'd slipped the pepper spray into her right pocket and the switchblade into the left.

He plonked himself next to her on the sofa but didn't crowd her, so she felt a little relieved. Picking up her glass, he handed it to her, with a smile and a 'Drink up'.

"Tell me about yourself, Emma," he said. With that, he sidled up too close and the alarm returned as he slipped his free arm round her shoulder. She was glad the other hand was occupied with his glass or she suspected that one would be on her leg.

He's going a bit too fast for me.

There was no-where to go, she'd sat at the end of the sofa as she'd placed her drink again back on the coffee table. When he leaned forward and placed his glass on the floor next to him, as she suspected, the now free other hand landed on her leg.

"If I do anything you don't like, just tell me," he said, but his soft words didn't sound sincere.

"Well, you can take your hand off my leg. Not so sure I like that this early on in our date."

He didn't remove his hand, but instead slid it round to the inside of her leg, easing them apart.

"I said no."

His leer as he half turned to her was in complete contrast to his previous friendly smile and told her everything she needed to know.

"Enjoy."

"I said no." She attempted to push his hand away, but being stronger, his hand stayed put. Emma didn't like using weapons, but she couldn't take the chance and wriggled forward to take the pepper spray from her pocket. He was too quick for her and grabbed her arm, pushing her to the floor.

Rolling onto her back, she didn't like the gleam in his

eyes and rolled further away, giving her time to retrieve the knife. Although never used in anger, she had practiced many times, and her finger found the button immediately. She heard the blade whistle as it leapt up from the handle. Matthew was wearing shoes, but fortunately they were slip-ons, with narrow fronts leaving plenty of room for her to strike the blade into the exposed part.

His roar of pain reeled around the room. The racket prompted Emma into action. She leapt to her feet, legging it towards the door.

Snatching her coat from the coat rack in the hall, as her hand touched the front door handle, she heard him bellow,

"You bitch, you fucking bitch."

Emma didn't wait for more, she yanked open the door and fled for what she presumed was her life. Running into the dark garden, she headed in the direction of the gate. The street ahead of her was as equally dark as the garden but she didn't hesitate, dashing to the right, although having lost her sense of direction while she was in the taxi, her sharp brain recalled they had turned left into the driveway as they had arrived at the house. After two yards, she kicked off her high heels, snatched them up, even in her dilemma recalling they had cost her two weekend pay packets, and she wasn't going to ditch them. She then ran as if like the devil and all his mates were chasing her.

"That was a shite evening," she called to the few stars that gleamed in the narrow band of dark sky showing through the gap left by the tall trees. "Real, fucking shite."

The stars winked back as though to say, you can never be too careful!

Chapter 15

"Boss, I think I detect a pattern here." DC Mesbah glanced up from the computer screen across the room to where Dan Blake was sitting at his desk. She noticed he was running his fingers through his unruly red hair, causing it to stick up at various angles, whilst attempting to catch up with the paperwork from the previous two years that had accrued in his in-tray while he had been absent. She didn't realise he was finding it hard to concentrate with his mind continuously harping back to his meeting with Lucy Hamilton.

Hearing Meena's voice, he was glad to have a few minutes respite from his swirling thoughts whilst attempting to absorb details of past investigations that had occurred while he was seconded elsewhere, including the current, harrowing investigation into a child's murder. Dan took in a deep breath before leaning back in his chair. Picking up his coffee cup, and being very aware that Meena was a conscientious, intelligent officer, who picked up on many relevant points that sometimes slipped by her male colleagues, he asked,

"Pattern? What have your sharp eyes detected, my meticulous friend?"

Meena leaned forward in her chair, picked up a pencil, and tapping it on the desk side like a woodpecker pecking for insects, she frowned as she thought through her words, not wanting the lean facts she had noticed to sound insignificant.

"OK," she started, her eyes still glued to the screen. "March 20th of this year, we had a report in about a missing woman, Stella James, twenty-nine, unmarried who lived on her own. She went missing one night, and it was only noticed when she never turned up for work after three days. Going missing without explanation was most unlike her. The usual inquiries were made, but as absolutely nothing turned up, obviously it eventually became a lower priority, and no-one's actively working on it now as far as I know."

"Presumably the case is not closed."

"No. I was involved with the initial investigation, but still recall the details. It was probably put on the back burner because on April 2nd, a young lad went missing. Tommy Deadman, ten years old. Again nothing, no sightings, no body, and…"

"A vulnerable child. Yes, I heard about that case. I assume all the normal processes were gone through."

"Yes, it was thorough. After a week of investigation, we find out he has gone missing before. In fact, a couple of times and in due course turns up. He's often absent from school and his mum eventually told us he was out of control."

"A missing woman, a missing boy, possibly a run-away, I don't see the pattern."

"Hang on, I'm getting there."

"Good. Just give me the bare outlines at this stage."

"OK." Meena touched the screen with the pencil. "Next. Another woman goes missing on…umm, on May 5th. Sandra Murphy aged twenty. Still not turned up. Then another lad, Harry Davy, twelve years old on May 29th. Again, a bit of a hooligan from our investigations and also prone to running away but eventually comes home."

"But hasn't so far?"

"No. Again, no-one saw anything despite a re-enactment of his last known movements. Right, where am I? Oh yes, then a third woman. Again, no sight nor sound of her. Molly Carson, aged eighteen, on June 20th. Apparently, a real home bird. Her parents insist she wouldn't disappear. Then a Jack Walsh, just 10 years old, at the beginning of July. Then a blip, because we have our present case, Jason Stone, 11 years old, but not another woman missing as yet."

Dan sipped his coffee and peered over the rim at Meena, but she was aware he wasn't seeing her, but his 'diamond-brain coma' was working overtime and evaluating what she had told him.

"Woman, boy, woman, boy, woman, boy and …boy... Jason." Dan put his cup onto the desk. Leaning forward, he sighed loudly and put his elbows on his desk and cupped his hands around his face. Taking a deep breath, he said, "Let's hope another woman doesn't turn up even if it breaks your pattern. So far, anything that connects them?"

"Certainly nothing that's listed in the files. I think that would need further investigation."

"How's this gone unnoticed until now? The obvious pattern I mean?"

"Different Investigating officers, different areas, so no-one connected them. As we're all being amalgamated under the Thames Valley Standard, connections are now becoming obvious. With this new software coming online for that event, DI Coles asked me to do the collating of past investigations and get them under this one heading for simplicities sake."

"OK. Right, here's what we do. Firstly, give me a hard copy of all these details so I can take it home to read tonight. Tomorrow I've got a progress meeting with dear Coley. I can get his thoughts on it." Dan was aware DI Roy Cole was himself being nagged by higher authorities on lack of progress on the Jason investigation, and his way of dealing with it was to pass the stress straight onto his subordinate's shoulders. Dan was prepared for a painful meeting, but Meena's theory had captured his imagination, although he knew the guv wouldn't take kindly with the lack of connections so far.

"Just coincidence, boss?" asked Meena, interrupting his contemplations.

"You know what our esteemed guv, the wonderful Coley is often heard to quote, there's no such thing as coincidence, and the longer I'm a police officer, the more I think he's right. I'm not sure we have enough evidence as yet to link these cases unless there is a common denominator, but I think we need to keep these events at the front of our minds. Let's just hope no-one mentions the word…" He paused, and then lowering his voice, whispered, "Serial killer. Jesus H Christ, that's all we need. So, currently, our top priority is Jason, but if there is a connection, I don't want it missed while it's in our lap."

Meena winced, then whispered in return. "Serial killer, please no. Mind you, they, he, she, whoever, hasn't aimed at the same targets, our victims are women and children." She winced again, and mouthed, "Serial killers!"

"Wash your mouth out, young lady. The women are only missing at this point, no bodies. Still it's dodgy…as for the missing children..." He shook his head in despair.

"I know we have a body in Jason's case, but it could be that Tommy's and Harry's bodies haven't been found. Jason's body was only spotted because the jogger pushed his way into the undergrowth for a pee. The houses in the Warren are large and detached with a lot of ground between them; otherwise, it could have lain undiscovered for weeks, months even. The area around his body has been thoroughly searched so if the other lads are dead, their bodies weren't located in that region."

Dan stood up and smiled at Meena. "Well spotted, mate. Until we have proof let's try and be positive, or should I say hopeful. If this comes to anything and there is a link, I owe you a large drink for moving things forward. I'll read the files tonight and if there is any spare capacity, I might get you investigating and seeing what does connect them."

Collecting the jumble of files littering his desk, he walked towards the door. "Off to the Lion's Den. See you later, presumably with my ears well burnt so I might need a large pot of cooling cream when I get back. Well done, mate."

As he pushed open the swing door with his elbows to avoid dropping the files, he winked at his colleague, but failed to see the blush that painted her cheeks as he left the room. She had worked in Dan's team for almost four years, and although unaware her stunning looks attracted a great deal of attention from most of the other male officers, the one that interested her merely treated her like a *'mate'*.

Sod him. But her heart wasn't in her thoughts. She wondered if he ever thought of Lucy Hamilton. He seemed so keen, yet nothing came of it, so maybe there was hope for her yet.

Chapter 16

"You ought to report this to the police," said Heidi, passing a cigarette to Jose. The two girls stared at Emma who was sitting cross-legged on the other side of her double bed, twirling a long lock of hair round and round from the side of her head, a child-hood habit rearing itself as it occasionally did when she was worried.

"Don't be stupid," said Emma, looking contemptuously at her two friends sitting in similar ways on the edge of her bed. "Christ, me mum would kill me for lying about where I was going."

"No, she wouldn't," insisted Heidi, wringing her hands in frustration. "She might be cross first off, but then she'd be relieved you wuz safe."

"Oh yeah, till she found out I was carrying a knife and pepper spray."

"Yeah, but you was only carrying 'em for protection in case anyone whacked you," said Jose. She blew out smoke from the cigarette, waving her arms through the cloud to disperse the smoke in case Mrs Bradbury came in with the promised cups of tea.

"Remember what happened to Hannah. She carried a knife 'cos her ex wouldn't leave her alone and threatened to do her in."

"Em's right," said Heidi, turning to look at Jose and

taking the four centimetres of the cigarette left for a last drag. "When he attacked her and she defended herself and cut his arm, the bastard cops did her and he walked free." She took a deep draw and on hearing footsteps on the stairs, ran to the open window, blew out the mouthful of smoke and threw the butt into the garden.

"Remember to pick that up when you go," whispered Emma as the door opened and her mum appeared with a tray of mugs steaming with the tea that she regularly made for her daughter's friends.

"Not going out tonight, girls?" Mrs Bradbury asked as she handed round the mugs.

"Nah, just staying in for a chat and a catch-up, mum." Emma watched as her mum left before shouting her thanks through the closed door. Turning back to her friends, she continued to talk quietly aware her mum could win a gold medal at the Olympics for over-hearing things she wasn't meant to hear! "Cops aside, can you imagine how she'd hit the roof if she knew I carried a weapon. Try and tell her it's for protection and then she wouldn't let me go out if it was that dangerous."

"Well, what are you going to do?" said Jose. Watching Emma's nervous hair twirling she started to emulate her and twiddle her own long hair that was a similar colour to Emma's. "Where'd you say you met him?"

"Prada, but if he's got any sense he's not going to visit there again, is he. He'll think I've reported it and the cops'll be crawling over the place like ants. No, don't reckon he'll go there again."

"Maybe we ought to warn everyone. You're good at drawing, why don't you do one of your portraits like you do of us? We'll photocopy it and hand it out to our mates. You could take it into your course and dish 'em out and I'll take one into mine." Heidi glanced from Emma back to Jose. "Whad you think, Jos, good idea?"

"Yeah, good idea." She looked at Emma to check her

reaction. "You don't look too keen, but your drawings are great. Can you remember what he looks like? Maybe save another mate going through the same thing."

"OK." Emma closed her eyes. "I can see him clear as anything." Jumping from the bed, she hurried to her dressing table and started sorting through the piled-up mess.

"What you looking for?"

"Whad you bloody think, Heid? Me drawing pad." After throwing most of the jumble onto the floor, Emma eventually retrieved the pad and a pen from the heap and hurried back to her position on the bed.

Silence reigned as she turned to a blank page, placing the end of the pen between her lips, and then stared at the pad. Jose and Heidi supped their tea; not interrupting their friend whom they knew would not speak as she concentrated on her efforts. After a minute had passed, she put the pen onto the paper, and with her tongue poking out of the side of her mouth, began her endeavours.

The teas were finished, and the two friends waited patiently for the end-result. They knew better than to interrupt Em 'in full flow' as it was known. When Emma held the pad out in front of her for a last scrutiny, both the girls jumped off the bed and raced round to look at the efforts. They both gasped their admiration for the picture before them.

"Can't say if it's a true likeness 'cos I don't know the bastard, but it's a great drawing," said Heidi.

"Bloody great. Christ, rapist or not, he looks definitely fit," said Jose; 'fit' being teenager parlance for a real dish.

"Yeah, that looks like him." Emma's muttered words sounded bitter.

"You got a scanner on your PC, Em?"

"Yeah. I'll knock up a half dozen for each of us and we'll pass 'em out. Tell everyone, if you see this man; don't let him charm your knickers off. Leave well alone."

Her two friends stared at the portrait of the dark-haired

man that Emma, with just a black pen on plain white paper, if accurate, had illustrated and displayed a handsome man with beautiful eyes.

"Certainly looks rare fit. Think I'd have been taken in too," said Jose. "Whad you say he was, 'bout thirty-ish?"

Emma was still staring at her efforts, and ignoring Jose's question, looked up at her friends, her eyes sparkling with enthusiasm. "Got an idea. Can't remember exactly where it is, but let's find the house." She looked from one to the other. "Don't look like that. We don't do nothing. We just suss out the right address, then we can report that to the cops. Just phone them, say I got attacked and this is where the bastard lives."

"Thought you said you couldn't remember as you were legging it, and were at the top of Castle Street before you stopped."

"I think it's a good idea," said Jose. "Christ, Coley ent that big an area. We can go out on our bikes on Saturday and ride round. You said you had sort of an idea where it was."

"OK, you're on," said Heidi. "Anyway, though we know this Loddon House is a false name and don't exist 'cos we checked on the internet. Whatever it's really called, the house is there somewhere. Another thing, what about his mate, the taxi driver. D'you reckon she was kosher?"

"No, I reckon she was in on it."

"What about drawing her too?"

"Didn't really get a good look at her. Not good enough to draw. I know she had long black hair, badly done blond streaks, parted in the middle and was fucking ugly. She was definitely in on it, 'cos she kept praising him up, said she'd known him for years. Her taxi badge said she was… Linette…or Yvonne...then some foreign name." Emma jumped up from the bed. "No, we go looking for the house."

"Then you phone the cops."

"Maybe. I'll think about it. Maybe we get ten of us go around there and sort him out, whad you say?"

The two girls hooted with laughter at the idea.

"Yeah, no-one messes with my mate without paying," said Heidi, feeling safe in the security of her friend's bedroom.

The bedroom door opened, and Mrs Bradbury's head appeared around the door.

"You girls sound happy. Up to planning some mischief?" She withdrew to make more tea, grinning at the girls' protests of 'Would we? Course not.'

Chapter 17

Meena glanced across the room at Mel who was drinking coffee whilst checking a report.

"Hey Mel, WPC Mandy French's got a personal number plate for her twenty first birthday from her boyfriend."

Meena sipped her coffee, waiting for Mel's reply, knowing her colleague wasn't keen on the Woman Police Officer who was known to think rather a lot of herself. Mel sat back in her chair, squinted over her cup before replying. "Hmmm, bet it reads FAT MF1."

The irreverent but apt reply caused Meena, not known for being bitchy, but in this instance unable to contain her mirth, to splutter a mouthful of her coffee over her desk before saying, "Mel, that's an awful thing to say."

"Yes, but very appropriate to the size of her arse, you must agree."

Meena giggled as she wiped up the mess with a tissue, trying to think of a witty reply but her telephone ringing broke the moment. Trying to sound more professional than she felt, she swallowed hard before saying, "DC Meena Mesbah, how can I help?"

"Meena, its Simon on the front desk. Got a lady here, Mrs Taylor, reporting another missing person. Her daughter Lilly, aged twenty-five, missing for four days. Phones her mum regularly every other day normally. Never misses.

Thought under the circumstances you might want to deal with this."

His words caused a sensation resembling a sharp, frosty digit to scrape along her backbone that inevitably occurred when she was alarmed. Not wanting to sound as anxious as she felt, she just thanked the police colleague and said she would come to the front desk immediately to deal with the matter.

"Anything wrong?" asked Mel. "Your golden looks have diminished to a distinct shade of cheap white bedsheets."

"Another missing lady. Although there are no bodies, but to use our esteemed leader's least favourite word, coincidence… I think now four missing women is definitely not a fluke by any body's reasoning."

"That was not the most succinct sentence I've heard you say, but I get your drift and inclined to agree with you. Four, blimey, that's dodgy."

Meena picked up a writing pad and pen from her desk and hurrying towards the door looked over her shoulder to Mel, saying, "Very dodgy. I'm just going to reception to talk to the mother who's reported her missing."

Walking through the swing doors into the reception area, Meena looked at Simon Leadbetter, the police officer manning the desk, who nodded her towards a smartly dressed woman perched on the edge of one of the chairs. Meena approached her, noting the woman's twisted face as she anxiously chewed the side of her mouth. After introducing herself and confirming with Simon that one of the interview rooms was free, she invited the woman to accompany her.

Refusing the offer of a tea or coffee, and before Meena could ask her anything, the woman gabbled out her concerns, her face showing her distress.

"As I explained to the policeman at the desk, it's my daughter Lilly. She phones me regularly and I haven't heard from her for four days. She's never, ever done that. I tried phoning her on her landline and her mobile, but I just get the answer phone. I live in Pangbourne. Haven't got a car now so I caught the bus and went to her flat. She lives just off the Oxford Road. I've got a key, so I let myself in. She wasn't there. No sign, nothing."

As though a balloon had burst and all the air had escaped, the woman flopped back in her chair, seemed to shrivel into herself, and the words dried up. Her eyes were wide and hysterical, and Meena deemed this was the moment to take control of the situation.

"Right, Mrs Taylor, understandably you are concerned, but let's go through this slowly and we'll sort out the details. Now, why don't you let me get you a drink and we can discuss this further."

Still deflated, Mrs Taylor just nodded her confirmation for a coffee. The machine was outside the door, so it only took Meena a minute to get two cups of something that poorly resembled the beverage, smelt uninviting, and tasted even worse. The woman was obviously in shock, and Meena hoped the foul liquid wouldn't add to the woman's anguish. Giving her the time to sip some of her drink before she questioned her, Meena studied her as she supped her own drink. She was dressed in a smart navy blue cotton suit beneath which was a crisp, pale blue blouse. On the lapel was a large brooch of a peacock, small diamanté, and sapphire coloured gemstones covering the feathered tail. Meena wasn't one for sparkling jewellery, but the brooch went well with the plain clothes and the women's whole persona was of a smart, intelligent woman who cared about her appearance.

"Mrs. Taylor, are you feeling alright now to continue and answer some questions?" Meena asked gently. At the woman's nod, she continued. "When exactly did you last see or hear from your daughter?"

"Umm, Saturday…no, Friday last. We chatted for a few minutes. Then she said she had to go because she had a date. Sounded really excited. She'd make a lovely mum, but she's just never met the right man."

Meena wrote the details in her notebook before asking. "Did she say anything about the date? Who she was meeting? Where they were going?"

"No, I asked her all that, but she just laughed and said he was a real dreamboat, and if the date was as good as she hoped, she'd phone me the next day and tell me." Mrs Taylor finished her coffee and placed the plastic beaker on the table. Meena didn't want to hurry her, and experience had shown her that if you wait long enough, the speaker will say something else. She watched as the woman poked her hair behind her ears, heard her sigh before she continued, "But she didn't phone. I waited all day, then another day, then another...I hadn't wanted to rush her, but...I had been as excited as she was. By nine o' clock last night, when she never answered her phone again, I had an awful feeling of... dread. Like a premonition. Maybe you think I'm daft, but I've had them before and I'm not wrong. I'm not a hysteric, believe me, something's not right."

Meena saw before her a sensible woman not given to panic and with what she already knew, she silently agreed with Mrs Taylor, something was definitely not right, and that cold feeling of the frosty digit was back, manipulating her backbone with a vengeance.

She also knew that now Lilly was the missing woman on the extended W listed on the white board in the front of the incident room.

Chapter 18

Mrs June North handed her son the purse containing a ten-pound note. "Don't lose it, Pete, or you'll get scalped. Hold it tight. The shopping list to give Mr Ramsheer is with the money. Just give him the purse and tell him the order's inside. Here's a carrier bag. Now all you're getting is half a dozen eggs, sausages and a pack of bacon so it won't be heavy, but don't swing the bag around like you usually do or you'll break the eggs. Is that clear?"

"Can I buy something for me? Something for going." Peter's big, appealing brown eyes set in his angel face was so serious it triggered a gentle smile to break out on his mum's face and a happy skip in her heart. She often wondered what she'd done to get such a sweet kid. No trouble, not like the older two toe-rags. Ruffling his fair curls, she said, "OK, you can spend about fifty pence. Just get yourself some smarties or jelly babies. No bubble gum."

"OK, mum." Peter slipped the purse into the carrier and walked to the door.

"Hey you, where's my kiss?"

Peter ran back to his mum, throwing his arms round her waist and she bent and kissed the top of his head. "Fancy going off," she chided him, "before giving you're ol' mum a smacker."

He untangled himself from his mum's clutches and

hurried to the door again, the thought of sweets beaming like a beckoning, welcoming beacon.

June never saw him walk along the garden path, and then turn right to the corner shop as she normally did when her little cherub went off on an errand because the phone rang and distracted her. She hesitated before answering because although the corner shop was only at the end of the street, she loved watching him as he skipped so happily down the road, but guessed this call was from her sister who always phoned at this time on a Tuesday, and as Tessa suffered from depression, she often contacted her for a pacifying chat.

"Mum, can I watch tele?"

"Finished your homework?" June asked in a pre-occupied fashion. She was gazing out of the window, arms folded, heart beating with anxiety, and so didn't hear her eldest son's answer that he had finished everything. When she didn't reply, he just shrugged and walked into the living room to watch his favourite programme.

June looked at her watch for the fifth time in ten minutes.

"What's wrong, Mum?" asked Katie as she sauntered into the room. June's eleven-year-old daughter was 'the little sod of the family' in the fashion of her mum's words, but underneath the mischievous exterior beat a sensitive heart, and Katie didn't like her mum's agitated appearance.

"It's our Peter. Sent him off to the corner shop fifteen, twenty minutes ago. He should be back by now." As though the explanation had made up her mind, June North pulled on her cardigan and said, "Right, I'm not waiting any longer, I'm going to check on him."

"Mum don't bother. I'll go," said Katie. "Your hips still playing up and I can run up there in two minutes. Bet he's talking to ol' man Ramsheer. You know what chatter boxes they both are."

Before her mum could argue, Katie dashed from the room. Her mum's concern was catching, and as she ran down the street, looking in every direction for her young brother, her heart was pounding so fast she felt as though someone was inside her beating it with a hammer. On dashing into the shop and only seeing a bemused Mr Ramsheer behind the counter, the hammering detonated like an exploding sun. Katie shrieked from the pain of something evil that she felt in every cell of her being and intuitively knew this moment was the end of her family's happiness in this world forever.

Chapter 19

The three girls skidded to a halt at the end of the long lane that stretched out before them. The heat from the last of summer that was racing over the horizon into early autumn had hardened the muddy path, and despite a couple of days of rain last week, the solid ruts that extended into the distance resembled an impassable abyss.

"Shite," said Jose as she delved into the left pocket of her skimpy shorts for her cigarette packet.

"Damn," agreed Emma. "We've been this way before."

Heidi eased herself slowly off her saddle. "Oh God, my arse is killing me. I haven't cycled this far in ages. Not since I biked to school." Lowering her bike onto the grass bank that lined the small road that led to the seemingly impenetrable track, she rubbed her backside, groaning at the discomfort. "Who suggested this bloody madness?"

Emma, used to her friend's whinging if exposed to the least amount of discomfort, ignored the remark. Holding the bike's handlebars, her legs straddled either side of her bike; she screwed her eyes up against the low sun's brightness despite the light being fragmented into a myriad of broken pieces as it pierced through the thick leaves of the row of trees in front of them.

"It's not up this track, I know," she muttered. "The taxi would've bounced all over the place. Road was not made up, gravelly, but never this bad. Christ, this looks like a sea of muddy waves. If it was water, a surfer'd be in his element."

The piercing wail from Jose made her two friends jump. "Fucking hell, Jos, what the hell's the matter?" said Heidi. "You been stung or some'ink?"

The ear-splitting wailing continued, and both Emma and Heidi, even though used to their friend's tendency to hysterics, became concerned.

"I've lost me fags," she yowled. "They musta fallen out of me pockets. Twenty frigging fags, untouched. Haven't even opened the packet. Sod and bum."

Heidi smirked, not able to contain her mirth, really believing Jose had been seriously hurt and now relieved it was not the case.

"Jeez, Jos, you scared me to death, you stupid cow," snapped Emma. "Don't panic. This isn't the way anyway so we'll re-trace our steps so keep your eyes open for them." Easing her bike round, she pushed on the pedal, lifting herself onto the saddle and rode back the way they had come.

"Not too fast, Em," Jose called, "We'll never spot them otherwise."

The three girls biked through the leafy lanes that surrounded the Coley Park Council Estate, jolting slowly over the stony path that cut along the side of the wide stream to the north, that eventually turned left bringing them back towards the main roads of the town. Emma braked to a halt as she spotted the cause of Jose's consternation.

"Found 'em," she called to her friends who were lagging more and more behind. Lowering her bike to the ground, she picked up the packet and handed it to a relieved Jose as she skidded to a halt, her brakes not being very efficient.

"Thank God," puffed a red-faced Jose, her colour and laboured breathing showing clearly her habit wasn't making her fit. "I'm knackered. I'm not going another metre till I've had a drag and a rest."

The three girls extracted their coke bottles from their backpacks and sunk down onto a large tree trunk conveniently lying by the side of the road. Jose lit up, took a deep drag, offering the cigarette to her friends who shook their heads as they gratefully glugged their drinks.

The muted noise of distant traffic didn't disturb the peace of the countryside, and the girls sat in silence, still breathing heavily from their exertions, and enjoying the noisy twittering of the birds.

"Peaceful, ennit," whispered Heidi.

Emma was about to agree when she noticed a chimney through the thick growth of trees opposite where they were sitting.

"Hang on a minute," she said, getting to her feet. She crossed the narrow road but could see nothing. Turning to the left, she scooted down the road and disappeared out of sight from her friends.

"What's wrong with her?" said Jose, blowing the last of the smoke from her cigarette into the air. "She want a pee or something?"

Heidi didn't answer but got to her feet after a minute, wondering if they ought to follow her friend, and was then relieved when Emma re-appeared, sprinting towards them.

"I've found it," she said, great satisfaction colouring her voice. "Don't know how we missed it, though there's quite a sharp turn before you get into the garden." She snatched up her bike. "Come on you two, hurry up, we gotta check this out."

Emma ran down the road, pushing her bike with Heidi close behind when Jose's familiar wail slowed them down.

"Uhh… Em…Heid, don't think we ought to do this. If it's definitely the house, let's phone the cops. If he's there, it could be well dodgy."

She saw them say something to each other, and then they carried on running, ignoring her remark. Disappearing around a corner, Jose's concern escalated sky-high like a Houston rocket. Snatching up her bike, she ran after them as if the mad rapist was on her tail; being on her own was definitely worse than being side by side with crazy friends and facing the enemy. Rounding the bend where they had disappeared, she almost collided with the pair who had discarded their bikes and were kneeling and peering through a gap in a large bush.

"What're you doing?" she whispered, lying her bike next to theirs and then crawling on her hands and knees to where they were positioned. "Can you see some'ink?"

Emma stood up.

"Get down," hissed Jose, peering through the gap in the hedge. Then to her horror, Heidi stood up and joined Emma.

"Don't worry, Jos," explained Emma. "The house looks empty."

The words only slightly re-assured Jose, but not wanting to appear a total wuss, she joined her friends, although she was not able to control her shaking legs. When she saw the boarded-up windows, the relief was slight.

"This definitely the place?" said Heidi.

"Yes, definitely," said Emma. "Anyone up for some breaking, and entering?"

Jose whimpered as her friends opened the garden gate and boldly walked to the front door.

Chapter 20

The Incident Room was full to capacity and except for the overwhelming smell of coffee, the reigning silence would have fooled someone without sight that anybody else was present. All eyes were glued to the white board at the front of the room; even the breathing of the officers seemed suspended by the chart before them suggesting something stomach-turning.

Across the top of the board were photographs of four women, their names, ages, and the dates they were reported missing. Listed below in large letters were the sad words, 'MISSING…NO BODIES'. On a lower level were photographs of five missing boys, including Jason, the only boy whose body had so far been recovered. An arrowed line joined the photographs in the date order that they were reported missing, making the shape of an extended letter 'W'.

Feeling that the Officers present had had enough time to grasp the situation, Dan Blake stepped forward.

"As you can all see, four missing women, five missing boys, the latest one being Peter North. DI Cole and I have just returned after visiting his family again. With all of these disappearances, only one body has currently come to light." He indicated the photograph of Jason Stone, the boy's smiling face showing front teeth that looked too large for his child size mouth. "Jason, aged 9, whose body was spotted by a jogger. The women's disappearances were important, but obviously eventually set at a lower level in terms of priority; firstly, because no bodies have turned up and secondly, as we know, many adults go missing on a daily basis, although all of these disappearances were out of character, and were thoroughly investigated.

"We know some missing adults eventually turn up, and the remainder usually don't want to be found. However, the reports on these women suggest that families are concerned because for all of them, just disappearing, as I said, was out of character." Dan looked round the room and asked if there were any questions so far. When none were forthcoming, he continued. "Naturally, vulnerable children are a different case altogether. What didn't help initially was the fact that Tommy, and Harry had gone missing on several occasions previously. They both had poor attendance records at school, and it was believed they'd scarpered again.

"Meena spotted the pattern when she was merging information on various current and cold cases into the computer, although until that time, each case had a different investigating officer in other areas in the Thames Valley and the connection wasn't spotted. I think there's no excuse for that, but we don't want to waste time on blame, bad police work or what could have been poor chance.

"We need to focus our energies on what's ahead of us. Under the circumstances, the cases have been merged, headed up by DI Cole as the S.I.O. answering to DCI Jacobs. I'm running the day to day. Adam Kennedy's seconded to the bank robbery at the Nat West Bank; consequently, for this investigation, I'm reporting to DI Cole with two sub-teams, one headed up by DC Luke Steiner and the other headed up by DC Meena Mesbah."

Dan paused and walked to the front table and picked up his coffee cup. He swirled the cup, peering at the uninviting contents and then shuddered as he sipped the cold brew.

"Christ, that's awful." The shocked silence had slipped away, and he could hear mutterings swirling round the room. "Any questions, so far?"

"Boss, although you said all the cases were previously dealt with as separate incidences, have we discovered any connections yet? There must be some, I can't believe there isn't."

"OK, Tom, I'll get to that. As I said, Meena to head the team that will look again into the disappearances of the women whilst Luke will head up the investigation into the missing children. I will liaise with the two of them, and naturally all information will be shared across the two teams.

"When Meena noticed the pattern originally, I asked her to look for connections. I agree with you, Tom, there has to be. As to whether there is also a connection between the women and the children's disappearances, Mel is concentrating on that area specifically and will report to Luke and Meena because I think if there is a link, that could be the key to the investigation." Dan turned to Meena. "Have you managed to find anything that connects these cases yet, Meena?"

"Not as such, boss, but now it's our top priority, I'll keep on it. The one link I did notice is that the women all went missing either from nightclubs or telling friends or family they were going out on a date."

"OK thanks. Luke, connections?"

"The thing that connects the kids is they all go to church schools. Tommy and Jason, and the latest, Peter, all went to catholic schools, not the same ones and the other two, Harry and Jack went to C of E schools. Again, not the same ones. I couldn't find anything that connects the lads to the women."

"Seems the sequence of dates suggests a connection," a female voice from the back of the room called out. "Plus, the fact the dates of those going missing are getting closer and closer."

"Do you think he, she, they, the perpetrators, are getting…cocky, needing more and more...victims? I won't say murders 'cos so far we have only one body... to get their sick kicks?" asked Luke Steiner who was sitting in the front row next to Meena. The broad -shouldered detective's face was pink with the heat of the room, and his blond hair plastered to his face with sweat. He glanced round, saying,

"God it's hot in here with all these people. Can someone please open the damn window?"

Dan, also feeling the heat, waited until someone opened two windows before he continued. "Yes, I think the dates clearly indicate an escalation in activity, and that is really worrying. Uniform are still out questioning regarding the Jason Stone's disappearance, and another team is also out going door-to-door on the Peter North enquiry. There are officers still looking into the other missing lads, although realistically with the time lapse, we know it'll be searching for bodies and not the lads themselves. We know that every minute that goes by reduces our chances of finding Peter alive, so speed is essential."

"CCTV or house-to-house been productive?" asked Tom Carter.

"Nothing's turned up yet. No-one seems to have seen anything, but if we keep it high profile maybe it'll jog a memory or two. Of course, the worrying thing is, if the pattern, ie the extended W is an indicator of a pattern, we're a woman short. Could mean nothing, could mean there are two perpetrators and no connection. I would suggest there is a connection, so either the perpetrators are out of sync, or as yet, the woman hasn't been reported missing. Let's hope that's not the case. However, until we know or hear anything, we go with an open mind, consider all possibilities."

Dan picked up some work sheets from the front desk. "OK, list of Actions and your assigned teams. Luke's team to stay here and Meena's team meet up in Incident Room Two for your Actions. I know you'll all do your best." Dan turned to his two DCs. "See you outside for just a minute.

After retrieving their paperwork, Luke and Meena followed Dan into the corridor. He was gazing out of a window and didn't turn when they stood next to him. Running his fingers through his hair, he shook his head in frustration.

"Damn and hell," were his only words but the venom in his voice confirmed their rising doubts.

"Boss, you thinking what I'm thinking?" said Luke.

"What *are* you thinking, Luke?"

Luke didn't answer, but just looked at his colleague and Meena spoke for them both.

"We've been talking, boss. No evidence yet, but we've both got these feelings, intuition. I don't know, call it what you want. This smacks appallingly of the horrors of four years ago. I've got iron insects with lethally sharp wings flying madly round in my stomach."

Dan continued to stare out of the window. "Yeah, but Tomas is dead...she's dead," he shrugged and eventually murmured. "It can't be her. Anyway, their sick leanings were to children, and in this instance, we have women and children missing. Women...that wasn't their bag at all."

"Then why, boss, do the three of us have the same fears, that other nonces are out there again, and getting very organised?"

He turned to face them, his normally cheerful face vampire white with trepidation. "Yeah, but our deadly enemies, Tomas and Van Looy are dead. Tomas, absolutely no doubt, I saw the body myself, albeit what was left by the time it was found. That was him! The devil in woman's clothing...well, I was seconded elsewhere by then." He turned to his white-faced colleagues. "Either of you see the remains of the body found in the Thames.

They both shook their heads

"The DNA matched that found at the old men's murder," said Luke.

Dan nodded, and murmured, "Yeah, but why do we all

feel…? Still, I wouldn't trust her as far as I could throw her… and the DNA matched our findings, you say?"

"Close families share similar DNA, Boss," said Luke. He shrugged and continued, "OK, similar maybe, maybe not identical, but it was the same DNA as that present at the old men's murders, definitely, and although no proof, we strongly suspect she was present."

"Unless she was a twin," muttered Meena. She looked at her boss. "Only joking, bad joke, too much of a coincidence."

Dan turned to her, "Family members! Christ, wasn't that checked?" His green eyes were huge with horror.

"We had no need to," said Luke. "As I said, the DNA from the body found in the river definitely matched that found at the murder scene of the three dead men. We had no need to think it wasn't hers. Despite investigating, we couldn't trace down any family."

"Well, with this going on, we'd better make a bloody hundred per cent sure, hadn't we?" Dan strode down the corridor. As he pushed opened the swing doors at the end, he called back. "Get Mel on it straight away. You two are already up to your eyes in it. She's not back to haunt us, but let's make two hundred percent sure."

"Up to our eyes in shit if we discover she's got a twin sister," said Meena. "We should have checked."

"Nah, don't worry," Luke assured his colleague," that would be a horrible, convenient coincidence and you know DI Cole assures us they don't exist. Things like that only happen in films or on the tele."

The two stared at each other, their feelings not on a par with his confident assurances, because if the female anti-Christ was not dead and back in town, then something nasty and evil had raised its head.

Chapter 21

"Right lads," the Irish teacher said, "homework. Remind me of the research topic I asked you to investigate?"

Four chubby hands shot up, arms ramrod straight, each desperate to be asked. Mr Declan O'Leary was very popular in the school. His gentle accent, soft as melted chocolate rolling off the tongue, and obviously forged in a fairy factory in Southern Ireland, supported his popularity. He never raised his voice in anger, and no boy came into his class for a lesson dreading the next hour, or left at the end of it feeling down at heart.

Not overly given to hard work, his humour and life experiences often unwittingly swayed the topic of the hour down a very meandering path, usually not connected to the theme of the lesson. He taught sports, and a very loose mixture of geography and chemistry, or whatever took his fancy on the day, and the content of the two subjects could ramble from the life of frogs, his alleged prowess at ju-jitsu, different baits needed for fly-fishing as he was an avid angler, or whether or not his geraniums had flowered well this year right through to his walking holiday in the Welsh Hills.

With the exception of the class swat, a plump but angelic faced boy with the unfortunate name of Bernie Pratt, and consequently known to his cruel-tongued classmates as

Fat-Pratt-Face, none of the boys were one bit interested in geography, chemistry or any lesson that needed brain power. However, the boys rarely interrupted his diverse musings unless they suspected the subject was running dry, and then some bright spark would dredge up another open question to pump him up and keep him going.

Mr O'Leary decided to choose the lad nearest the front of the classroom to answer his question.

"Johnny Payne, you tell us."

"Sir, we had to find out about precious stones. How they were formed, where they're found, and what colours they were."

"Good lad," said Mr O'Leary. "Me sister Mary had a beautiful emerald engagement ring. Stone big enough to look like a gobstopper. If it was a gobstopper, what colour would it have been?" Silence followed the question because none of the boys actually believed the homework would be pursued. Only Bernie Pratt had done any work, and he was so fed up with the lack of knowledge he was obtaining from geography cum chemistry lessons, that he had mostly given up listening, and was currently gazing out of the window watching Father Francis. The master had his finger pointing like a lethal knife as though to stab through to his heart should it penetrate a certain Daniel Bigley's navy-blue jumper, obviously giving him and two other fifth formers a right bollocking for being late for a lesson. "Right, come on lads. Surely everyone knows the colours of emeralds are a similar colour to a *gooseberry* flavoured gobstopper...hint hint."

When the penny dropped, six hands shot up for attention and Alec Carter was pleased to be selected to answer an easy question, but still earn a favour mark from Mr O'Leary.

"Green, sir."

"Good lad. OK, Alec, now answer me this. How were emeralds formed and where are they to be found?"

It took a great deal of skill for Alec to side-track

the question. Like a siren from Greek mythology, Alec, although not singing as beguilingly as the sea nymphs, nevertheless lured Mr O'Leary, not to doom on the rocks, but onto a subject not remotely aligned with gemstones. Golf was another of the teacher's weaknesses and having been a six handicapper in his youth, if the pupils could get him onto this subject, the class was pretty much assured that his recollections would take at least half an hour. Alec's deflecting question as to whether Mr O'Leary had ever won a first prize at golf, might, to an innocent onlooker, have seemed stupid and wholly unconnected, but the intention worked, and emeralds, as such, were forgotten and the teacher's success at his golf club's championship day was duly discussed.

Unfortunately, five minutes before the bell was due to sound indicating the end of the lesson, Mr O'Leary somewhat gathered his thoughts, had a pang of conscience that he had strayed from the subject, and felt he might have a small stab at focusing on what he was actually paid to do.

He took a deep breath, his eyes sweeping the room for a victim, and Tom Gardner, slumped on his chair and indulging in his favourite past time of doodling, was selected.

"Tom, me lad," boomed the Irish voice, making Tom break the lead in his pencil as the shock caused him to jab it into his notebook, "tell me where we find rubies?"

Tom, not given to great intelligence and having just drawn a rather good design of the sun, moon, planets, and other heavenly bodies, panicked. His brain went blank and he stuttered, "Umm, rubies…. Rubies…on the moon, sir?"

Luckily for Tom, the bell ending the loosely connected geography cum chemistry period peeled out, and Mr O'Leary, having a good sense of humour, instead of extra homework or detention for not paying attention, slapped his textbook closed, roared with laughter at the silly answer, and dismissed the boys. Tom was first from the room, in case 'sir' changed his mind.

Mr O'Leary was as popular with most of his fellow teachers as with the pupils and when he entered the staff room a cup of strong, sweet tea was thrust into his hand by one of the Jesuit Priest teachers, Father Ignatius.

"Bless you, Father," said Mr O'Leary, and plonking his heavy frame due to a liking for both whisky and cream doughnuts, although not taken together, he began to regale his colleagues with tales from the classroom.

"I had a right bloomer today from Tom Gardner," he chuckled.

"Oh, do tell," said Father Francis, his voice laced with sarcasm, knowing nothing halted the Irishman in full flow. The black looks from the other seven members of the teaching staff stopped further nasty comments. The Priest was jealous of his colleague's popularity. The staff were aware Father Francis's tongue had a spiteful edge to it, and that didn't make him well liked in the staff room.

"Carry on, Declan," encouraged the quietly spoken teacher of maths who loved and admired the Irishman for his large heart and generous nature.

Between sips of his tea and chuckles at his recollections, Mr O'Leary said, "When I asked the lad where rubies came from, he just said, 'Rubies…on the Moon, sir."

Seven of the staff joined in with his mirth except for Father Francis. The colour drained from his face and he felt a lump with the consistency of concrete form in his throat. A violent pain formed around his heart, whipping a sting across his chest and for a few moments, he thought he was experiencing a heart attack. Placing his teacup onto the coffee table with a shaking hand, he whispered to be excused, and hurried from the room.

Despite orders not to use this telephone number unless it was an extreme emergency, using his mobile, he dialled the forbidden number, sensing the incident he had just witnessed was an urgent situation.

"I must report an occurrence," he hissed quietly when

his call was answered with a sharp 'Yes'. "Someone's just used the password."

"Does he know anything?"

"I don't know. He must do. I think he was testing me. Yes, he was. He glared at me when he said it." Father Francis's thoughts were out of control with panic.

"Then if it's not your imagination working overtime, you know what to do. Dispose of him as soon as possible."

The phone went dead.

Chapter 22

"What the fuck do you mean, she got away?" Yvette Van Looy's voice was shrill.

"Don't use that language," Matthew Nielson muttered, irritated by his companion's vulgar language. "It's no big deal. There's nothing to trace. We've stopped using that location; she doesn't have my real name. She was nothing but a kid; bet she didn't even tell her parents about the date. Young kid, much older man, can you imagine what they'd have said."

The woman glared at him, and if the piercing look had become physical, it would have scarred the handsome man's face. "How did it happen? I should have refused to drive her. When you asked me to drive her and I hadn't vetted her beforehand…"

The man shrugged. "Look, I've just explained, I'd spotted her one night when you weren't at the night club for some reason. I just fancied a bit of dark haired, teenager for a change. I had the North kid lined up for you so I was saving you a job."

"Because, you stupid bastard, we should have waited for a while now a kid's body's been found. Plus, getting yourself a woman, girl, whatever, without me vetting her was idiotic. All hell's broken loose now the cops have found this kid's body, so we should have played it cool for a change. It's no good carrying on regardless if there's danger. One thing I'll say about Gerry Tomas, he didn't take any chances."

"Well, he got caught in the end, didn't he? He's six feet under now, I don't call that successful."

"He never got nicked by the cops though. We covered our every move. He only got caught because those bastard kids stabbed him, and the Brothers found out about our whereabouts."

Matthew winced at the word stab, but so far Yvette hadn't noticed his bulky sock due to the bandages and his new limp that he had taken great steps to disguise.

Matthew thoughts bounced back to their present conversation. He knew that Gerry Tomas and Yvette had escaped from arrest by the police whilst the rest of the cell to which the two had previously belonged had been apprehended during their planned operation.

"You just got lucky," he snapped. "As I understand it, you just happened not to be there when members of the Brotherhood went to the house seeking vengeance for the killing of the Committee of Elders. If you had, you wouldn't be sitting here now. So, I repeat, you got lucky, so don't preach to me, you supercilious cow."

"The stupid old dodderers were blaming us for the undercover cop infiltrating our cell. We did all the checks possible to check his authenticity before he could join us. His credentials were perfect."

"Oh yes, but you couldn't control yourselves, and so you foolishly abduct three kids to use as bait to lure him in and punish him as retribution. That defies belief! You then get into a rage, stab the whole damn committee of Elders when they were questioning you, understandably, about the abductions. Oh yes, very careful…very controlled, not!"

"I hope the Elders are rotting in hell. As regards the cop, Adam Kennedy, our plans worked, didn't they? We got him. He shouldn't have played Mr Nice Guy, offering himself in exchange for the kids. We never did intend to let the kids go. I'm glad to say, Kennedy suffered a great deal. The punishment we inflicted on him was terrible."

"How was it, then, that you couldn't even keep him and the three kids? All of them escaped. You never even thought to search that street wise hooligan who was armed with knives that he eventually used to stab and injure your dearest mate Tomas."

Matthew threw back his head and laughed. When his mirth finished, he leaned forward and pointed his finger at Yvette. "Don't you lecture me about Emma Bradbury getting away. Just so happened the little whore was armed with a spray." He glared at her; glad he hadn't mentioned she'd also had a knife for protection. He continued, "Anyway, you couldn't keep those kids and a cop from escaping when they were locked up in a cellar. You've got nothing to be so high and mighty about. I'm surprised you even told me about it. Plus, and a big plus at that, if you hadn't dumped that Jason kid in the Warren where you did, he wouldn't have been found because the cops won't find the other kids' bodies in a thousand years. They'll never find the women in a *million* years, so actually our present dodgy predicament is down to you, because you panicked!"

"I only dumped him there as a temporary measure because of the accident along the road and I had the kid's body in the boot, and just couldn't take the chance he would've been found."

"Why would the police search your boot? You were just in a line of traffic waiting until the accident was cleared. You panicked, so despite your nagging, it's your fault."

Yvette held her breath. She could feel her dislike for this man coursing like an army of marching red ants through her veins. Slowly letting out her breath, she controlled herself. No-one spoke to her like that and lived to tell the tale, but today wasn't the time. His skills were still advantageous so until his usefulness finished, she had to restrain her feelings and anger.

"OK, let's stop arguing. It's getting us nowhere. What do we do about that little cow?"

"Nothing. I told you, she has no idea who I really am. We won't use that nightclub again for a time. She's no danger to us."

"The cops must be getting suspicious. All these women and kids disappearing. As far as the papers and news tells us, only one kid's body's been found." Yvette took deeper breaths; glad she was back in control.

"Why you dumped it in the Warren I can't understand. That was dangerous."

"Don't keep repeating yourself. I've just said, it was well hidden. You know I had to dispose of it quickly with that police car patrolling back and forth 'cos of a burglary the night before in one of those big houses that overlooks the river and backs onto the Warren. Appears a jogger taking a leak found him. As you said, they won't find the others where we've dumped them".

"Don't change the subject. Even the cops, thick as pig shit, must be getting the message something's going on. So far, this Bradbury girl's the only one that's got away. She'll go to the cops sooner or later, even if she hasn't been already. We can't take the chance. We've got to get rid of her." Matthew leaned forward in his chair, his eyes narrowing as he considered. "Let's think, how do we find her? You picked her up on the corner by the Calcot Estate bus stop, near to the library, so we don't even know her address." He didn't add that he should have got her address, even if he wasn't the one going to pick her up.

Matthew sat back in his chair and picked up his whisky. He was getting bored with this conversation, going around and around and getting nowhere, and his dislikeable companion was getting on his nerves. Swirling the contents of his glass and watching the amber liquid coat the sides, he lifted the glass to his nose and inhaled the peaty bouquet.

Taking a sip, the drink soothed his tubes and nerves and he felt some of his irritation at this conversation drift away. He looked over the edge of the glass, and keeping the sharp edge out of his voice, he finished, "Ok, so it's best we deal with her. What's your wonderful plan?"

Yvette stood up, finishing her large drink in one go. She leaned close and her alcoholic breath lashed his face. "Don't give it a thought. You may be handsome, but you don't have an original idea in your head. In this day and age, anybody can be traced. Let's hope your lack of brain cells is inversely proportional to your strangling techniques. That's a mathematical relationship should you wonder. I'll find her and do the job properly."

Matthew winced as the door slammed loudly. He finished his drink, wondering what the hell inversely proportional meant. With his annoyance, the urge came back, and he knew he needed to do something very soon to quell the desire. If it spiralled out of control, he might be careless. He put his glass on the coffee table, stood up and went to look for the key to the crypt. After that, he knew what would stop the craving.

The moon was full and bright and as the man drove down the country lane, despite the lack of streetlights, the cats' eyes in the middle of the road and the silver glow from the lunar body above were enough for the road ahead to be clearly seen. After a quarter of a mile past the 30mph sign, he took the next right into a single-track turning. He opened his window a few inches, knowing that in the silence of this wooded area, he'd hear the lonesome cry of the owls that lived here. He loved their cries. Wistful sounds, always reminding him of the creepy films he used to watch as a kid, and yet despite sounding so forlorn, he found it comforting. He never could understand why, he'd hated his home, his childhood and his parents, yet the sound soothed and re-assured him.

Another quarter of a mile on, he came to the old cottage and the lock-up. There was no electricity in either accommodation, so he always came prepared. It was dark here; the moon's glow not able to penetrate the overhanging branches, so a torch was a necessity to be able to see to get the key into the heavy lock on the chain that secured the door.

Everything was as he'd left it ten months ago. He hadn't wanted to leave the area, but the three missing women had caused too much attention from the police. He'd covered his tracks carefully but realised that his pool of clients was compromised, and he'd have to move on. Father Matthew had secured him a position at St Anne's when he innocently explained he had to move back home to look after his parents in the village of Pangbourne, just outside Reading. His parents were long-time dead; he'd made sure they paid for their wickedness to him when he was able, but Father Matthew hadn't known that.

Realising his musings were taking too long, he hurried to the table and lit the hurricane lamp. The light's glow was soft, and he felt an easy comfort spread over him. As he opened the clothes box in the corner the smell from the clothes and the blond wig was musty, but he'd just have to put up with that.

He was dressed and ready to go in ten minutes. He poured himself a milky coffee from his thermos that he'd brought with him. This time he wouldn't use his knife. Although no clients' bodies had been found thus far, he couldn't take the chance at some time in the future they might be, and he didn't want the MO to appear the same as his new intended victim in this area. Some nosy cop might put two and two together and realise that he had lived in both areas where women had been stabbed.

Tonight, I'll use the hammer. Just as quick if you hit them hard enough on the back of the head. If it was good enough for Jack the Ripper, its good enough for me.

Driving away, he felt the thrill of the chase; the kill, the taking of the trophies and then the dumping of their bodies in the long-disused Roman drains, all of which caused a spiral of excitement to escalate up from his toes and accelerate through every part of his body.

He parked up near the night club. Already the whores were spilling out, laughing and yelling to each other. Eventually, as on other occasions, one lone girl waved goodbye to her drunken mates and staggered away. He followed about twenty steps behind. He felt the need spiral through his body. Fondling the hammer in his jacket inside pocket, he whispered to it.

Not long, my friend. And you'll be put to good use.

Chapter 23

The three girls were again in Emma's bedroom, with Jose sprawled over the stack of discarded clothes covering the bed; Heidi slumped uncomfortably in the dressing table chair that contained another heap of underclothes delivered to the bedroom by Emma's mum for tidying away into her chest of drawers. Emma, sitting with her back to the wall, legs drawn up under her chin as she contemplated Heidi's question as to what she intended to do next.

The girls had returned from their breaking and entering enterprise at Loddon House. It had actually turned out to be an easy endeavour. Having crept stealthily around the right side of the house even though the boarded-up windows had indicated the house was not currently occupied, Emma noticed there was no boarding across the large French window that spanned across a large proportion of the back of the house. After peering in, hands cupped around her forehead to keep out the light, she beckoned the girls to join her.

"What are all those white shapes?" said Jose, being the least brave of the trio and her voice wavering with nervousness. "Ghosts?"

"Covers," said Emma. She stood back from her examination, hands on her hips in a knowing posture. "Bloody furniture covers. Either they've lit out of the house or they borrowed the place for dear friggin' Matthew's rape games."

Jose lit up a cigarette and offered it to Heidi for her drag. Shaking her head in an absent-minded refusal, Heidi asked. "OK, Sherlock bloody Holmes, how the hell do you deduce that?"

Emma irritably waved away Jose's offer, coughed on the lingering smoke before saying, "For Heaven sake keep those blasted fags away, Jos. You're smoking too much." She turned to Heidi to explain her meaning. "Well, the furniture in the room where we sat, which come to think of it could very well be this one." She peered again into the room, once more cupping her hands to keep out the light. "It didn't match. The taxi driver had said the house was wonderful, but it was just a mishmash of odd furniture that didn't go together. I reckon the house was only semi furnished and he dragged furniture from other rooms to make out it was well appointed."

"Yeah, 'cos if you'd come into a room with just a bit of furniture, he probably guessed you'd be suspicious." Heidi joined Emma with gazing into the window. "Whad you reckon, they broke in and just used it for their own use?"

"Dunno. Maybe. Yep, bet that's what they did. Mind you, big gaff like this must have a burglar alarm. They must have disarmed it. If we get in, we'll have to watch out that they didn't re-set it, and that a great big clanging sound calling up the local cops doesn't make us jump out of our skins."

"Shouldn't think so," called Jose, cigarette dangling from her mouth. "Look, back-door's open, not even locked. I tried it and it opened easy peasy. Leads into the kitchen."

She beckoned them over to where she stood by an open door, looking pleased with herself, obviously proud of her discovery. Emma didn't have the heart to tell her off and that by opening the door she could have set off the alarm.

"Oh well, no harm done," she muttered at the thankful silence.

She walked past Jose who, although still beaming with pride at her finding, wasn't brave enough to be first to cross the threshold. Emma entered cautiously with Heidi a close second. Jose wavered in the doorway, but the empty garden behind her held many mad murderers hidden in the bushes and shrubs so following them into the house was preferable to the empty, silent garden full of all those potential killers.

"I watch too many horror films," she murmured as she caught up with her friends who had left the kitchen and stood looking into a doorway on the left.

Emma strode into the room and the others followed, watching as she yanked dust covers from a large sofa and two armchairs. "Told you. Look at this load of rubbish. This might be a posh house, but they didn't have any style in decorating or furnishings."

"Looks OK to me," laughed Heidi. "It's just your arty farty side coming out."

The shrill sound from the ceiling startled the girls, who without exception had leapt so high they would have won gold medals if a leaping-straight-up-from-the-floor competition were available at a sports competition.

"Jesus Christ," shrieked Jose. "What the hell was that?"

"You stupid cow," yelled Emma, her heart beating as though Thor's hammer was thumping it to death. "Your bloody fag's set off the fire alarm. We've discovered what we came here to do, let's leg it before we disturb the whole bloody neighbourhood."

The total body mass of the three girls 'legging it' proved fortuitous. Their combined weight as the three impacted in quick succession against a man standing outside the kitchen door ready to phone the police about house breakers knocked him to the ground. Luckily, he dropped his phone in the chaos and it was snatched up by a quick-thinking Heidi who, as she ran past the front gate, tossed it into a thick bush.

Emma's mum was out visiting her sister when the three girls tore into the front garden, threw their bikes on the ground, and hurried into the kitchen. When they had slaked their parched throats with a week's supply of orange juice just bought that very morning by Mrs Bradbury, they hurried to Emma's bedroom to decide the next steps after their discovery.

"I still think you gotta tell the cops," said Heidi. "It's not like you were strapped."

"No, I'd never have a gun, even if I knew where to get one, not even for protection."

"Just phone them. Tell them about Loddon House. They can go there with all their fingerprint stuff. Maybe this Matthew's got a record."

"If he's that smart, he'd have cleaned up. The only fingerprints they're gonna find are mine."

"Anyone fancy a fag?" asked Jose.

"No," two voices said in unison.

"I still reckon I can find him. We start trawling the night clubs together," said Emma. "This time we stick together. You given out those sketches I did?"

Her two friends nodded. "Good, then we start hitting the night clubs. Three against one. We'll be OK."

She didn't realise that three relative innocents against such evil characters was not nearly enough.

Chapter 24

"Luke, think I might have found something. Mel's busy looking at the CCTV around the area of the missing children searching for a link, so I thought I'd help out and check these." Meena looked up from examining footage from local cameras that she had been trawling through to see if anything could assist with their slow progress in the search for the women and children. Where they were available, she was examining events outside the various venues that relatives or friends of the women reported they had visited on the evenings that they were last seen or known to have visited.

"OK, what've you got?" said Luke. Leaning over his colleague to view the screen, he could smell a combination of her clean hair and the slightest hint of a subtle perfume.

"Haven't managed to get all the footage we could usefully trawl through," explained Meena. "Some of it's already been erased. Other footage they can't trace for the pertinent dates." Meena mimicked a man's voice, showing her frustration.

"Yes, Mel's having the same trouble with footage needed for where the missing lads were last seen. Anyway, what's turned up?"

"OK." Meena flicked forward the frames of one of the films. Pointing to the screen, she continued. "Notice this tall man and woman. Images aren't very clear, but they go into the Hades Night club." She fast forwarded the film. "Right, here, this is the pair emerging at midnight."

"Mm huh, and…"

"This was a few days before the date that Mrs Taylor reported her daughter had a date and then went missing. Then the same again, two days before the date that Sandra Murphy went missing in May, we traced her on film going into the Prada Night Club." Luke waited until Meena switched to this particular footage. "There she is. Now wait, guess who we have following her in?" She fast-forwarded the film until she got to the relevant place. "See, the same tall guy and the woman again. Not very clear image but I'd lay money it's the same pair. Then last and not least…here." Meena brought up another film frame. "The date that Molly Carson was reported missing. She went to a pub in centre of Reading where there's a small dance floor. Again, hard to see because she's in the middle of a group of girls entering at the same time, but that certainly looks like her. Now… look, just here."

Luke leaned in to get a better view of the screen and at where she was pointing. "Christ, the same couple." He stood up, running his fingers through his fair hair, causing it to stick up. "I agree, it's hard to see, the quality on most of those is not good, but they, the tall guy and his companion, don't look like teenagers trailing round the night life of Reading."

"And last but not least, the day before Lilly goes missing. First, we have this same woman leaving Hades, then later Lilly and the tall man come out…together."

Meena turned to face him and despite the seriousness of the situation, Luke noticed her beautiful toffee-coloured eyes. He knew she had a 'thing' for the boss, but Dan always seemed unaware of her attractiveness, treating her just as a colleague. Luke forced himself to focus on the job in hand.

"I think they're stalking, sizing up what's available."

"And then pouncing. Yeah, you could be right."

Meena stared at her colleague, speaking quietly and her worried tone made Luke uneasy. "You haven't notice then?"

Having just been momentarily side-tracked by being a 'man' before a police office and noticing her eyes, he blustered. "Umm… noticed?"

Meena turned back to the screen and pointed at the outline of the women on the frozen screen. "This person. Who does she resemble?"

Again, Luke bent over, screwing up his eyes to bring the fuzzy image into view. After a few moments of concentration, an uncomfortable sensation of dread punched through his chest. "Jesus H, it can't be." He straightened up and knew the colour had plummeted from his face, with the sensation of having an ice pack wiped all over it.

"I know. I can see by your face you're feeling the same as I felt when I saw her. It's like a re-occurring nightmare has returned."

Both police officers were silent. Luke strode from the room. Meena re-ran the film, feeling almost close to tears with trepidation as she watched the familiar figure enter the building that she was observing.

The swinging door burst open and Luke returned, two plastic cups in his hand. He handed one to Meena, pulled a chair from a nearby desk, and sat down near his colleague.

"Fuck and double fuck. Dan asked us to get Mel to check out familial siblings, and the links, also particularly close relatives that could have the same or similar DNA as Yvette Van Looy. You said you'd ask her to get on it pronto. Has she got back to you yet?"

"No, haven't seen her this morning. There's loads of cameras to check, that's why I'm helping her out. She's been checking local security cameras covering the areas of the missing children, so I think she delegated the DNA enquiry to Tom. I've seen him today. Downstairs, talking to someone on the front desk. I'll give him a call."

Turning her back to Luke, she dialled the number of the reception area. Luke was irritated with himself as he watched her because he noticed a small strand of her hair had come loose from her bun and was dangling by the side of her cheek. He had the urge to tuck it back behind her ear.

Bloody concentrate. Stop ogling.

Pulling his thoughts back to the more urgent matters at hand, he heard Meena questioning Tom and knew from the conversation that he hadn't yet obtained the information, but was hoping to hear that afternoon from the Statistics Office in Southport who were checking for her birth certificate and any family details. Replacing the phone, she swung back round, and faced her colleague. Their knees were touching as they gazed at each other, dismay at the prospect painting their faces.

"He's chasing them up now. Luke, I feel sick," she murmured. "We didn't do our job properly if she's still at large."

"No way. Close sisters, twins, as I said before, they're the stuff of fiction."

The feeling in his stomach didn't agree with his words. He could only stare at her, seeing his colleague's normal Asian complexion turn from a light golden shade to an unhealthy ashen. He guessed his pallor wasn't a great deal different.

"Look, we're police officers, until we have proof we shouldn't panic. We shouldn't rely on…what, intuition… umm…feelings." He finished lamely.

Meena gave a half-hearted laugh. "Yes, you're right."

"Finish your drink, there's nothing to worry about."

Meena's hand shook as she brought the drink to her lips.

Chapter 25

To any onlooker, it would appear that Father Francis was praying. In fact, he was, but not to God for the usual reasons, he was pleading with God for inspiration. He had been ordered to get rid of Mr O'Leary, and whilst in itself the Irishman's disappearance would be a great benefit, the actual act of achieving that aim was far outside Father Francis's usual remit.

His lips twitched, not in adoration or devotion, but in a hope his entreaties would miraculously produce a vision of ideas if God wouldn't answer his supplications.

Poison. Quite handy if you've got the stuff. Must check the chemistry labs though probably any dangerous chemicals will be under Father Aloysius's care. He has a key. Heaven only knows where the idiot keeps it. Stabbing… no, too messy, too dangerous… umm, strangling… not really my bag as the students say.

The priest tried to visualise putting his hands round O'Leary's throat and although the thought of the act was very attractive in one way, realism meant that to die in such a way would mean the police would soon be at the school, and any investigation into everyone's backgrounds could, nay, would be extremely risky. He felt he had covered his tracks well, but with the technology currently available to the police, and also the nosey press, should either get a whiff of 'a dodgy priest situation', neither would stop until a great deal of sifting and digging uncovered some, in their opinion, stimulating information.

Drowning…yes, drowning in the bath. He takes a hot bath every night. Usually after a large whisky.

This idea was not too fantastic, and well within his abilities, causing a spiral of excitement to coil through his being, and Father Francis knew he would be capable of this deed.

Not that I'll enjoy it. I might have some bad habits, but murder's not one of them. I can't afford any scandal and spending the rest of my life in jail doesn't appeal one bit.

The man rose to his feet and hurried from the church, nodding to Father Ignatius who passed him on the way to his devotions in front of the altar. Walking to his room, plans whipped through his mind with great ease.

Lash him up with plenty of whisky. Make it fairly obvious to the others that he's participating in the whisky rather more than usual. After Father Ignatius and Father Aloysius have retired to bed, they always go first, I'll feign tiredness and go shortly afterwards. Then I'll not be the only teacher to have left the staff common room early and won't be under any suspicion. Soon as it's clear, I can get into the bathroom. He always uses the one on the second floor near his room. I can take the key from the lock so he can't secure the door. Have one hand round his mouth and the other pushing him quickly under. Back into my room and 'asleep' in a second should he be discovered promptly.

The relief in finding a solution to his worries put Father Francis into such a good mood, he whistled as he entered his room, a habit he normally abhorred in the common mob. His easy life with its unusual pleasures on the side could continue undisturbed. Congratulating himself on his inspiration, he forgot his normal nightly prayers and heaved himself straight into bed.

Chapter 26

Matthew pushed the cup of coffee over the table to Yvette as she slid along the opposite bench in the cubicle. They had arranged to meet in the coffee shop at 12 o'clock.

"Can't stop long," said Matthew. "Have some foreign dignities visiting the church from South Africa and I have to entertain them; I'm taking them to the cathedral and show them round, that sort of thing, until the Bishop arrives."

"Oh, you're so important," his companion replied, her voice laced with irony. Sipping her coffee, enjoying the strong taste of the cappuccino, she glanced over the rim of the coffee cup, wondering what the hell she was doing partnering this stupid tosser, who except for his good looks, was a total waste of time in her opinion.

Matthew sighed, sensing, as seemed to be the usual thing of late, that this meeting wasn't going to be easy. His dislike for Yvette was growing daily, and up until the Emma incident, their skills had worked well for both of them, but now her constant sarcasm was annoying him.

"Look, stop with the sarky remarks. We've chosen to work together and so far, it's worked out fine. We've both benefited. OK, one mistake isn't the end of the world. Remember, it's two mistakes, one each, me choosing that damn girl and you putting the kid's body in the wrong place. If you keep harping on about my mistake, continue to get digs in, we may as well call it a day. So, let's be adults, and have a civil conversation."

Yvette carefully placed her cup back onto its saucer, leaning back in her chair while she thought through his words. After their last conversation, her long-term plans were to punish him for speaking to her in the way he had. However, she had decided he still had his uses, at least for the short term, so she knew she must control her tongue, her temper, and her true feelings.

"So why did you phone me?" she asked.

"Two things. One, to tell you about a change of MO I'm proposing and secondly, have you managed to discover where we can get hold of the infamous Emma Bradbury?"

"I think I'm almost there. There were quite a number of Bradburys in the Berkshire phone book. We know she lived in the Calcot area, and there are six there with that surname. I'll go to the main library tomorrow and look for her or her family in the Census documentation there. Also, didn't you tell me that night you talked to her at the Prada that she said she was at the local tech college doing some sort of course?"

"Yes, think she said it was…uh, Art and Design or something."

"That gives me another lead. Don't worry, I'll find her in a few days. So, what's this good idea of yours?"

"It came to me during one of the church meetings. We and most of the other denominations have weekly meetings for various groups of disadvantaged people. We take it in turns, one week at our church, the next week at the Methodists, then the Church of England and so on." He leaned forward, elbows on the table and whispered because although there was nobody in the close vicinity, he knew the need for absolute discretion at all times. Fortunately, he could not sense Yvette's impatience at what she thought was unnecessary rambling. "Yesterday we went to the Baptist church in Caversham. The meeting was for single mums." He relished the last sentence; then leaned back, arms folded, waiting for the penny to drop.

"So? Great, sure they all thought it was worthwhile." This time, Matthew caught the insincerity, but chose to ignore it.

He leaned forward again. "Right, we've decided we have to be careful at the moment. The police finally have put together the fact that women and kids are going missing. It's all over the newspapers and news, but luckily for us where I met the women is not being published, maybe because that's something they want to keep under their hats for the moment. So young women haven't stopped going to nightclubs and such, and perhaps later we can exploit that avenue again.

"But think about it. I'm involved with these young mums' meetings. It suddenly struck me, right here in front of me were twelve young mums, ranging from fifteen to twenty-five years of age, usually with their snotty little brats with them. They're being handed to us on a plate. I could see a couple of them eyeing me up. What I need to do is quietly arrange a meeting with one of them. There were two ideal candidates. The best target is called Wendy Groves, she's got a six-year-old boy. She's only twenty. Apparently got kicked out of home when they found out she was pregnant. She's been struggling ever since. Lives in a council flat but even with assistance, is battling to make ends meet."

"You're saying you befriend them and..."

"Exactly. It's not even on our turf."

"Was she one of them that was eyeing you up?" This time Yvette's comments were without any taint. She realised they might be on to a good thing.

"Yes. She said she was coming to the meeting next week. It's in Tilehurst, the Church of England hall. With all the different venues, you don't always get the same people attending so if she fell off the radar, no-one's going to be suspicious. At the end of the meeting, I could surreptitiously ask her to stay behind, have a quiet word. Make out I'm really sorry for her circumstances. Normally the church's approach is to talk with them, encouraging them to think of ways out of their difficulties themselves. Our role is to give support and encouragement. I could arrange to meet her, emphasising that this is over and above our normal help."

"And during this so-called chat, give her the stare to suggest she's the best thing you've laid your eyes on in a long time."

"You've got it. Lonely, vulnerable, broke. Is chatted up by a good-looking bloke. Don't look like that, I'm kidding."

"Not God's gift to women then?" Yvette grinned as she spoke. His idea had great potential and had put her in a good mood. "Two for one. Could do the taxi role again. Maybe you could suggest she brings the kid, and I'm a reliable friend and I'll baby-sit while you two…do whatever. You have Wendy and I've got the kid. You said two potential punters, who's the other?"

"Can't remember her name, but similar circumstances. If we're successful, then we bide out time before the next one."

"Right! So, when does this all kick off?"

"As I said, next week's meeting. Will it be bad luck to celebrate in advance?"

Sliding herself along the bench, Yvette stood up and slinging her bag over her shoulder, said, "Young man, I'm going to treat you to a large drink of your choice. Follow me."

"I'm meeting these people from South Africa and what about the Bishop?"

"Bugger the Bishop."

"Nah, not my type. One foot in the grave."

They both laughed as they left the coffee shop, their

faces glowing with anticipation and wearing expressions that looked as though they had won the lottery. However, it suddenly struck the man that for the moment he was in the driving seat, and he didn't need her. Still, he wasn't one for rushing things, so he'd have to think that through!

Chapter 27

Five elderly men sat round the table; the smell of brandy and the thick cigar smoke curling like pale grey ringlets of cloud into the air was reminding the oldest man, George Hampson, of the aromas he associated with Christmas when a child. As the evening light was fading, he stood up and hurried to close the curtains and switch on the side light on the antique sideboard next to the table.

"Can't be too careful," he said.

"No-one can see us through the thick hedge you have along the garden front, George" said Bob Vause, the youngest man of the company, although he had just celebrated his sixty-fourth birthday.

The first man ignored him, and on taking his seat, turned to the man on his right. A tall man with white hair neatly combed back and dressed immaculately in a business suit.

"Arthur, as chairman, would you like to tell the meeting what I discovered? About the leak."

"Thank you, George." Arthur leaned forward, putting his elbows on the table and clasping his large hands, his manicured nails clearly revealing he was not a blue-collar worker. "We all have people that supply us with useful information. I've just had a very worrying incident reported to me. You are all aware of our password, without which you cannot attend any meeting and have any electronic information passed to you or participate in any of our pleasures. *Rubies on the Moon*. A password we purposely chose because it was silly, had no connection to any of our operations and in my opinion, even a code-cracker or a technical whiz-kid with some knowledge of the usual daft, obvious things people select for their pass words, wouldn't have guessed."

He glanced round the table, savouring the attention. His words, spoken with a soft, west-country burr, were easy on the ear. Still enjoying the moment, he leaned back in his chair and took a sip of his brandy before continuing. "One of my informants has recently heard this password spoken quite openly." With the exception of George, the three remaining men gasped with dismay and astonishment.

"Quite! It was apparently quoted by a teacher at the St. Stevens Jesuit Academy in Sonning, a Mr O'Leary. Not one of the Jesuit Brothers himself. The person who reported this occurrence, Father Francis, felt that this Mr O'Leary, the chap who used the password was aware of the implication of what he'd said, because he then stared at Father Francis who reckoned that he was goading him."

George let the other men present digest this fact totally before he spoke, a cut-throat edge to his voice. "Unless, of course, there *was* a leak."

"What! Leak! Is something being done to plug this betrayal?" said Bob, his voiced laced with concern, and always one to jump in and speak before he knew all the facts of a discussion.

"Naturally, Bob." said Arthur. "That will be done as soon as possible. As George said, there appears to have been a leak. However, I think the most worrying thing is that the disclosure comes from a teacher at the Jesuit School in Sonning, this Mr O'Leary, who has no connections what-so-ever with our Brotherhood of Elders at any level, so how he found out about this very secret code is a total mystery? He will of course, be quickly disposed of if necessary when we investigate this worrying issue."

In unison, as he spoke, all heads swung round in his direction, with looks of disbelief painting their faces. The silence at this information seemed to hang in the air above the table like smoky phantoms delicately tiptoeing on the cigar smoke. Suddenly the reality of his words became clear, and words of denial and protest climbed and coiled around each other in the men's efforts to be heard and believed. Arthur elegantly held up his hand, shaking his head at the turmoil.

"Friends, friends," he asserted. "Hush. I am not necessarily saying the leak comes from this top layer. Nevertheless, we must face facts. There is a layer beneath us, comprising of probably eleven men and four women, and only we and they know this password. Perhaps one of the fifteen has leaked this, whether intentionally or not because there is no way this teacher would have known it."

"Then perhaps we shouldn't get rid of him," said a small set man with a Hitler haircut and moustache. Placing his cigar in a cut-glass ashtray in front of him, he tapped the table with a nicotine-stained finger. "What's the use of getting rid of him until we know how he knew the password? Once he's dead, we'll never know."

The silence around the table this time was different, razor sharp, as though to break it would mean a deep cut for the speaker. Arthur sat back in his chair, steepling his fingers, considering the words.

"True. Quick thinking Dennis." He turned to George. "I believe you gave orders to dispose of this teacher. Do you know if this has been carried out yet?"

"I've heard nothing, and I'm sure if he'd carried out the job I'd have been informed immediately. Do you want me to contact him to call off the elimination? I think it would be sensible to do this as soon as possible in case he intends to move quickly. He's never disposed of anyone before as far as I know, but he might have got inspired."

"Yes, phone him and explain we need to ask this teacher some questions and therefore for the moment, we need him alive."

"Are you saying that he, this Father Francis chap, should interrogate him or that we will kidnap this Mr. O'Leary, and find out ourselves exactly how he discovered the password?" These words came from John English, the only man not to have spoken. John was the quiet one of the five, but he was the deep thinker.

"No, that will need thinking through as to what our future actions will be. However, I know someone I can call on who is an expert in the field of high jacking. He's capable of snatching someone from under the nose of the police without them noticing a thing. I suggest, George that you leave the room now and contact Father Francis as he was the person who reported this incident. Then return here quickly and report back."

"But most of the 'heavies' so to speak who could physically deal with this sort of situation, that is, securing this O'Leary, are still incarcerated after the collapse of Operation Hobbledehoy four years ago," said Bob.

"My dear Bob, think about it," said Arthur, patting his companion on the shoulder in a re-assuring manner. "There are plenty more 'heavies' in the world. When you are in our business, for everyone that falls, there are three waiting to be allowed the honour of joining the Brotherhood." His eyes travelled around the table, looking at each of the others in turn before he continued, "When George returns, we need then to discuss the case of the missing five boys that are currently all over the news. Some-ones queering our patch and we need to find out who. I think we have rivals. If that's the case, things may have to turn very nasty. Our mole at the police station will be very useful." He sniggered, then rubbing his hands, said, "I'm really looking forward to some excitement. Things have been too quiet these last few years. Right, here's what I suggest we do…"

His elderly companions leaned forward to hear more.

Chapter 28

Jose hurried into the cake and coffee shop where she'd arranged to meet her two friends. Spotting them at the table in the dark corner at the back, she hurried over, her grin so large it looked too big for her face.

"Progress, progress," she said to Emma and Heidi as she flopped into the third chair around the table. Waving a piece of A4 paper, she explained, "Your sketches, Em. Handed them out to me mates at the riding stables last Sunday. Both Petra and Charlene recognised him."

"You're kidding," said Emma. "I can't believe he'd be so brazen. What, they both knew him?"

"Yeah, honest." She turned to the waitress who had walked to the table and ordered herself a pot of tea. Twisting back to her friends, she continued. "Charlene and her boyfriend, Frenchie Morgan, were at Prada. They'd 'ad a row and he stalked off. She sat there for yonks, making her drink last 'cos she didn't have any dosh. She thought he'd come back, but he didn't for ages. Anyway, he," she waved the sketch of Mathew Nielson and placed it onto the table, "came up and started chatting her up. Bought her a drink, asked her to dance. Everyfing like. Then he asked if he could see her home. Charlene said he was real fit, bit old but still dead fit, but then Frenchie turned up and started getting nasty. This bloke was much bigger than Frenchie, but he obviously didn't want no trouble. Just held up his hands, palms forward like and said, 'Sorry mate, didn't know she was your property, and walked off."

"When was this?" asked Emma.

"Dunno. She weren't sure? Thought maybe a couple of weeks, a month ago."

"Was it before Em had a date with him?" asked Heidi.

Jose shrugged. "Didn't really ask that much detail. 'Spec she'd know if you got her to think about it."

"What about Petra then, what happened to her?"

"Not sure about her. She's a real drama queen. Listening to Charlene, she might've just jumped on the band wagon. I had to hurry away, but we can talk to her again." Jose looked round the coffee shop. "Suppose I can't smoke in here either."

"You know you can't smoke anywhere indoors, Jos," said Em. "Come on, tell us about Petra, what *did* she say?"

"She reckons she was at Hades with her usual gang, Donna, Sammy and Carly. The others were dancing, but she sat out 'cos she had stomach-ache. Apparently, there was this blond, older woman who gets in there. Often on her own. Maybe in her late twenties. Anyway, Petra who loves to nose around and see who's being chatted up, reckons she sees this guy on your sketch with this older woman. He buys her drinks and eventually they go off together."

"You sure it was him?" Emma picked up her sketch. "It's a pretty good likeness but it's dark in Hades. She sure?"

"Well, she said he was definitely shaggable, first date shaggable. Umm, maybe she's not making it up. Anyway, said he was tall, dark, real good looking. Yeah, she said she could pick him out in a line up, no trouble."

"Em. I think this is getting serious." Heidi leaned forward towards her friend. "I was watching the news on the tele last night. There's some real funny stuff going down. Missing women from this area and missing kids. I never recognised any of the women from the news, but their photos are bound to be in the papers so why don't we buy one and if they're in there, we show Petra and maybe Charlene as well. If Petra recognises the blond woman in Hades that left with the guy in your sketch, and Charlene recognises him as the bloke what chatted her up, I really think you should report it to the law."

"No way. I think your idea is a good one though. If Petra or Charlene should recognise him, then we phone and tell the law what we know, but I don't tell them my name."

"We could send 'em one of your sketches, Em," added Jose, determined to get back into the conversation now her moment in the spotlight had finished. "You said it was a good likeness, and you're real good at drawing. If the cops had a picture of him, that'd probably help them." Clapping her hands suddenly, she squealed, "Maybe there's a reward for giving the info and he gets nicked. Oh, Em, you could be rich. Take Heidi and me to Majorca for a treat. Loads of blokes go there."

"You wish. Still, sending them a copy's a good idea. Right, finish your coffees kiddos, let's go and buy us a newspaper."

"Me teas not even come yet. Let me just have a drink before we go. Here comes the waitress. I won't take a min to throw it down me throat."

Her two friends waited impatiently as Jose sipped her drink that she couldn't 'throw down her throat' because it was too hot. The last drop had barely gone down before Emma snatched up the bill and she and Heidi headed towards the pay desk situated by the front door. Jose jumped to her feet quickly, hating to be last and feeling indignant that her remarkable suggestion hadn't caused more admiration from her mates.

Three sets of ridiculously high heels clicked and

clattered down the High Street as the girls headed for the late-night newsagent to buy a newspaper that was to change their lives.

Chapter 29

Father Francis smirked and watched as Mr O'Leary heaved himself from his chair, staggering under the influence of rather more whisky than usual. He promptly plonked himself back in his chair again. As predicted, Father Aloysius and Father Ignatius had already retired to their beds and there were only six teachers left in the common room where they went for their after-dinner coffees and brandies. Four younger priests, discussing the forthcoming sports day, hadn't noticed Father Francis frequently topping up Mr O'Leary's glass. At first, the teacher had protested that he'd had more than enough, but the whisky was very 'more-ish', and he didn't need much persuasion to 'just have another sup to help him sleep.'

"My goodness, I think I've definitely had more than enough now. I don't know if I can even be bothered to have my bath. Maybe I'll leave it until the morning." As he spoke, Mr O'Leary put his hand on the arm of his chair to steady himself as he tried to hoist himself up again.

Father Francis felt the panic coupled with annoyance spiral through his body. "Just have a *quick* dip then. You know you're not good at getting up promptly in the morning. Nice hot bath after the whisky and you'll have a wonderful night's sleep." He wondered if he should offer to run the bath, but knew that was totally out of character, and might draw attention to the fact he was the last to see O'Leary alive.

After Mr O'Leary had tottered erratically from the room, he gave the inebriated teacher twenty minutes, having previously estimated that it would take him five minutes to reel to his room, another five to undress and put on his dressing gown, and then another five to get to the bathroom, run the bath and lower himself in. During the last five minutes of this estimated time, he stood, wished the remainder of staff a good night, reminding them with a chuckle that Mr O'Leary certainly had enjoyed himself that evening.

Arriving on the second floor, he hurried to the bathroom door; checking that no-one else was in the corridor, he listened for the splashing sounds and the normal out-of-tune singing of Irish ballads filtering through the slightly ajar door. He had taken the key from the lock just before going to dinner ensuring O'Leary couldn't lock it. There were no sounds coming through the space left by the small opening of the door, which was a good sign because that meant O'Leary had probably dozed off, would not therefore see him enter and prove troublesome as the job was done.

Checking again that the corridor was empty, Father Francis eased open the door and peered in. Steam filled the large room and from his angle of view, he could not see the top of the bather's head where he estimated it should be. Taking two steps forward gave him a clearer view of the bath; to his horror, he saw that O'Leary was already submerged.

His brain took seconds to analyse the situation and realise this was the ideal state of affairs; the man had obviously fallen asleep and slipped under the water. He was relieved he didn't have to do the dirty deed. Indeed, he could explain his presence in the room by saying that he had entered the room because of his alarm at the unusual silence. All staff members were aware and amused at the warbling emerging nightly during O'Leary's bathing activities. Another second passed before guilt shot up through his body like the rise of mercury in a thermometer when placed in boiling water. Despite orders and previous plans, there was no way he could let the man drown, annoying and maddening as he was.

Stepping forward to pull the man out of the water, his heart leapt like an Olympic pole jumper going for gold as the 'body' suddenly rose up and a spluttering and broiled O'Leary sat up in the bath. Wiping the soapy water from his eyelids and catching sight of Father Francis leaning towards him, hands outstretched, he shrieked, "Mary, Mother of God, what the hell are you doing in here? You frightened the life out of me."

The active brain cells saved the potentially embarrassing situation and instantly a believable explanation issued from his mouth. "Thank goodness. I was passing the bathroom and was uneasy about the lack of the usual melodies that normally come issuing forth. The door was ajar, so I just peered in for fear you had dozed off and slipped under. When I saw you submerged, I panicked, fearing my worse doubts had been realised. I was just going to drag you out when you sat up. In fact, you nearly scared *me* to death."

"How kind of you. Thank you for your concern." Mr O'Leary was glad of the bubbles covering much of his face as he was sure that surprise for the priest's unexpected alarm must show in his expression. "I…umm, often duck under for a few seconds to wash off the shampoo. Sorry to alarm you."

Mr O'Leary's sincerity created a molecule of remorse in Father Francis when he considered his original intentions. He pacified this shame by remembering that whatever his objective, he couldn't bring himself to actually kill the man.

"Sorry to intrude," he said. Turning around to leave the room, he muttered, "Glad you're safe."

The shouted "Thank you, kind sir," that followed his exit somehow exacerbated his guilty conscience.

Deep in thought, Father Francis hurried down the corridor to his room, realising he still had a problem. He was pulled two ways. One, he had a great fear of the consequences of his inaction, and secondly he now knew he didn't have the guts to kill anyone. He realised in the eyes of the world his leanings were abhorrent, but at least he wasn't a murderer.

He wiped the sweat that was forming in small beads on his upper lip. His hands shook as he attempted to put the key in the lock of his door, and he had to put his left hand on his right to stop the tremors. After a few moments, the door opened and he hurried in, closing it quickly and then leaning against it in the attempt to get air into his lungs from the pain of the stress sitting heavily on his chest.

After taking in deep breaths, he felt better, and as he turned to switch on the light, his mobile rang.

There was no introduction by the caller, merely a snappy, "Have you done the deed?"

"No, I…"

"Good. There has been a re-think. Do nothing for the present although watch the intended victim carefully. If you get the opportunity, get into conversation, bring up the remark that he made concerning the password and see what he says. Only report in if there is something that is…umm, useful to our enquiries. I'll contact you when plans have been discussed and some decisions made."

Before Father Francis could answer, the call terminated. Now shaking from head to foot, he pushed himself away from the door and hurried to his wardrobe. Groping to the back, he withdrew a bottle of Jameson's Irish Whisky. Pouring a large measure into a glass by his bedside table, his legs felt decidedly unsteady as he sunk onto the bed, and even the smooth and triple distilled nectar barely soothed his nerves.

I'm getting too old for this lark. He poured a second large amount, downed that in one and cursed his luck

Chapter 30

Dan was quiet, closely studying the stills that Meena had obtained from the security cameras situated outside various night clubs she had been scrutinising. She had passed them over to her boss for his opinion.

"What do you think, Boss?" said Luke. When Dan didn't reply, he glanced at Meena and shrugged. Giving Dan another minute, his patience then ran out and he asked, "Could it be her? Meena and I, despite the poor quality reckon it's a dead ringer."

Dan looked up from his inspection; put the photos in a neat pile on his desk, biting his lip as he thought.

"Mel was checking on a sister. Twin or maybe close sister for the DNA to be identical, unlikely as that is. Too coincidental for real life. She come up with anything yet?"

Meena winced as she handed him some documentation. "Just come through from Southport. Mel delegated to Tom, and he's just brought the info for us to examine. We purposely didn't say anything before you looked at the prints. Didn't want to influence your take on it." Dan's eyes, cat green, bored into hers making her gulp as she explained. "Sorry, boss, we let you down. Tom pushed for results, knowing we needed them for the investigation. Seems Yvette Van Looy had a sister, an identical twin. Lived in Birmingham. She was a widow and suddenly went missing last year. Her daughter actually reported her absence. Said there was no way her mother would just disappear like that without contacting her or her brother. The brother was equally puzzled and agreed with his sister.

"They had no idea that their mum had a twin sister so nothing like that was mentioned in the investigation. When neither she nor her body turned up after six months, the investigation was run down, although obviously still an open case. We all know how many people go missing daily. There was no connection obviously at that time to our operation in any way, so the Birmingham investigation put it on the back burner." Meena turned to Luke for support. He was staring at her.

Luke hurriedly looked away and continued. "Knowing what an evil person she was, although only surmising, Meena and I wouldn't put it passed her to get rid of her sister so when a body was found, we'd think it was her. DNA matches. End of the case. No more looking. Bit coincidental, but…" He shrugged his shoulders. "No proof of that, but a good motive."

Dan was still silent. Suddenly standing up, he stacked the photos in a pile on his desk. His voice was brisk as he said, "No use tearing ourselves to pieces about past mistakes. We update the Birmingham police; they will need to speak to the son and daughter. We move on from here. We don't make any assumptions, but I believe we must trust the evidence in front of us. Women and children are missing. Yvette Van Looy aka the evil Delilah is probably not dead, and we have images that suggest she and an accomplice are frequenting places where young women have gone missing. Currently, we do not have the identity of her companion. Her preference is for children. We have children going missing."

His flow of words stopped, and he sat back down at his desk. He glanced up as Mel's back appeared through the swing doors. As she turned the welcome smell of coffee filtered through the room. Sensing the atmosphere, she didn't speak but just took the cups from the moulded polystyrene tray and handed them to Luke and Meena, placing one on the desk in front of Dan. Absent-mindedly Dan picked up the cup and sipped the beverage. The three police officers waited in silence while he did his well-known, silent deductions. They supped their own drinks, watching and waiting until Dan tipped the cup back and finished his. Placing the cup carefully back on his desk, he took a deep breath before looking back up to his colleagues, a smile playing around his lips. Not a beam of joy, but a look of satisfaction.

"Think about this. The two working together. Of course. *Her* predilection is for children. I bet his preference is for young ladies. They work together for the other's fulfilment. Maybe he gets the kids for her." His eyes focused and he looked at Luke. "The children mostly came from church schools. Bet he's connected in some way. Maybe a teacher, an assistant, a priest, a Curate, a Deacon, whatever. She gets the women. Maybe susses the vulnerable ones out for him. Without exceptions their families maintain the women weren't the types to disappear, just quiet, home loving types."

"That's a big leap, boss. Just because the two are seen together." Luke shook his head, unsure of his misgivings even as he spoke. "If he is connected to a church school, I can see how that can fit together, but her...I dunno. You reckon she could be getting him the women, but how? She's not exactly young and beautiful and able to befriend them. Agreed, we've seen them together on the cameras but...not sure"

"No, I agree with Dan," enthused Meena. "Think about it, it all fits. Women and children going missing, on alternating dates. Think about the extended W shape on the white board, how the dates fitted together...umm, woman, child, woman, child and so on. They work together to find the victims for the other one.

"Now, women overall tend to trust other women so she's probably doing something that doesn't make them suspicious. You're right, boss, she susses out the women. I don't know how, and as Luke says, that connection is tenuous, but I bet it's there. He susses out the kids. Knows the ones that have a history of truancy, maybe troublemakers. When they go missing, the initial assumption is they've run away, giving them more time."

"What about Peter North. He hasn't got a truancy record… still…you're right, he went to a church school. That just can't be coincidence, and is a good connection," said Luke, enthusing to the idea, knowing that both Dan and Meena were brilliant when it came to analysing facts, and making an entire picture from a puzzle of disjointed pieces.

"We need to get the image of these two characters out into the news media, wide circulation. Someone out there will have seen these two. We say they are wanted to help with our enquiries in connection with the missing women and children. That may well jog some one's memory on the nights they went missing." Dan picked up the photos again, turning them over one by one. "And back to the clubs and pubs where they were last seen. Take these images with you. I think we've taken a big step forward." He looked up and his cheeky grin that was his normal expression returned. "Quick celebration. One more quick coffee, what d'you say, Meena?" Seeing her expression, he turned, "Uh, Mel?"

"No, boss," said Mel. "Just got you all one, against my better judgement."

Meena turned and walked towards the door, calling over her shoulder, "Equal Ops, boss. Come on Mel."

Mel followed her colleague, leaving the two men. Dan looked hopefully at Luke who shrugged, saying in a sympathetic voice. "Never said it would be easy when they gave women the vote, boss. When they made them equal… phew, dodgy." He blew out a long blast of breath. "I think it foretells the end of the world. 'Till then, I'll get on with my enquiries."

As his colleagues deserted him, Dan studied the photos again, knowing that the more he looked, the more he was convinced he knew the woman. For years they had battled with her, but he knew he mustn't give in to despair because sometime, somewhere, she would make a mistake and they would get her. She was the last evil member of the paedophile gang that they had worked so hard to overthrow. His mind reflected back four years when DS Adam Kennedy had worked undercover and he had been his first line of contact. The team, mainly due to Adam's unpalatable work, had foiled the operation, but somehow this wicked woman had slipped the net, like a serpent disappearing into the jungle undergrowth. The police investigation had found out the cell used code names for members of the paedophile gang, and hers, ironically, was Delilah.

His thoughts were disrupted as a hand holding a cup of coffee appeared, placing it on his desk.

"Could see you were desperate for more sustenance. New drinks machine tastes OK for a change," said Luke. "Not trying to curry favours, but when you're on the promotion panel and it's between Mel, Meena and my good self, just remember who looked after your needs."

Dan grinned as he watched the well-built police officer hurry through the swing doors, remembering how Luke's broad shoulders had been useful when they were involved in a small riot in the town centre earlier in the month. Uniform were being over-run and all the detectives had fallen in besides their colleagues to bring peace to that unruly evening.

Returning to the task in hand, he sipped his coffee, still staring again at the woman's image, wondering how he was going to break it to the Guv, DI Roy Cole, that Yvette Van Looy, the female anti-Christ, Delilah the seducer, now a siren bringing women to their doom, had arisen from the supposed dead, and was back in town! He didn't panic; he intuitively felt to the very core of his being that it was his future, eventually, to track down and snare this evil woman predator.

Slowly finishing the coffee that for a change actually tasted and smelt like the real thing, different from the garbage that the previous machine had dispensed, he allowed himself the luxury of thinking about Lucy before he strolled into the Lion's Den. He wondered if he would be brave enough to phone her, maybe test the waters for a second chance. Checking his watch, he saw it was five o'clock, she'd be home from her teaching job at the school. He picked up the phone.

Chapter 31

"The church meeting with the single mums is tomorrow. One thirty in the Tilehurst Church of England hall. We're treating them to a light lunch, sandwiches, sausage rolls, cups of tea." Matthew leaned back in his chair. The two of them were in a dingy corner of the equally dingy Red Lion pub in a quiet part of town. They varied their meeting places, very rarely phoning one another, as phone calls were easily traceable now, and confident that by not having habitual meeting places, their movements could not be located.

"Right. What do you want me to do?" Yvette swirled the red wine in her glass, bringing it near to her nose to savour the rich bouquet of the Spanish grape.

"Nothing yet. I think it best if you wait outside the hall. I'll endeavour to delay her until the Church of England minister has left. Then I'll walk outside with her and you can get a glimpse. This is when I'll imply suggestively that I feel particularly sorry for her position and feel it's an awful shame that such a lovely young person should be in such a situation. Give her the long stare into the eyes. I can always tell immediately if they've fallen for it. If it works out OK, I can introduce you at that point; say you're a friend and that you'll give her and the brat a lift home."

"Who else from the churches will be there? If her disappearance finally gets noticed, we don't want you connected to her in any way."

"The gods are with us. The only other person is the Reverent Daley, who's as blind as a bat, deaf as the proverbial post and has as much common sense as a pillar-box. If his sermons are as dull as his wit, I feel mightily sorry for his congregation. If her name was plastered all over a billboard right outside the church, he wouldn't notice, and it wouldn't register.

"As I've said before, the charm of this operation is that because we meet at varying locations, there are very rarely the same attendees, so our lovely Wendy Groves won't be missed or noticed by the other women. Certainly not for a while, thus giving us more time." Matthew leaned back in his chair, lifted his Guinness glass from the table, sipping slowly, his brow furrowed as he thought through his next words. "Yes. That'll work well. I'll chat her up. You be outside and give her a lift home. That way we know where she lives, and you can check her potential suitability."

"Don't you have their addresses?"

"If they don't want to give details, we don't force them. Remember, we're just there mainly for support. We do help in lots of ways, although rarely give them money because that encourages some of them to buy alcohol or drugs if they're using."

"We'd better get my introduction thought through carefully. It's a bit thin just saying I'm a friend, conveniently waiting outside."

"I'll say my cars up the chute, and you've given me a lift to the meeting, and you waited to give me a lift home. That won't seem so suspicious."

"If I'm there, you can't make a date."

Matthew leaned forward, placing his elbows on his knees, and then rubbing his eyes. "Mm, true." He was silent for a few moments while he contemplated his moves. He straightened up, took another sip of his drink before saying, his expression showing that he was pleased with the idea. "In the car, I'll tell her that I've a friend who has a small property that he wants looked after for at least a year. Doesn't want it to be empty for that length of time, encouraging burglars, or the like."

"She won't necessarily like that. Even if it's a year, she'll lose her council flat after that time."

"I could spice it up. Say that he's even willing to pay the housekeeper. She's broke; the thought of easy money and staying in a great property might just do it. I can say she can still keep her flat on, no-one need know she's not there. She can go back to it when he returns, having in the meantime, made some money."

"I don't know. Doesn't seem very plausible."

"Well, you come up with an idea then," he snapped. "Everything I say and you're pulling it to bits. What you're forgetting, you're looking at it from a sensible, adult point of view. She's a thick, desperate kid. This will sound like manna from heaven, she'll leap at it."

Yvette downed the last drops of her wine. "Yes, you're right. I'm just trying to make it believable. If she's as thick as you say, then yes, this will probably seem like a gift. It's just that we had such a good thing going before; it's such a shame we've got to shelve it for the moment."

"Don't fret, this will be good. Two for one this time, woman and a kid. I've a good feeling about this. I'll hint that if she takes this place, I'll visit her as often as I can. She won't be able to resist."

"OK, we try it. Nothing to lose. Still, you can't chance meeting at her place, so where you going to take her?"

"I've been thinking about that. The house at Coley is obviously out of bounds now just in case the Bradbury girl did report the incident. I think we take the chance and go back to the house near Pangbourne where I took the blond woman, what's her name?"

"Lilly Taylor."

"Yes, that's the one. I'm still looking after it for Father

Harry Fellows until he returns from Africa. It's out of the way enough to be safe." When Yvette didn't argue, he continued, "Emma Bradbury. Found her yet?"

Yvette smirked and put her hand into her trouser pocket, withdrawing her cell phone. After much clicking, she handed it to Matthew.

"Who's that, coming out of college like the proverbial lamb to the slaughter?"

Taking the phone and using his hand to shield the screen from the lights above him, he nodded. "That's her alright. I loved the long dark hair. Well done. How did you run her to ground?"

"Easy. Found out what course she was doing and sat outside the college and waited. She wandered out, not a care in the world, within half an hour of my parking."

Matthew lingered over the picture.

"She certainly was a stunner. Shame..." He handed the phone back. "Who's the blond she's with? She's nice too."

"No way. You've got yourself into enough possible trouble as it is. Kids like that are street wise. Some even carry weapons."

Matthew inwardly winced, recalling his foot that was still sore, and just said, "Don't blame me. You're the one that vets them for me."

"No. If you recall, that particular evening you met her, you'd spotted her yourself. I wasn't there. I did warn you to keep to the usual lonely, vulnerable type but you didn't. I must admit she did seem to take to you immediately if your version of events is to be believed, but when we're back on track, remember it's always safer for me to sift them first. She turned out to be a wild card, or more likely a wild cat. You've never had that sort of trouble with my choices. In future…"

"Well for the moment we're not going down that path."

"No, that's true. The thing we are not sure about is if she has been to the police and given your description. Not that anything has been in the news to that effect, but she might have given them enough details for them to compose a photo-fit."

"Even if she did, and described me, a police artist's impression, from what I've seen in the papers or the television news, is never a true likeness. I'd just look like a hundred other blokes. Another thing, in my position, people aren't going to be looking at me with suspicion. Most people see me with my church garb on. It's not like I'm usually walking around in my jeans and leather jacket."

"OK, but we still need to dispose of her. I'll take the first couple of evening's surveillances and then you take your turn. She's a young woman, you can bet your life she's out and about most nights. We get to know what dark road she constantly walks down, and we strike. The two of us can get her easily."

"How? Strangling? Knife? Mmm, which do I fancy?"

"Your predilection if for the knife. Might as well have two bonuses, getting shot of her and a knifing to boot. That way, the cops will probably think it's a random mugging. We'll take her shoulder bag to ensure it looks like one."

Matthew nodded and relaxed back into his chair, draining his glass.

"Yes, I must admit I do like a piece of carving up. However," he paused, analysing his thoughts. "I think a variation might be both enjoyable and also confuse the plod. If they're building some sort of picture, a MO of some sorts, it might be a good thing to bamboozle them. Change things so there is no obvious connection to us." Leaning forward, he carefully placed his glass back onto the table. He looked up at Yvette, and a nasty grin appeared over his handsome face as he said, "Hey, how about we bring her back to the hide-out for a bit of enjoyment."

"That's damn dangerous, and you know it."

Matthew mused for a few moments, but the more he thought about some prolonged punishment for stabbing his foot, the more he warmed to the idea. Knowing his companion wouldn't like the plan, he just said, "Fancy another?"

She shook her head and stood up as she finished her drink.

"No, got a few things to do." She had to discipline her expressions not to reveal her true feelings. More and more, unless they were actually out and about getting some action, his company was getting difficult to cope with, even with his new suggestions that for a short while should prove enjoyable and beneficial. Staring at him for a few moments, he raised his eyebrows in a 'what's up' expression.

"Nothing. What time shall I pick you up tomorrow?"

"Quarter to one. Meet me at the corner of Castle Street."

Nodding, she walked away, her mind busily working on how long he'd be useful before she had the joy of disposing of him. She was an expert at capture and torture, and the thoughts of how she could make him suffer for his words brought a smirk to her face. Brushing passed a young man as he entered through the front door of the pub as she was leaving, she failed to see the look of alarm suddenly sweeping across his face. Used to swaggering and being the threat himself, the murderous, evil expression on the woman's face cowed him, the local thug. He felt a shudder of unease judder down his spine, unaware that he had passed the equivalent of an antithesis of all that is good on this earth; the devil in woman's clothing.

Chapter 32

The three friends, lying on their stomachs across Emma's bed looked like three stripes, feet dangling down one side and heads hanging over the other. A newspaper was lying on the floor and Emma was slowly turning the pages to see if photographs of any of the missing women were on display.

"Sod, absolutely nada," grumbled Heidi. "Wouldn't it be easier to check our phones for the news."

"You know why," said Emma. "The moment something's not hot news anymore, the bloody press forgets them and moves on to something new. Anyway, I've checked my phone and there's nothing. We'll have to check past editions and the Library keeps them."

"Yeah, but that's terrible the newspapers lose interest," said Jose. "Those poor women disappearing, and probably getting knocked off. Not even like they were prostitutes and deserved it."

"Shuddup," said Emma. "Not even pros deserve to go missing. They're only earning a living."

"Yeah, but they're mainly working 'cos they're using, and they need the dosh for their drugs," Jose argued.

"No-one, whoever they are, whatever they do, deserves to go missing and probably knocked off. If that Matthew bloke was responsible for killing them, and from what thankfully didn't happen to Em, then God knows what he did to them. I think he was going to probably rape you, Em, and then murder you. That woman from Hades that Petra saw. She's gone missing. I bet she's dead, poor bitch. You've got to be grateful you got away with it. We must let the cops know what we know."

Emma pulled over the last page of the newspaper, rolled over and sat up. The other two mirrored her action.

She bit her lip, deep in thought. "Yeah, I suppose. If we can check old editions of the papers that had all those missing women's pictures in them, we could show Petra and see if she recognises the woman she saw in Hades. Then Charlene, and if she recognises Matthew, then we'd have something concrete to go on."

"What, then you'd phone the police?" said Heidi.

"Yeah, I'd phone them and tell them what happened to me. I'd refuse to give my name but say me mate saw the blond woman with this guy and that I drew him, pretty good likeness, and that I'd send them his picture to help their inquiries."

"You ought to tell them about Loddon House though," said Jose.

"You know why we can't do that. Since our break-in, our fingerprints are all over the joint. You can bet he made sure he wiped his off everything."

"The thing is, Em," said Heidi, for once siding with Jose. "It's not like any of us has got a police record, so our fingerprints won't be known. They might just end up with one of his fingerprints if he missed one. That'd be useful to them if they had to prove at some time that he was in that house."

"OK, so we haven't got a record now. What about the future, if by some chance we got involved in something that meant our fingerprints are taken? They'll be on their computer files forever and they'd match them up. Then they'd want to know what we were doing in Loddon House."

"If that event ever arises, and for whatever reason

you hadn't told the police all you know, and more women had gone missing, how would you feel?" Heidi paused for a moment, seeing the worried look on her friend's face. "Look, mate, if we don't give the cops a hand and more women go missing, you'll feel guilty forever, so telling them what you know might prevent more disappearances."

"Yeah, must admit I've been thinking about that." A determined expression spread over Emma's face. Jumping from the bed, she turned to her friends. "Right, action. We go to the library. We've searched the internet and can't trace any old pictures, but libraries often keep old editions of papers. We get a photocopy of the women's faces. Show Petra, and if she recognises the blond bird, we do what I said. We confirm with Charlene to see if it's the same bloke. I phone the cops, tell them what happened, and send them the picture I drew."

"Good. When we going to the library then?" Jose was keen to leave the confines of the bedroom as the need for a cigarette was becoming overwhelming, and Emma had forbidden her to smoke in her house anymore.

"Now, we go straight away." Heidi looked at her watch. "We've got an hour till it probably closes. The sooner we get going, the better it may be for the next poor soul he's gonna get his fangs into."

"Fangs," said Jose. "Christ, is he a vampire? If he is, they're well strong. We'll have to be well careful."

"Jos, dunderhead! Vampires aren't real." Emma shook her head in wonderment, knowing that Jose was serious.

The girls gathered their things together and headed downstairs. Jose determined not to let the vampire subject drop, said, "They must be real. They're in films, in books. There's just too much said about them for them not to be real."

"Jos, they're just fiction," explained Emma as patiently as she could. Loving her slow-witted friend as much as she did, it was hard not to keep exasperation out of her tone.

"What's fiction?" pursued the dogged Jose.

Heidi slammed the front door behind her before she snapped, not as patient as Emma, and her tone definitely displaying frustration.

"For God's sake, Jos, you're denser than me little brother Harry, and he's only ten and dyslexic. Fiction is… well…the opposite of…well… non-fiction. Christ, I can't think of another word for it. What's another word for it, Em?"

"Fantasy, imagination. Like in novels. Not real." Emma's words were quiet, her manner decidedly absent minded.

"What's wrong, mate?" asked Heidi, concerned for Emma, whom she knew, despite her brave face, hadn't got over the ordeal of the attempted rape and perhaps even worse.

"The more I think about it, the more I think that taxi-driver was in cahoots with him. I didn't see her face clearly, but I could give the cops a sort of idea of how she looked".

"Any info'd probably help them," agreed Heidi. "Did you get her name or anything. You said it was some sort of foreign name. Remembered what it was?"

"No, just can't think of it. If I saw it or someone said it, I'd remember."

"It'll come to you when you wake up one morning," said Jose, pleased she had something to contribute. "I couldn't think of the name of that really good film, ages ago, with Harrison Ford when he was like a cop chasing robot things. They've just made another one about it, but years later."

"Blade Runner," the other two said simultaneously.

"Yeah." Jose's voice showed her disappointment she couldn't now make a point. "Anyway, woke up the next day and the first thing I thought of was..."

"Blade runner," said Heidi.

Emma ruffled Jose's hair. "Never mind, ducky. You

can't help being a nerd. I bet your IQ's around 2."

Jose looked puzzled. "What's IQ stand for?"

Emma and Heidi proceeded to have hysterics.

"But we love you anyway," added Heidi.

The three girls laughed, linked arms, and hobbled quickly down the road together, once again their high heels causing passers-by to look in amazement that young girls could actually move on such huge monstrosities.

The heavy clouds in the sky, as yet undecided to release their load, swirled with amazement at the balancing skill of the three young humans.

Chapter 33

As Dan hurried down the stairs, he glanced sideways at the view. The rain was beating against the window, streaming down and distorting the distant trees into bloated bizarre shapes.

"Bloody weather," he muttered. "Bloody murderers, bloody Cole, bloody everything."

He shrugged off his bad mood as he hurried into the meeting room, aware that he was late, but unable to get away from DI Roy Cole who was still giving him a bad time about lack of progress, despite the fact the team having made the development by deducing Yvette Van Looy wasn't dead, but back in town. His boss hadn't even shown pleasure from the headway made from the images obtained from the CCTV cameras, even though when he studied the pictures, he'd agreed with Dan that the woman struck a remarkable resemblance to the 'female anti-Christ'.

The poor quality of the pictures didn't prove categorically that it was her, but with the results from Southport Statistics Office confirming she had a twin sister, suggested, as far as Dan was concerned, that these points were slotting more puzzle pieces into place, and almost certainly revealing the motive behind the disappearances of the women and children. Also, now discovering this sister had mysteriously gone missing just after Van Looy and her side kick Gerry Tomas had escaped the police net, certainly supported the belief that the sister's DNA could have fooled them, but now, on the positive side, they were getting back on track.

DI Cole had just nodded, handed back the photos and said with a voice grating like wheels on gravel that he needed these people apprehended sooner rather than later!

Meena and Luke were sitting facing each other at the end of a long table with their files spread on the table before them. Dan noticed that Meena's files were placed in neat piles, whereas Luke's looked as though he'd just ditched them onto the table in a haphazard fashion. Dan wasn't deceived, he knew despite appearances, Luke would be as well informed and organised as his Asian colleague.

Walking to the other end of the table, Dan dropped his paperwork and sighed heavily.

"Getting a load of grief?" asked Luke, aware of DI Cole's infamous reputation, very short on both patience and understanding with the apparent lack of progress, and his suffering a dire dearth of humour badly needed in this line of work. However, all three police officers were also conscious that the guv would give them his full support if the chips were down. He wasn't politically minded in terms of climbing up the promotion ladder by making his team a scapegoat to the higher authorities when investigations seemed to stagger. Upfront he gave them a hard time, but the end-result was they worked even more diligently, and the end game was normally a successful investigation.

"Yes, definitely lots of grief. Enough of my troubles. Hopefully you two have got some good news." He leaned forward, elbows on the desk, and rubbed his eyes. When he opened them, the cup of coffee being pushed towards him lifted his spirit a tad. "Thanks, mate." He took three sips before he continued. "OK, what have we got? Meena, you first."

"Some good news, some bad. I'll start with the bad and

sad, and then cheer you up. None of the missing women have turned up, or their bodies found...yet. The good news; the pictures of the couple shown on the television news and in the papers have proved successful. We've had many responses although no names as yet. Also, going back to the places the women visited before they went missing proved profitable. In every case when friends or people frequenting the clubs on the night our women were there, there was always someone who remembered the couple. In two of the cases, Lily Taylor and Molly Carson, people actually recalled a tall man talking to them, obviously on separate occasions. When questioned why they hadn't recalled this on initial interviews, they all admitted they had other things on their minds but seeing the photographs had prompted their memories. Shows persistent police work pays off."

"Good. Anything else?"

"No. 'Fraid not. This certainly puts the couple in the frame though. I'm getting Paul Fisher from research to work on getting better quality from the surveillance camera shots, see if we can get some clearer images. We're pretty sure we know the female. To date, Van Looy's name, as you know, hasn't been published in the news. Don't want the wierdos calling in giving wrong info. If we can get some clearer images of the male and get them into the media, that might help."

"Good thinking." Dan turned to Luke. "OK, Luke, what's the progress on the missing children and the image of the male. Any development on his connection to these children? We think it certain that he was tied in with something akin to church schools, so any headway there?"

"Like Meena, there's good and bad. I'll start with the bad. As you're aware none of the other missing children have shown up. On the positive side, surveillance cameras have found images of two of the missing children, Harry

Davy and Jason Stone, taken, we reckon, just before the last time anyone saw them." Luke spread some still shots over Dan's desk. He pointed to one particular image. "Here. This is Harry Davy. He went missing…late May. Look whose holding his hand. The picture quality is extremely poor and in black and white, but you can still see, a tall, slim man. Then this one." Luke pushed another picture forward. "Again, bad picture quality but we think this is Jack Walsh, missing early July. Again, a tall man walking beside him. Whether it's the same tall man, it's hard to tell from the poor-quality images."

Luke straightened up from his position of leaning over the desk and waited patiently whilst Dan studied the photos.

"Good work." Dan looked up and stared at his colleague but said nothing. Luke was aware the 'Diamond Brain' was doing its famous sifting of the facts and waited for the question. He repeated the two words again before saying, "Tommy Deadman, anything on him?"

"Not so far. The team keeps trawling in case we've missed anything. As you know, often camera tapes are wiped fairly promptly for reuse so that didn't help."

"Harry Davy. Any pictures of him found by the first investigative team?"

"Not at first, but when Simon got grounded with a sprained ankle from rugby, he used his time and spent hours on looking and eventually spotted what we believe to be the images of Harry. Funnily enough, French was helping out the first team but reckoned she never spotted him. Mind you, it was an old tape, poor quality that was due to be wiped and re-used but luckily wasn't. Simon reckoned he got lucky and wasn't surprised the first investigation team missed him."

"Anything on Peter North?"

"No, the kid had only gone to the corner shop, and there were no cameras on the housing estate."

"OK, good, some progress. But no names on the tall

guy…or guys." He sank back in his chair, screwing up his eyes with frustration as Luke shook his head. "What about the schools, church connections, anything?"

"No, but we're still questioning. Obviously, we interviewed the various staff and showed them the stills from the security cameras at the relevant schools that the four missing lads attended. No-one recognises him, the tall guy, at all."

Meena, who had been studying the pictures as her two male colleagues talked, placed the coffee cup from which she had been drinking onto the desk. Her voice was laced with excitement as she said.

"Appearance, his appearance." Dan and Luke looked at her, puzzlement painting their faces. "Yes, the quality of the images are poor, I know, but looks like he's wearing tight trendy fitting jeans and some sort of bomber jacket." She picked up one particular picture and showed the other two. "Here, he's under the lamp. See his jacket, it's got a shine to it. Cloth doesn't shine like that so it's probably leather. If you look at the man with the two boys, unfortunately not clear enough to see what he's wearing."

"OK, good," encouraged Dan, "so now we conclude the tall guy's probably wearing jeans and a leather jacket... so?"

"What if people don't recognise him because the clothes he customarily wears, when they see him in the workplace for instance, are so different, they don't *think* they recognise him because here he looks so dissimilar. Out of context. I think maybe the tall guy is one and the same…with the kids and the woman accomplice."

Luke caught Meena's drift and enthusiasm. "Could be. At work though, school or church, different attire. Like a… umm, uniform."

"The kids all went to church schools. That is not coincidence. What about the 'uniform' of the church?"

"Meena, you bright spark. If you weren't a police

officer and spoken for, I'd marry you," said Dan, grinning from ear to ear.

"Spoken for? I'm not spoken for," Meena said gruffly.

Luke glanced at Dan and saw he was unaware of the insensitivity of his words, but he also knew that Dan was oblivious of her feelings. To his surprise a small coil of jealousy twisted in his stomach and glancing at Meena he felt sorry for her as she glanced down to hide her hurt feelings.

Luke leaned forward and took her hand, attempting to make a joke to soften the blow, but this was also a small gesture to indicate feelings that surprised him as they were growing by the day. Raising her hand almost to his mouth as if to kiss it, "Beautiful and intelligent. Hey, DC Mesbah, maybe rich too, and with all that going for you, you're definitely in my league."

Meena snatched her hand away, but his words made her grin and she muttered "Hey, sexual harassment", and the moment passed. Turning back to Dan, feelings now under control, she just said, "Surplus, cassock, robes, all those sort of things."

"Yes, definitely that sort of thing." Dan congratulated her again before adding, "You probably know, DCI Jacobs is doing an appeal on the TV news. The boss and I have written most of his speech, but I think that idea about his usual garb could be added."

"You couldn't put the idea of vestment or the like into those words, Boss. The press would have a field day, and without anything definite to go by, we'd get it right in the neck," said Meena.

"Maybe not use the word uniform either," added Luke. "Police and the army immediately spring to mind. Again, the weirdos would love that."

"OK, give me some alternatives that won't incorrectly influence the public's thinking."

"Clothing, garb… attire."

"Outfit, um, kit," added Luke.

Dan scribbled the words on a pad. "I'll have to get this to DI Cole toot-sweet. He was about to email the speech to Jacobs as I left." He stood up, picking the note pad up as he did so. "OK, thanks for the update. I assume the two teams are up to date on all this?"

"Yes," said Luke. "Meena and I've just left the briefing, both teams and each is aware of the other's progress."

"Good work," said Dan as he walked towards the door. Opening it, he glanced back and said to his two colleagues. "I know you will, but remember to tell your teams to add this thought about his 'normal work appearance' versus the 'jeans and the leather bomber jacket look' when they talk to people."

"Will do, Boss," they said together. Dan nodded, looking from one to the other. "Chins up, mates. We will crack this one, I know." He went to leave, stopped, and looked back at them. "OK, we've interviewed at local church schools and churches. I want you to arrange for photographs, of all medium to tall males based or working in some capacity at all local schools and churches. We need to match up and check how they compare to our poor-quality images we have from the security cameras. You can often tell a lot by some ones…how shall I put it…body profile." He half waved as he turned and left.

"Sure, Boss," acknowledged Luke. Both officers stood up, gathering their files.

"I'm knackered," said Meena.

"OK then, how about I treat you to a quick glass of wine round the local before we police plods plod on? Anyway, we're off duty in half an hour."

Meena picked up the remainder of her files, hesitating for a minute before she looked up, smiled and said, "Silly not to. Half an hour it is then."

The door opened and Mel walked in.

"Mel, when we've finished, we're going to the pub for

a drink, you want to come?" asked Meena.

"Sounds good to me," she answered. "What time?"

"'Bout half an hour.'

"OK, see you in reception."

Luke was typing up his briefing on his computer. Looking forward to having an hour or so with Meena, he swore his disappointment under his breath.

Chapter 34

Three elderly men hurried into the room as their host, George Hampson, was leaning over a fourth man, Arthur, pouring him a large brandy. He turned as he heard them, removing the cigar from his mouth, saying, "Aah, gentlemen, just in time." He raised the decanter that sparkled as the radiance from the chandelier above the table caught the fine cuts in the glass and reflected the shafts of light onto the ceiling. "A little drinky poos to start off the evening on a merry note."

Bob and John nodded their agreement so he poured them generous doubles, but Dennis, always dour, both in appearance and character, shook his head before sitting at the opposite end of the table to Arthur, who was already noisily slurping his refreshment. Dennis glowered at him, but Arthur was either unaware or chose to ignore the frown.

As soon as John and Bob had taken their seats, Arthur smoothed back his hair, picked up from the table a pile of A4 pictures, and handed them to the other four men. Giving them a few moments to put on their reading glasses and study the images, he coughed for their attention before saying,

"Gentlemen, at the end of our last meeting we decided that I was going to start investigating what the police's thinking was in relation to the five missing lads. George's responsibility was to liaise with Father Francis who'd been instructed to keep an eye on Mr O' Leary until the time and place for the kidnap could be arranged. George suggested the kidnap happen in half term, giving us hopefully five clear days before it's noticed that he's missing. Apparently, in the holidays he returns to his cottage in Bournemouth where he lives on his own. He has no near relatives to check on him as far as we know.

"The rest of you were to start making enquiries from other *associates* in the same business as to their thinking on these boys' disappearances. Our network of knowledge on the ground, so to speak, is far wider than the 'bizzies' as my Grandson calls them. If they had our resources, they'd have solved these disappearances long ago." Arthur stopped for a moment and topped up the liquid in his glass. Taking a sip, he pursed his lips and then nodded in approval at the smooth yet slightly peaty slant, before continuing. "Nice. Well, as we all know, and that's one of the main reasons we have met again so soon, very helpfully, the police and news media solved our problems by publishing images of two characters they suspect are involved with the missing bitches and probably the missing children. So, I need to hear from you regarding progress. George, we'll start with you. By the way, I assume we got to this Father Francis in time and he didn't knock off the person who quoted the password?"

"Yes, I got to instruct him in time, and O'Leary's right as rain at the moment. Not much to tell. I've had some interesting conversations with Father Francis. He has no idea how this O'Leary chap came to find out about the password. He's carefully questioned him, and O'Leary maintains that one of the boys in his geography class, when they were studying countries that supplied most of the world's gemstone, allegedly said, 'Rubies on the Moon'. Francis doesn't believe this and is convinced he just said that to make up for a slip of the tongue."

"Has that been checked?" asked John. "After all, if one of the kids did actually say that and this O'Leary just repeated it, then we don't want to waste time and energy kidnapping, questioning and then disposing of this teacher. The less you get your hands dirty, the less chance that things lead back to us."

"Yes, I agree," said George. "I have asked him to check this kid actually said the words, but Francis maintains that he questioned the class as subtly as possible, and they all deny saying it."

"Well, they would, wouldn't they?" Dennis spat out the words. "As just words, the saying is stupid, and no kid will admit to being stupid."

"OK, so I'll push Francis into having one more go at verifying what's going on, but if O'Leary did say it, with no connection to the kids, then we must question him." George turned back to Arthur. "That's all I have to report I'm afraid, Arthur. Not really progress."

"That's fine." He turned and looked in turn at John, Dennis and Bob. "OK, anything from your end?"

"I'll start." Bob picked up the picture that had been passed to him. "Speaking to an *associate* who does not want his name mentioned has been keeping an eye on the media coverage of the missing children. He's been asking round, but none of the usual, shall I dare use the term 'in-crowd', have any information. That's most unusual in our business. It's a fairly small, intimate pool of people, and if someone is on the prowl, he or she has usually mentioned it to someone, and word gets around." He leaned back in his chair and studied the pictures before he continued, his words sounding as though he wasn't concentrating on what he was saying. "So… to sum up…I suppose what I'm trying to say is, most unusually, there is no info whatsoever going around about these disappearances." He then stopped talking, put his hand inside his jacket pocket, and drew out a small magnifying glass. Placing the picture on the table, he poised, putting the glass over the images, moving it backward and forwards in order to focus. The other four men watched his actions, all looking as puzzled as each other.

Eventually Arthur could wait no longer and snapped, "Bob, what the hell are you doing? Well, I can see what you're doing, but unless you're going to explain, I feel a lot of time is being wasted here."

Bob said nothing at first, just passed his magnifying glass to Arthur. "Look at the image of the woman. It's not clear, I know, but who does she remind you of?"

Arthur almost snatched the magnifying glass, his patience wearing thin. He peered at the picture, looked up, and said, "It's just a poor-quality picture of a woman who..." He paused, and leaned over the image again, moving the glass as Bob had done moments before in order to obtain the best focus. He studied the picture from various angles, taking a full minute, before he leaned back in his chair, and looked round the table at his colleagues. His face had turned from a healthy tanned glow to uncooked pastry pallor. "Right, I'm not going to influence you. Pass the magnifying glass round, and tell me who you think either of these people are? I want everyone who hasn't studied the picture to do so, but not say anything until we've all had a chance to see it, so we don't contaminate or unduly influence each other's thoughts."

He and Bob glanced at each other, both very disturbed by the image and thinking the same thing. *Plans might have to change...and quickly.*

Chapter 35

Emma was hoping that the cutting look she had given the unhelpful librarian would slice off the top of her head, spill her brain onto the desk and then she would brush the bloody remains all over the floor and stamp on them. Swallowing her anger away, she bit her lip, and then hoped the pleading smile on her face wasn't too false as she again asked, "Please, closing time isn't for fifteen minutes. Can we please just have those precious minutes to look through a few recent and also back copies of the daily newspapers?"

The old, fat, unhelpful, stupid bat, in Emma's opinion, carried on checking through the stack of books in front of her, and without bothering to look up, replied in a prim voice, "I'll explain for the third time, shall I? The back room containing the old microfiche, the computers and the back copies of the newspapers is now locked. This is done for security reasons. The computers are expensive, and thieves have broken in twice this year and stolen them. New regulations quite clearly state they have to be locked away in that secure room." The woman slammed closed the last book on the pile, looked up, and squinting aggressively through her thick glass lenses, added, "Therefore, not even for the Queen could I unlock the door and allow you after closing time, which," she looked at her watch, "is *imminent*, to go in there to look at newspapers. Come back Monday morning and the room will be open."

"But its Saturday," interrupted Heidi, who, until now had been rubbing Emma's back in an effort to encourage her friend to be patient and remove the sharp edge that was cutting into her voice. Now the woman's negative bordering on rude attitude, and despite on a scale of 1 to 10 in tolerance terms she graded herself at eight and therefore regarded herself as very lenient, and Emma's tolerance being two on a good day, yet this unreasonable stance was also beginning to annoy her.

The woman opened her mouth to reply but before the words spilled out, Jose with a face depicting a sad portrait, said, "It's a matter of life and death. It's about them two what the police fink have been knocking off them women and kids. Em's got attacked herself and she finks she can identify the man. Please, please, five minutes is all we ask. What happens if someone else gets topped this weekend? You'll be to blame 'cos you wouldn't let us look. If we recognise him, we're going to the cops."

Both Emma and Heidi turned in amazement at their friend whose capabilities in terms of long, sensible explanations were normally extremely limited, so therefore before Emma could tell her to save her breath, 'the cow won't budge', she was surprised when she heard,

"Why didn't you say that? You'll have to wait till I've locked the main door. I'll have to come with you and keep an eye on things. Five minutes that's all." She stalked away, throwing a curt 'Wait here' order over her shoulder.

Jose smirked, wallowing in her friends' looks of surprise that she interpreted as admiration. She shrugged her shoulders intimating they could always rely on her! She wasn't to know that although her words had worked the seemingly unlikely miracle, the fact was that the librarian, Miss Brown, was a neighbour and friend to one of the families of the missing children. Her usual unbending attitude for not breaking rules and regulations was overruled by common sense, and the heart-felt sorrow she felt for their grief. If bending a few regulations for a good reason helped to ease the anguish she witnessed daily, then so be it.

The turning of the key in the lock echoed through the lofty library and the three girls waited in the silence, not wanting anything they said or did to change the librarian's mind. The echoes of her heavy, sensible heels striking the highly polished wooden floor as she strode back into the main part of the library, for some strange reason, caused a sensation of anxiety to wind itself round Emma's innards. She felt as though this was a pivotal moment in her life. Not given, in her opinion, to such hysterical inclinations, she attempted to push the sensation away, but as the foot sounds boomed closer, her intuition hung on, refusing to let go of the threads of apprehension.

The girls followed like well-behaved children from kindergarten as Miss Brown strode passed them, beckoning them to follow her. Round her neck, hanging from a red string with a brass attachment on the end, hung a large bunch of keys. The stillness in the room was filled with the keys clanking against each other as the librarian sorted through them, muttering to herself as she did.

"Gold one, that's the front door. Silver, upstairs. Pink blob, lady's lavatory." The three girls leaned forward in unison, peering with interest at the 'pink blob'. It was a silver key with a splodge of nail varnish, that, if Miss Brown's short, unpainted nails were anything to go by, indicated she was not the supplier of the pink daub. "Ah, ha, this one. That brat Sylvia always gets them in a muddle."

Emma opened her mouth to say that Sylvia surely was not to blame; the bundle of keys could never be held together in one bunch as huge as the one clutched in Miss Brown's hands, and not inevitably become mixed up. The kick on her ankle from the side of Heidi's six inch black patent sling backs reminded Emma that Miss Brown's unhelpful nature could return as soon as it disappeared, so she closed her mouth and just dug Heidi in the ribs to pay her back for the bruise that would almost certainly form on her ankle.

Jose of course, despite her earlier success, couldn't be relied on to keep her thoughts to herself. She giggled as she said, "Bet that isn't Sylvia's nail varnish."

Heidi and Emma froze; the librarian looked up, the squinting, aggressive look back in her eyes, before she snapped, "What?"

Jose, oblivious as usual to the possible recklessness of her remark, before her friends could shut her up, continued, "Well, Sylvia's an old person's name. That nail varnish is bright pink. Me mates would wear that, not some old…" Perhaps the pinch on her bottom from Emma started to put doubts into the thoughtless ramble. Jose's words slowed. She glanced at her two friends but was unable to interpret their warning glares. Consequently, when Miss Brown raised her eyebrows for her to continue her wordy blunder, the gaffs issued forth, totally out of control, as though on a steep, highly polished, playground slide down on which she was hurtling them forth with wild abandon, "Well, what I mean is, when you're old…well, Sylvia might not…but then even if she wasn't...then you are...well, sort of, not... young…although maybe….it's a nice pink, but…"

It was the second pinch from Emma and her muttering, "For God sake, shut up, Jos!" that thankfully stopped the reckless torrent mid its turbulent flow.

Three sets of young eyes, one blue, one speckled hazel and one deep green, gazed with apprehension at the librarian, all owners' expecting the door Miss Brown stood before to now remain firmly closed until the following Monday. Indeed, the identical thoughts did race across Miss Brown's mind, but the bloated face due to constant sobbing of June Davy flashed across her mind. She considered. If these three lunatics could help in any small way to identify the people wanted by the police, she had to ignore their obvious insanity, and believe their crazy tale, and let them into the room.

It took Miss Brown exactly four minutes to locate national newspapers that had the pictures of the missing women on their front page. The three girls and the librarian stared at the pictures of the smiling women, none of whom could have realised their moments of fame would be due to tragic consequences.

"Can we have one of these pages, please?" asked Emma. "We want to show a mate if she recognises one of the blond ones."

"No, I'm sorry, you can't; these are kept for our files. However, if that's all you want, those photos, then I'll gladly scan that page for you."

Emma nodded, thanking Miss Brown but unable to take her eyes away from the smiles of the victims.

Walking back to Emma's house, the girls were silent. Jose, although not sure of the actual reason for the sadness now surrounding their adventure, was wise enough to maintain the hush.

Even Heidi's mobile ringing and her unusually quiet hello didn't break the mood.

"What? Really. Great. OK. Hang on, I'll check. It's Petra." Heidi's voice was now full of anticipation. "She's just seen the news on the TV. They showed some pictures from a CCTV camera of a man and a woman they want to speak to in connection with the disappearances. Petra says the quality was terrible but even so, she recognised the man straight off."

"OK, great." Emma caught her friend's change of mood. "She at home for a while?" At Heidi's nod, she continued, "Tell her we're coming around now. We've got the pictures of the woman she said she saw at Hades. We need her to look at it."

Heidi passed on the information, snapped the phone closed.

"She'll wait but we gotta hurry. She's seeing her boyfriend in an hour or so."

As they hurried away, Heidi informed Emma very firmly that if Petra recognised the missing woman as the person being chatted up by the tall guy, and Emma also recognised him from the pictures now on the news as her attacker, she *had* to contact the police.

Emma bit her lip. "Yeah, don't nag. I will, but like I said, I'll phone, tell 'em all I know and send in my drawing. That'll be enough to really help them without me getting sliced up by me mum."

"Better being sliced up by your mum, Em, than that 'orrible guy. Wouldn't put nuffink past 'im," added Jose, not realising the prophesy of her words."

Chapter 36

Yvette Van Looy studied the girl as she and Matthew walked towards the car. Noticing the youngster in her arms, she muttered, "Bloody hell, a slobbering kid. Hope the little horror doesn't puke in the car. Can't stand the smell of sick; it'll taint the car for weeks."

Her face changed to a welcoming smile as Matthew opened the car door for Wendy and helped her into the back seat. He hurried round to the other side and got into the back beside their target.

"Wendy, this is Gail, a great friend of mine who constantly does God's work by driving me around. It's her car and she does it out of the kindness of her good heart. What would I do without this angel?"

Yvette turned around and smiled. "Hi, Wendy, pleased to meet you. And who's the little 'un?"

Wendy smiled back and as she fastened the seat belt around her child, whom she had placed in between her and Matthew, replied, "Hi, Gail. Fanks for the lift. This is Dominic."

"Hi, Dominic, hope you enjoy the ride with Auntie Gail."

It was all Matthew could do to control himself, and not laugh out loud at the remark. Yvette constantly annoyed him, but sometimes she could be witty in a taking-the-mick sort of way. He turned and patted Wendy on the hand and gave her one of his eye-penetrating looks that usually melted the punters, and the resulting putty could then be easily moulded in his hands. Although he wasn't wearing his 'pulling-the-chicks-gear', he knew that his eyes were beautiful and beckoning behind his rimless glasses, and his straight nose and full mouth made him attractive.

"As I was saying to you earlier, Wendy, I have a suggestion that might help out your current situation that I understand is not easy." He paused, eye contact still piercing and suggestive, and waited while the stupid punter returned the gaze. Her grey eyes, outlined in heavy black kohl and eyelashes dripping with gobs of mascara, resembling a victim caught in the headlights of an on-coming car, were stuck like gunky glue to his gaze. "You realise why I had to speak cautiously to you."

He drew out his words slowly and waited for her to nod, while trying hard not to smirk whilst noticing the furtive twinkle from Yvette's eyes that he could see out of the corner of his eye reflected in the front mirror.

"I'm doing this especially for you because...well..." He lowered his gaze, acting the cautious, shy lover. Looking back up, he continued. "The other girls might wonder why I'm singling you out, so I would ask that you tell no-one about this. Can I ask you to swear on my bible?" He held out the black, leather bound book and leaning past Dominic, placed it in her lap. After she had duly sworn, and this time he didn't dare look at Yvette or he knew he would definitely explode with laughter, added, "I have a good friend, a very trusted friend who has gone abroad to fill a missionary position in Africa. He has a beautiful property in Pangbourne that overlooks the river, and in this day and age of high crime rates, he is loath to leave it unattended. He asked me whether I could recommend a housekeeper. She or he could live in it rent-free for a year, and he is willing to pay wages to ensure the person cares for this property."

Pausing again, he saw that her overly made up eyes were large and staring, her expression resembling a child utterly fascinated by a fairy tale. "Rent free." He was pleased with the last two words, ending the drama better than any story he had seen on any television play.

He watched as her revolting mouth, lips much too full for his liking, drop open in a very unflattering fashion. She drew a breath before she was able to reply.

"And...and you fort of me?" Pausing, a tear slipped from her left eye and trickled down her face. "How sweet, how nice. No-one's ever done nuffin' like that for me in all me life. Thanks so much. I will pray for a long and happy life for you every night for the rest of my life." Bending over her son, she kissed the top of his head, murmuring. "Oh Dom, I do believe our luck has changed. There is a God up there watching over you after all."

Just for a micro-second, Matthew felt guilty. If she'd said, "A God watching over me," he wouldn't have had that reaction. The fact that she'd put her son first found a way to a feeling at the centre of his heart that he thought was buried and extinguished long ago. The face of his hated mother wafted before him. That cruel bitch wouldn't have ever said that, her only thoughts were to look after herself and inflict as much physical and mental pain onto her son as possible. Again, he felt emotions threaten to awaken and bring back memories long submerged. He gulped, and luckily at that moment glanced up into his companion's evil eyes in the mirror, and sense prevailed, returning him to the present and the plan in hand.

He patted her hand again. "You're more than welcome, my dear. Now tell Gail where you live, and we'll drop you home. Pack a case; tell no-one and we'll come and pick you up tomorrow."

"What should I do about my flat? Its council, I ought to tell them."

"No, you needn't. You ought to keep it on for the time

being. With your wages you'll easily be able to afford the rent, and when you vacate the Pangbourne property, you'll still have your own flat."

They dropped Wendy and her son a little way from the block of flats, being aware that security cameras might well be located to help control vandalism in the area. Matthew glanced round the dingy neighbourhood, concluding that the cameras were a necessity by the look of the obviously damaged and vandalised properties in the vicinity, but as long as they were careful, they wouldn't be a threat to their plans.

As the couple drove away, the laughter, suppressed by both during the drive to Wendy's flat, erupted like a dormant volcano suddenly celebrating the release of its lava load.

"Success, don't you 'fink,'" mimicked Matthew.

Yvette smirked. "Yep. Kid's a bit young for my taste, but as things are a bit thin on the ground currently, he'll do!"

Both laughed hysterically again.

Chapter 37

Despite the seriousness of the occasion, when Petra's mum opened the door with her hair in rollers, the three girls could barely contain their mirth.

"Hey, you three scrags, take those grins off your ugly mugs. Me sister's doing me hair and I don't want no wise cracks from you."

"Mrs. Black, would we?" sniggered Emma.

"Wouldn't dream of it. Anyway, you look wonderful, rollers or not," added Heidi.

Mrs Black was an extremely overweight woman who regularly changed the colour of her hair, had no idea about fashion, had a deep and contagious smoker's laugh and all Petra's friends loved her to pieces.

"Lippy kids. Come on in then, don't want the bloody nosy neighbours to see me in this state." She opened the door wide and the girls trooped in. "Petra's only just got out of the shower. Go on up, but apparently Tom's due any minute so don't keep her yakking or she won't be ready, and you know what a moody little sod he is."

"Thanks, Mrs Black, we won't be long. You putting the kettle on?" said Heidi.

"Cheeky moo. You want tea, you bloody make it," she retorted. "You drink enough of my tea. You know where the tea bags is kept."

"Thanks." Emma, halfway up the stairs turned to Jose who was on the bottom step. "Go on, Jos, brew the tea."

"No way, I want to hear what Petra's says. You do it, Heidi. You make the best cuppa."

"OK, in a min. Let's show Petra the photocopies first."

Trooping along the landing to their friend's room, they could hear the high pitch whine of the hairdryer. Consequently, when the door opened and the girls spilled into Petra's bedroom, she jumped in alarm and dropped the hairdryer.

"Bloody hell, you bloody startled me. Didn't hear you coming," she shrieked.

"Sorry, mate," said Emma. "We just got some photocopies of the women that went missing and Heidi said you saw this tall guy chatting up that blond woman that gets in Hades."

"Yeah, just phoned Heidi 'bout it. Saw it on the news. Like I said, terrible quality, dunno why they bothers with such crap cameras, but I'd swear on me sister's life it was him; you know, the bloke what you drew."

"OK, mate, look at this." Emma pulled out the picture tucked away in her handbag. Unfolding it, she handed it to Petra. "D'you recognise her. It's Lilly Taylor. One of the women that's gone missing. Is this the bird he was chatting up?"

Petra studied the photocopy, biting the side of her mouth as she concentrated. She nodded, then looked at Emma. Her voice was quiet as she said, "Yeah, that's her. He was jawing to her. Seen her in there quite a few times. Nearly always on her own. Bit older than us really, so none of the guys ever ask her to dance. Sometimes she just gets up and joins our group when we're up dancing. You know, me, Sammy and Carly. We always feels a bit sorry for her really." She looked again at the picture and her face was sad when she looked again at Emma. "Poor bitch. Missing you say. Since when?"

Emma shrugged. "Dunno. Don't tell no-one, and I mean no-one, but I had a run in with this guy. Nearly scared the shit out of me. I got away, but I reckon this poor Lilly didn't if he was chatting her up and left with her, and now she's missing, poor cow."

"Bloody hell, you reported it to the cops?"

"No, I wasn't meant to be on the date. You know what my mum's like. But if you recognise him, this woman's missing, then I'm gonna phone and tell them." She withdrew her own sketch of Matthew from her shoulder bag and showed that to Petra. "Is this him, you sure?"

Petra gasped as she took the likeness sketch, and studied it. "Yeah, that's him. He was older than the usual guys, but real fit. Jos showed it to me the other day at college and I told her it was definitely him. You draws real good. Looks a dead ringer for him. Much better than the pictures from the cameras what they showed on the tele."

At that moment a toe appeared around the door which was then pushed opened and Mrs Black entered with a tray of steaming mugs of tea. "Don't say I ent got a heart of gold and I am a really wonderful person."

Heidi laughed and took the tray. "Mrs Black, despite the 'orrible things the others say about you, I think you're my most favouritist person."

"Cheeky moo. Don't keep our Petra gabbing. Misery guts Tom's just drawn up in that pile a shit he calls a car."

To the ringing tones of 'Thanks, mum', 'Love you lots' and "what a sweetie', Petra's mum left the room. As the girls sipped the hot beverage, they discussed their next move.

By the time, Jose, at Petra's request, had finished blow drying her hair, and the tea almost finished, the girls decided that they ought to contact Charlene as soon as possible. Despite two calls on her mobile, there was no response.

As Petra slipped on her jacket, picked up her handbag and headed for the door, she informed them that Charlene was probably going to be in the pub with Frenchie. "If she is, I'll tell her to call you."

"Tell her it's urgent." At Petra's nod, Emma continued, "What pub you going to? We haven't got nothing planned; we could go for a drink anyway."

"The Hanging Man. Might see you later. Don't leave them mugs in me room, put 'em in the kitchen."

The three girls said 'See yuh' to the closing door.

"OK, drink up, we're going to the pub. I think we gotta do this as quick as we can."

"Em, I haven't got no money. Can you stand me a drink?" said Jose, standing up whilst finishing the last dregs of her tea.

"You've never got no money," complained Heidi. "It's 'cos you spends your allowance on bloody fags. Come on, I'll get you one. Just a cheapie, mind you."

The clattering of heels on the stairs brought Mrs Black out of the living room. "Put the mugs in the kitchen, girls. You going to the pub as well?"

"Yeah, we just gotta see Charlene," Heidi explained. "Petra reckons she's at the pub as well. Thanks for the tea, Mrs Black, it was up to your usual real good standard."

"You're welcome, ducks. See you girlies." The woman opened the front door and the girls kissed and hugged her as they passed.

Emma checked her watch. "If we hurry, we'll catch the Number 33. Goes right by the Hanging Man".

Once again, the wonder of such high heels amazed a passer-by. A Mr Henry Jackson was walking his dog and seeing the achievement of three young girls moving so quickly on such monstrosities caused his and the dog's eyes to open with amazement.

Chapter 38

Father Francis waited until Mr O'Leary had finished talking to Father Aloysius, and then watched him carry his coffee cup to his usual seat near the sideboard where decanters of brandy and whisky were kept. Predictably, the Irishman placed his cup on the coffee table and sauntered to the cut glass flasks to pour his usual measure of whisky, 'My little night-cap for sleeping purposes only' he repeated on numerous occasions should anyone remark on his drinking. Any such retorts would not have been ill meant, merely tongue in cheek comments as his popularity far outweighed any weaknesses his fellow teachers might consider he had.

Normally Father Francis would sit as far away as possible from O'Leary but knew this evening he must not miss this opportunity if he was to gain any knowledge about the unlikely, preciously guarded password that this annoying Irish teacher had blurted out in front of the whole staff. Francis had reported that O'Leary had made the statement in a gloating manner, but on sensible reflection, he was not sure that was the case. Sometimes panic and shock misconstrue context and sensible thinking.

He waited until the Irishman went through the normal routine of picking up the whisky glass, lifting the decanter, which he swirled round as though to mix the alcohol. Next, he slowly poured himself a single measure. Placing the glass next to his coffee cup, he predictably picked up the decanter again, swirled the contents and then lifting the glass up to the light as though this somehow measured the correct quantity. Obviously and unsurprisingly satisfied this was not the correct measure, he then poured another amount, thus ensuring his nightcap was in the order of a treble. He did this nightly, and Father Francis had witnessed the routine countless time.

Waiting for him to settle himself into the armchair with his coffee and nightcap on the small coffee table next to his right arm, Father Francis picked up his own cup and walked round the room towards his target, studying the black and white pictures of former brothers that garnished the walls. Gradually he moved towards Mr O'Leary until just a few feet away. Slowly turning, he glanced at the other brothers present, and when satisfied no-one was taking any notice of his progress, he moved to the empty seat alongside his objective.

He nodded and made a remark that it was a shame the heavy wind and rain had caused the cancellation of the football match that afternoon. Mr O'Leary agreed, and for a few minutes the two of them made polite conversation. As Father Francis had previously planned how he would introduce the matter, his conversation flowed easily toward the subject.

"It's funny how odd things come into your head," he said. "I couldn't get to sleep the other night and for some strange reason the subject you spoke about came into my mind. How exactly did that arise?"

When Mr O'Leary didn't reply, Father Francis immediately interpreted his enigmatic look as one that was either adopted to mask guilt or to mock him further. In fact, the Irishman was somewhat confused by the question, thinking for a moment that his companion was referring to the episode in the bathroom when the teacher had shown surprising anxiety for his wellbeing. Mr O'Leary hoped that by nature he was a reasonably affable person; he certainly made great efforts to be, but he felt even a genial character can only take on board a limited amount of unpleasant and sarcastic digs without human nature taking over. Despite great efforts and a lot of praying to the Almighty for assistance to control his feelings, he found himself disliking Father Francis more and more. So when he'd shown such unexpected kindness by coming into the bathroom, and being so concerned, remorse for such evil feelings had cascaded over his body like rain from a cloudburst, and he had felt extremely guilty about his thoughts, and had continued to suffer these disturbing pangs ever since. Consequently, his troubled conscience and then confusion had momentarily blanked his mind.

    Realising suddenly that the words 'the subject you *spoke* about' could not refer to the bathroom episode, and not having given Tom Gardner's unfortunate comment further thought recently, O'Leary was still puzzled and couldn't recall to exactly what his companion was talking about.

However, his silence and unreadable expression yet further convinced the Jesuit teacher that he was being goaded, and even when the Irishman's forehead had furrowed into a frown, and he hesitantly asked to which subject he was referring, Francis wasn't convinced of his innocence.

His voice was therefore sharp as he continued, "Come, come, don't tell me you've forgotten. You were highly amused by the remark. What's happening, your memory failing you this early in life?"

When O'Leary shook his head and continued looking puzzled, Francis' voice had slid from merely sharp to a scalpel cutting capacity as he continued. "The remark in your class, geography I think, about where rubies came from." He could not bring himself to use the actual words of the preciously guarded secret passwords that had slipped from O'Leary's mouth so carelessly. Plus, the virtual brainwashing that all members of his cell received to ensure absolute security made him paranoid about the use of loose utterances.

"Oh, yes, of course, I do remember. Yes, you've mentioned it before if I recall." Mr O'Leary threw his head back as he laughed at the recollection. "Where do rubies come from? Rubies on the Moon. How ridiculous, how truly silly." The laughter, now issuing forth with great gusto unfortunately fuelled Father Francis's uncertainties to combustion point, and he had to control himself from not leaping over and squeezing his hands round the man's throat to quell the laughter, and the careless use of the sacred password. Only the appearance of Father Aloysius suddenly appearing with the coffee pot stopped homicide at that moment, which was a shock for Francis as he recalled how previously he had convinced himself he was not capable of murder.

Realising that if ordered again to finish the job of getting rid of his fellow teacher, perhaps if he worked himself into a fury, he could accomplish the mission.

Taking a deep breath and nodding his thanks, his hand was surprisingly steady as he held up his cup for a refill. As Father Aloysius walked away, he was about to pursue the subject when his companion helpfully continued.

"Oh yes, the subject was the source of gemstones. I'd asked the boys for their homework to research how gems stones were formed and where they were mainly to be found. I thought I'd told you that previously. Why are you so interested?" He refrained from mentioning Tom Gardener's name, still not convinced that his new feelings in regard to the teacher's changed character were secure enough to mention it, in case the spiteful nature so prominent in the past returned, and in Father Francis's lesson, Tom was made to suffer.

Consequently, he knew his answer wasn't probably

convincing, and even when further questioning forced him to produce equally vague answers, O'Leary didn't realise his hazy replies further fuelled his companion's suspicions and enhanced the danger to his life.

Chapter 39

Dan had once again left DI Cole's office with his ears burning. Despite the investigating officers persistently questioning people who had come forward as being in the nightclubs when the women went missing, and the appeals and images from the cameras splashed across televisions news programmes and displayed in both national and local papers, no fresh leads had emerged. Although Cole had assured his subordinate, he understood everyone was working diligently to get results, the upshot was that there had been *'no bloody progress'*. Naturally, as not much else was on the news front, no footballer was found to have three mistresses, nor a twice-married film star confessed to being gay, aliens hadn't unfortunately invaded, so the news media was still dragging up the stories of the missing women and children. At first the press had been supportive of the investigation, but that angle was not fresh news now, and therefore something different was needed to sell more papers, so recently they had taken a new stance, 'Why the lack of progress?'

Stopping by the drinks dispensing machine to buy a coffee, Dan eased open the door of the Incident room, precariously balancing the coffee cup and the pile of files in his arms. The moment he entered the normally noisy room, he was aware of the atmosphere. All the officers had obviously stopped whatever task they were doing and were staring in his direction. Hurrying to the front table, hastily dropping the armful of files onto it in an untidy pile, but carefully placing the precious coffee in a safe spot near a pot full of pens, he looked around the room.

"OK, tell me the news. Something's just happened I know; you can cut the atmosphere with the proverbial knife."

Luke stood up, putting on his jacket. "You'd better bring that coffee with you if you want it hot, boss." He picked up his car keys and a buff A4 file from his desk and walked towards Dan. "Just put the phone down on a call. A body of a boy's just been discovered."

Dan felt the colour drain from his face. Although the boys had been missing for too long for the officers not to realistically think the worst, while there were no bodies, there was always that small spark of hope. That hope was now sadly extinguished! Not bothering with his drink, Dan just said, "We'll go in your car. Update me as we go. Where's Meena?"

"In court with Adam Kennedy. The Whitley Wood burglary case."

"OK, let's go."

As Luke eased the car out of the crowded police car park, he explained the details of the phone call.

"You watched the local news recently?" Glancing sideways at the oncoming cars, he joined the flow of traffic before he continued. "At the end of the Warren Road in Caversham where Jason Stone's body was found, approximately a mile further along that road are the remains of some chalk pits. That's what we used to call them when I was a kid. Mostly built on now, but behind the houses there remains a small area not used for further development yet.

"Yesterday, early evening, a man was out walking his dog when it ran off. The man searched for ages, and eventually heard it whining in the distance. Turns out the dog had fallen into some sort of vent or drainage shaft that's at the back of the undeveloped zone. The area has a substantial fence round it, but there are quite a few, large holes in the wire that the dog obviously slipped through. The dog's owner called the fire brigade out, but they couldn't do much till it got light. Too dangerous and inaccessible, and obviously the dog wasn't going anywhere.

"This morning the fire brigade turns up again to rescue the dog. Apparently, the shaft is very deep, but down about twenty, thirty feet there was some sort of half grid that the dog had landed on, luckily. As the firefighter was lowered down to put a harness around the dog, he noticed a strong, bad smell. He guessed what it was and shone his torch further down the shaft. About ten or twenty feet below him was what looked like the other half of the grill which had broken in half and fallen further down, but had got jammed on a big plant or maybe tree roots growing out of the walls. Lying on the grill was the body of a child. The fireman could see he was dead and was beyond saving and guessed he shouldn't do too much investigation as it was a crime scene. Said he'd read about kids going missing.

"He said nothing to anyone at the time, not wanting to cause a panic, especially as the local television crew were on hand to televise the dog rescue and would then have had a field day. He just rescued the dog, the cameras loving it, and even did a short interview afterwards. Once the cameras and press were gone, he reported his find to his chief, and they phoned straight away."

After his dialogue, Luke took a deep breath. Dan said nothing, just sat quietly looking out of the side window. Luke knew better than to interrupt his thoughts. Eventually, he murmured, "SOCOs etc been informed?"

"Yes, on their way." Luke glanced at his boss again, still deep in thought. "Umm, Mel was phoning around just as you came in. She'll update DI Cole. Thought maybe we could have a quick survey just in case it was an accident, although somehow, I doubt it. We can have a gander you know, hopefully get there before the SOCOs arrive. What d'you reckon, boss?"

Dan suddenly came out of his musings. "Yep, still need the facts though, and an investigation's still necessary should it prove to be an accident…which I also doubt. OK, you're right, if we get there before the SOCOs arrive, we'll have time for a recce ourselves. Once the boys turn up, and the crime scene tapes erected, we'll have to wait for them to finish." The DS turned to his companion. "Did you bring the photos of the lads for checking? Hopefully he'll still be recognisable, poor little so and so."

"Yeah, file on the back seat."

The traffic as usual over the Caversham Bridge was stacked nose to tail, forcing Luke in this area to switch on the blue light to enable him to force his way through the chaos. Once free at the bridge end, he then continued through the next set of traffic lights, and it didn't take long to reach the end of the Warren. A man in fire service gear waved them down, and as they halted, without an invitation he opened the rear off-side door and climbed into the back.

"Bit complicated to get there. Charlie sent me down to guide you in," he said without introduction. "Take that next turning right. Goes uphill, passed the sides of the end house for about fifty yards." He waited until they did as he had ordered, and Luke realised that without his guidance, they would have had great difficulty finding their way. Twisting and turning through some muddy lanes, they eventually pulled up beside the fire tender. Four white-faced firemen stood round their vehicle. Dan couldn't decide who was the palest and sickliest looking.

A tall, dark haired man with sideburns walked towards them, held out his hand and introduced himself as Charlie Walters, the fire chief. "Bobby here was the person who found the body. It's a bit inaccessible. Follow him. He'll show you the way."

Both Dan and Luke nodded their thanks, shook Bobby's hand, and followed him as he pushed himself into some thick-growing, prickly undergrowth.

"It's only thirty feet in or so," he explained, pushing back the overhanging branches for them to follow. "Just overgrown."

Walking to a small clearing, he bent down and indicated a hole, about three feet in diameter, with a rusty grill lid lying next to it. The two officers bent down beside him. A faint whiff of a sweet, sickly smell was apparent even from their position outside the shaft.

"Presumably the lid wasn't in place when you got here," said Dan. "Looks very substantial. No way a dog could move it if it was in place."

"Apparently half off according to Mr Turner, the dog's owner. When I quietly told Charlie my find, he asked the man to stay. Explained he obviously needed some details for his report. We waited till the news people had scarpered and phoned you straight away."

"Where is he now?" asked Luke.

"We sat him and his dog in the vehicle. He's getting a bit impatient now he's got his dog back, but we insisted."

"Have you told him about your find?"

Bobby shook his head. "No." He straightened up and looked at the entrance to the shaft. "As a fireman I've seen some awful things. I think this beats all." Obviously at the memory of his find, his face went from white to green.

Dan looked at him sympathetically. "Thanks, Bobby. Go and sit yourself down or something. We'll take it from here and get back to you in a minute."

"Don't try and go down there on your own," said Bobby, even with his distress, showing professional concern for the two officers. "You'll need a harness and…"

"Don't worry. Initially we're just looking. We can't do anything until we've decided what further action is needed." Dan retrieved his torch from his pocket. "Will we be able to see anything from here?"

Bobby took a large flashlight from his overall pocket. "One of ours. Doubt you'll see anything with that little one. You will with this. Poor little begger's on the right side as you're looking at the hole now. Maybe thirty to forty feet down."

Handing over the flashlight, he turned and scrambled back through the undergrowth.

Both officers pulled on plastic gloves, Luke carefully shifted further around the hole allowing them both to peer down. Dan shone the light, appreciating that Bobby was correct, and that without the flashlight, they wouldn't have spotted anything. Even so, he doubted that unless previously informed about the position of the boy's body, even with the strong light, what they could see was just a vague shape. Knowing that it was in fact a body, with careful examination it was clear the corpse was barely suspended at the edge of the broken grill, a part of his clothing snagged on a spike.

"Absolute luck that the poor little so and so got caught up. If he hadn't, I guess he'd never have been found." Dan shone the beam passed him, but the blackness swallowed the light.

"You know what this means," murmured Luke. The two men looked at each other. He continued. "One, as you said, his body would never have been discovered. Two, if it's one of the missing lads, chances are, if this is where they are being dumped, there are other bodies down there."

Dan sat back on his heels. "I agree. When you think that Jason was found only a half of a mile from here. Can't have been coincidence."

"Yes, maybe the dumper panicked or had to make a quick get-away."

"Wonder how deep this shaft is. I'll phone back to the station, get Mel to find out which council is responsible for covering this area, see if there are any maps or plans.

Looks like some sort of drainage system. They must have some record."

"Going down there will need an expert. Looks years old."

"Yes, and probably very unstable. If this is a mass grave so to speak, except for our good luck, if you can call it that when so much heartbreak for the families is about to happen, then we'd never have found the bodies."

Both men breathed in deeply, depression slapping over them in great waves; not wanting to find more bodies, yet knowing if this was the boys' final resting place, the case could move forward hopefully in leaps and bounds, and at least heart-broken families would have the doubtful peace of knowing what had happened to their beloved children. That was heart breaking in itself, but still a minute amount better than a lifetime anguish of never, ever knowing.

Chapter 40

The five elderly men that formed the Brotherhood of Elders walked into John's dining room. Each meeting was held at a different venue. Security, secrecy, and utmost care ruled their actions. The fiasco during Operation Hobbledehoy, despite being almost four years before, was still fresh in their minds, and they were aware that despite stringent precautions, things could still go amiss. They were determined such a costly shamble was not going to be repeated.

Taking their places around the highly polished rosewood table, as one body they looked towards Arthur. He, always aware of his position as absolute leader, liked to appear calm and aloof, so he casually ran his hand over the shiny surface. "Elsie certainly keeps this beautiful piece of furniture in top notch condition, John." His voice, despite the compliment, had a patronising tone.

"Yes, housework is the top priority in our house." John spread out A4 papers on the table as he spoke. "She thinks during our get-together today we are discussing the forthcoming church bazaar. Luckily, she doesn't come in the office much where the computer's kept. Not that she'd know how to access it, but one can't be too careful."

"Why would it matter?" said Bob, "Assume you don't keep anything on it that would prove interesting and damaging should our friends in blue get their hands on it?"

"No, of course not." He looked Bob in the eyes as he answered, pleased with his ability to lie so adeptly.

"Ok, let's get on," interrupted Arthur. He was feeling grouchy having been to the dentist not three hours previously for an extraction of a back tooth and the effect of the painkiller was wearing off. He needed to get home to take more paracetamol. "At the last get-together we almost certainly identified the woman from photos in the newspapers as the supposedly long-dead Yvette Van Looy, Delilah to her so-called friends, and we were all pursuing various avenues of investigations to support this thinking. OK, Dennis, I'll start with you. What did your contact at Reading Police Station have to offer?"

"Obviously he doesn't attend the meetings in the Inci-dent room when progress of the investigation is discussed. He keeps his eyes and ears open as people pass by his desk, often still discussing developments, and the details of plans for moving forward. He's not absolutely sure, but believes the police now know that Delilah is not dead. The body found last year and identified as her is in fact her twin sis-ter. So, what's the conclusion? She, the Numer One Most Wanted is alive. Tomas is definitely dead, as we know. The thinking is they wouldn't put it past the She Devil to knock off her very conveniently identical twin sister. Solves all her problems. As far as the police are concerned, once they com-pared her DNA, they had their man…or woman actually."

"Identical twin sister. Sounds a bit coincidental," said George who had returned from the kitchen as Dennis's monologue had begun and was now handing round mugs of steaming coffee kindly made by John's wife.

"True." said Bob. "However, people do have twins. I have a twin sister. OK, not identical, but twins happen."

"Right," said Arthur, keen not to let the discussion run on too long. "We have a picture that we all agree is a dead ringer for her. The police have found out she had an identical twin and have probably also concluded that she's back from the dead, so to speak. Almost certainly the correct conclusion, knowing that she's a demon in woman's clothing, and I for one would believe she conveniently bumped off her sister to make it look as though she was dead and gone. Hence, nobody's chasing her."

"Yep," said Dennis. He leaned back in his chair and took a sip of his coffee before he continued. "The source says he wouldn't bet his life on it, but he would offer his nag of a wife's life that the woman in the picture is definitely Van Looy."

"Umm. OK, we conclude it's her then." Arthur looked back up at Dennis again. "And the man in the picture with her… they got any names, suspects, any identification at all?"

Dennis shook his head. "As far as I can make out, they've no idea who he is. Connected to a church or church schools maybe, but they've no clue as to which one."

"Yes, I remember reading the names of a couple of schools in a newspaper report, St Anne's Primary and St Bernard's Convent if I recollect correctly," added Bob. He turned to Arthur. "What about St Stephens Jesuit Academy in Sonning, where the password was used. Any of the kids come from there?"

"Interesting point," said Arthur. Turning back to Dennis, he raised his eyebrows.

Dennis shook his head. "Don't know. Source never said. Still, it's been in the papers. I could check that if I can get hold of some back copies."

Arthur interrupted, his voice now taking on a sharp whine. "Bob, I believe it was actually your task to find out about the tall man with Delilah the Devil woman?"

"Yes. Dennis helpfully informed me that the police have suspicions that he was connected with either church schools, churches themselves or certainly something along those lines. That was helpful, and so that was where I focused my enquiries. I made a list of all the church schools in the immediate Reading area, including the Sonning one. I delegated to the Watchers and got them to watch outside the schools. They had two each. Needless to say, despite supplying them with copies of the photos of the man, not one of them reported seeing anybody resembling him. The closest we got was a tall fellow who was seen leaving Saint Bernard's. I made some enquiries, but apparently he is the choir master who comes in a couple of days a week."

"Did you get a name or a photograph?" asked Arthur.

"Yes. His name is David Sinclair." Bob lifted his brief case onto the table and extracted two photos, one he passed directly to Arthur, and the other he gave to his neighbour for passing around the table. "Tall, yes, as you see, but he has close cropped gingery hair and glasses. Also, he has a slight limp that certainly wasn't reported in the news."

Arthur compared the original photo and Bob's contribution. Pursing his lips, he shook his head. "Mmm, see what you mean. Similar build but otherwise not really a likeness. However, I think it's worth pursuing." He passed back his copy to Bob. "Can you find anything more? Where's he stationed permanently? Whether he visits other schools? That would be a good source of knowledge for him about potential lads, victims. See what else you can dig up."

Bob nodded as he took back the photograph and slipped it into his briefcase.

Arthur finished his coffee and placed the cup onto the saucer. Rubbing his fingers across his eyes, he knew he'd have to get home soon as the pain was reaching an unbearable point.

"You OK, Arthur?" asked George. "You seem really uncomfortable."

"Mm, not really. I've had a tooth extraction and it's beginning to play up."

"We can call it a day, maybe reconvene..."

"Not yet, George. Just need to hear if there has been any progress about the teacher, O'Leary?"

George looked at some notations he had made in a spiral notebook. "I phoned just yesterday evening, wanting the most up-dated report as our meeting was this evening. Father Francis once more carefully questioned O'Leary but got no-where. He, O'Leary, still maintains it was an off-the-cuff remark from some kid in his class, yet Francis is very aware that the kid's name is never mentioned, and when questioned, he is still vague and unhelpful. Francis says he keeps his expression very...umm…enigmatic I suppose is the word."

"You did mention that he'd changed his mind, that he decided his first panic was shock, and maybe he'd got things out of perspective."

"True, Arthur, he did say that, but because one-minute O'Leary is acting as though he just thinks the incident was a boy making a silly remark, the next moment he looks vague and uneasy. This has Francis believing he has something to hide, and consequently thinks O'Leary needs to be questioned. If some-one has got a loose tongue, then we need to bring in the man and find out exactly what he does know."

Arthur, the pain now almost out of control, knew he'd get no further with his investigation and was now desperate to bring the proceedings to a quick close.

"I think you're right." He stood up and hastily piled his files together. "OK, I'll arrange something. I suggest we meet next week. I think it's your turn Bob, your place?"

At Bob's nod of affirmation, he finished, "Carry on with your enquiries; I'm particularly keen to find out more about this tall fellow. So, follow up about the red-headed choir master, Bob… this Sinclair, I think that might be interesting. All of you, keep your ears to the ground, eyes peeled and keep talking to your sources. Someone must know something. We've more contacts than the men in blue, and we need to break this before they do.

"Goodnight gentlemen, I've got to go and get some

painkillers down my throat. John, as the others have assigned tasks, perhaps you'd like to poke around to see if any gossip is circulating. I know Bob couldn't dig anything up but keep trying." At John's nod of agreement, he added, "And John, feel free to use the brandy I brought, I think you all deserve a drink."

He closed the door quietly behind him, not wishing to wake up John's three grandchildren who he knew were currently staying with their beloved grandparents. It didn't occur to him to wonder that someone with John's predilections should, on the surface, be a happily married man, devoted father and grandfather.

Chapter 41

The three girls tumbled off the Number 33 bus, giggling loudly at the driver's remarks. He was a handsome, young Indian looking man with eyes and eyelashes to die for, brilliant white teeth and a cheeky grin. When the three good-looking teenagers climbed on the bus, he thought heaven and paradise had arrived in one package.

Once they had individually paid their fare, all three girls being aware of the dishy driver, they had conveniently arranged themselves near to his seat. The four soon entertained themselves with a great deal of banter during the ten-minute drive despite a miserable grey-haired woman in a black beret pulled well down over frizzy, permed hair telling him to concentrate on his driving. Apparently, Aarav Khatri, as he introduced himself, was leaving this temporary job at the end of the week and going to Oxford to study law, so he just winked at the woman and carried on with the repartee.

At the end of the journey he had attempted to get a date with Heidi, who although very tempted, had not agreed a firm meeting despite his numerous requests, but had told him that she frequented the Hanging Man pub which was their destination that very evening. As the doors closed behind the girls, the driver's last words of 'See you there about 10 o'clock after my shift finishes' caused the girls to collapse into more fits of giggles.

They linked arms as they tottered along the uneven pavement towards the pub, and Emma could hardly talk coherently as she repeated the past events. "I thought I'd die when he said you had a sexy mouth."

"Yeah, but I hope he never bloody believed you when you said I had false teeth and farted when I coughed."

This remark caused even more laughter, and the girls were still enjoying the silliness of youth when they fell through the door of the Hanging Man pub into the lounge bar.

Staggering on their high-heeled shoes to the bar and annoying the barman by merely ordering three orange juices due to a cash shortage, they picked up their glasses and surveyed the crowded room. Eventually Charlene, Frenchie, Petra and Tom were spied in the corner by the wall covered in ink sketches and oil paintings for sale by local artists studying at the local Art Academy, and as the four were deep in conversation, they hadn't spotted the girls' arrival.

The teenagers pushed their way through the crowded room to sit near their friends and noticed three girls whom they knew sitting on the next table, and worked at the local riding stables. They were still rigged-out in their riding boots, jodhpurs and oiled jumpers. Emma asked if they could join them, and at their agreement, drew up unused chairs from surrounding tables. There was a distinct smell of horse manure hanging in the air, probably emitting from the girls' boots, and Jose, not being over-run with tact, screwed up her nose and said loudly, "Phew, what's that pong. Jeez, horse shit I know."

Momentarily, a micro-second of silence hung alongside the odour before Donna burst out laughing and the awkward moment passed. "Yes, Sammy's horse crapped all over her boots as we left."

"Well, I think she didn't make much effort to wipe

it off," added Emma, producing further mirth. The girls continued to gossip until Emma noticed Charlene get up and walk towards the bar.

Glancing sideways, she noticed Frenchie was deep in conversation with Tom, so she quietly left her seat and followed her. She wanted the opportunity to speak to her, and as she didn't get on with the boyfriend Frenchie Morgan, who had at one time been her boyfriend, she didn't want him to overhear their conversation and butt in with sarcastic remarks. When she had eventually sent Frenchie packing because of his possessiveness, they had not finished on friendly terms and had not spoken since. Emma was aware that Frenchie was just as possessive with Charlene, and wouldn't even like her talking to Emma, particularly as she was his ex.

As Charlene ordered the drinks she smiled as Emma squeezed passed the crowded bar and stood next to her.

"Charlie, Jos tells me you recognised the fellow whose mug shot is in the papers. You know, the one the cops want to interview." She withdrew her sketch from her shoulder bag, unfolded it and showed it to her friend. "Just wanted to make sure. Is this the guy that chatted you up when you were sat on your own?"

Charlene took the change for the drinks and put it in her purse, frowning as she looked at the picture. She nodded. "Yeah, that's 'im. Real good looking, dead fit. Dark hair, lovely eyes. Real dish. Real dangerous."

Emma looked at her in surprise. She always considered herself a good judge of character, but that hadn't been her impression at all when she'd first met Matthew. "What makes you say that, dangerous?"

Charlene shrugged. "Dunno. Thought he was creepy. Too nice. Blokes, especially older blokes, that gets in Night Clubs, well they're well weird. It's a place for youth, not old gits. If they're in there, they're sinister, nasty, up to no good."

Charlene picked up the tray of drinks and pushed her way through the crowd. Emma was shocked. She looked again at her sketch. It was a dead ringer for him. A cold chill blew round her heart. Without even realising it, she'd caught a look in his eye. Hoping she wasn't kidding herself, she knew she had some talent. She didn't realise how much until she saw the mocking look that she had inadvertently, but so accurately caught in her drawing. She murmured, "Mr Evil, up to no good. Dangerous. A killer. Jeez, why didn't I see it?"

"Fancy a drink, beautiful?" a voice asked. Emma looked up, a short guy with a cheeky grin and a crew cut was staring at her, his eyebrows raised questioningly.

"No thanks, mate," she absent-mindedly replied as she walked away, still annoyed at her stupidity.

Chapter 42

Dan and Luke watched in silence as the SOCOs erected the tent over the four small bodies now lying side by side, and just a few feet away from their last resting place. Dan hadn't smoked in four years, and during the last six months the lingering smell of smoke from a passer-by's cigarette hadn't even brought back the urge, but seeing this terrible sight before him, he felt a desperate need.

"Suppose we knew this day would probably come," murmured Luke. "Still, doesn't make it any easier to bear. Glad the fireman kept quiet about his find. The television crew there filming the dog rescue would have loved to be the ones to break that news to the public, a real coup for them. If we hadn't got to the parents by then, how terrible to hear the news from the television."

Dan just nodded his reply. No experience as a police officer made this occasion any easier to bear. He felt as though there was a tight band squeezing his heart. His hands clenched into fists at his side, and he silently vowed that when he caught the perpetrators, he wouldn't be acting like a police officer. *In fact…I'll kill the fucking bastards*.

His unprofessional thoughts were interrupted as the tent to cover the heartbreak was finally erected, and the SOCOs disappeared inside to complete their job before Dan eventually spoke.

"DI Cole's on his way. We'd spoken previously that unless we got a break on this case, we'd call in more officers from other constabularies. Shame Adam's on the burglary investigation, we could do with him. Still, I think that investigations almost concluded, so hopefully we'll get him on board soon enough. We need fresh eyes, new thinking. If we're not getting the breaks, not progressing, then we do need fresh blood, rethink our strategy."

"You saying different blood on the team will look at it with new eyes?"

"Yep. We're not making enough headway. None of our lines of enquiry are going anywhere. Door to door, appeals on the news, interviewing the nightclub goers, all moving us forward, but not fast enough. A creative look, an innovative edge, and an untarnished view may well provide something new. We round everyone up. Put together all we have, and we go over it with a fine-tooth comb."

"Brainstorm, boss, as we've done previously. Everything, however seemingly crazy, gets listed. Yeah, it's amazing what comes out of that."

Dan nodded again. Before he could reply, he looked up as Luke tapped his arm and inclined his head towards the opening that led to this place of heartbreak and death. DI Cole squeezed through the bushes, followed by Meena.

The two officers both murmured an acknowledging 'Guv' towards the Senior Officer. He curtly nodded in reply, walking past them to the tent. They watched as he picked up the door flap, bending his head as he entered.

Meena joined her colleagues, her face displaying the same anguished expression that she saw on their faces.

"Three more bodies then as well as the one that the fireman spotted?" she asked.

"Yes. We suspect Tommy, Harry, young Peter North. Jack was the body the fireman spotted, and we retrieved first. Not definitively identifiable at this moment, but from the files detailing descriptions, size, clothes they were wearing when last seen, I'd say it was them."

Meena quietly spoke some words that neither Dan nor Luke understood. They guessed it was some sort of prayer in her language, but neither thought it was the time to question the meaning.

DI Cole appeared out of the tent. His face was ashen. Standing still for a moment, obviously collecting himself, he rubbed a hand over his face. He took a deep breath and joined his colleagues.

"Christ, almost certainly the four missing lads then," he said. "Obviously won't know for sure until the parents identify them, but in my own mind, I've no doubt."

"Yes, Guv, I agree. However, I think we need to get to the parents as soon as possible. There's a big crowd gathering outside the taped off area. News will get around. The cameras will be here any minute you can bet. They'll put two and two together and probably come up with the correct four for a change. We don't want one word, phone call, news item getting to the parents before we do. Mel's on her way. I'll go with her. Luke and Meena can go to another set of parents. I'll arrange…"

"OK, good thinking, Dan," Cole interrupted. "I'll get another female officer and I'll do the third set of parents. WPC French's is on standby, she's experienced in family support. I'll pick her up and give her the heads up about the situation. OK, let's go. We need to be out of here before the press turn up. I'll arrange for two officers to get to the fourth set of parents. Speed is of the essence."

The police officers hurried away to visit the parents with the news they most dreaded. They dispersed to their transport; heads bowed with sadness. Pushing through the bushes and walking to their cars, their hopes of secrecy were dashed as a 'gaggle of press', as they were known at the station, had obviously heard the news and were already crowding around the area containment tape. Climbing into their cars, no-one answered the piercing yells of the questions that were too near the mark not to urge the police officers to make Mach speed to the poor families who were about to have another devastating day in their lives.

Chapter 43

Yvette saw Wendy struggling to open the glass door of the council flat entrance. The girl was holding her uncooperative son's hand, and at the same time was attempting to drag her case through the opening, but the door kept swinging back before she could get the case and the boy through safely. Yvette was tempted to go and give her a hand, not to be helpful, but just to speed up the process, and get the stupid cow out of the vicinity as soon as possible. Being aware that CCVT, sneaking bloody lenses that were supposedly there for checking on criminal activities, she therefore wasn't sure that more cameras wouldn't be positioned around the flats to protect against the vandalism that was obviously prevalent by the look of the area. Not wanting her car to be spotted she didn't dare move it from the dark corner where she was parked.

She sighed with relief when she saw a young black man appear from behind Wendy and hold open the door enabling her to get past the obstacle. He then evidently offered to carry the case because she saw Wendy laugh and nod, and the three of them, with the man towing the case, began heading to where Yvette was parked, and where she had previously informed Wendy she would be situated. Yvette silently cursed. Luckily the girl hadn't questioned why Yvette wasn't going to be parked in front of the main entrance that would have been the most practical option. However, Yvette was in a dilemma.

She could not chance the black boy seeing her face, and yet if she drove away, the girl might not linger long, and she would lose the opportunity of picking her up. Deciding she had better not chance being seen, she switched on the ignition to drive away, when fate took charge. A car, a battered old Mercedes, appeared out of seemingly nowhere, and reversed back close to her bonnet, effectively blocking her in.

Shit. Yvette was afraid of no-one, and even when a very large man extracted himself slowly from the vehicle, and began walking towards her, she wasn't alarmed for her safety. It was just that she did not want to be spotted, and perhaps later remembered and described as the last person identified in the area where Wendy was last seen.

She wound down her window, and preparing for an argument, was disconcerted by his non-confrontational voice, so at odds with his giant frame. "Excuse me, mate," his said. "Know there are spaces either side of you; sounds picky but the council have allotted us particular car spaces and we have to keep to them. 'Fraid you're in mine."

Keeping her head back in the gloom of the car, she said, "Oh, sorry. I didn't realise. Just waiting for my passenger." Glancing to her left and seeing Wendy, Dominic and the pain-in-the-arse-knight-in-shining-armour approach, she said. "Oh, they're just coming now. If you move forward a tad, I'll soon be on my way."

"Thanks, mate," said the friendly giant, and walked back to his car and drove forward to give her room. Giving a friendly wave as she eased out the car, she rationalised that he'd be more likely to remember a stroppy individual than a helpful one.

By this time, the trio were only yards away. Yvette flashed her lights and pulled alongside them. She noticed the giant then park in her previous space and walk away from the approaching pair. Not wanting to get out of the car and again be seen, Yvette bumped open the boot from inside the car and was thankful the black guy helpfully loaded Wendy's case. Easing down the window; she heard Wendy thank him and then saw her wave as he walked away down the road. The girl opened the rear offside door and asked whether she and Dominic should sit in the back. On Yvette's confirmation that it would be fine, the pair climbed in.

Waiting while Wendy seemed to take an age to belt up Dominic, and then slowly slide into the car and secure her own seat belt, Yvette felt her patience wearing very thin. She might not have been spotted by cameras, but there were now two potential witnesses. Hopefully, neither had secured a clear view of her, but should Wendy's disappearance hit the headlines, they may both remember this situation. Whilst not being able to describe her, the damn giant would know she was a woman, and unfortunately men always seemed good at recalling a car's model.

"It's well good of you to come and pick us up, loik," simpered Wendy.

Yvette shuddered at the grammar and the council-oik speak, but her reply didn't reveal her thoughts as she replied, "My dear, you're more than welcome. I'm always pleased to help out someone in need of a leg up in life."

"Well, I think Matthew's right." Yvette looked at her in the rear-view mirror, wondering what she meant. "He said you were an angel, and I think he's right."

"Nonsense, I'm definitely no angel," protested Yvette. *And how true that is*.

As the antithesis of an angel drove Wendy and Dominic to their doom, she decided she wouldn't tell Matthew about the possibility she had two witnesses. *What he doesn't know won't hurt him*.

Chapter 44

"Can I talk to the cop what's in charge of the disappearance of those women that's all over the news," a young sounding voice asked the female policewoman who answered the phone.

"Who shall I say is calling?"

"Don't matter who's calling. Just say I got some info on that tall guy whose picture has been in the papers and on the tele. The guy the cops want to talk to about being involved with those poor missing women."

"The person heading up that enquiry is DS Blake. He's not here at the moment but if you'd care to tell me what information you have, then I will pass it on. If I can take some details…?"

"No details, just listen," Emma interrupted. "Well, it's like this. I had a date with this same guy. Tall, dark haired, good-looking, real fit. He takes me back to this place and then gets real nasty, threatening. Anyway, I manage to escape. Me mates said I ought to report it, but I wasn't meant to be on a date and if me mum found out, she'd go ape shit. Anyway, then I see on the news all these women and kids going missing, and this guy's wanted in connection with it all."

"This sounds useful, interesting information. I really think it's necessary that you come in and talk to us. You won't get into trouble and..."

"No way. Just listen. I've drawn a sketch of the guy and showed it to me mates. I met him at Prada nightclub, but me mates also saw him at Hades. One of them saw him talking to that Lilly Taylor that's missing. Then they go off together and she's not been seen since. He'd already tried to chat up Charl...I mean, another mate, but her boyfriend told him to piss off. I reckon he'd been picking up girls at night clubs and then knocking them off 'cos they disappear."

"Please listen to me. This is information that may well aid us in apprehending this person. He could well continue to act in this manner, and your information may well prevent this happening. If you come in and help us with our enquiries ..."

"No, no way. I'll send you the sketch. I'll even send you a sketch of the taxi driver that drove me to his place. The more I think about it; I reckon she was in cahoots with him. Yeah, sure she knew him."

"Can you describe the driver?"

"Yeah, a woman, real ugly, long dark hair with blond streaks. Got a foreign name, but no foreign accent. I noticed her name on the identification card in the front."

"I'm WPC Maggie Smith. Call me Maggie. Perhaps you would give me your first name so that I can at least address you properly."

"I'll tell you me middle name. You can call me that… Louise."

"OK, Louise, if I can't persuade you to come in and speak to us, would you phone and talk to DS Blake or one of his team. I have recorded what you have said to me, and I know he would be very interested in talking to you."

"Do you want me to send in the two sketches then?"

"Yes, that would be helpful. Do you think you have managed to capture their likenesses?"

"Yeah, me mate said it was a dead ringer of him."

"Are you gifted in drawing and painting?"

"Yeah, not bad I suppose."

"Louise, if you had a date with this fellow, he obviously told you his name."

"Yes, he told me to call him Matthew…um…Nelson, or similar. No, Nielson."

"And you said he took you back to his place. Do you have the address?"

"Uh…no, I didn't notice where we was going. A taxi with this woman with the foreign name picked me up. Said she knew him, come to think of it. It was in Coley somewhere, I know that."

"You stated you managed to escape. Did you not notice the street or area you were in?"

"Well, I panicked and ran and then eventually ended up at the top of Castle Street."

"Louise, I…"

"Right, I've said enough. I'll send the sketches in."

"We could do with them as soon as possible. Can't you drop them off or get a friend to or maybe fax or email them?"

"Yes, OK I'll do it tomorrow. I'll scan them and send it by email."

"Good, thank you. His email address is danblakeDS 62@btinternet.com. Please phone DS Blake tomorrow. He or one of his team will be here first thing. The number is, shall I wait while you write it down… OK, 01189 665531. That will bring you straight through to the Incident Room. Ask for DS Dan Blake. I will pass on all the information you have given me, but I'm sure he will have more questions relating to this enquiry. We really need you to help out, Louise. Are you sure I can't persuade you to come in. I promise you that…"

"No, I've done what I can. I'll phone tomorrow morning. 'Bye."

The phone went dead.

Chapter 45

The well-dressed, white haired man walked into the Blue Bird coffee shop and stood by the small portable notice board that requested customers to wait to be seated. It was nine thirty in the morning; consequently, most of the tables were free; presumably, shoppers had not yet finished buying their purchases before the need for a morning coffee.

A diminutive waitress, hair tied up in a ponytail, wearing too much eye make-up in Arthur's opinion, walked from behind the counter at the other end of the room and hurried to smile at the smart customer.

"Morning, sir. Table for one?" On being told he needed a table for two, she continued, "Yes, sir, Follow me." As she hurried forward, she half turned to check as whether a window seat would be acceptable. Normally Arthur would have welcomed a view, even if it was only Broad Street and its passers-by, but on this occasion, he didn't want to advertise his involvement with his 'date'.

"I'd rather have the seat in the corner, my dear." Using, in his opinion, his most disarming smile, he continued. "Bit of a headache, so a dark niche will be fine."

"Fine, sir." The waitress smiled in return, and handing him a menu, informed him she would return in a minute for his order.

Arthur had no sooner opened the menu, when

he noticed the person whom he had arranged to meet standing by the noticeboard. The waitress duly escorted the unusually short, stocky man to Arthur's table. The two men nodded a greeting but didn't speak until the girl had walked away.

Arthur wanted this rendezvous over as soon as possible so quickly got to the point. "We need to…umm…shall I say, interview someone. I need him picked up, blindfolded, and then brought to an address that I'll give you in a minute. I don't want any details written down, so you'll have to memorise them. Next week, half term for the schools, this person retires to his cottage in Bournemouth. He's a teacher at St Steven's Jesuit Academy school in Sonning. As I understand it, his normal routine is to drive there on the Friday night. He'll shop for food on Saturday, attend mass on Sunday and play golf on Tuesday and Thursdays. Return to the school on the Sunday afternoon.

"I leave it to your expertise in these matters as to when you pick him up. It's just that he's a bachelor, has no family in the UK as far as we know, so the earlier we get him, the longer it will give us to extract our information from him."

"Right, I need a few more facts. If this fellow gives you this information, is it your intention to let him go, or do you intend to dispose of him?"

At this point, the men noticed the waitress returning and ceased their conversing. After ordering two cappuccinos, a jam doughnut and an apple turnover, the girl walked away, and the men continued.

"There is a reason for my question. Whatever answer you give will determine my MO."

"If the man is co-operative and gives us the information, his answer will actually decide the outcome. We suspect he is in possession of information that is seriously damning to the organisation. We have taken all this into consideration and now modified the information we suspect he knows so it won't now affect our plans." Arthur was referring to the changed password but didn't want to mention it. "Anyway, in the unlikely event he can convince us of his innocence, and what he...knows... is quite coincidental to the issue concerning us, then we return him unharmed."

"Umm, dangerous on two counts. One, he will recognise you and two, he will certainly report the incident to the police."

"He will not see or recognise us, I assure you. He will be warned not to contact the police, or he will pay the penalty. Even if he does, the police will have nothing to go on."

The coffee and cakes arrived, and the two men sugared their drinks, and munched their food for a few moments before resuming their conversation.

Arthur's guest, after sipping his coffee, wiped his mouth with a napkin, leaned forward and lowered his voice as a couple had been shown to the table next to them.

"May I make a suggestion?" As Arthur nodded, he continued. "Why take the chance of picking him up? Always risky. Why not let me vet the cottage? That won't take long, and then *interview* him there if suitable. If he's innocent, just tie him up loosely enough that eventually he'll escape. If, and not knowing the facts, but shall I say he's found *guilty*, then dispose of him there. If you're careful enough, you...I, can make it look like suicide, or an unfortunate accident. It's easy to do. If you have to dispose of him elsewhere, and his body is found, however long that takes, that always causes a great fuss." He leaned back in his chair and continued to eat his cake as though he'd been discussing the bad weather.

Arthur looked at the cotton tablecloth, not seeing the blue check pattern, and sipped his coffee. His mind was busy thinking through the advice. After two minutes he looked up.

"You're right. I'll give you the address. If you can vet the place and it's suitable for an interview, I think we go with that. Remember this." He leaned forward and whispered all the relevant details. "Don't write this down. When will we know if the Bournemouth venue is suitable?"

The tall man drained his coffee, stood up and said quietly, "Wednesday pm latest."

He turned and went, neither man worried about the formalities of a normal farewell.

Chapter 46

Dan walked to his desk, his slumped shoulders conveying his sadness. The last few hours spent with the parents of Harry Davy had been depressing, made worse because he had to behave professionally, keeping his own emotions hidden. He obviously had to be seen to be sympathetic yet not so heartbroken that he wasn't thinking clearly by the dreadful news he was having to give these poor people. His heart went out to them; their grief had been almost tangible. Their flowing tears had made his eyes water in unison.

Sinking into his seat, he shrugged his shoulders, trying to disperse the depression. Glancing at his watch, his eyebrows rose in surprise.

Seven o'clock. Where's the day gone? Christ, this must be the worst day of my life.

Noticing his note pad open on his desk, his eyes were drawn to the cut-out red arrow often used to draw attention to an important note or point.

DS Blake

At 1420, (you were still at the crime scene in the Warren/ seeing the parents of the murdered boys), I received a phone call from a young girl. She would only give scant details about herself, but I estimate she was between sixteen and twenty. Refusing to give her name, she did agree I could address her by her middle name, which was Louise.

She referred to the man we are looking for in connection with the missing women. I'll list what she described in the order she said it.

She described him as tall, dark haired, good-looking, quote 'well fit'.

He took her to a posh house where he quickly got threatening. She managed to escape. She had met him at the Prada nightclub. And one of her mates called 'Charl…. (realised her mistake and stopped, could be ie Charlie, Charlotte, Cheryl??) also recognised him from a sketch she'd drawn and shown her. This mate had seen him in Hades and said she saw him talking to Lilly Taylor, who they know from the news has been reported missing.

She says she will send in a sketch, both of him and the taxi driver who, to use her words, reckons is 'in cahoots with him'. I asked her whether she could describe the taxi driver and she said, quote, 'a woman, real ugly, long dark hair with blond streaks.' She noticed a foreign name from the identification card hanging from the front mirror but couldn't remember it. The woman didn't speak with a foreign accent.

She said his name was Matthew Nielson but maintained she couldn't recall the address although confirmed it was in the Coley area. I pushed this, but she insisted she was panicking when escaping, and ended up eventually at the top of Castle Hill.

I asked if the likeness was a good one, and she said her mates had said it was a dead ringer for him. Obviously good at drawing. (Art College, Art Course at local college, Charlton Road, Reading?) I said we needed the sketch as soon as possible and persuaded her to either fax or email it to us. She says she will scan it and then email it to us. She's canny so I doubt she'll use a traceable computer.

"I did my best to persuade her to come in or say more, but she was adamant she wouldn't. Said she shouldn't have

been on the date, and her mum would go …quote…'ape-shit' if she knew. After much persuasion, she agreed to phone tomorrow morning to speak to you.

Sorry I couldn't get more from her, but hopefully she will phone, and you can obtain more information. I had to treat her with kid gloves because I didn't want her ringing off. I gave her your email address, hope that's alright.

I'm off duty now but please feel free to phone me at home. Phone number listed below.

WPC Maggie Smith.

Chapter 47

Dan re-read the note, a small nub of hope building in his chest.

"You ok, boss?" Dan was suddenly aware that Luke and Meena were standing in front of his desk. He'd been lost in his perusals of the letter and hadn't noticed their arrival.

Leaning forward to switch on his computer, he handed Luke the note. "Maybe, just maybe, our luck's turning a small amount to the positive side." Waiting for his computer to boot up, he told Luke to show Meena when he'd finished reading it.

"Boss, yesterday I thought the world was black, now I can see a small spark of light at the end of the tunnel." Luke watched Dan as he got his emails up. "You hoping she's sent the scanned picture already?"

"Yes. If she has, and it's a good likeness, that's a big step forward."

Meena placed the note back on his desk. "The note says tomorrow. That's if she phones, please Allah."

Her two colleagues looked at her, neither of them ever having heard her use the phrase before. Luke walked around the desk and stood looking over Dan's left shoulder at the screen. As Dan went into his emails, he leaned over eagerly to see what his boss had received. Dan scaled down the list of unopened emails, and Meena saw his shoulders dip in disappointment.

"Nothing?" she confirmed. Dan, lips pressed together and shaking his head sadly with the setback. "Look, give the girl time…" She took a deep breath and was about to continue when she was interrupted.

"Excuse me, DS Blake, someone posted these through the front door a short time ago. Says on the front to hand to you directly, and as soon as possible." The duty Sergeant had arrived unnoticed and stood to the left of Dan's desk. He handed over an A4 envelope.

Hope once more flooded Dan as he tore open the envelope and extracted two pieces of paper. Meena hurried round his desk and peered over his right shoulder. Seeing the sketches that Dan was holding, simultaneously their eyes opened in amazement and smiles so large they were almost falling off the sides of their faces.

"If these are true likenesses," crowed Dan, "we've taken giant league steps forward." He held up the pages and three eager pair of eyes took in the details. "If that's Delilah, then the person who will be able to confirm that absolutely is Adam Kennedy. In my opinion, that's definitely the person who was in the gym where…" For a second, he just couldn't bring himself to say the words about his best friend, 'where Alex was murdered'. He took a deep breath, and continued, "Personally my memory says it's her, but I only saw her briefly. As I said, Adam'll confirm it one way or another." He turned to Meena. "When he's around, show him for confirmation."

She took the sketch from him and nodded.

"Adam's in court again today. If you want a quick answer, how about I check the woman's sketch against the pictures on file of the body of her sister. Twin sister so must be a dead ringer. We all thought it was Van Looy." Luke peered again at the sketch. "Until Adam confirms it absolutely, it'll give us an in initial heads-up."

"If this is a true likeness, and there's no reason to

think it isn't, the gods are on our side at last. Right, now... Matthew…let's have a look at you."

The three of them peered at the other sketch.

"The girl, Louise, said she met this Matthew at the Prada nightclub." Luke looked from Dan to Meena and back to Dan. "There are cameras at the entrances; after all, that's how Matthew and Delilah got spotted. Wonder if we could identify the girl?"

"If we knew what she looked like, yes, no doubt we could. As we don't know, I think our time would be wasted trawling through those again."

"Yeah, true. No doubt there are hundreds of girls going through the doors most nights. Still, I'll get someone to check the cameras on our front door in case we can see who posted this envelope."

"You know," said Meena, "from a woman's perspective, I can see how he could be attractive to women. But look at his eyes. If Louise has really captured his likeness, there's a look about him. He's...sinister, dangerous." She didn't realise she had seen the same as Charlene, and the fact that Emma had cursed because she had missed noticing how accurately her sketches had portrayed his evil eyes. "I wouldn't want to meet him unless I had my Taser or someone with very large shoulders with me."

"Ah-ha," said Luke, "bet you were referring to me." He flexed his shoulders and arm muscles.

"Don't kid yourself," retorted Meena as she walked away.

"Boss, I think, she fancies me."

Dan shook his head at the DC's cheek, and grinned as he added, "Quote…don't kid yourself."

Chapter 48

Yvette handed Matthew her phone. He stared at the image for a few seconds before nodding.

"Yep, that's her. Tall, skinny, dark hair. She was wearing that long dark coat on our date. So, what's the plan all of a sudden?"

"We've got Wendy and the off-spring settled, so I think we deal with this Emma situation as soon as possible. We don't know if she's contacted the police yet. If she hasn't then we need to shut her up as soon as possible to stop her doing it."

"What if she's already spoken to them?" He handed back the phone.

"Well, her description of you isn't going to help them, is it?

"True. I've considered how we attack her, and I've come to the conclusion I knife her. It's quick. One strike and it's all over."

"I agree, but I've given it a lot of thought as well. Obviously, we don't want witnesses, but if she has gone to the filth, what we mustn't have is any connection to you. It doesn't matter that your appearance is different, I still believe we shouldn't take any chances, and you may still be recognised and..."

He frowned and interrupted, "By whom, I can't think..."

"By some of her nosey, bloody friends for instance." She glared at him, her dislike of him that she had managed to submerge suddenly erupted, and her voice sounded as though honed to steel as she snarled. "Probably friends of hers in one of the night clubs."

He considered her words for a few moments before reluctantly nodding his agreement.

"I think although we go together, you stay well hidden in the shadows, and I do the attacking."

"You! Knifing someone!" He stared at her for a few moments, surprise causing his eyebrows to rise. "I didn't think violence well, not to adults, was your thing."

She controlled her urge to smirk, and say that he might think he knew her, but he only knew the part of her history that she had selectively provided. "I'll manage," was all she answered.

"OK. You say I come with you but stay hidden. What exactly is my role then?" He knew her thinking was sensible, but he had to manage his disappointment in front of her. He hadn't told her the cow had stabbed his foot when escaping and he was still in pain from the wound. He hoped his next meeting with the bitch would be pay-back, big time.

"We need it to be quick. You're the driver. I've got it all worked out." From her pocket, she took a colourful A5 leaflet and handed it to him. "I picked this up from the college. An end of half-term disco. This Friday evening. There was a list for those wishing to attend next to a large advertising poster on the main news board. I scanned the list and hey ho, halfway down was our target. We wait till she comes out and…"

"That could be risky. She'll probably be surrounded by friends."

"Don't keep interrupting. You asked me my plans, and all you do is chime in with thoughtless, stupid comments. Wait me out." The pair glared at each other; both sets of eyes flashing with infuriated sparks. "Just outside the college gates is a lay-by. We park there. There is a line of small trees that will keep us hidden. Just before the disco finishes, I'll be outside. I'll make sure I'm there in plenty of time should she come out a bit early. As she comes through the gate, I'll be there, waiting. Do the deed. Then I run to the car and we'll be away before she hits the ground."

Matthew was silent when she finished her ideas. He took a deep breath, considered her words, and not wanting to annoy her again, used a calm voice as he spoke. "I appreciate your hard work, but I just think it's not watertight." He ticked off points on his fingers. "One, she might not appear for some reason, maybe sick. Two, if she does attend, she may leave *very* early…or very late and we can't loiter too long. Three, she may well be surrounded by a lot of people. Big, burly youths. You may not be able to get passed them, and if they should see what you've done, may well be able to stop you easily. Please don't get annoyed, but it's ...loose."

She stared at him, biting her lip, knowing he was right. When she'd planned it in her mind, it had seemed straight forward. Now, his points highlighted the impracticality of her plan. Chewing her lip as she re-thought her strategy, but being experienced in devious tactics, it didn't take long for an idea to form. "I know, it's easy. A diversion! You cause a diversion, and while everyone is looking in your direction, I strike. The moment I run, you drive, picking me up."

"It's got possibilities, but I thought I had to stay out of sight."

"True. OK. We'll think of some sort of diversion which keeps you in the car. And you'll have to wear some sort of disguise as well, so should you be seen, the description given will be misleading."

Yvette went into her kitchen to pour the previously prepared tea that after their heated discussion was now brewed. Walking back into her living room with two cups of instant coffee as she couldn't be bothered to make another pot of tea, she placed his cup on the table before asking him if he'd come up with any other ideas.

He took a sip of the drink before explaining what he had in mind. For once, Yvette agreed with his idea and the plan was set.

Chapter 49

As Arthur entered the dining room, Bob was pouring coffee into cups at the end of a long table.

"Just arrived in time," he said. "One of those for me, I hope?" He walked and sat at the other end of the table.

"Of course," agreed Bob, and passed a cup to the seated John, indicating he could pass it down the table to Arthur. "Toothache gone?"

"Yes, it's fine now. Right, we're all here, so let's get started. I've begun proceedings into the interview of our Mr O'Leary, but before I update you on that, let me hear if there's been any progress. Dennis, anything new from your source at the police station?"

"He overheard an interesting phone call. A young girl, wouldn't give her name, phoned in to say that she reckoned she had come across this fellow, the tall one, that's in the news. Had a date with him, but he got nasty and luckily for her she managed to escape. Said his name was Matthew Nielson. Ring any bells?" Glancing around the table to check, and as they all shook their heads, he took a deep breath and continued. "OK. More interestingly, she did two sketches, one of him and one of his companion. They believe the woman is Van Looy. They're getting that verified by one of their officers who apparently had dealings with her in the past. When no-one's around, he'll try and get photocopies of the sketches for us.

"Anyway, the police don't recognise this Matthew, but according to the girl, her sketch is a dead ringer, her words describing him. No doubt, these images will be in the papers and on the television news pretty soon anyway. That should scare the chemical out of him. If he is connected with any school or church, some ones bound to recognise him."

"Good work, Dennis." said Arthur. "That's progress. We'll keep an eye open for any news article or television news that carries the sketches. Anything else?"

"I'll go next," said John when Dennis shook his head. "I've carried on asking around if there's any gossip on what's been going on. All these kids going missing I mean. Like Bob reported previously, no-one's heard anything on the underground, and we all know that's strange in itself. I've been thinking about that fact. If there is no connection between these two and any of our …umm...compadres in arms…then they are either, one, new to *this game*." He glanced round the table for comment, but when none came, he went on, counting on his fingers as he went. "Two, new to the area. That's not likely as we suspect Delilah is the woman. Or three, they are taking great care not to be visible to anyone."

"Except their victims," added Bob.

"Obviously," John agreed. "Now that we know Delilah is involved, have the original safe houses been checked?"

"Surely she's not going to be stupid enough to hole up in one of those places. She knows the addresses will been known to the old Brotherhood, and thoroughly inspected," said Bob.

"Yes, but that was well over a year ago," added George, who had been drinking his coffee. "We all thought she was a goner, so no-one would have thought to check that she was hiding up in one of them now."

"True," agreed Arthur. He looked thoughtful and passed his cup back down the table for a refill. "I don't believe she would be stupid enough to do that. Most of the bolt holes have long since gone, changed hands. Still, there's a couple left. I'll get their locations. George, can you check to see if there is any sign of them being inhabited, or any sign of the evil bitch."

"Will do."

"OK John, both you and Dennis's investigations seem to indicate that there is no rumour-mongering as such, and we have to draw the conclusion that Yvette aka Delilah has hitched herself up to someone new. Either new to the area, or perhaps someone who's been clever enough not to be noticed previously, but with all that's now happening, has now come onto the radar." Arthur looked back at George. "Anything new from Father Francis that will change our plans?"

As George shook his head, Arthur turned and asked Bob if he'd made any progress in checking out the tall, ginger fellow, the choir master, David Sinclair.

"I used the same Watchers again. Explained I needed a breakdown of this choir master's movements." He leaned forward, perched his reading glasses on the end of his nose and read his notes. "OK, he seems to go around all the church schools, St Bernards in Woodley, St Anne's in Caversham and also The Holy Angel in Tilehurst. He hasn't been seen going to St Stephens Jesuit Academy in Sonning."

"If he visits all the schools from where the kids went missing, that must make him *very interesting*," added Dennis. At Arthur's nod, Bob continued.

"Apparently he plays the organ at St Anne's most Sundays. He's been in the area for just over a year. That means he's newish to this area, so as John pointed out, that is another factor we have looked at. Mind you, the women and children have only gone missing over the last six months, so if he's our man, he's either laid low, not gone into action, or his previous activities haven't registered with anyone." Glancing round and seeing nods of agreement, he continued when no-one commented. "What really goes against him being this Matthew, except being tall, he's got ginger hair cut really short, glasses, and the hint of a limp as I said previously."

"OK, but let's not rule him out yet." said Arthur.

"Anyway, this David Sinclair…interestingly, he's also the Deacon at St Anne's church besides playing the organ. Seems a quiet, studious type and his hobby is stamp collecting." Bob shrugged his shoulders. "I think he's not our man. Except for being tall, we have nothing else…well, except him being fairly new to the area as John suggested."

Arthur thanked him for his endeavours and agreed it didn't sound like Matthew but emphasised they all keep listening to the 'gossip' and report back immediately they heard anything interesting or helpful.

He then proceeded to tell them the suggestion by the prospective kidnapper that in his opinion the interview should be carried out at O'Leary's cottage rather than take the risk of picking him up and transporting him to another venue. Their nods and murmurs of 'good idea' prompted him to add that if necessary, the kidnapper could make it look like suicide or an accident, which was a great bonus, and a lot less hassle for them.

On deciding that the 'interviewers' would be himself, John and George, plus the 'heavy', the meeting was adjourned. The men, all having finished their drinks, rose from the table, congenially bade each other goodnight.

As they were leaving through the front door, Arthur paused and turned to Dennis. "Your source at the police station. Tell him. If the police do find out the identity of this girl who allegedly can identify this Matthew, remind him that he'll be greatly rewarded if we get to know who she is as soon as possible. I know he's not in the inner circle as such, but I'm sure a monetary remuneration will encourage him to work late, and maybe have a gander at the detectives' files."

"Right, I'll tell him." Dennis nodded. "Yes, you're right; speaking to this young lady could be *very* rewarding for our cause. I'll do what I can. The moment she turns up, you'll be one of the first to know."

The elderly men drove to their individual houses, with not one of them suffering with a shred of conscience about their intentions.

Chapter 50

Emma, sitting at her dressing table applying make-up, glanced up when her bedroom door opened, and Heidi and Jose walked in.

"Bloody hell, you two're early. What's going on?"

"We wanna hear what you say to this cop fellow," said Jose. "I think you're well brave talking to the cops. I'd be dead scared."

"Nosey cow," laughed Emma. She leaned forward towards the mirror and started applying mascara to her eyelashes.

"Yeah, and also to make sure you phone in again," said Heidi, plonking herself on the bed.

"I will. Jeez, I swore to you I would, and I promised that woman copper, didn't I. I don't break my promises."

"OK. Still, another thing. Maybe you need protection." Heidi stared at Emma's surprised look in the mirror. "Don't look like that. I've been thinking. This Matthew knows you can identify him. That's well dodgy. He doesn't know whether you've reported the incident to the cops or not. But both ways you're bad news for him. If you've already reported him, then he'll want to get rid of you so you can't identify him should the cops pick him up. You know, like in one of those line-ups they have on the films. If you haven't reported him, he'll still want to get rid of you before you do."

"But he won't know if I have or not."

"Yeah, but like I already said, either way you're dangerous for him."

The two friends gazed at each other via the mirror.

"I'm gonna do my hair the same as you tonight, Em," said Jose, as usual, short of concentration on anything she wasn't involved in. "Can I borrow your long coat so I can sneak some vodka into the disco?"

Her two friends ignored the inane remark, well used to her limited attention span.

"OK, I've said I'll phone him," said Emma. "That's why I got up early. I'll put me make up on, wait for me mum to leave for work and then we'll walk to the phone box and I'll phone. You can listen in; check I'm telling him everything. Alright."

"OK. Just worried about you, that's all. From what you said, and from what the news says, he's well dangerous."

The bedroom door opened, and Mrs Bradbury came into Emma's bedroom.

"Hullo girls. Em, your rooms a disgrace. You're not going out tonight till you've cleared it up a bit. Your sister's room's as neat as a pin. Why you don't take after her, I don't know."

"Don't nag mum. Promise I'll do it tonight before I go to the disco."

"You'd better. 'Bye girls. Don't forget to put the dishwasher on when you've put your cup and plate in it. 'Bye, be good, I'm off to work."

The three girls sat still until they heard the front door slam close. Heidi jumped off the bed and picked up Emma's mobile from the dressing table. She thrust it towards her friend.

"Right, no excuses, phone the bloody cops."

"Not with my mobile, you thicko, they can trace it." Seeing the look of exasperation on Heidi's face, she held up the hands, palms forward, as though warding her off. "I'll do what I did before; use the phone box by the bus stop."

She stood up, picked up her mobile and handbag lying on the bed. "Come on then, what're you waiting for? Chop, chop."

The girls flew down the stairs, into the kitchen, and while Jose proceeded to eat grapes from the fruit bowl, Emma and Heidi loaded and switched on the dishwasher.

They giggled and laughed their way down the road until they got to the phone box. The three stopped when they saw it had a resident. It was occupied by a tramp, who, from his sitting position, obviously wasn't making phone calls. He was squatting, knees up round his drooping chin, looking as though he was dozing and dreaming, his head jolting forward intermittently; then jerking up and down.

"Oh shit," said Emma. "If we don't move him soon, the bus'll be along."

Heidi opened the door, and using her 'I'm very important, you'd-better -listen -to -me' voice for which she often used to entertain her friends after too many drinks. "Right, my man," she boomed. "What do you think you're doing? This abode is not for dossing in, get up and vacate this property immediately."

The tramp, slowly lifted his head, opened one eye, peered at Heidi and said. "Bugger off. I ain't going nowhere."

"Right. I'm a plain clothed detective. You're under arrest. I'm phoning the police station immediately for back up. I'll give you one more chance. Leave now and you won't be arrested."

"Oh please, DC Jamieson, give him a chance." Emma bent down and spoke in his ear whispering something inaudible to Heidi and Jose, but the words had an immediate effect on the recipient.

With a lot of mumbling, in which a few curses could be detected, the tramp heaved himself to his feet, and slowly stumbled from the box and headed off down the road, not before they heard clear references to 'bossy, hostile police bitches."

"Whad you say to him?" Jose looked at Emma with admiration. "He moved well fast."

Emma shrugged. "Just said if he didn't move, I'd kick him in the balls and then use my Taser that'd give a damn great shock for good measure."

"God, you haven't really got one of those, have you?" Jose's eyes were open so wide that the whites were visible round her hazel irises. "Fought they were outlawed or som'ink."

Emma opened the telephone box door, and shaking her head, said, "Jose, you're really something else." She turned and looked at Heidi. "You coming in then? Check what I'm saying."

At that moment, the tramp's voice could be heard echoing down the road. "You might as well get your fat arses out of there, it don't work."

Heidi squeezed in by her friend, while Jose, determined not to be left out, held the door open a fraction in order to also hear the conversation. Emma picked up the receiver, and the two friends watched as she jiggled the buttons up and down. "Blast, he's right. Dead as a dodo. Dunno where the next phone box is."

At that moment, the number forty-eight bus appeared around the corner. Heidi opened the door, exasperation colouring her voice as she said, "Sorry, gotta go, I've got my half term assessment at nine thirty. Petra's coming in for a cut and colour."

"Same as me," said Jose. "Got me mum's mate coming in for me assessment. Sorry."

Emma joined her friends at the bus queue and stood in the line to show her student card. "I've got to get in on time too. My design folder's being assessed."

"*When* you going to phone then?" persisted Heidi.

"One day won't make any difference. Told you, Charlie

Johns put his hood up and poked the envelope through the police station letterbox. Even if they got those security camera thingys, they won't recognise him. Anyway, they got the sketches to work on. I've given them all the info I know. Come around in the morning and I promise I'll phone. Like I said, one day won't make no difference."

She wasn't to know how she would regret those words.

Chapter 51

Dan checked his watch for the third time in an hour. Luke looked up from his desk.

"Boss, it's nearly twelve o'clock. Doubt she'll phone now."

"Yes, I know."

Meena walked by, placing a buff file on his desk, and said, "Except for persuading her to come in, what more information d'you think you would get from her?"

Dan shrugged. "Not sure. I would have pushed on the date, location, more description. I know we have the sketches, but I would have pressed on how he talked. Words he used. You can get a lot of information with details like that."

"The sketches and his name are going to be featured on the midday television news and in the papers tomorrow. That should scare the couple to death." Luke smirked. "Love to see his face when he sees his image plastered over the screen for all to see. He'll feel vulnerable even if he does alter his garb or appearance."

"Let's just hope it doesn't send him to earth," added Meena.

Dan stood up. "Funny you should say that, Meena. I've been thinking about something I could do with clarifying in my mind. Maybe the three of us could retire to Incident

Room Three. It's not being used. I want to run some thinking passed the two of you. We spoke about having a brainstorm; maybe we'll have a mini one now."

Luke, following his two colleagues from the office, said, "By the way, Boss, I caught Adam on the way to court and mentioned we wanted him to have a gander at the sketch of Evil-in-Woman's-clothing. That should give us a definite ident one way or another. He'll be back about 5."

"Good." Dan nodded to the two of them to pull up their chairs opposite him as he settled behind the table in front of the white board exhibiting the photos of the missing women and children. He leaned his elbows on the table, put his head in his hands, and remained there for a minute. They didn't interrupt his deliberations, knowing he was doing his 'diamond brain analysis' of the situation for which he was well known. Eventually he looked up.

"OK. Serial killers. I've been talking to profiler, Gordon Ward. I know Coley doesn't have a lot of time for him, says it never makes up for good police work, but a couple of things Ward said were interesting. Serial killers normally work alone, but they can work in pairs. Now Delilah aka Van Looy is a paedophile, and doesn't really, according to him, fit completely in either the psychopath or sociopath groups. Psychopath… normally low intelligence, maladjusted, often without a job. Sociopath, normally intelligent, living a normal life. When eventually caught, neighbours and friends are shocked. She's in neither category as far as I'm concerned, although a psychologist might not agree."

"What about him, Matthews? Except now knowing what he looks like, we don't know a great deal about him," said Luke.

"Not necessarily true," added Meena. "He's not a psychopath, low intelligence etc. He went to these nightclubs, we believe had women carefully vetted and then chatted them up if they were suitable, i.e. lonely, vulnerable etc.

Now we've more or less deduced they, Matthew and the she-devil, are working for each other's benefits. She vets the women for him. He's somehow has connections with kids for her.

"We think maybe he looks quite different on a day-to-day level, probably wearing a uniform or something quite different to his jeans and leather jacket that he wears when he patrols the night clubs. Therefore, I think we're building up a good picture of him. We know his name, or the one he uses for his stalking. OK, might not be his real name I know, but progress even so. We know what he looks like; that he's almost certainly a sociopath; therefore dangerous, so we don't underestimate him. He's almost certainly local. Yes, I think we're getting more facts about him."

Dan nodded. "Good. You're getting it. We have the dates these women went missing, and for a time it appeared as though the dates were getting closer, which as we know, is when the serial killers are exercising less control because the urge to kill is growing. This is often when they are nearer to getting caught, because the crime scene gets messier in the rush. So even if he was, shall I say, new to the job, she's experienced and keeping him in check.

"Plus, if they are doing one for one, ie woman, child, woman, child, the time between must wait until someone convenient for their particular needs comes on the scene". Dan stood up and pointed to the photos on the white board. His finger followed the extended W line that joined the victims. "Right, note the dates, the times between." His finger rested on the last victim, Peter North, then traced the line to the first one, "As far as we know, Stella James. Right, we've found the children's bodies, I know, but look at the dates, the times, what do you see?"

The two officers, both with deep v's between their eyebrows as they perused the board and deliberated Dan's words. Meena was mumbling the dates. She went quiet.

"They've stopped. Nothing's happened since..."

"Exactly, Young Peter North in late August. I know the W shape is uneven, we thought there was a woman missing and we can now deduce it's probably the elusive and mysterious Louise. We need to find out the exact date of her attack when she phones in…but if the W's the correct shape, then she was attacked before Peter, probably early August."

"Perhaps because they know we're onto them now the children's bodies have been discovered," interrupted Luke. "They're having a breather."

Dan shook his head. "No, serial killers don't, can't stop, in most cases. Some even leave clues, both to exasperate us, and for some weird reason, deep down, they almost want to get caught. For some, they love the chase, love the challenge. They think they're better than us, arrogant. As you know, that often gets them caught."

"Now, if they don't, *can't* stop, and I agree with that, but they might be having a breather as we're onto them. If you don't think that's likely due to the urge, what's your thinking as to what is going on? Why the gap in time, unless there were more murders, and we haven't discovered them?" Meena frowned as she asked her questions.

Dan took a deep breath. "Maybe but consider this. They know we've found where they dumped the children's bodies, so they can't use that anymore. I think they're so up themselves and believe themselves so clever, or so they think, they've not stopped. We haven't spotted it yet, but I bet you a month's pay they're carrying on, they've just got themselves a new MO."

Dan sat back, looking slowly from one colleague to another. Luke swore under his breath and Meena's golden skin became pale.

"I know it's my intuition, no hard facts, but it hasn't finished, others are in deadly danger."

Luke swore under his breath, and Meena's skin faded even more to the deathly pale of an anaemic person desperately in need of a transfusion.

"Oh fuck." Luke shook his head as he muttered the oath.

Chapter 52

Emma, Jose and Heidi were standing with a crowd of people in the entrance lobby outside the main hall where the very successful disco was just ending. Everything had gone well. The music, varying from 'golden oldies' to which the lecturers had mainly danced, much to the amusement of the college students who had taken every opportunity to verbally and loudly 'take the mick', and shout for more modern music. The ribbing had all been good humoured because the lecturers then did the same when the students had lived it up to the more modern sounds of Calvin Harris or The Chain Smokers.

From Heidi's perspective, the evening had been particularly successful as the good-looking Indian bus driver, Aarav, had turned up with an even more handsome friend, Shahraan, whose name no-one could pronounce properly despite repeating it several times. Eventually everyone was in fits of laughter, helped enormously by the large quantities of vodka disguised in three coke bottles that Jose had sneaked in beneath the long black coat she had borrowed from Emma. They had all eventually compromised and called him Aragon, the hero from the Lord of the Rings that they had studied in their GCSE levels in English literature when at school.

Aarav had explained to the girls he was due to go back

to Oxford college on the following Monday, so this was a night to let his hair down before the serious studying began again. The three girls needed no excuse to go over the top, and with the aid of the vodka, the dancing and the great company, by the time everyone spilled out of the hall at midnight into the college's front entrance hall, no-one was in a hurry to leave and go home.

The three girls, the two Indian guys, plus Charlene's gang were loudly discussing which nightclub should become the next venue for them to hit and drink and dance away the night. No-one wanted to be home before dawn.

The din caused from the many excited, shrill voices, aided by prohibited drink and becoming more strident with every word, caused the home-going lecturers to wince as they crept passed, firmly shaking their heads as their noisy students begged them to accompany them to Hades or Prada. All memories of previous dodgy events at those venues forgotten in the excitement of youth, and their capacity for the enjoyment of the moment, and not worry or care about what had been!

"Going outside for a fag," Jose shouted in Emma's ear. "Wait for you there, when you've made up your mind where we're going, come and tell me."

Emma nodded, and was only half-aware as Jose pushed open the double doors accompanied by Charlie Walsh, who had a spliff hidden in his hand that he intended to light up outside to impress Jose, whom he strongly fancied.

As more people spilled out of the hall, the clamour and chaos continued and then expanded. Emma thought she heard a scream but ignored it as she was laughing at a joke that 'Aragon' was attempting to tell over the uproar. Suddenly aware of someone frantically shaking her arm, she turned to get rid of the offender, annoyed at the distraction. But catching sight of Charlie's hysterical expression, and suddenly becoming aware of sobbing gasps as an uneasy hush slowly descended over the hall, an awful premonition swept over Emma, causing icy fingers to spitefully dig into the bottom of her spine and cut their way up to her neck.

Tears spilled from Charlie's eyes, and his words were garbled and choked as he sobbed, "Jose's been stabbed. I think she's dead. We gotta phone for an ambulance real quick."

For a moment, the world stopped, the silence became complete… painful in its intensity, no sound whatsoever hovered in her ears, just the raw silence of outer space. In this moment, in this cold world, Emma wanted to die herself. Heidi had been right about her predictions, and Emma knew who the victim should have been. Her lack of action had caused this tragedy. Her heart felt as though it had turned to stone.

Chapter 53

Declan O'Leary walked through all the rooms of his Bournemouth cottage, opening the windows as he always did whether summer or winter, when he returned home for the school holidays. Although he loved his job at St. Steven's school, he loved coming home more and spending a few days or weeks, depending on the occasion, enjoying the solitude of his own company, and squeezing in a couple of games of golf, of course.

He rinsed out the electric kettle before half filling it with water ready for his coffee. Opening the new instant coffee jar, he inhaled the strong, fresh aroma. It wouldn't be as tasty as the drink he would later brew in his percolator, but it would suffice for the moment. Once the water had reached the correct temperature which was not quite at boiling point, as a Dutch colleague had once assured him boiled water makes foul coffee, he poured the liquid into his freshly washed mug, heaped in three teaspoons of sugar, topping it up with full cream milk.

The drive from St. Stevens to home had been fraught with heavy traffic, and slowly sipping the welcome beverage, he realised how thirsty and tired he was. After checking that all the windows were open to freshen the rooms, his next job was to phone his friend Shaun Murphy to arrange their two, or three golf friendly matches that were institutions for them both during the school holidays. Shaun was a teacher at a local comprehensive school, and consequently shared the long, welcome school holidays. As though expecting the call, Shaun answered immediately, and after the usual discussions of health and the sad state of the world which they always endeavoured to rectify during their golf matches, they agreed to play on the following Tuesday and Thursday as usual. Shaun, being a member of a local golf club, offered to phone and book the tee-times.

Shaun then informed Declan that it was his birthday on the following Monday, so suggested they go for a drink and a pint or two at a local pub they frequented whenever they met together. Declan agreed enthusiastically, and as it was Shaun's celebration, offered to pick him up so the birthday boy could have a few celebratory drinks. As he put down the phone, Declan decided he would not drive, but pay for a taxi both ways so he could join in the celebrations.

Now in a thoroughly good mood, Declan carried his case upstairs to the spare bedroom. Opening the case, he tossed most of the clothes into the wash basket, and then, in his opinion, getting his priorities right, walked to the landing cupboard and extracted his golf bag and clubs. Deciding the washing should be delegated for a tomorrow job, he lumped the heavy bag downstairs to the kitchen in order to give them a good clean and polish. Always finding this task very therapeutic, he decided another coffee was in order, and enhancing the taste with a large slug of whisky as he was celebrating the start of his holidays, he did not kid himself that it was for medicinal purposes. He hummed happily as he started buffing his beloved golf clubs.

By eight o'clock he was feeling pleased with himself, and having cleaned his clubs to perfection, he then indulged in treating himself to a large portion of cod and chips from the local chippy and washing it down with a cold Guinness. All thoughts of difficult, spotty, temperamental teenagers now firmly banished from his mind, he felt life was definitely for enjoying this week.

Putting the last of the washing-up into the kitchen cupboard, the sharp knocking on his back door took him by surprise. He wasn't expecting company, and anyway the only person who would use the back door was Shaun who had a key to the lock that fortified the side gate. As he was away from his cottage a great deal, he made sure he securely locked his doors, windows, and side gate.

Cautiously opening the back door, he was surprised when he couldn't see anyone. Pushing it further ajar, he stretched out his head, glancing right and left. Again seeing no-one, he shrugged and was about to withdraw indoors when from both sides his arms were grabbed, and a hood dragged over his head. His shock was so great he didn't cry for help, and by the time he came to his senses, he'd been pushed back into the house, hauled through the kitchen and plonked into a chair, and then realised it was too late to cry out. The next hour was not hell, but as he later told Shaun, it was damn confusing.

With his arms securely tied behind his back, the hood was removed, but his eyes were quickly covered by a mask, and a tight gag stretched over his mouth, Declan decided his final hours on earth had come. Obviously, burglars had burst into his house, presumably with the intention of robbing him blind…literally, as he could see nothing! Even in his present predicament, he was clear thinking enough to know they wouldn't get much for their troubles. Living away during term time, and spending minimal time at home, except for his furniture and his beloved golf clubs, there was not much to take. He was therefore surprised when a cultured voice said, "Mr O'Leary, we mean you no harm. We just need to ask you some questions, and if you give us the correct and truthful answers, we will leave here quickly, and you will be unharmed. Now I want you to nod if you understand what I'm saying." Declan was puzzled, having no idea what he would know that they so badly need to have information about. Deciding he was never going to find out by not co-operating, he duly nodded. The questioner continued. "Good. Now the next thing is, if I remove your gag, I want you to promise not to shout. All the doors and windows are now closed so I don't think the neighbours will hear, and unfortunately you will have to be further restrained, and that will be… painful. Do I make myself clear? Again, just nod if you intend to be co-operative and quiet when I remove the gag?"

Still totally confused by this ridiculous situation, Declan nodded again.

"Good." The voice cautiously removed the gag and when Declan remained silent as requested, he heard the voice repeat, "Good". Despite the eye covering, light shone around the mask like the corona produced by a total eclipse of the sun, and Declan deduced his desk lamp was shining straight into his eyes. *Presumably so there's no chance should this mask fall that I'd recognise them.*

His thoughts were interrupted with a question, although this time he could tell it was from a different person.

"Mr O'Leary, we know you are a teacher at St. Stevens School. Now, straight to the point, can I ask you where or how you came across the phrase, 'Rubies on the Moon'? I need you to be honest here. As my colleague said previously, you tell us the truth, we can all move on from here. We can go home, you can have your life back, and you'll be safe and sound."

Declan couldn't answer due to amazement. Of all the questions they might have asked…possibilities swirled through his brain…his relationship with the IRA, or should he say, his dislike of the said party; the Big Bang Theory, judo, golf cheats, fractal geometry, or any other subject on which they could imagine he was important enough or cared to have an opinion, he was staggered to be asked about a young pupils silly answer in a geography lesson!

This absolutely beggars belief!

Due to his astonishment, when no words issued from his mouth, a third voice said sharply, "Well, what's your answer? A simple enough question surely."

"Yes, a simple question sure enough. However, if someone broke into your house, tied you up, put a mask or some such over your eyes, and then asked a really stupid bloody question, would you not be at a loss for words?"

There was no immediate reply to his remark. Declan knew he was taking a chance at being so forthright, after all, he hadn't any knowledge about his abductees, but from their voices they sounded educated, and didn't sound young and/or thug-like. In fact, as far as his ear could tell, they sounded at least middle-aged, and some-how he didn't feel as intimidated as he might if they had been younger and threatening hoodlums.

The silence continued and what Declan did not know was that his words had completely fazed the three questioners. This was not the response, from all the facts fed to them from Father Francis, that they were expecting. Indeed, they had expected shock, then panic and stumbling excuses until they were forced to get 'heavy' with him.

Declan wasn't to know they had glanced at each other in bewilderment. John had raised his eyebrows and shrugged. George had shaken his head. Arthur realised things weren't going as expected even this early into the process and decided he must take control and get things moving. The 'heavy' just shrugged at him, indicating he'd done his bit, and didn't care about the outcome as long as there was no come-back on him.

He leaned forward and said, "Mr O'Leary, this is not a stupid question. This phrase had a special meaning in the security of the country. It was reported to us, and as members of the government…umm, and MI6." He looked at John and George who were looking at him in astonishment and winked. "Well, I can say no more than that, but when we hear that phrase that may well endanger the security of this country, as I said previously, I urgently need to know how that phrase came to your knowledge." He sank back in his chair and folded his arms, pleased with his quick thinking, and from the corner of his eyes, could see George and John gazing at him, he assumed with admiration.

He was then astonished when the reply from Mr. O'Leary was a very firm, "Bollocks." Before he could pull himself together and retort with a suitable reply, O'Leary continued. "I repeat, bollocks. Now I don't know who you really are, but bloody government agents or whatever you maintain, is a load of total rubbish. If you want the complete and absolute truth, I'll tell you. Some time ago, in a Geography lesson, I gave the class some homework research on finding out about how precious stones were formed, and where they could mainly be found in the world. Young lads of fourteen probably find this topic very boring, and I don't suppose much effort went into this venture. When I asked one of the pupils where rubies could be found, he looked totally confused for a moment, and then said, and I quote, 'Rubies...on the Moon, sir."

Declan could hear three sets of heavy breathing, the wind whispering outside his window, and the kitchen clock melodically ticking, so when someone banged very loudly on the window just two feet from his left ear, and screeched, "Open up, Police," he didn't know who out of the four men or himself who screamed the loudest.

Chapter 54

Dan and Meena gazed at the young girl before them. She was deathly pale, as though her skin was coated with a fine layer of frost. Two streams of tears slowly trickled down her cheeks and dripped onto her jumper.

"Drink your tea whilst it's hot, Emma." DC Mesbah's voice was soft and sympathetic. "The best thing you can do for Jose is to tell us all you know so we can find out who did this terrible thing."

As Emma raised her head and gazed at them, both the police officers noted her big, green eyes overflowing with guilt as well as tears.

"I'm Louise," she said softly. She looked at Dan. "As in the Louise who phoned, and sent in the sketches of Matthew, and his dead ugly female mate. Heidi said I should phone you again. I intended to. I tried to, but the phone box was broken."

"Aah…so you are in fact Emma *Louise* Bradbury. Nice to meet you, Emma. I'm sorry we eventually meet in these sad circumstances but…"

"She will be alright, won't she?" Emma interrupted, her voice rising hysterically. She put her face into her hands, sobs erupting through her fingers. "It's my fault. It's all my fault. I should have…"

Meena leaned forward and gently grasped Emma's

wrists. Easing her arms away from her eyes, she said, "Emma, listen. We all do things we regret, but what's important right now is that we move on and make progress. We need you to go back to the beginning, and for you to tell us all you know. This way we can make headway and catch Jose's attacker."

Emma leaned back in her chair, took a soggy tissue from her pocket, wiped her eyes, blew her nose, and nodded. "Yeah, you're right. I must stop being such a bloody wuss. Yes, I do feel guilty, but that's not gonna help catch those fucking bastards."

Emma started her story, and both police officers were impressed how she told the tale in a succinct fashion, keeping to the timeline and including appropriate dates when relevant to the plot. She told them how, when and where she'd met Matthew; their first disastrous, perilous date and her lucky escape. She related the bike ride that she, Heidi and Jose had undertaken, and how they tracked down the infamous Loddon House, as they continued to name it, in Coley, where the taxi had taken her on her first date. Explaining how they then decided to trace Nielson by trawling the nightclubs, and checking friends' recollections, and subsequently discovering that he had been recognised from Emma's sketches as the man who had gone off with Lilly Taylor.

At this point, someone entered the room with three more cups of tea, but Dan and Meena were so involved with the story, they did not glance up, merely nodded their thanks. Emma gratefully sipped her second drink; her throat had become parched with the telling. She finished off by explaining once they had some proof, that she had phoned with all she knew and spoken to a policewoman and then asked a friend to deliver the sketches. Fully intending to contact them the next day as she promised, she told them again about the broken phone booth, and not wanting to use her mobile as she could be traced. That night they had gone to the fateful disco. At this point, her lips trembled, and she could hardly bring the cup to her lips because of her shaking hands.

Meena questioned her as to what school she had previously attended, and whether she regularly attended any church. Emma noticed her persistence about whether she had any connections with a church or church schools. When she pointed out that there was no connection, Dan took over.

He asked a few more questions filling in details before asking why Emma thought the attack was aimed at her.

"I didn't give it much thought till the other day me mate Heidi said she was sure I was in danger. She said he either wanted to shut me up before I went to the cops, or if I'd already been to see you, then he wanted to shut me up anyway so I couldn't identify him." She finished her tea before continuing. "I think him and his ugly friend, the one who owned the taxi and took me to Loddon House, were out to knock me off before I identify them."

"The female taxi driver, she was the one you referred to in your telephone call?" Dan continued when she nodded her affirmation. "You said she had a foreign name, but you couldn't recall it. Can you remember it now?"

Emma pursed her lips as she considered, looking over Dan's right shoulder as she contemplated his question. "Mm…I know Yvonne de...something or other. De Borg, that was it. Me dad always says the brains are well better than your memory."

Dan glanced at Meena, who knew what he was thinking; not Yvette Van Looy, but near enough for someone who wanted to change her name but retain a similar impression.

"Emma, we were impressed with your sketches. You say that all your friends confirm that the sketch of Matthew Nielson was an accurate likeness." After she nodded, he continued. "Both representations have previously and again today been published in local and national newspapers, and shown on the television news, but except for what we consider crank calls, no-one has contacted us to say they recognise him. Can you tell me what he wore for instance?" Although Meena had already spotted from the security cameras that he wore jeans and a leather bomber jacket, he needed to hear Emma confirm this or otherwise.

"Yeah, when I met him at Prada, he was wearing… umm… jeans, white shirt and a black leather bomber jacket. When I was dropped off at Loddon House, he wore… umm, yeah, jeans again and a plain, white tee shirt, and a cashmere jumper. He'd just had a shower; had the towel slung over his shoulder and apologised he couldn't pick me up so he'd sent the taxi for me." She suddenly frowned, and then whispered, "Though when I think about it, his hair wasn't wet, maybe…I dunno, probably not important."

Both Meena and Dan had been leaning forward, listening carefully to her words and as though mirror-imaging, they both sunk back in their chairs at the same time. They didn't realise they were thinking the same thing, was he wearing a wig so perhaps that was probably why his hair was dry!

"When you were in Loddon house, and thinking back to that evening, did you notice any other clothing in the room or house?" Dan raised his eyebrows at his question.

"Other clothing. Not sure what you mean."

"We suspect, Emma, that his normal attire may not be casual jeans, bomber jacket, but perhaps more formal clothes. So, now thinking about it, was there anything there that you noticed that might lead you to think his normal attire, his everyday working clothes for instance, were along uncharacteristic lines to casual jeans and tee shirt?"

Emma shook her head, explaining she was sure she would have noticed, as she had at the odd furniture, and that she was normally quite observant.

"Right. Now this Yvonne de Borg. You say this sketch you provided is a good likeness."

"Well, I didn't get such a good look at her. She had her back to me in the taxi, but I'm OK at remembering how people look, but I think it's not far off."

The door of the interview room opened, and Mel walked in and handed a page of A4 paper to Dan. After reading it, he passed it to Meena. As his colleague read, Dan , smiling, said to Emma, "Good news, Emma. Jose is out of danger. Although the stab wound was deep, it wasn't quite as bad as initially thought. Some glass was extracted from the wound. The doctors believe that a large glass bottle containing vodka she'd hidden under her coat saved her from being mortally wounded. However, of course, any stab wound is dangerous."

Emma put her hands over her eyes again, muttering through her fingers. "For once I'm glad she's got some bad habits."

"I'm pleased the news is good, Emma," said Meena. "After all you've told us, I agree that Nielson may well have been after you to keep you quiet. I'm just surprised that Jose, if our presumptions are correct, was stabbed in error."

"Well, she's my height and age. She's got long dark hair like mine, although often she ties hers back in a ponytail, but for the disco she had it down. I think the main things were though; one, it was dark; two, they were probably in a rush, and thirdly; Jose borrowed my coat so she could sneak in the vodka." Both officers smiled at her words. Emma smiled back, silently thanking a God she didn't really believe in, but just in case he was around and had been kind on this occasion, she thanked him out loud before adding, "Anyway, *that was the coat* I wore on my date with that bastard Nielson. He was after me, I know."

Chapter 55

"I quote…a young girl, Jose McDonald, was stabbed outside the local Technical College after the half term disco had finished." Matthew glared over the newspaper at Yvette, who was sitting with her feet resting on a stool, sipping a glass of red wine. Her nonchalant shrug in response to his words infuriated him even more, and he continued his rant, shaking with fury. "After all our plans, you stab the wrong, fucking girl."

"Well, you were with me. If I remember correctly, Mr oh-so-bloody-perfect-Nielson, you pointed her out. Said, ooh, weren't we lucky, she had left the disco earlier than expected. No-one around, but some tall, lanky lad who wasn't going to be any trouble. In fact, it was so convenient, we didn't have to phone the fire brigade saying there was a fire as a diversion. She even stood by the gap in the fence around the edge of the college, so I could sneak up easy as pie and stick the knife in." Yvette swung her feet back onto the floor, leaned forward, and placed her glass next to a bottle of wine on the coffee table before her. "Well, I did just that. The brat even conveniently turned around so I could stab her around the heart area, and not a hit and miss stab in her back."

"How the hell then, if she *conveniently* turned around, did you not see it was the wrong girl?"

Yvette saw that in his fury, his eyes bulged, and the whites of his eyes showed round his iris; white birds' eggs with black spots on the middle of them. His pupils were huge in his rage. She fought down the urge to giggle; he looked so ridiculous. He didn't scare her, and her scorn for him grew with each hour and at every childish outburst.

"If *you* recall, I only saw her briefly in the taxi and for a few seconds when I dropped her off at the house in Coley. Yes, I did get a photo of her on my phone, and you confirmed it was her, but obviously I was a distance away. We agreed she was tall, slim with long dark hair. I remember she was wearing a long, dark coat and this girl, this Jose, had on a very similar coat. You weren't situated that far away you know, so how come you never recognised that it was the wrong girl?"

"You took your phone with her photo on it with you, so you must remember what she looked like. Anyway, it was dark, and I was about twenty yards away. You were right next to her, for God's sake."

"Oh, taking the Lord's name in vain. Naughty man. Yes, you said it, *it was dark*. As I said, the same description with the same coat, an easy mistake. I obviously didn't see her clearly enough. Why don't you stop shouting like a kid having a tantrum, throwing your toys out of the pram, and let's plan what we do next to retrieve the situation?"

Matthew took a deep breath, folded the newspaper and placed it on the coffee table next to the wine bottle. Yvette could see he was still trembling with rage, but as he sat down and spoke, he was obviously trying to control his feelings.

He took another breath before he asked, "Plans? What do you suggest? The cops will be all over the place now. Our likenesses are in the newspapers. What chance will we have?"

"Forget the sketches. Yours doesn't resemble you in everyday life, and I'm wearing a blond wig at the moment. OK, so we got the wrong girl, but they won't necessarily know that. We all know stabbing is a common occurrence with youth in this day and age. Chances are, they'll think it was a lover's tiff gone wrong or some such thing. Case in the paper not so long ago, about a young thug who stabbed his ex because she'd thrown him over." Yvette drained the remnants of her wine before she continued. "But it will be wise to lay low and forget any action for now until this has all blown over. That way, this'll soon be over and forgotten."

"That's alright for you. They may not connect what happened last night with our true intentions, but we now know that Madame Emma probably has contacted the cops, because our likenesses are all over the bloody Nationals and the TV news again. You say they don't resemble us, I'm not so sure. Anyway, these sketches must have been supplied by her. None of the other bitches have *escaped and lived*."

"Think about this. The papers reported that these likenesses were in the police's possession, but never mentioned they had a witness. Maybe she hadn't gone to the cops for whatever reason but sent them somehow. Anyway, the face did bear a resemblance to how you look when we were *stalking*, but I very much doubt your everyday colleagues will see the resemblance to the working you."

"Let's hope you're right." Matthew bit his lip as he thought about her words. After a few seconds of deliberation, he looked up and said, a touch of gleeful malice smearing his voice. "What about you? They have your likeness all over the news as well."

Yvette shrugged again. "No problem. As I said, I wear a wig. I intend to bleach my hair, tie it back, put on some glasses and I'll look completely different. Now whether or not the annoying bitch Emma sent in those sketches and has spoken to the cops, I say again, we must lay low for a while."

He nodded. "What about Wendy and Dominic. We've got those stashed away safely." Walking to the sideboard, he picked up a wine glass, and filled it from the bottle on the coffee table. He glanced up and smirked. "Maybe cheer ourselves up with one more celebration if we must lay low for a while."

She smirked back. Much as her dislike for him was growing by the day, and her long-term plans were to dump him and move on, sometimes he could have a good idea. "Why not?" she agreed.

He walked over to the window and peered into the darkness. He wasn't sure he *could* 'lay low' for a while, but better not to say anything to her, she wasn't totally aware of his cravings which were escalating to boiling point as each day passed.

His need for a client's 'breast' was becoming a burning sensation. He hadn't been to the tomb for what seemed like ages. Wendy's breasts were full; he could almost sense how fondling one would feel before he cut off his token piece. He guessed this was how an addict feels when desperate for a fix. He was desperate for a kill. He hoped his outside demeanour didn't reveal his inside feelings. The compulsion started at his toes and marched and slithered upwards and through his body like an army of angry red ants, gnawing on every nerve.

Still, when I've satisfied that urge, before long I'll dispose of her…the annoying Van Looy. I'll find a space for her in one of the tombs. Yes, that's cheering me up already.

Until that time, he could take a day off, go back to the 'old place' again, scrutinise all his souvenirs concealed there and those might temporarily satisfy the all-consuming urge that had occasionally overwhelmed him in the past. That had worked a couple of weeks ago and he'd felt so good afterwards. He knew he shouldn't go back this soon, but he had to do something to ease the compulsion. He took a deep breath and controlled the craving for the moment. The thought of going back made him feel a whole lot better. Maybe a stroll in the night would throw up 'another client'. *Yes, I feel better already.*

He put down the newspaper, took his coat from the back of her dining room chair and slipped it on. "Right, I've got to go." As he walked to the door he half waved and left, saying,

"See you in the usual place at seven. I'll bring a bottle of good wine to celebrate our …occasion."

He twitched as he walked away. He hadn't mentioned the fact that all clerical officials had been called to attend the St Anne's hall the next day to be photographed for the purposes of assisting a police investigation. He knew what the investigation was of course, although his colleagues were none the wiser, and he didn't enlighten them. He felt certain his day-time look would suffice, but he sensed that if his annoying companion knew what was about to happen, she'd start with her normal irritating tirade, so silence was the best option.

Van Looy, unaware of his thoughts, just nodded. Watching him leave through guarded eyes, she emptied the remainder of the wine into her glass, and considered which gratifying method she could use to dispose of him, after the 'enjoyment' of Wendy and her kid Dominic, of course.

His days are numbered. He's getting to be a burden, and a threat. He's out of control. After the Wendy and Dominic indulgence, he's a goner.

She chuckled and finished her drink.

Chapter 56

He was sweating, breathing so heavily his chest hurt. The panic at the close shave coursed through his body like a whirlwind.

Jesus H Christ, that stupid bitch nearly did it for me.

Checking his watch and realising it was 3am, he decided that despite the perspiring he would just fall into bed and shower in the morning. Glad that he'd left off his bedside lamp so that any passing nosy parker would not wonder what he was doing staying up so late, he changed into his pyjamas and lowered himself gingerly onto his knees to say his prayers. Despite the care, as his knees touched the carpet, he winced with the pain.

"That fucking bitch could have caused me permanent damage. Bad enough being stabbed by that Emma cow, now this fucking Pauline bitch kicked me on the knee and in the balls! Jesus H, what's this country coming to when you can't have some enjoyment without the client inflicting unnecessary injuries."

Placing his hands together in the praying position, he closed his eyes to gain some peace and murmured,

"Dear God…well, if there is one which after tonight's debacle I very much doubt, what the hell, excuse the pun…" He giggled at his wit. "Repeat, what the hell are you doing, or not doing in this case, by not looking out for your own?

I'm a Deacon of your church with all the boring responsibilities that go with that; I play the bloody organ all over the place; I help with choir practice so what the fuck else do you want me to do in order for you to watch out for me?

"I'm warning you, one more incident like last evening, and I'm off. You can do your own Deaconing or whatever it's called. The organ playing will have to fall on the shoulders of that useless twit Father David and as for helping out with choir practice to spot potential kids, that ugly evil cow Yvette Van Looy can do what she likes to all the brats. Not that I intend to procure any more for her, I'm finished with all that milarky. Right, after tonight, I'm finished, making plans to move on. Amen."

He heaved himself off his knees, wincing again at the pain, pulled back the bed covers and flopped thankfully into bed.

Closing his eyes, he waited for sleep and peace to arrive. He stayed awake. After a few minutes he attempted the regime he sometimes used by relaxing his toes, slowly working up through the muscles in his body. Despite all his exertions, the incident kept playing itself over and over in his mind and interfering with all his efforts.

Deciding to give into it, he knew the remedy was to go over everything, analyse what he should have done in order not to repeat the mistake in the future, to avoid a dangerous re-occurrence.

Despite his anxiety, a smile creased his lips, spread across his face until a giggle slipped out like a gentle breeze. He replayed their meeting in his mind. The girl was already three sheets to the wind by the time he'd hit the disco pub. Her friends had either already trapped or just abandoned her from the state of the discarded chairs and empty glasses spread untidily over the tall, round table.

She was precariously half sitting and swaying on a tall stool, slouching over her glass, and he didn't need pain-in-the-arse Van Looy to tell him she was vulnerable and ripe for picking. Using the same ever-successful approach, he noted what she was drinking, hurried to the bar and bought her a large version. Sidling up to her, he placed the glass in front of her, and gently stroked back the long piece of hair falling over her face. Her reaction was identical to all the other idiots…she looked surprised, glanced up to observe her saviour, her overly-made-up eyes opening in admiration, then the mouth fell open like a cod fish, not realising she was reaching the end of her useless life. At least that's what occurred ninety percent of the time, and so far, this was exactly what happened.

He took a deep breath. Unfortunately, it was the second part of the evening that had failed so bloody miserably. Initially it was OK, they'd chatted…well she'd grinned like a fool, so he'd chatted; then they'd danced and then gone outside for the proverbial fag and snog. By this time, she could barely stand, let alone walk, so it didn't take long for him to offer her a lift home, knowing that he'd better hurry things up or she'd either collapse or even worse, puke all over him.

Driving to the usual place, which was only a hundred yards down the road, he turned into the small space just beyond the edge of the trees and concealed the car from passers-by. This was when he made his mistake. Deciding on a quick shag before murder for an amusing change, he moved her easily onto the back seat. She never even twitched as he yanked off her knickers, but as he moved inside her, he could hear quiet moans of pleasure, which was quite gratifying for a change.

Change is as good as a rest.

That part had gone well. What happened next was a bloody pain. As she lay there, legs akimbo, he manoeuvred himself from the car, did up his flies, grabbed her ankles, and yanked her outside onto the grass. Her head hit the edge of the open door's sill as she tumbled. Even as she flopped onto the grass, she stirred, groaned but didn't fully wake up although he sensed she was coming to as the cold night air slapped her face, so he knew he'd better work quickly before the cow woke up and became a noisy nuisance.

Then the manure really hit the fan. He recalled shouts suddenly coming from the direction of the road, then car head lights pierced through the wooded area. In an instant he knew it was more dangerous to bolt and leave her there than to heave her back into the car and drive away along the narrow path that he had always used to escape along on previous occasions. The shit then developed into huge vats as he heard the voices getting nearer and calling her name. "Pauline, Pauline, where are you?"

She groaned and attempted to sit up. Heaving her to her feet in order to throw her onto the back seat, knowing this wasn't the time and place to cut her throat because her body would mean the police would be called and on the scene in minutes, he attempted to shove her into the car. Unfortunately, they must have both been standing on a muddy patch, because he wasn't sure what happened next, but both her and his feet slipped, her weight tipping her back and her legs coming up and kicking him in the balls as he was stumbling to his knees. In agony, he yelled, fell and this time his knee smashed against the metal sill on the open door's frame.

The voices were close. He shoved her away, jumped into his car, and thankful the keys were still in the ignition, switched on the engine and screeched away on squealing tyres, aware of faces momentarily appearing in his headlights as he turned left onto his get-away path.

Oh well, disappointing, but I got away, that's the main thing, and the shag was ok for a change.

He turned over on his side and fell asleep immediately and dreamed the peaceful dreams of a sociopath.

When he woke up at 7am, he stretched contentedly until he suddenly recalled his DNA was inside her!

Fuck!

Chapter 57

It was three o'clock in the morning and Declan was still trembling. Shaun went to top up his friend's glass with more whisky, purely medicinal he explained, but Declan covered the glass with his hand.

Shaking his head, he explained, "No more. I need a clear head to think this through."

"Declan, mate, I think you need to take yourself to your bed. I'll kip on the sofa. There's a policeman positioned outside. Have a good night's sleep and we'll work this out in the morning when you're over the initial shock and can think clearly."

Shaking his head again, Declan said. "Funnily enough, as I told the police, I didn't feel really threatened."

"Maybe because they weren't young thugs as you explained and were well spoken. However, as we all know, that doesn't actually mean a thing. Heaven knows what would have happened if I hadn't come knocking."

Declan finished the dregs of his drink before he continued, "Mmm, I suppose. I'm used to you knocking like you're trying to break down my back door, but your thumping even made me jump, and the 'Open up, Police' was hysterical... well, from my point of view."

"And I heard you tell the police it frightened the willies out of the men."

"Yes, it certainly did. With the lamp shining in my face I couldn't identify them." He placed his empty glass on the table, and then sniggered as he continued, "When you hammered like a pneumatic drill trying to dig into hell and back, all of them musta jumped six feet in the air by the sounds I heard. It wasn't until I heard them grabbing up their things and heading like bats out of hell for the front door that I realised there were probably three or maybe four of them."

"But up to that point, you think only three of them were questioning you."

Declan nodded. "Yes, but I definitely heard four different voices during their panicked whispering and scarpering. Anyway, I just don't get it. They were asking me about something so stupid…"

"Rubies on the moon thingy."

"Yes. As I told them, it was just a stupid remark made by one of the pupils when I asked him where rubies originated and could be located. Why is it so important what the lad said?"

"Maybe it's not so important what the lad said as to what this saying means to someone. A code for something, perhaps."

"Yes, maybe something like that." He shrugged, picked up his glass for a refill, and nodded to the whisky bottle that Shaun had placed back on the sideboard. "I will have another one. I'm never going to get to sleep tonight unless I partake enough of the amber nectar to knock me out." After Shaun had poured the equivalent of a double into his glass, Declan said, "The more I think about it, I believe you could have put your finger on it. One of the Fathers at school, despite my trying hard to find his better nature, is not a particularly nice bloke. He's talked about this a couple of times. Pushed me into how this phrase came up in the lessons. I've always been a bit reticent about telling him the lad's name who said it, because I wouldn't trust him not to pick on the boy."

"Is he involved then, this Father?"

"I've no idea."

"You got a computer?"

He nodded and knocked back his drink, before replying. "A laptop but I left it at school. Didn't intend to do anything but doss around and play golf this week. Why?"

"This internet gadget's a marvel. We could have put this phrase and see what comes out."

"Yes, but if this was a code or password or something, chances are they'd have changed it by now."

"True, but I still think it's worth a go. Tell you what; I'll get my nephew Connor onto it. He's one of these geniuses on the computer. Can get into anything he wants. Luckily for the government, he's an honest chap. He could have found out and sold all their dirty little secrets."

"Like a... what's the word they use on those films... hacker?"

"You hit the nail on the head, boyo." He lifted the bottle again.

Declan wisely shook his head. "No, there's a limit even for me."

"Shall we offer a noggin to the young chap outside?"

"I doubt he'll partake, him being on duty. He might welcome a hot coffee though."

"Could always lace it with a wee drop, it being bloody freezing out there."

The two men rose together. "Feel a bit better now. You get young Connor on the trail, maybe something'll come out of the woodwork."

"You never know. Now get yourself to bed, I'll make the coffee. Keep your mind off things by planning how you'll beat me. You've never got passed the sixteenth hole in over a year now."

"Bollocks, man, you've a memory of convenience."

As Declan climbed the stairs while Shaun went to make the officer's coffee, and while not usually nervous by nature, he was very glad of Shaun's company.

Chapter 58

Meena glanced up from her notebook at Jose who was sitting up in the hospital bed, propped up by two large pillows, and despite the nasty wound, was looking very pleased with the attention she was getting.

"Jose, we've almost finished. You OK for another couple of minutes? Not too tired?"

"S'fine," Jose said. Leaning forward slightly she winced, and then eased herself back to her original position. "Damn sore. Not allowed to smoke in here, you know. I'm dying for a puff. Just one puff."

Luke, who was sitting on the other side of the bed and used to be a smoker himself, said sympathetically, "Can't smoke anywhere except outside in the designated areas, Jose, sorry."

Jose, sensing a like-minded individual, nodded and said, "Yeah, I know, a bugger, innit."

Meena, keen not to lose the moment and keep Jose focused, said, "Not long, and hopefully you'll be discharged, and you can have a ciggy at home. Anyway, I'll summarise what has been discussed so far. Firstly, to check if you agree it's correct, and secondly, to jog your memory should something important have been missed." She coughed, apologised, and read from her notes. "You say that you and a friend, Charles Walsh...?" She stopped when Jose giggled.

"Charles, ooh, posh. We calls him Charlie." Her grin faded as Meena raised her eyebrows and opened her eyes in a 'shall-we-continue' look. "Sorry, miss."

Luke and Meena looked down, both trying not to grin. Jose was obviously a scatter-brained individual, but very likeable.

"You and Charlie went outside for a cigarette. You were both leaning over the match lighting your cigarettes when you noticed Charles…ok, Charlie, straighten up and say something like, "What the hell…" and the next moment someone pulls you around and you felt a terrible pain as someone stabbed you." At Jose's nod of approval, she continued, "Even though the incident was over in a few seconds, and you were in pain, you can confirm that the attacker was a woman. You have identified the woman as being one very similar to the sketch Emma Bradbury sent to us as being the person who drove her to the place you refer to as Loddon House."

"Yeah, 'ad me contact lenses in so I could see real well. Real ugly cow she was, awful hairstyle. Blond streaks in her hair, not done at a salon I know. If they were, it was a crap job, not worth the dosh she paid for it. Anyway, weren't I lucky? Knife glanced off the vodka container. Doctors said it probably took away the full imp…imp..."

"Impact."

"Yeah, said I might been a gonna otherwise."

"Charlie's version of events ties in with yours. Is there anything else you can remember that would assist us with our enquiries?"

As Meena and Jose chatted, Luke was closely watching his colleague. She had dressed casually for this interview in jeans and sweater. Her dark glossy hair, normally tied back in a bun, hung loosely down her back, black and gleaming like a swaying pool of oil, turning an extremely attractive officer into a beautiful woman.

"Thank you, Jose. I believe we've finished here."

Meena glanced across at Luke to check whether he wanted to add anything. Their eyes locked and held; Meena's because she read the penetrating stare as him trying to relay some sort of message which she couldn't interpret. His look because he suddenly realised his attraction to his colleague was growing by the day, and he did not know how to control it. They both slowly dragged their eyes away from each other, one puzzled, and the other perplexed by the rapidly evolving allure.

The moment passed as Jose screeched. The officers both jumped to their feet, but relaxed when they realised the noise was Jose's welcome to her two visitors, Emma Bradbury and Heidi Roberts.

The officers said their goodbyes as the two girls leapt across the room and smothered their friend in hugs and kisses.

Outside the private ward, the two officers nodded to the young Police Constable who was present for protection purposes. Walking along the corridor, Meena flicked through her notebook. "Didn't really get anything that moves the case along. Almost certainly the attack was made by Yvette Van Looy, but we knew she was tied into the case."

"I think it helps in terms of showing us they're getting desperate. Emma was probably correct when she says Nielson is keen to shut her up. That reminds me, did we manage to get anyone assigned to protect her when they realise their mistake?"

"I believe Dan assigned young PC Simon Leadbetter. Anyway, I know someone's been assigned, not full time, but checking on her whereabouts quite regularly. She's been advised not to go clubbing or such."

Meena murmured a thanks as Luke opened the door for her at the end of the long hospital corridor. "But we're still no nearer to knowing Nielson's everyday identity. We have his description. His face has been on every newspaper and on the TV news, but except for the usual quacks, no firm, sensible sightings have been reported. Plus, it appears as though he's getting Satan-woman to do his dirty work."

The two police officers walked through the hospital main entrance, down the steps and hurried to the police car. The rain that had been threatening to soak everyone caught in its downpour had arrived whilst they were in the hospital, making them break into a sprint to avoid getting soaked. To make matters worse, a spiteful wind had also turned up and both officers were damp and cold by the time they were safely inside their vehicle. Luke switched on the engine and turned the heater to high.

Looking at his watch, he said, "Seven thirty. Right, back to the station, write up the report. By then my shift'll be over, so it's off to the pub. How does that sound?"

"Mmm, don't know, I..."

"Come on, DC Mesbah, how does a nice cold white wine sound?"

"Your treat?"

"You bet."

"You're on. Our drinking's getting to be a habit. Step on it, officer."

Jose was still basking in the attention and enjoying opening her presents. Emma had bought her a beautiful matching pink dressing gown and stripped pyjamas set. Heidi had bought matching slippers with a small bunnies' heads on the top, and a bling jewellery bracelet set that comprised of seven bangles, ranging from golden, ruby red and rose gold, tied together with a pearly chain.

"I love it," screeched Jose, and continued to swoon over it while Heidi pushed it over her hand onto her wrist.

They all laughed at Emma's present of a silver tot bottle for her vodka so in future she would be more discreet when sneaking in her drinks for topping up her orange juice, emphasising that it was more substantial than glass!

The laughter subsided when Emma's face became

serious and she said, "I'm going to be up front with this, but I don't want you two to be involved in what I'm planning."

Heidi groaned and shaking her head said, "Here we go again. After all of what's happened, I hope you're not planning on any more searching."

"Well, yes and no." She glanced at Jose, concerned that she might be upsetting her friend, but Jose, whose attention span had not improved since her ordeal, wasn't concentrating on her friend's words and was still admiring her bracelet. "It's just that the cops kept on asking me about whether I had any connections with church schools, went to church regularly or had any links with the church?"

"Well, you don't go to church and Wellborough Comprehensive wasn't churchy or anything."

"I know and I said that, but they kept on a bit, and I've thought about it. The cops also asked about his clothes. Maybe his normal clothes, you know, business clothes like, are different to his clothes that he wore at the nightclubs. Well, what about if he was a priest or something. You know, wears those hassocks or cassock thingys."

"If they think that, they must have been round those schools, and checking churches and priest and things themselves until the cows come home."

"Yes, I expect they have, but they don't know what he looks like."

"They've got your sketches now. They *know* what he looks like."

"They only know from my sketch and from the CCTV cameras. He's wearing his evening gear. I've met the evil bastard; it wouldn't matter what he wore. I've looked into his eyes, it wouldn't matter if he was wearing a frilly dress, I'd recognise him."

"You're un-bloody-believable. Well, you're not going searching and spying on your own, I'm coming."

"No, you're not. He's well dangerous, and so is his bloody ugly mate."

"When I'm out of hospital," said Jose, who had finally looked up from admiring her new jewellery, "can I come too?"

"No," the two girls answered in unison.

"Well, you're talking about church schools and things. I knows loads about that. What about what Alfie Smith posted on face book? He goes to a church school where that Jason what's missing also went."

She smiled liked the proverbial cat who'd found a saucer full of his favourite condensed milk when her two friends looked at her with intense interest that she misread as admiration.

Chapter 59

"So, you didn't find out a thing. Sounds like this so-called interview was a big fiasco," said Dennis, his voice smeared with a smirk.

The five men were sitting around Dennis's dining room table with large goblets of brandy before them, and the haze from comforting cigars floating like gossamer fairies dancing tiptoe in mid-air. Arthur blew a misshaped smoke ring, frowning as he collected his thoughts to give himself a few seconds to plan his answer. The tone of Dennis's voice was annoying, and he had to control himself not to snap as he replied. "You weren't there so I don't think you should take that attitude. I agree things did not pan out as we hoped and…"

"And you didn't find out thing," interrupted Bob, who had been some-what miffed because he, like Dennis, hadn't been selected to 'interview' the teacher, and was therefore pleased the event had obviously failed miserably.

John's modulated voice quietened the threatening disagreement, "Please, gentlemen, control yourselves."

Arthur continued, "We carried out this task with the best of intentions. If this O'Leary had somehow discovered our password, the result could have been disastrous. After the failure of the Operation Hobbledehoy, we need to be ten times more careful. Everything we do now we think through very carefully. I know the Ruby password has been changed, but I understand there are people with knowledge that means they can dig and dig and find anything that has been sent electronically despite firewalls, passwords etc. We needed to investigate this worrying penetration into our system."

He took a sip of his brandy, puffed on his cigar before he continued. "I'm sure that it was coincidental that the police arrived. No-one knew about this meeting, and I'm also sure none of you mentioned it to anyone else." He glanced around the table, and as the others nodded their agreement, continued, "We got away safely, which was the main thing, and I agree, we found out nothing for sure. However, what I would say is that this O'Leary was amazed by the question, and was adamant that it was just a stupid answer that one of his pupils gave during a project about rare jewels, and where they are found." He took a deep breath as he leaned back in his chair. "I, for one, believe his answer."

"I do as well," supported John. He looked at George, who nodded his agreement.

"So, I repeat," said Dennis, "you didn't find out a thing."

"Not at all," said Arthur, "we found out that we have been wasting our bloody time. I think Father Francis got it wrong and just saw what he wanted to see."

"Or *thought* he saw, or heard," said John.

"Thank you, John, for your sensible words," said Arthur. "I agree it appears we may have wasted our time and found out nothing, but we had to make sure of those uncertainties, and I think we now have. I feel we have nothing to worry about with the password, so that in itself means we have made progress. Do you all now agree that?" His voice was firm, and his eyes travelled round the table with an 'I'll take no more nonsense' glare. When no-one challenged the statement, he continued. "This now gives us more time to concentrate on this David Sinclair, and also this Matthew something or other that our helpful mole has informed us about. If one of them is indeed queering our patch, we need to find out who he is and shut him down."

"Well, we don't have a lot to go on," said Bob, his voice tinged with a sulky tone.

"We have enough to focus on." Counting on his fingers, he explained, "Firstly, this Mathew…umm, apparently is tall, good looking, and secondly, whoever *he* is, we are ninety-nine percent certain he's working with the delightfully, foul Yvette Van Looy aka Delilah. Thirdly, he's new or fairly new to the area because there's no info on him. Fourthly, he, in fact, or should I say *they*, do not move around in the usual circles because there is no gossip whatsoever." Glancing round the table, he continued, "Agreed so far? Now, Bob, I believe you were going to check a bit more on this David Sinclair chap because he ticked three of those boxes. Any more on him?"

"Yes and no. He certainly visits all the schools from where the kids were taken, and others. He hasn't visited, as far as I or the Watchers have discovered, St Stevens in Sonning. He's a church deacon at St Anne's, and apparently a gifted choir master who travels to schools, and also plays the organ at many other churches when needed, so except for being tall, he doesn't resemble this Matthew. I think however, we need to…umm… interview him. Mind you, I can't quite see any connection between these two, this Matthew and Sinclair. Except that the mole's report suggests this Matthew is after attacking women and Sinclair has associations with children, and women and children are missing."

"True." Arthur was thoughtful for a few seconds. "However, consider this, although Sinclair is ginger with a limp and glasses; anyone can dress himself up completely differently, and appear, especially on poor quality pictures that we've seen in the news, a completely changed person."

"Are you saying they could be one and the same person?" asked John.

"Not necessarily, but I don't think we discount anything or anybody." He turned to his right. "George, while I think about it, you were going to check the few safe houses left in case Van Looy was holed up there. Find anything?"

"'Fraid not, Arthur. There were only two not accounted for, and they've been sold on with families occupying them."

Arthur nodded towards Dennis, "Anything new from your source?"

"No, not really. He couldn't get hold of the sketches that are displayed on the white board in the incident room, but they were in the papers again the next day, so there was no need."

"Right, we go one step at a time. We need to investigate Sinclair. Bob, with the aid of your Watchers, can you get a rough timetable of where he goes and when. We need to move on this pretty quickly."

"Certainly. We know he plays the organ at various churches. When we find a church he plays at on a certain occasion, it might be prudent to pick him up after the service. If he doesn't turn up when due to at one of the schools, that might be investigated pretty quickly."

"Just get a timetable, and we'll make a decision on that." Arthur lifted the decanter of brandy. "I feel we are moving on a pace now. We've stopped wasting our time on O'Leary. So, little noggin anyone, to celebrate a small success?"

"Yes, please," said Dennis, holding his glass up for a refill. "I'm not being awkward, and I understood why it was necessary to check out O'Leary, but I'm not sure why we're chasing down this Matthew. If he's taking a few women, who cares. If somehow, he's involved with taking kids, again, who cares? Why are we getting so worked up? After all, there's plenty of kids to go around."

Arthur topped up Dennis's glass before snapping, "Because this cell area is ours. We decide what's going on. After the shambles of Operation Hobbledehoy, we've learnt the difficulty we incur when people do their own thing. Even those within the local Brotherhood cell, French Larry and Lawman, doing their own thing before Hobbledehoy was extremely dangerous if you re-call. That could have brought us all down, and a lot of our comrades are still suffering in jail.

"I know the operation failed, but that was mainly due to a cop infiltrating the cell. Although our organisation structure has changed, and security stepped up, we are still vulnerable if people step out of line. In this area, and the other cell zones, all those with our interests and leanings understand they belong to their particular groups, and they do as the top level instructs them. If they choose not to, then they either control their urges or pay the consequence. Plus, plans for the next operation are well underway, and nothing must jeopardise that coming event." He leaned forward, his face red with passion. "Kapish?"

Dennis, eyes wide with fear, nodded demurely and looking down, sipped his brandy without further comment.

Chapter 60

Wendy smiled as her friend Paul Johnson pulled up outside her new accommodation in his large car, a battered old Mercedes, his pride and joy. Although she was very grateful to Matthew for bringing her to the wonderful house in which she was now living, after seven days of doing nothing, she was bored. Although her flat was dingy compared to her present housing situation, she missed seeing her friends who lived in the same council flat's building.

As he alighted from the car, she walked over and hugged him. Taking him by the hand, she dragged him towards the entrance to the apartment.

"Christ, this looks well posh, Wendy. What the hell are you doing here?"

She laughed as she said, "Wait till you get inside. Now that's real dead posh. Never seen a place like it in my life. Hurry up, Dom's asleep but I don't wanna not be there if he wakes up."

The two hurried through a marbled tiled entrance; displaying in the centre an octagonal centrepiece filled with old money three pence pieces and covered with hardened glass causing Paul to whistle with admiration at the classy arrangement. "Christ, that's like, dead good. It wouldn't last five minutes in our flats. Some thieving bastard'd have that smashed and nick the dosh before you could blink."

"Yeah, I know. Posh people don't act like that, though." She took his hand again. "Hurry up, I've called the lift. You'll never believe it. It goes straight into the living place. The bottom floor's a huge garage and storage area."

Paul was practically speechless for the next ten minutes as Wendy showed him around. When he sank himself onto the kitchen bar stool, shaking his head in wonder, Wendy explained as she filled the kettle to make the tea, that she wasn't supposed to contact any of her old friends, and had been sworn to secrecy.

"I know, but you'd already told me."

"Yeah, I know, suppose I was trying to rile you 'cos you're so bloody possessive."

"Why's he so secretive? After all, according to him, that priest fellow at the church, he was just helping you out and you were doing him a favour; looking after this place while some one was abroad or summit."

"Not really sure why I didn't have to say nuffink. Anyway, he's been really kind, but I don't think he's meant to show any favour…fav…ism."

"Favouritism. Mmm, I'm not really sure about this you know. Sounds a bit dodgy to me. He ent tried anyfink on, loike, has he?"

"No, they're not like that at all."

"Well, I'm not so sure. In fact…" he nodded to Wendy to heap a large teaspoonful of sugar into his tea. He saw her stare at him. "Sorry, just trying to make sure you're safe, that's all."

Wendy duly poured the tea and stirred it before saying, "What you worried about then?"

"Sit down. I've got something to tell you. I don't want to worry you, but I think things are well dodgy." He withdrew a creased newspaper from the inside of his jacket pocket. It was folded around a large picture. Handing over the paper, he asked. "Look at that image. Who does it look like?"

Studying the picture, Wendy's eyes were large, her

brow furrowed with confusion. "Not a dead likeness, but it looks a lot like…umm…that friend of Mr. Sinclair's, Gail som'ink I fink he said, his friend what drives him."

Wendy started to unfold the paper to read more, but Paul shook his head and took it from her. He said, "I saw this Gail the night she came and picked you up. When Billy put your case in her boot."

"Yeah, and you ignored me 'cos we'd had a row about my going."

"Sorry about that. I know I'm jealous, I can't help it. Anyway, she'd parked in my spot. She stayed in the car, but that new street lighting's pretty strong and I got a good look at her face."

"So?"

"I didn't think anything of it at the time. Too annoyed, but when I read the headlines, I got dead worried. That's why I phoned you." Paul unfolded the newspaper and handed it to her.

As she read the words, Wendy's eyes bulged in their sockets and her mouth stretched back over her teeth in horror. Looking up to Paul, she gasped, hardly able to speak. Eventually she stuttered, "Jesus Christ, the coppers think she's sort of responsible for all those missing women and kids. Bloody hell, me and Dom... oh no, do'you fink…?"

Paul looked grave; he nodded. He unfolded the rest of the paper and handed it to Wendy. "What about this fellow. Is that your friend?"

The girl screwed up her eyes bringing the paper back and forth to get it into focus. "I dunno. Sort of, but nah, Deacon Sinclair wears glasses and his hair's different. This guy, well, his hair's longer, wavy. The Deacons is close cropped. Still, his face...yeah, looks sort a similar. This geezer in the photo, jeans and bomber jacket don't look like 'im. But this, whats 'is name, Matthew Nielson looks different. David, he told me to call him that, and he just looks…like innocent. Their faces are similar, but I'm not sure…" She shrugged as she handed the paper back to Paul.

"But you don't know. He looks familiar. Anyone can look different if for instance, they wears a wig. This picture could be when he didn't have his glasses on or maybe wearing a wig. Look again, just look at the face."

She took the paper, studying the picture intently; Paul noticed the deep v between her brows as she concentrated. After a minute, she nodded, and her whispered reply was painted with concern, "Yeah, could be him. In fact, dead ringer for 'im round the nose and mouth an' that. Still, it's somefink to do with, you know, how your face shows fings."

"You mean, his expression." At her nod, he continued, "Wendy, we can't take no chance. Think about Dom if nothing else. I think you should scarper from this joint."

She jumped up. "Christ, they're coming here tonight." Glancing at her watch, she said, "Fucking hell, it's five. They said they'd be here about seven. Bringing a McDonalds for us for a treat."

Paul stood up. "Ok, let's get you out of here. Let's get packing."

"They knows where I live. They'll come and get us."

"No, they won't. I'll take you to me mums. She's got a spare room. Then we go to the cops."

"No, no, not the cops. I'm on probation, remember, for shop lifting. If they find out I changed me address without telling me welfare woman, I'll be in dead stuk. Got warned last time if I didn't behave, I could maybe lose Dom."

"Look, don't get worked up. For now, we get you packed up and we scarper. We'll think this through later, when we've had time to sort it out."

Within twenty minutes, the three of them were speeding away in the rusty car, unaware of the horror that might have been that night.

Part II
Suspects Galore

Chapter 61

Dan, with Luke and Meena, was huddled over his desk, studying the photos of seventeen men previously taken of possible suspects fitting Nielson's description who were either teachers at church schools or some sort of official representative at local churches, including two priests.

"We didn't just stick to church schools even though we believe that's where our suspect is located. I felt we couldn't leave any proverbial stone unturned." Luke then went on to explain that he had used three of his team to visit all the schools in a five to eight-mile radius from the centre of Reading. They had photographed all the tall, slim male teachers for comparison. They had then done the same for tall associates or leaders of local churches.

Dan nodded, murmuring a "Sensible thinking," as he perused the photos. For comparison purposes, all three officers were examining pictures that had been altered to a similar size image they had obtained from the security cameras of Matthew Nielson entering the nightclubs. They also used Emma Bradbury's sketch for evaluation as she had suggested it was an accurate image.

"Almost certainly that's not his real name," said Meena, working as she talked. "D'you reckon he took it from that Nielson that killed those young gay guys. In the 1970s/80s I think. Mind you, the spelling's different, think that was N-I-L-S-O-N."

"Why would he?" asked Luke, pleased to look up from his studying, and able to admire his colleague's lovely face. He knew he was thinking more and more of her as a potential girlfriend, and he wasn't sure it was a good thing. He was always aware of her when she was anywhere in the room near him, and some days he had to force himself to focus on his job.

"Because he's arrogant, thinks he's beyond the law and uncatchable."

Luke laughed. "Uncatchable, is that a proper word?"

Meena shrugged. "Ok, can't be caught if that's what you'd prefer."

"I can see where you're coming from, Meena," agreed Dan. "Sick bastard like that would probably take pleasure in using another sick bastard's name. Bet if we checked, there'd be many equally perverted *Matthews* now enjoying her majesty's pleasure." He picked up two pictures as he spoke. "OK, these would be the two I'd pick out. What have you two got?"

His two colleagues studied the photos he was holding up for them to check. Luke tapped the one on the right. "Yep, I picked him out. Not so sure of the other one; looks a bit too stocky." He picked up two from the selection before him. "These two are my choice."

"I agree with those two as well," said Meena. Pointing to the photo in Dan's right hand, she continued, "I agree with that one, and this is the one I think looks similar."

"Ok, that's five. Put the others away for the moment and let's study these five prime suspects for clarification."

Dan placed two poor quality pictures of Mathew retrieved from the nightclub CCTV cameras either end of the five suspects plus the sketch. The room was silent as the three colleagues perused the photos again, so focused on their task that none of them were aware of the storm raging outside, with the rain beating so hard against the windows as though someone with sharp nails was tapping on the window panes.

"Mmm, hard to say," murmured Meena.

"I agree," said Dan. "We investigate these five thoroughly. I want to know everything about them. I want them to account for their whereabouts and actions on the nights both the women and the kids went missing. I want…"

"Why when the kids went missing?" asked Luke. "I thought we agreed that Matthew was interested in the women."

"True, but we don't know anything for sure, and if he's getting kids for the she-devil, then she could well be in the vicinity. Emma told us she was his driver, so if one of these is Matthew, we need to check on their movements for each and every abduction case." Dan stood up and shuffled the non-suspects into a pile and placed them into a buff file. "As I said, I want to know every detail of these five, from their Grandmothers' maiden names to what brand of toothpaste they use."

"Why don't we bring them in and start questioning them now?" Luke said.

"We tread carefully. Currently we have no proof, no evidence, it's all circumstantial. We don't want to show our hand and forewarn them, or anyone else. We check and re-check their alibis. When we're ready, fully prepared, we bring them in and grill them till we know their lives better than their mothers."

"Has Emma seen these? After all, she's seen him. I know she looked at some mug shots and was sure none were Nielson. She should be looking at these."

"Yes, she's popping in tomorrow. Can you deal with that Meena?" Dan stood up. "I want Emma to look at all suspects' mug shots first, so we get a good feeling where we're at with this. Then we go from there. Let her filter out her choices, see if she comes up with the same five. Hopefully she'll come up with a definite."

Luke and Meena nodded; the feeling that at last they were making progress, the puzzle pieces gradually falling into place ready for the final big picture was giving them the high buzz that police officers inevitably experience.

"OK, I'm off for the night," said Dan.

Luke looked at his watch, and then at his boss, a grin spreading over his face. "You sound keen. Got a hot date?" Out of the corner of his eye, he noticed Meena glance sharply at Dan, who just grinned back at him.

"Suspicious, dirty mind you've got. I'm going to see Sara. With all that's been going on, I haven't seen her since I got back. Phoned her a couple of days ago, and she's offered to cook me a curry. Can't say no to that. Lived on stale sandwiches and cold coffee since this all went down, so I think I deserve a hot meal."

"If you say so." Luke pushed back his fair hair that continuously fell over his eyes. Grinning again, he continued, "She setting you up with a date? Anybody you happen to fancy be there too?"

Dan walked to the door. As he opened it, he glanced back at the pair, both waiting in anticipation for his answer, but with different reasons. "Nosey bastard! You might be wrong; you might be right." His grin was so broad they knew the answer without being told. He walked back into the room, rummaging in his jacket and bringing out a well-worn leather wallet. Handing a twenty-pound note to Luke, he said, "Buy yourselves a drink after your shift's finished. Then first thing in the morning, you get your arses into gear. I want to find out who of those five is our man." He hurried away, whistling tunelessly.

Luke noticed that Meena was looking at the door that her boss had just gone through. Her face was expressionless. Once again he experienced a small stab of jealousy.

"Cheer up, Meena, things can't be that bad."

She looked back at him, giving her colleague a strained smile. "You're right. If the boss can go on the razzle, so can we. Will that twenty stretch to a nice cold glass of Pinot?"

Luke waved the note in the air. "Think it will stretch to two, maybe three. We could get pissed on it especially if the Red Lion's got a happy hour going."

"Lead on, my man. I fancy a hangover in the morning. Might need to stretch to a taxi though."

"No worries, we share the taxi and it'll be my treat."

Luke followed Meena through the door, admiring her pert bottom in her jeans, wondering if tonight was the night!

Luke put a large glass of Pinot Grigio on the table in front of Meena. She was busy texting someone. Putting her phone away, she looked up and smiled.

"Thanks." Glancing down at the glass, she said, "Hey, I said a small one. That looks large to me. I've had a large one already, and two small ones are my limit."

Luke supped his pint, looking over the rim of his glass. "Get it down your throat, young lady. This was Dan's treat. That doesn't happen that often, so let's make the most of it. We walked here and I've already said I'll treat us to a taxi to your place."

"My place…hope you don't think you're kipping on my sofa again."

Luke just grinned and downed the rest of his beer. He burped quietly before saying, "The trouble with you, young lady, is you're too serious and you've gotta learn to relax and enjoy yourself. We've worked enough long hours on this case that our brains are starting to frazzle. I've learned…" he put his hand in front of his mouth as he quietly burped again. "'Scuse me.. Now, where was I…oh yeah…we've got to unfrazzle our thinking, have a relaxing drink, a friendly chat and unwind."

He stood up, and before Meena could object, walked once more to the bar. Sipping her drink, she shook her head with incredulity at his audacity. "He'll never change," she murmured to herself.

When Meena reflected on that evening, she never could remember exactly when it all went wrong, or maybe, from a different point of view, when it all went right.

All she could recall was that they continued drinking, despite her objections, although she did remember Luke drank a great deal more than her. At 'throwing-out-time' as Luke called it, she definitely retained the memory of her legs feeling wobbly, and Luke was certainly staggering.

The taxi that she had called was waiting impatiently outside the pub. Luke refused to give his address, insisting her sofa was comfortable enough for him, and Meena was forced to give the driver her address as he was threatening to drive away, saying very clearly he didn't usually drive drunks. It was only Meena's warrant card and her assurances of no trouble that mollified him somewhat, and he allowed them to get in.

Forced to let Luke into her flat, Meena hurried to her linen cupboard to find some blankets for the sofa as she strongly suspected he would be getting amorous before long. Throwing the blankets onto the sofa back, she hissed, "Don't snore so damn loudly this time."

Turning around quickly, she was startled to find him really close to her. He smiled, pulled her to him, and kissed her gently on the mouth. Releasing her as quickly as it had happened, he whispered, "I'm only saying this 'cos I'm pissed, but I strongly suspect I'm getting too fond of you."

With that, he took two steps to the sofa, flopped onto it, closed his eyes and was asleep in ten seconds. With her heart beating ten to the dozen, she covered him with the blankets and hurried to her room. Her legs were still wobbly, but she suspected it wasn't the wine.

Chapter 62

Declan, Shaun and his nephew Connor sat round the kitchen table drinking coffee. The two teachers watched with anticipation as the boy fired up his laptop.

Declan glanced at the young man who had long black hair tied back in a ponytail, and eyes as green as Irish grass after a summer shower. He was a tall, handsome young man and Declan, despite his great affection for his childhood chum, couldn't see any physical resemblance. Shaun was short, his ginger hair having receded to an unruly halo around the back of his head. However, Declan ruefully admitted to himself, that didn't stop him being a two-handicap golfer.

"You're grinning like an eejit, Shaun. You obviously know what the lad's found."

"Declan, me friend, you are going to be amazed at the depths this laddo of mine has had to dig through, and what he eventually came up with."

Connor glanced up and shook his head at his uncle's remarks. "Ignore him, Mr O'Leary…"

"Just call me Declan, please."

"Declan it is. I have spent the most exciting and exacting thirty-six hours in my life, and I enjoyed every moment of it. I love a challenge. The investigative part that is, but shocked at the outcome." He leaned forward and pressed a few more keys before continuing. "Without meaning to boast, I'm probably one of the top hackers… umm, investigators..." He coughed, "Well, could be a top hacker, if I was so inclined, in this country. However, your problem almost, and I emphasise almost, beat me. After a day of trying, I got me mate, probably the number one hacker…umm, computer expert in the UK, on the job. Even he found the going tough." He leaned back and finished his coffee.

Declan picked up his percolator and offered to top up their cups. At Connor's nod, he filled all the three cups and nodded for the young man to continue.

"I'd bore you rigid with the fire doors, safety precautions etc, etc, we had to fight through. We'd get down three levels, and then boom, we'd be thrown out. But…"

"They hadn't reckoned on you two geniuses getting involved though," Shaun interrupted excitedly.

Connor grinned good-humouredly at his uncle's enthusiasm and pride.

"Well, we both got hooked before long, and weren't going to let the problem beat us. You've probably heard of the Dark Web." He glanced up for their affirmation, but they both shook their heads. "Well, I'll say no more on that but let's just say it was their mistake that gave it away. We looked at your phrase, 'Rubies on the Moon' in various ways, but decided it was undoubtedly a password at a top level in the system. If they were worried, almost certainly it would have been changed after you'd quoted it, because that obviously'd sent them into a flat spin from what then happened to you. Whoever set up the website was a very knowledgeable guy.

"My mate and I both reckon he was too clever to have made the mistake that eventually occurred, and that maybe had an assistant helping him who wasn't so bright." As he flicked through the screens, his Irish accent got more obvious with every word. "As I said, 'Rubies etc' was eliminated from the top level, but many, many almost impenetrable levels below, the eejit feckin' used the password again. And that's how we got through to this…" He hit a key and then swung the laptop round before adding, "Should warn you this is pretty gruesome."

Declan gasped when he saw what was on the screen. "Holy Mary, I don't believe…what gob shites…excuse my foul language." He realised there was something evil happening and somehow, he'd got caught up in it.

Chapter 63

Yvette pulled up behind the building. Switching off the ignition, she glanced round at Matthew. He was sitting, arms crossed, and not attempting to get out of the car.

"What's wrong?"

He shook his head, and she noticed a deep furrow between his ginger eyebrows as he frowned. His glasses had slipped down his nose, and he pushed them up before saying, "That's weird. We told her we were coming around seven. Yet look, it's almost dark and there are no lights on."

Yvette glanced at the house. "Yes, you're right. Maybe…"

Matthew opened the car door, his voice hoarse and laced with anger, and snarled, "Fucking cow. If she's gone anywhere, I'll bloody kill her."

He hurried towards the house, not hearing Yvette's ironic mutter, "Well, I thought that's what we were here for anyway." She followed him to the back door, where in his impatience he couldn't get the key into the lock.

"Give it here," she snapped, snatching the key from his fumbling fingers. "Hell, what's wrong with you?"

As she deftly inserted the key into the lock, Matthew was grateful she couldn't see him. He could feel sweat break out on his top lip, and the red ants were now armies of insects that had become vicious as his need for a kill was spiralling out of control. Biting his lip in a frantic effort to keep himself in check, realising he shouldn't have left it for so long before another kill. He just needed the thrill more and more often. The empty family crypt loomed in his imagination, and he longed to be in the dark chamber, laying his client into her rightful place, with the token folded in his hand.

"Hurry up. The doors open." Her voice snapped him back to the present. Taking a deep breath to control his emotions, he followed her into the dark and ominously silent house.

They searched the house not saying a word. He went upstairs whilst the woman hurried through the downstairs rooms. When they met together in the kitchen, he sank onto the breakfast barstool, while she walked to the kettle to make them a drink.

"She hasn't gone long," she said. "The kettle's still warm."

"Hot or warm?"

"Barely warm, but not that coldness you feel when it hasn't been used for, say, half a day. I reckon she made coffee or tea an hour or so ago."

She walked to the sink and picked up two mugs. "Used. She had some one here despite your orders. Maybe they've just gone out for a bite to eat or something."

He shook his head. "No, the little fucker's left. She wouldn't take her precious Dominic out this late. His cot hasn't been slept in, and all their clothes are gone."

She used fresh mugs to make them coffee. He sat quietly contemplating their position. Handing him his drink, she watched as he absent-mindedly sipped, growing concerned about his general demeanour. Usually so self-assured, he appeared agitated and certainly not in control. She didn't care if he was upset by the situation, only uneasy in case this emotional change was likely to affect her in any way. Planning to be rid of him in the near future, she had disciplined herself to act naturally, deciding that as this latest 'game' had so fortuitously fallen into their laps, she might as well partake of the enjoyment before scarpering.

Also, she didn't like loose ends. The fact that they had failed to eliminate Emma Bradbury also needed sorting, and two pairs of hands involved in removing her from the scene was going to make it easier. She sipped her coffee and continued studying him.

Is he losing his nerve? He's really been weird these last few days… so confident and cocky before. He's changed. Like he's two different people. One's totally self-possessed, assured…the other…quite the opposite. And it's more than unease…it's panic…desperation. That's dangerous for me! Right, after removing that nuisance Emma, he'll have to go. I don't want any loose ends that could lead to me.

He looked up suddenly. "I was so sure…did anything happen when you picked her up. Anybody see you or…?"

"Nope. Nobody," she lied. *Another loose end I need to tie up maybe.* Keen to change the subject, she said, "Your picture was in the paper again. Perhaps she actually reads the news and recognised you."

He tipped the last of his coffee into his mouth; stretched across the bar and tore off some paper from the kitchen roll to wipe his mouth. "*Our* pictures or likenesses don't you mean? Yours was more recognisable than mine. Whoever supplied that reproduction provided my night-time guise. They have no idea of my daytime character, and I don't think it looked like me as I am now."

"I agree to a certain extent. That dark wig is good, I'd be the first to agree. However, the likeness was in black and white, so colour doesn't feature. But if she drew glasses on the picture, your features are still there, and she may well see the resemblance."

"She's too bloody thick for that."

"Face up to it, she's gone. There's no bus route out of here for quarter of a mile. She couldn't afford a taxi.

Somebody else has been here, and helped her, and the two cups indicate that. Maybe he or she is way more intelligent and recognised the likeness."

"They wouldn't know me, so how the hell would they recognise me?"

"She's scarpered. She could be anywhere. I think you can't take the chance she's not gone to the cops. After all, she knows you set her up in this place. OK, I drove her, but that doesn't mean I'm implicated, just the driver. Until we know the situation, go home and pack. Get out of town, so to speak, and lay low till we know what's going on."

Again, she watched as he considered her suggestion. She couldn't quite work out what was going on, but she could see him almost twitching. It was as if he was a drug addict, desperate for a fix. She didn't realise how accurate she was, but not frantic for a drug, but the need to kill.

He stood up. "OK. I've got piano lessons tomorrow…"

"Forget that. Phone in and say you're sick. You're going to stay with your sister." Before he could interrupt, she continued, "Yeah, I know. You haven't got a sister. Get yourself away."

"I could stop with you. I…"

"No way. We need to split up… momentarily. You've got my mobile number. I'll run you home and take you to the railway station. Go to London. As soon as you've got an address, let me know it. Or maybe go back to Oxford."

"No, I'm not going yet. I feel confident that my disguise is good enough to keep me out of the frame. Over the next week, I've got a couple of really important meetings. If I don't attend, it will draw attention if I go missing. Father Bryan may well report my missing to the cops. If they start to investigate that could be dodgy. I might as well just give myself up to the cops now." He saw by her expression she was about to argue. He held up his hand, palm forward, and said firmly. "No, give me a week. I'll lay low, just attend these meetings and then I'll tell Father Bryan I'm going away for a short holiday break. That way, no-one will question my going for a couple of weeks."

Shrugging as though to indicate if that's what he wanted to do, then that was up to him. Her thoughts, however, were diametrically opposite to her body language.

If he gets nicked, that's his problem, as long as I'm not implicated. Bloody good riddance.

She washed the cups thoroughly and put them behind other cups in the cupboard. He followed her, but as she walked ahead of him through the front door, he took the opportunity to take a last look back at the dark hallway and inwardly sighed. He'd been so excited and trembling with expectation barely an hour ago, now…

"I'll be back," he whispered into the darkness, "maybe an Oxford visit's not such a bad idea."

Chapter 64

"Got a fag?" the kid asked Emma, obviously trying to look grown up and cool in front of his friend, who stood just behind him.

"Don't be stupid," said Emma. "Jeez, you're just a damn kid."

"How old are you anyway?" asked Heidi, shaking her head in frustration at the attitude and scruffy appearance of the small, cocky boy.

"Eleven," he replied, hand on his hips. He glanced at his friend to ensure he did not interrupt with the truth.

"You're never eleven. Maybe just ten, but probably nine. Eleven is a load of bollocks!" Frustration and irritation at his smug demeanour painted Emma's voice. "Anyway, that doesn't matter. Are you Alfie Smith?"

"Yeah, so what if I am?"

Emma clenched her hands. She had an irresistible urge to clock the irritating little sod round the ear, but knew if she did, she would not get the information she wanted.

"Who's your mate?" asked Heidi. Nodding her head in the direction of his equally scruffy companion, whose ginger hair was quiffed up in a hair style that looked more secure than the Eiffel tower by the huge quantity of gel that had obviously been used to safeguard its upwards path.

"Why?"

"Just wondered. I said, what's his name or shall I call him Sue?"

Alfie immediately disclosed his true age and immaturity by smirking. "Ah ha, Sue…I like that." He turned and grinned at his friend. "Sue, Sue, little Susie, innit."

"Fuck off, Alfie Welfy," the friend retaliated. He looked at Emma. "Ignore that turd, me names Joey, but everybody calls me Ginge, and 'e's Alfie Smith."

"Thanks, Jo…Ginge," said Emma. "Glad one of you's acting grown-up." Emma turned to Alfie. "Right, can we now have some sensible, adult type conversation like we discussed on Face book, or is that beyond your comprehension?"

"Beyond my what?"

"Beyond your understanding," said Ginge, obviously the brighter of the two.

"Depends," said Alfie. "It'll cost yuh."

Emma bent down, her face six inches from the youngsters' and snarled, "You listen here, you little *turd* as your mate so accurately called you, you agreed to meet us. Now all we want to know is what was behind the message that you posted on Face Book about your mate Jason Stone."

The boy's face suddenly changed. The arrogant look slipped away, the eyes widened and the childlike golden colour of constantly playing out of doors washed away. He fidgeted from his left foot to his right and back again.

"Dunno what you mean. Never said nuffink on Face Book." His voice became fierce. "It's a lie."

Emma realised that she had touched on a delicate subject and had to tread carefully if she was going to learn anything. "Look, Alfie. You're not going to get into trouble here. I understand your mum goes to church with Jose McDonald's mum. I think you know Jose too. Is that right? She's a friend of yours on Face Book?" She waited, wondering at the same time why the hell Jose would be a friend to such a little snot, and not tell them sooner about the message that had been posted after all that had recently happened, albeit 'not that long ago' Jose had explained defensively from her hospital bed. The boy cautiously nodded to her question. "OK, as I said, you're not going to get into trouble. But apparently, you posted something on Face Book a few weeks ago about your friend's disappearance. Just a few hints I know. If anyone didn't know the situation, they wouldn't have twigged, but I know the circumstances. I just want to know exactly what you meant by it. It was something like you saw Jason walking with some-one. Is that right?"

Alfie again shuffled his feet, looking at Ginge for support, who shrugged his shoulders as though to say, 'After-the-Sue-remark, you're-on-your-own'.

"Oh, for Christ's sake, Alfie," Heidi suddenly exploded. "This is important. The kid, *your mate*, got horribly murdered. Surely you want to help find who bloody murdered him. What are you afraid of?"

"His dad," Ginge answered quietly. He looked down at his feet.

The girls looked from Ginge to Alfie and back to Ginge in exasperation.

"His dad!" Emma held out her hands in a pleading manner. "Please Joey, *I mean Ginge,* help us out here. What does that mean, his *dad*!"

"Don't say nuffink," pleaded Alfie, looking at his friend, the cockiness now replaced by a begging look.

"I gotta, Alfie." Ginge turned to Emma. "Dunno what he put on Facebook. I know he saw something. He told his dad and his dad said keep stumn."

"But why?" Heidi shook her head. "Why would your dad say that? Why wouldn't he help?"

Alfie looked at his shoes and shook his shoulders.

"Cos he's a crook," mumbled Ginge.

Alfie suddenly became alive, swinging round and shouting at his friend, "He ent, you bastard."

He is," retorted Ginge. "He gets the Healy gang to nick

cars and he does 'em up at his garage and sells 'em on… mostly abroad. Me dad says he's probably making a mint so 'e don't want no cops knocking on the door."

Before the situation got too out of hand, Heidi interrupted. "Please Alfie, this is desperate. I don't suppose at this point in time the cops are worried about a few nicked cars. They're desperately trying to find a man and woman who are killing women and young kids, kids like you. If you saw something, please, please tell us. We won't tell your dad. You won't get into trouble; I swear on the bible."

The silence after her outburst was tangible, the very air between them seemed to vibrate with expectation.

"Please." Emma entreated softly.

So, tears slowly trickling down his face as he talked, the burden of the conscience that had made the child suffer tormented sleepless nights, and jagged nightmares when he did sleep, unfolded themselves in hesitant, stumbling words.

Chapter 65

As Dan turned into Sara's road, he passed a jogger. He recognised the long, slim body of the enigmatic Lucy Hamilton. He drove passed and turned into Sara's drive. Switching off the engine, he shook his head in amazement that Lucy would be exercising on this cold and blustery evening. Autumn leaves swirled along the road and he could feel the first drops of the forecast heavy downpour trickling down his face as he alighted the vehicle.

By the time he had locked the car, she had reached the driveway. She stopped, putting her hand on her hips, and breathing heavily, panted, "Gott im Himmel, the long-lost DS Blake at last."

A small grin creased his mouth, and shaking his head in wonderment, replied, "Aah, the totally mad exerciser, Ms Lucy Hamilton I presume."

She laughed, and thanking him as he opened the gate, asked, "Why mad? What sort of greeting is that when I haven't seen you in what, three, four years?"

"Not quite right, saw you at the Indian corner shop if you remember, just a few weeks ago."

"Well, not counting that occasion. Anyway, you're only here now because I touched your conscience about not contacting your friend, Sara."

He rang the doorbell. "Ok, touché. Jesus, only seen you

for ten seconds and you're nagging me already."

Before Lucy could reply, Sara stood in the doorway, the bright lights of the house looking welcoming, and silhouetting her petite stature.

Dan did not speak but stepped into the house and wrapped his huge frame around the tiny woman. Lucy looked down. She could feel tears fighting their way like determined invaders to the front of her eyes and blinked furiously to urge them away. When they eventually pulled apart, Sara pulled Lucy into the hallway.

"You don't normally grin like that when I get here," Lucy told her host, pulling off the small backpack from her shoulders.

"That's because you're not six foot five, red-headed and devastatingly handsome," Dan replied, his grin matching Sara's in its size. Lucy noticed that although he directed the remark to her, he was still gazing at Sara. She didn't mind, knowing their friendship went back many years, and although they had never explained their deep bond, she knew it was something special.

Sara's husband, Alex, had been stabbed some years ago. A woman paedophile had attacked Dan, and Alex had stepped in front to defend him. It had been a terrible incident, and obviously Sara had been devastated, but so had Dan, both with remorse for his friend's death and the burden of the guilt because Alex had lost his life in defending him. It all seemed a long time ago now, but Lucy knew how his death had affected all of them.

"Come into the living room," Sara said. "I want you to meet someone special."

"I'll go and shower quickly," said Lucy, and picking up her backpack, hurried up the stairs. She had stayed with Sara for three months after Alex's death, so this house was a second home to her.

Taking Dan's hand, Sara pulled him along the hall into the room on the right. As he walked in, he immediately recognised two of the men sitting either side of a log fire roaring away in the fireplace.

A tall, dark haired Freddy Mercury look-alike stood up and offered his hand. "DS Dan Blake. Long time, no see." He turned to his companion who then stood up and also stretched out his hand, "You remember my partner, Pete."

"Hi," said Dan as they shook hands. "Not sure we met, but you're a chef I believe."

"Yes, that's right. You've got a good memory. Still, suppose being a cop, that's no bad thing. I'm the drinks server, so what's your fancy, beer, G and T?"

"Beer's good."

"Thanks, Pete," said Sara. "OK, now the surprise." She turned and nodded towards a couple sitting on the couch. "This is my sister Debbie and her husband John."

Dan could not have been more astonished if she'd hit him on the head with the poker lying across the fire grate. He had known Sara for over twenty years, thought he knew every details of her childhood, and could never recall her ever mentioning a sister. The shock must have revealed itself clearly because Sara chucked and said gleefully, "It's not often I get to see that expression. I've really surprised you this time, haven't I?"

Dan nodded as he studied the woman sitting on the sofa. She smiled shyly and asked, "Can you see the resemblance? Freddy and Peter reckon they can."

"Yes," he admitted, "Different coloured hair but same nose and eyes."

Sara leaned over and held her face near her sister's, still grinning so much the expression was dancing all over her cheeks. "Dove grey, large and sexy. Is that what you're suggesting?"

"If you say so. Is Debbie as modest as you too?"

John stood up and the two men shook hands. "I can answer that. Debbie is the shy and retiring one. Sara's told us you've known each other for a long time, so I guess that you've probably known her character for years, but what *we've* discovered in a short space of time, is that Sara's the big, mischievous sister!" He glanced from his wife to a grinning Sara. "But discovering each other has made them both happy."

Before Dan could ask for more details, Sara insisted that they sit at the dining room table or the dinner would burn. She would explain everything as they ate. Lucy walked into the room at that moment, looking pink from the shower and her long hair still slightly damp. She wore tight fitting black jeans and a pink top with a sequinned heart in the front. Dan recalled how towards the end of their association, he had to control his feelings toward her.

Her dog had uncovered human body parts whilst they were out running together in the park. He was the investigating officer on the case, and for a time he was firmly convinced that her involvement and behaviour placed her very high on the list of suspects. This was mainly because a background check had shown her as uncommonly clean as the proverbial virgin snow, or more aptly, a religious zealot. Although he initially could not uncover a motive, it still made his naturally suspicious nature wary of her innocence. Later in the investigation, his boss had, right out of the blue, ordered him to remove her from his list of suspects unless something indisputable proving her guilt appeared, otherwise, she was not to be hassled and considered a suspect. Dan never did find out the reason for this, and when the true culprits were exposed, obviously other things took priority and he forgot the incident.

Sara conveniently placed Lucy opposite Dan. He guessed once more his dear friend was match making. Since his divorce six years ago, she had never stopped trying to marry him off, or at least, get him a steady girlfriend. He glanced across the table at Lucy and decided for once that he was pleased with Sara's 'girl-friend-meddling', as he called it.

Sara and Debbie brought in huge dishes full of delicious smelling food, and Dan felt his tummy grumble in anticipation, and remembered he hadn't eaten since a hastily woofed down two Weetabix that morning and was starving.

Curry was one of Sara's specialities, and no-one was disappointed in her efforts. The chicken dish was spicy without burning the mouth, and she had added chopped coriander that everyone agreed enhanced the taste and made it even more delicious.

Freddy was his usual crazy self, and after eating two huge bowls of curry and rice had leaned back in his chair and belched. Sitting on the right of Lucy, she batted him round the head with the serviette and told him not to be such a rude pig. Everyone had laughed and that had set the tone for the fun evening.

Dan had insisted on helping Sara clear the table and pack the dishwasher.

"Not that I'm house proud," he explained to the jeers from Freddy who said he was a creep, "But I want to hear the story of how the two sisters found each other."

Dan handed the crockery to Sara and as she packed it into the dishwasher, she told him the tale. "After Alex had gone, despite Lucy and Freddy being wonderful; around here pretty often, and taking me out and about, I still felt lost. I knew you'd been seconded to London or the north somewhere, so this isn't a dig at you. You've got a busy job and I know all these years of relentlessly searching for the paedophiles that took you when you were a kid are still eating away at you. Well, I started to understand your ... quest...mission, or whatever you want to label it."

She finished packing the plates away and picked up the bowls for the dessert. Leaning back against the kitchen cabinet, her eyes took a faraway look as she talked. "I started remembering that I had a little sister. I think I once told you, my dad had died when I was about four. Debbie was two, but I maybe didn't mention her. Anyway, Mum remarried about three years later and my stepfather was a sod. Mum died when I was thirteen, and within six months, he married a woman who was as equally cruel as he was. She gave my sister away, to a woman who couldn't have kids. I kept remembering we clutched each other as they came to take her away, really crying and sobbing. It didn't make any difference; they still took her. As you know, things went from bad to worse and I ran away to London... where I eventually met Stu."

She paused. Dan brushed away a lock of hair that had fallen over her right eye. "Slip of the tongue," he murmured. "I thought you agreed that Sharon and Stuart were forgotten, and forever you were Sara and Alex."

She sighed, "Yes, I know. That fateful day we rescued you..."

"And the even more fateful day when you and Stu... umm, Alex ran into me and my Nan in the supermarket, and I recognised you as my rescuers."

"Yep, fate I guess, and here we are today." She sighed even more deeply. "Anyway, as I said, I felt so empty. I decided to look for my sister. I hadn't worked for years. Alex had left me comfortably off, so I had the time and money. It was easy really.

"I knew her birthdate, where she'd been born, her... our parents' names. I then had a brain wave or whatever you'd call it. I suddenly recalled Debbie had been given to my stepmother's, may she burn in hell forever, sister-in-law, Susan. I remembered I had quite liked her, the sister-in-law I mean, on the couple of occasions I'd met her. Apparently, she was a good mum to Debbie, but whenever Debbie asked about her previous family when she was older as she knew she was adopted, her new mum clammed up. Susan's still alive today. Turns out my stepfather had told his sister Susan, after I'd run away, that I was a wicked bitch who'd run away with a drug dealer. So naturally, as the evil bugger intended, and Susan not wanting to upset Debbie, always maintained she didn't know any details or the situation. Which, to be fair, she didn't really.

"It only took me six months and I tracked her down. As soon as I contacted her and we met, it was like we'd never been apart." She bent her head and wiped away the tears beginning to form in the corners of her eyes. Dan hugged her, and a lump came into his throat as she sobbed, "I just wish she could have met Alex."

"Come on, honey, wipe away the tears. I'm so pleased you've found Debbie. That was fate too you know." Dan leaned away from her, and from his height of over a foot above her petite frame, he noticed a smile begin to form. "That's my girl, let's take the pud into those greedy pigs."

She giggled and the sad moments were over.

The rest of the evening was a great success. Peter insisted on leaving promptly at eleven thirty as he had to be up at five to leave for work, and although Freddy argued, his partner was adamant. "If you don't want to walk home in the pouring rain, we go now!"

Debbie and John were sleeping the night and not going home until the next afternoon. Lucy was going to change back into her running gear and run home, but Dan insisted that even a mad woman like her couldn't surely *want* to run in the storm that had now settled itself firmly over the area, and that he would take her home.

They drove in a comfortable silence. It only took ten minutes door to door. As Dan switched off the engine, he said. "Driving didn't take long, but running, you'd have got pneumonia by now."

"Yes, I know you're right. I'm grateful. I didn't want to put you out."

She went to open the door, but he told her to wait. He got out of the car, got an umbrella from the back seat, and covered her as he walked her to the apartment's front door.

"Didn't realise you were such a gentleman," she said, as she pressed in the numbers on the apartments front entrance's security pad. "You gave me a bad time, you know, during that investigation."

"Sorry, only doing my job."

"Yeah, I know. Yet you suddenly stopped hassling me. Right out of the blue. Why was that?"

Despite the umbrella, the water was beginning to trickle down his collar. Moving under the porch, he put down the umbrella and said, "Do you really want to know?"

At her nod, he continued, "It was weird. My boss told me to stop. Just like that. Unless I had evidence the size of a barn door, which I obviously didn't, to remove you quickly from the list of potential suspects."

He didn't say any more. Just stared at her. His job had taught him that silence often encourages conversation. The silence continued, which surprised him, and although it was dark, he could have sworn her pallor altered, maybe to a blush, or had she gone pale?

He bent down suddenly and pecked her on the cheek. "Never mind, you don't have to say a thing, sweet enigmatic Ms Hamilton. We all have our secrets. I have mine."

He put up the umbrella and walked away a few yards. He knew she was still staring at him. Turning, he said, "At the moment, I'm deep into an inquiry. When I'm not working all the hours under the sun, fancy going to the jazz club, having a few jars?"

She considered a few moments before replying. "Sure. That'd be nice. You thinking of re-joining the gym again?"

"No way. Only joined because I was keeping an eye on my undercover colleague."

"You're joking! I *knew* you weren't interested in getting fit. I thought you were there because you were watching me, convinced I'd killed those people, and dumped the body parts myself."

He grinned, and even in the dim light, she could see his white teeth gleaming. "You obviously suffer from a constant guilty conscience. I'll give you a call then."

He turned and walked away. As Lucy let herself into the building and walked up the stairs, she recalled how she had convinced herself that he'd suspected her. She was afraid his suspicions would mean he'd dig and dig and perhaps her secret would be exposed.

Turning the key in her front door, she prepared herself for her dog, Higgins, to throw himself at her in expectations of a walk. When he didn't, she went straight to her bedroom, where she found the guilty party snuggled up on her bed. He opened one eye, shook his head as though to tell her he wasn't that desperate for a pee, he could hear the rain lashing on the windows, thank you very much!

She walked to the kitchen to make a hot drink. "Dogs or men, don't know which are worse," she muttered. The thought of an evening with Dan was agreeable though. She felt somehow comforted by his comment that he had a secret too.

As she sipped her drink, she thought about the mystery in her life that forced her to be wary of whomsoever she met. Except for the person who had placed her in police protection when she was eleven, as far as she knew, he was now the only one who knew about her past. Presumably hidden deeply in some obscure files somewhere was the story of what had happened to her.

It was probably of no interest to anyone anymore, so when her contact died, the secret would die with him. In her heart, she knew her silence and wariness were redundant, but all the years of metaphorically looking over her shoulder was a bad obsession, but she couldn't kick it.

She still died her hair darker and wore coloured contact lenses to alter her appearance, and although often annoyed at her needless caution, the habit was unbreakable.

The murder of her father and brother by her mother that she had witnessed as a child was hidden in a file the back of her mind. Her testimony had ensured her mother would stay in jail for the rest of her life, but her mother's family had threatened her, even though still a child, and the authorities had been forced to protect her, hiding her away in police protection all these years. She knew her mother would always remain in jail and guessed most of her siblings were either dead or had forgotten her, and probably couldn't care less where she was or what she was doing, but the fear for her life was a deep scar and wouldn't heal.

Finishing her drink, she rinsed her cup and said out loud. "Ok, that giant of a red-headed man's...umm...dishy. When, ha ha, if he ever gets around to asking me out, I'm going to accept. If it comes to something, and I umm... should eventually marry him...or something, I'm bloody well going to tell him all about my past." She laughed as she dried the cup and put it in the cupboard, and shouted, "And then I'll stop dying my hair, stop wearing bloody coloured contact lenses. I'll stop keep frantically exercising to keep slim, I'll eat loads, have four kids and get fat!"

As she left the kitchen, she laughed to herself, realising they hadn't even had a first date yet! Walking into the bedroom, Higgins looked at her in amazement as though to enquire what the hell all that yelling was about that had so disturbed his forty winks!

Chapter 66

Meena randomly spread seventeen prospective photographs over the table in Interview Room 1 situated next to the incident room. She did not want to influence Emma's choice in any way when she came to check the images. Just because Dan, Luke and she had selected five photographs that, in their opinion, resembled the man both from the security cameras outside the nightclubs and the same person illustrated in Emma's helpful sketch, she needed the girl to make her own unbiased decision. She took the five they had chosen and randomly spread them between the seventeen.

Checking her watch, she decided she just had enough time to grab a coffee from the machine along the passageway outside the room. She had no sooner picked up the cup of foaming liquid, when WPC French, who had been staffing the front desk, walked towards her with Emma and another girl whom Meena hadn't seen before.

"Just in time," she greeted them. "Fancy a drink?"

Both girls nodded and Emma said, "A chocolate, please, if there's one of those."

"Me two," her friend agreed.

"This is me mate, Charlene," Emma explained. "She's seen Matthew too. He chatted her up once in the Prada Night club. She's got the day off, so she said she'd come and look at the photos too, if it helps."

"Excellent." Meena handed the two beverages to the girls and walked to the interview room. Opening the door, she turned and invited Emma in. Turning to her companion, she explained, "If you'd sit on this chair outside, Charlene, Emma can come and check these images first. I want one person's decisions not to influence the other's. So, Emma first, then Charlene. You OK with that?" At Charlene's nod, she led Emma into the room and indicated the photos that were spread out haphazardly over the desk.

"Who're all these blokes?" said Emma, looking at Meena with eyes wide open with shock. "They all suspects or something?"

"A selection of people we think bear some resemblance to the CCTV images and your sketch. Just take your time; we need you to be sure."

Meena watched as the girl sipped her drink, slowly looked over the images, moving from the left side of the table, to the right. She was thorough, and on occasions leaned forward, her face only six inches above the photographs. Eventually, placing her cup on the end of the table, she took a deep breath, and picked out three of the copies. She then took them to the end of the table where there was a space, laid them down in a row, and continued her perusal of the remainder. "It's none of these," she muttered. Shaking her head, she returned to the three set aside, picked up the one on the left and placed it back with those she had discounted.

She straightened, picked the two remaining pictures, and looked at Meena with a puzzled look on her face. She waved her selection. "Right, these two. It's weird. I thought I'd be able to pick him up easily. This is him…the one you've got in the security cameras is a def. That's Matthews. In my sketch, I'm sure I'd captured the evil expression in his eyes. When I talked to Charlene, she'd spotted that look too, and though this one's not a good enough quality, yet that's him." The girl glanced again at the snapshot, shaking her head. "It's none of the others. Except this one." She picked up the second photograph she had chosen, and Meena was shocked because neither she nor her colleagues had picked it out, recalling in fact, that he had been easily disregarded by all three of them because except for being tall, he didn't appear to resemble Nielson in any way. Before Meena could question her, she continued. "Yeah, really weird. I'm sure it's him, but it's like it's an…dunno…alter ego as they says in the films." Emma looked at Meena. "He doesn't resemble him yet…it's him as well, but it's like something's missing from his expression. Like he could be two characters, the one in this photo, and an identical person that's his evil counterpart, the one from the security cameras. I know this ones got glasses on, different hair style…but it's *his* face, but different."

Meena picked up the photo that Emma had selected and checked the number on the list against the names she had recorded of all the people whose photos they had taken. She put it back next to the security camera snapshot.

Emma looked at the two photos on the desk. "Sounds daft, I know." She stepped back and said, "See why you didn't want me and Charlene in here together." Looking at the police officer, she added, "Be interesting to see what Charlie thinks."

"Thanks, Emma." Meena took the photograph and once again distributed it amongst the others, moving a few here and there to place them in an unsystematic pattern. She was still in shock and could barely stop her hand shaking.

"Shall I sit outside?" asked Emma.

"No, you needn't, but as I said earlier, I wanted you both to make your selection without influence. Sit over by the window. I'll call in Charlene."

Meena opened the door and beckoned the girl in. Indicating the selection distributed over the table, she explained. "Take your time. I want you to look at them all. Then select the one, or ones, that in your opinion, is the man you saw at the Prada nightclub talking to Lily Taylor and asked you to dance. On the other hand, if none of them resemble him in your opinion, then that's your call."

Meena sat herself next to Emma and watched as Charlene peered at the images. Like Emma, she bent over and put her face close to them. She hummed, and one by one tapped them with her fore finger of her right hand, shuffling along inches from left to right to cover the area. Straightening up, shook her head, then bent down again, moving from the right to the left this time. She performed this action three times, before straightening up again, saying, "It's confusing. They're so many. They looks…well, not the same, but well similar so it's hard to choose."

Emma leaned over and whispered into Meena's ear, "She's a Gemini or som'ink, never can make a decision. Tell her to take out first the ones that are definitely not Nielson. We'll be here all frigging day otherwise."

"Good thinking." Meena, surprised by Emma's obvious common sense, suggested, "Charlene, why don't you take out, say five photos, that are definitely not Nielson, in your opinion."

The proposal seemed to untangle the girl's muddled decision-making, and quickly she had put five aside, remarking, "It definitely ent them."

"OK, now do the same. Take out the next five. That way you whittle them down to a few, and you can study them and make a decision."

Again, this worked, and gradually she placed more and more on the 'definitely not' pile. Eventually, with four images left, she once again hummed and tapped on her chin. She then took out two and put them aside, leaving just the two, and continued to study them.

Turning to Meena, she shocked her by then using practically the same meaning as her friend in expressing her feelings, yet they had not conferred. Picking up the photo on the left, she said, "I was so sure I'd be able to pick him out …but…umm… this is a dead ringer for him. Yet it isn't. He hasn't got that dangerous look. I'd recognise that anywhere. If he walked in now, I'd know him. This…" she waved the same photograph, "well, looks like 'im with all the madness let out of him. Well weird. This other one is him like he was at the night club. Not just his clothes and hair an' that, but it's him, the mad version. The other one is where it's him with all the madness gone."

Meena took the photo that Charlene had selected and thanked both girls for their efforts.

"Did we both choose the same bloke?" asked Emma.

"Yes, you did," she answered. She could barely get the words out. The shock was making her feel cold, as though her limbs were encased in ice.

"Can you tell us his name?" said Charlene. "Well, we knows he calls himself Matthew Nielson, but I reckon that's not his real name."

"I am extremely grateful to you both. However, as the enquiry is still on-going, I cannot reveal that information at this time. We still have to make further investigations, and obviously I cannot compromise those."

Meena noticed the two girls glance at each other, and was about to query whether they had a problem, when Charlene said, "The one we picked out. Not the Matthew going into Prada or Hades, but the other one. Is he David Sinclair, the Deacon at St Anne's?"

Meena took a deep breath. "Umm, I can't confirm his name due to the on- going inquiry. However, I must ask, what information do you have that makes you suspect him and then pick him out?"

"You tell her," said Charlene, looking at Emma. "You're better at telling them sort of fings than me."

"Tell me what?"

"Yeah, we know he's the Deacon at St Anne's, and he plays the organ, I think. It's something Jose told us. Her mum goes to that church though Jose don't if she can get out of it. Anyway, Jose's always on Face Book, talking to some-one. She's got loads of 'friends'. One of them's an Alfie Smith, he's only nine so God knows why she talks to him on it, or that his mum allows him to use it. He goes to St Anne's as well…in the choir. Anyway, apparently a few weeks back he posted something on there about Jason Stone."

"Jason Stone, the child who went missing some time ago?" Meena's eyes were open in surprise, her shock apparent in her words. This was the last thing she had expected to hear.

"Yes, that's right. Anyway, apparently Alfie was hanging around the graveyard one night, having a fag. He filches them from his dad who leaves his ciggy packet on the coffee table. He saw Jason walking away, hand in hand with David Sinclair. He plays the organ like I said and helps out Father Bryan with the choir practice as well sometimes."

Meena took a deep breath. "He's absolutely sure about this?" Both girls nodded.

"He told his dad, but he told him not to interfere. Not to say a word."

"What? His *dad* told him to not say anything."

Emma nodded again. "Yes, his dad's the local crook. Pays the Healy gang, the local thugs from Whitley Grove, to nick cars. Rumour has it he does 'em up in his garage lock-up place and sells them on."

"Surely a missing boy takes precedent over that. Even if he'd phoned in anonymously, it would have given us a lead. What about Alfie, wouldn't he…" Meena stopped, realising that in her disbelief and shock, she wasn't sounding very professional.

"It's not just that, Miss," interrupted Charlene. "It's what else he saw that frightened him, and that's also why his dad insisted he didn't say nothing."

"What in the world *did* he see?"

Charlene looked again to Emma. She said quietly, "He reckons he saw the devil."

Meena looked from one girl back to the other. "The devil! I don't understand…"

"No, you wouldn't. We didn't know whether to mention it or not. You'll think it's ridiculous. You see, Alfie's got the gift."

"The gift. What gift?"

"Look," continued Emma. "I don't believe in religion, God and all that bollocks. Alfie's mum's a catholic, so when, as a kid, she found she had the gift, she was well choked because she believes in heaven and hell and all that. But she can see halos round peoples' heads. The church lot don't like things like that. Apparently, her great grandma was a Romanian gypsy or something, and loads of them have this gift. When people are evil, apparently their halos are so black, it hurts their eyes." Emma paused. "I know it sounds well stupid. I can see from your face what you're thinking, but even I, the biggest non-believer in Reading, have heard about her gift. She could tell good from evil."

"She and Father Bryan have prayed and prayed for the gift to go away, 'cos, you know, it's not what Christians believe in." continued Charlene. "It did go away a bit, but all that happened was that it passed to Alfie."

"And he saw the devil with Jason," said Meena, the disbelief still painting her voice.

"Yes, David Sinclair was holding his hand, but the devil was behind them, disguised as a woman. She had a long, black coat, and long, black hair with a blond streak. Alfie said the halo round her head was so black, so evil, he nearly passed out, and he felt sick." Emma paused, but Meena just stared at her. "When we questioned Alfie, he used words a thick, nine-year-old doesn't normally know. He said, I quote, 'she was the devil incarnate, personified in the body of a woman'. When he's 'touched by the gift', he says really grown up things."

Meena was still speechless, but despite the crazy words, a feeling of dread cut spitefully along her spine as though someone with a sharp knife was carving her back. Despite her different religious convictions, and in spite of her normal reaction to anything that was not hard evidence, she had the over whelming conviction that what she was hearing was the truth, and that sometimes in this world there are things outside our normal understanding of life as we know it.

"What's this got to do with Mathew Nielson, the person you've picked out from the photos?"

"Maybe they're in cahoots; maybe brothers, the good one and the dead evil one," offered Charleen.

"As Alfie was telling me," said Emma, her face now white with the trauma of her story, "I had, like an image come into my brain, and I saw her as clear as anything. Not the halo or nothing, just her face. It was the taxi driver who took me to Loddon House that night. Matthew's friend. She's that devil! I'd bet my life on it."

Chapter 67

Arthur checked his watch. Ten past ten; he'd arranged to meet the 'kidnapper' as he labelled him at ten o'clock at their previous meeting place, the Blue Bird coffee shop.

The same diminutive waitress with the ponytail and overly made-up eyes had welcomed him and smiled a greeting of recognition. Being acknowledged as a previous customer probably pleased most people, but Arthur did not want to be recalled, so although too late on this occasion, he resolved not to use this venue again.

Arthur hated unpunctuality and could feel the annoyance creeping up his limbs like nipping bugs. Luckily, before his annoyance soared too high, and the nipping turned to biting, his invitee walked through the door. He spoke to the waitress who was hovering by the notice board near the entrance who pointed in Arthur's direction. The short, stocky man waddled through the tables to the quiet niche where Arthur was seated.

Pulling the chair from under the table and plonking himself down into it, he wheezed and coughed before he said, "Sorry I'm late. There's been a prang along the Oxford Road. Everybody's been held up for ages." Leaning back in his chair, he took a deep breath. "I know you hate lateness, but it couldn't be avoided. To make up for it, cakes and coffee are on me."

Somewhat mollified, Arthur thanked him. A stout black woman appeared and asked them if they were ready to order.

"Coffee and lemon Danish for me," said Arthur's guest. "What's yours, Arthur?"

"The same."

As the woman hurried to the kitchen, Arthur leaned forward, his voice, quiet but decidedly sharp and snapped. "What the hell are you doing, saying my name? Now, if ever asked, she'll remember me. Names facilitate memories."

"Oh, for God's sake, she probably couldn't tell anyone your name if asked in the next five minutes."

"We stay safe, keeping steady with the Plimsoll line as it were, because our security should be watertight. Just remember that; never mention anybody's real name."

His guest looked discomforted and muttered an apology. At Arthur's nod of acceptance, he whispered, "Thought you had nicknames anyway."

"We used to have code names, but that was Gerry Tomas's stupid idea. He's dead and gone so we don't bother with those. However, our security is strict, and it works."

"Ok, sorry. What did you want me to do this time?"

"We want you to pick someone up, for questioning. After the last debacle, we are not going to question him at his house, as you suggested last time. Before you comment, I don't blame you for that. I think it was an unfortunate coincidence that a policeman turned up, I assume just one, because as we hurried out of the house, we only saw one person peering in at the window." Arthur took a deep breath before continuing. "When I look back on the event, I believe maybe O'Leary was expecting him …"

"Has anything come of that? Any ramifications?"

"No, and as O'Leary has no idea who we were, I don't expect any consequences. Hang on, the waitress's coming with our order; wait until she's out of earshot."

The two men were silent as she put the cups and plates on the table, and both sipped their drinks and bit into their cakes before continuing. Swiping the crumbs from his hands over his plate, Arthur leaned forward and continued his instructions, his voice still low as the coffee shop was beginning to fill up with customers, and he did not want eavesdroppers.

Handing a photograph and some written instructions under the table to the kidnapper, he explained. "That's him. His name's David Sinclair. His address and schedule over the next three days are listed on the paper. I'm hoping you can pick him up tomorrow, or Thursday at the latest."

The guest glanced at the photograph and the details. "I'll need help on this one if he's to be picked up efficiently and without fuss. It'll cost."

"That's fine. I've taken account of that in my planning."

"Where do you want him taken? The usual, or why not at his place the same as we did for O'Leary's? I know that didn't work but…"

"No, this way will be safer. The address to take him to is written in red. There'll be no trouble. It's a quiet country cottage of a member of the …umm, shall we say, of our committee. He's happy for the interview to take place there. No near neighbours, no snoopers. Fortunately, his family are away at his wife's sister for a week. We'll need you to be there to restrain him."

The waitress appeared again, and they ordered more coffee. The men's heads were almost touching as Arthur finished explaining the entire plan, and they only moved apart when their drinks arrived.

"All clear? Any questions?" asked Arthur.

"No, it's clear. The only thing is, you don't like me having your mobile number, so how am I to contact you when we've appropriated him, then when we're on our way with the 'goods', as it were."

Arthur handed him a mobile phone. "It's new. Never been used. There's just one number on it. When you have him, phone the number, and say where you are and how long you will be before he is...umm, delivered. Then destroy the sim card and the phone. Do not keep it or ever use it again. Understand?" At the man's nod, he said. "Good."

The two men finished their coffee, tipping back their heads in mirror images of each other. Replacing the cups on the saucers, they left the coffee shop together, one walking east and the other west. Neither said goodbye, it was just a business deal, not friends parting.

Chapter 68

Dan nodded to the young female police officer staffing the front desk. Despite only having walked forty yards from where he parked his car, the pouring rain had managed to find the gap between his coat collar and shirt, and he could feel a cold trickle of water creeping down his shoulders and back. About to make a remark to the WPC about the foul, English weather, she nodded towards a grey-haired man in a smart navy-blue suit and a young man with a ponytail, more casually dressed, sitting to the left of the desk, and whispered, "There's a Mr O'Leary and a Mr Connor Murphy, waiting to see you, sir. Said it's extremely important. Wouldn't see anybody else except 'the boss'."

Dan glanced towards the man. "OK, I've got a meeting now with 'the boss', DI Cole." He needed to update his boss on the surprise of the two girl's revelations and discuss picking up Sinclair. He was as shocked and puzzled as Meena when she had relayed the facts that the girls had supplied and knew his boss should be informed as soon as possible. Raising his eyebrows and giving a slight shake of his head, as though to emphasise he was therefore not the person to see at this point, he said, "What about…"

"DI Cole's been called away, asked me to tell you. Won't be back until later this afternoon."

Dan attempted again to delegate the meeting to either

Meena or Luke when the older man stood up and walked over to Dan. He held out a laptop and said in a Southern Irish accent, "I assure you I won't be wasting your time, sir. This is me best friend's nephew." He nodded towards the young man. "What he has discovered is unbelievable. It's disgusting, revolting and foul; all rolled into one. Child pornography."

Dan went to speak, but the man, his accent getting stronger as he progressed with his story, interrupted, "Excuse me, sir, I have to explain, and you'll soon know why. Me name's O'Leary. I'm a teacher at St Steven's Jesuit Academy. I've been reading in the papers and hearing on the news and such like about all these children gone missing from this area, and it said you yourself were leading the investigation. Well, sir, this may well upset a good man like yourself, but on the other hand, it may well help with your enquiries."

With his meeting with DI Cole obviously delayed, Dan knew he had time to speak to the two men, and if what the elder man inferred was correct, it could prove helpful in moving forward the investigation.

"Right, Mr O'Leary and Mr Murphy, follow me. We'll use Interview Room 1 if it's free, through these swing doors."

As Dan passed reception, he glanced towards the young policewoman sitting there on duty and cupped his hand towards his mouth as though drinking. She grinned and nodded, used to Dan needing constant hot drinks.

The three men entered Interview Room 1 where Dan formally introduced himself and they settled themselves around the smaller round table in the far corner away from the oblong table used for interrogations. No sooner than they were seated, O'Leary pushed the laptop towards his nephew. "Right, lad, show this good man what you've found."

It took Connor two minutes to switch on and make his

way through the barriers constructed within the software to stop anyone finding the site by chance unless they possessed the critical passwords and knowledge to penetrate the various levels. He moved his chair nearer to Dan so they could both see the screen clearly.

His finger hovered over the enter button as he said, "I think I should warn you, sir, what I'm about to show you is extremely unpleasant. I'm sure as a police officer, you've seen some horrible things, but unless you've served in a vice unit, this may well shock even you. I've had nightmares these last couple of days since I've seen this site." His words, although dramatic, were not varnished with an over-the-top theatrical tone.

Dan nodded. "OK, I appreciate that." He looked as the screen as Connor hit the entry button. As picture after picture of young children in implicit, sexual poses passed over the screen, Dan was glad of the warning, but even so, a lump of horror slowly formed in his throat, and his insides flinched with painful cramps as he viewed the nauseating images.

Connor shut the screen down. "I don't think you need to see anymore."

"No, I don't but…"

"DS Blake, I think I need to go back to the beginning and explain just how this all came about." O'Leary then explained what had happened from when he had gone to his house at half term: men breaking in and overpowering him there, their questions and how his friend's prank of banging on the window had disturbed them, causing them to flee.

"And you've reported this to the local police I assume."

"Yes, naturally."

"And what did they say?"

"They were extremely helpful and thorough, and although their attitude was positive in terms of doing all they could to investigate why this happened, I think we all knew they weren't going to get too far. I don't know who these people are, I never saw them, and I didn't recognise their voices. The police said they were going to have local security cameras checked, but unfortunately there's none in my road."

"Right. And what was their reaction to this?" Dan gestured towards the laptop. "These images."

"They haven't seen them. My friend Shaun, the one that banged on the window and interrupted the interrogation, was talking with me after the event. Although not hurt, I was pretty shaken up as you can imagine. I just had no idea what these eejits wanted. Their stupid questions about this equally stupid phrase…"

"Rubies on the Moon, you mean."

Declan nodded. "Shaun suggested it might be some sort of code, or password. That got me thinking. I'd first mentioned it in the staff room, just telling the other teachers how I'd set this homework. Form 9 had to research about precious jewels. How they'd been formed, where they could be found, etc. One lad was obviously not paying attention, so I asked him to tell me what he'd found out about it. He just looked vague, and then probably panicked and answered, Rubies, umm, on the Moon, Sir? Everybody in the staff room laughed except Father Francis."

Declan stopped his story for the moment when the door opened, and the young WPC walked in with a tray of coffee. After thanking her, taking a sip of his drink, the Irishman continued. "This character, a fellow teacher at St Steven's, Father Francis, then kept pestering me about it, asking what it meant. I've got to confess; I don't like the man. The other teachers are splendid. He's a gobshite, if you'll pardon the expression. I didn't want to get the lad into trouble, and I thought if I tell him who said it, he might pick on the lad. I'd heard he's done it before. But he wouldn't let up, kept pestering and asking. Why would that be, I thought, unless it meant something to him?" He shrugged. "Anyway, back to the facts that we do know. When Shaun said it could be a code, password, whatever, not thinking we'd get anywhere really 'cos we're not computer experts, he spoke to his knowledgeable nephew," Declan nodded towards Connor, and continued, "to do some research on the internet. Connor's a right whiz kid, and bloody hell, this is what he came up with."

Declan sank back in his chair, took a deep breath and noisily slurped his coffee.

For a few moments, Dan pondered, a deep frown of concentration furrowing his brow. Pursing his lips, he narrowed his eyes before he turned to Connor. "And…well, what did you do? I should imagine this kind of thing isn't easy to access. It'd be well hidden, deeply disguised…"

"Yes, sir, you're dead right. It took a long time, with a lot of digging." Connor went on to explain how he and a friend, both very capable with computers, had spent a lot of time digging through the safeguards put in place that had been set up to stop anybody just hacking into the website in error. "Whoever set this up," he continued, "knew exactly what he or they were doing, and unless you had very specific information, it's extremely unlikely you'd be able to access it."

Dan stared at the young man, his mind racing. His natural suspicions as a police officer began whirling like a spin ball in his mind. "But you managed?"

Connor read his expression. "I understand what you would be thinking, sir. How would a lowly guy like me be able to access this. In my defence, all I can say is I have a first in computer studies at university. Without meaning to boast, I came first in my exams every year. My mate who helped me crack this has a top job, works at a confidential Government place set up to uncover serious government hackers. Believe me, he's the best in the world at this game.

"As I told Declan and my Uncle Shaun, we both got hooked in the end and weren't going to let the problem beat us. But eventually we discovered it was their mistake that gave it away. We considered the phrase, 'Rubies on the Moon' and decided it was, or had been, almost certainly a password at a top level in the system. If they were worried about being compromised, almost undoubtedly, they'd have changed it.

"Whoever set up the website was a very knowledgeable guy. We reckoned he was too clever to have made the mistake that was probably made, but someone else involved who wasn't so bright. As I said, 'Rubies etc' was eliminated from the top level, but many, many almost impenetrable levels below, some eejit feckin' used the password again. And that's how we got through to the website. Down deep as hell, but we cracked it."

Dan sat for a few minutes saying nothing, staring into space. The two men eventually thought he'd lost it, and coughed and shuffled their feet, wanting to bring him back to the present. They didn't realise, as did his colleagues, that he was doing what was called, 'Dan's Diamond brain thinking." Dan had also obtained a first at University, and his logical brain was working overtime, fitting all the bits of information together. The disjointed puzzle was slowly beginning to slot into place.

Eventually, leaning back in his chair, a deep frown creasing his brow, he asked, "This Father Francis. It might just be…"

"I know it isn't much to go on, but he was relentless. Believe me, that stupid phrase was very meaningful to him."

Dan took a deep breath and considered his options. It might be he was grasping at straws, but just a little word with the man may take them a step nearer the truth. He let out a sigh, suddenly aware he was holding his breath, and muttered, "I think we may have to have a conversation with him."

"Good. I just hope I'm not wasting your time, but the more I think about it, it's not my imagination running away with me. Excuse me repeating myself, but my gut feeling is that no-one can be that interested in that stupid phrase unless it's meaningful to them."

Again, Dan stared at Declan, just nodding. He stood up. "Right, gentleman, where can I contact you when I need to?" He turned to Connor. "I need to keep the laptop. I want to discuss this with my boss. I think we'll be paying a little visit to this Father Francis. Just persistently asking you a few questions isn't necessarily a crime, but when I add all the pieces, I think nothing will be lost in questioning him."

"Good. However, you can imagine, it's awkward with my working with him, and I know I've only got suspicions, but for the moment, if I needn't be named that would be helpful. I'm thinking of the school you understand. Course, if anything does turn out to be useful, you know where to find me." He shrugged.

As Dan watched the couple walk through the front door, a feeling of the puzzle slotting together nicely once more came into his mind. They might only have the corner pieces, but some of the middle parts were falling gradually into place.

Part 3
Kidnapping

Chapter 69

David Sinclair was having a wonderful evening. He had discovered an extremely rare stamp and now, with his stamp books spread out on the desk before him, his excitement was escalating as he decided where its position of pride should be in his collection book.

The unexpected knocking of his heavy door knocker made him jump. He sipped the last dregs from his cup of coffee before hurrying to the front door. Not expecting anyone, he attempted to peer through the glass panel in the door, but except for seeing a man's outline, the darkness prevented him discerning the caller's identity. He attempted to switch on the outdoor porch light, but the switch was already in the 'on' position which he thought was weird, and nothing happened.

"Odd," he mumbled, "bulb must have blown."

Slipping back the bolt, he carefully opened the door a small amount and peered into the gloom. Even the light from the streetlamp did not reveal the visitor's face, so still David could only make out his outline.

"Good evening, sir," the stranger said, his voice low and friendly. David felt re-assured and half opened the door. "Sorry to call so late," the stranger continued, his voice still soft and not threatening. "I am calling on behalf of Father Bryan. He said you could help me with my enquiries. I'm from the Church of England in Caversham." The man shivered. "Brrr, it's a bit chilly tonight. Although my questions will only take a few minutes, do you think it possible I could just step into your hall? I really hope I haven't called at an inconvenient time?"

Although his face was still in shadow, Sinclair noticed his white teeth as the caller smiled. Reassured all was well, he opened the door fully, stepped back and waved in the man, who muttered a thank you and moved passed him into the hall. Turning to shut the door, when a bizarre smelling object was clamped over his mouth and nose, it took him by surprise, and the few seconds of shock he experienced was enough for the sedating fluid on the pad to do its work. The room swam, there was a ringing in his ears, and that was all David remembered until he roused in a strange, cold room.

The room seemed to sway for a few seconds, and David gagged, and was sure he was going to be sick. Despite a light shining into his eyes, out of the brightness, a glass of water appeared on a table in front of him. Leaning forward, he went to pick up the glass when he realised his arms were pinned fast behind him. A shadow appeared at his side, lifted the glass to his lips and despite the astonishment of being in this strange situation, he gratefully glugged down all the water.

Sitting back in his chair, he took a deep breath before he quavered, "Where in the world am I? What is happening? Why…?"

Before he could ask further questions, an arm appeared from the brightly lit area before him, and a picture pushed across the table.

"Do you know this woman?" a disembodied voice asked from behind the light.

David, despite his uncomfortable position, obediently leaned forward slightly and peered at the picture. Studying it for a few moments, he leaned back, looked straight into the light, and with his voice still quivering, he said, "No, I don't know her. I've never seen her before in my life. What has this got to do with me? Why am I here?"

Another voice snarled, "You don't know her! Huh, what a load of nonsense. We believe that you and this woman are in league; and for the past few months have been abducting children."

David was now visibly shaking, and all colour had drained from his face. "This woman, who is she?" Leaning forward, he again studied the picture, his expression showing total bewilderment. Shaking his head, he said, "No, I assure you I don't know her. In fact, I can absolutely state I have never seen her before in my life." He looked up and squinted again into the light. "Why would I kidnap children? I mix with children most days, so why would I be abducting them? I wouldn't have to go anywhere, because I am surrounded by them. If I wanted to, if I was that way inclined, I suppose it would be easy just to…" He faltered, looking as though he was going to cry.

"It would be easy to just what?"

"I don't know. If I understand from your implication, it would be easy to invite them to my home and…"

"And what?"

"Please, I don't know. All I'm trying to say is…I don't know. I'm not who you think I am." Tears slowly slipped down his face. "I don't know this woman. I'm just a music teacher, and the Deacon at St. Anne's Church. I play the organ there…and at other churches if need be. I collect stamps for a hobby. I just…"

A third voice interrupted. "Now listen, stop all this I'm-so-innocent-act. We've had you watched. You attend all the schools and churches where children have gone missing. This started not long after you came into this area. It's not a coincidence."

"You're talking about the disappearance of Tommy and Jason. How can you draw these conclusions? I helped Father Bryan and some of the church congregation when we went out on our own search, as the police didn't appear to be getting anywhere." The tears streamed down his face. "With God as my witness, I swear I haven't had anything to do with these disappearances."

The questioning continued for almost another hour. The interrogators' voices grew louder and harsher with frustration, but Sinclair continued to deny any knowledge of their inquiries, and his voice and answers becoming more distraught.

Eventually the inquisition ceased, and Sinclair was aware that the cross-examiners were mumbling together, their voices mixed with frustration, presumably with their lack of progress. He was still unsure how many men were behind the light, but he suspected at least three. Hearing the scraping of chairs, and then fading footsteps, Sinclair concluded they were leaving the room, maybe for a rest. The ensuing silence was welcome, and he dropped his head forward onto his chest, took a deep breath, and appreciated the break.

The respite did not last long. He heard the door open and by the sound of the footsteps, estimated two people at least had re-entered the room. Someone slipped behind him and undid one of his hands. A cup of tea slid across the table towards him and a friendly voice said, "Ok, David. Have a cup of refreshing tea."

No other questions were forthcoming until Sinclair gratefully gulped down the drink. His throat was sore from his continual denials. As soon as he finished drinking, his free hand was tied up again.

"Better?" the same soft voice asked. He just nodded his reply. "Now David, here's where we are with this. My colleagues seem to think that you are guilty. As we explained previously, children have been going missing. According to the news, children's bodies have now been discovered in a manhole at the end of the Warren Road.

"Now, you've continuously denied being involved

in this and personally, I believe you. However, you can imagine how this looks. As my colleagues stated previously, you are often present at the schools where these unfortunate children attended." He took a deep breath, and suddenly raised his voice and said, "Right, I want this room cleared. David and I will have a private conversation."

A loud voice from the right-hand side of the light said, "No, why should we? He's guilty and I for one think we should now use more persuasive tactics to force this pervert to talk."

"No, that is not going to happen," said soft voice. "David and I are going to have a private conversation. I'm in charge, so please leave us alone."

Sinclair heard annoyed mumbling, but he estimated that two chairs scraped back in unison and detected the sound of footsteps as they left the room.

Is this good cop, bad cop?

"OK, David," good cop said, his voice still laced with a smoothing tone. "Just us two now. As I said before, I believe you. Unfortunately, as is probably obvious to you, my colleagues do not. Now, if you can just tell me what your connection is in all this, maybe we, you and I, can work this out. Then we can take you back home to your comfortable life and forget all about tonight."

"Thank you, thank you, you are so kind, but I have no idea what is going on. Yes, I know children are going missing. As I told you, I do personally know Tommy and Jason. Tommy comes to church where I play the organ and the other lad attends the school where I take music lessons on occasions when Father Blessed is absent. He's elderly now and suffers from chronic arthritis. I often have to stand in for him."

"Right." The soft voice was then silent for a few seconds. His hand pushed forward the photo of the woman once again. "And this woman, you say you don't know who she is; you have never met her."

Once again, Sinclair leaned forward and regarded the picture. Leaning back, he shook his head and looked straight into the light. "No, I don't think so." This time his voice sounded uncertain. He bent over the picture one more time, took a deep breath before saying, "Well…I'm not sure…not sure at all…but…"

He paused, waiting for his magnificent performance to convince the 'good cop'. He almost smirked when the listener, breathlessly said, "Yes, yes, you're not sure, but… what?"

The prisoner gazed into the light, assumed a doe-eyed, proverbial butter-wouldn't-melt expression as he said, his voice quivering nervously, "Well, I suppose it could be the woman…I've only seen her through the window…and she doesn't get out of the car…" He stopped for effect.

"Yes, yes," good cop said impatiently.

"I don't know her name, and I can't be sure, but there is a likeness I suppose…" Pausing again, he did not know whether to laugh at his over-acting or silently reprimand himself for taking things too far. He waited again.

"Yes, and…" the voice was now louder and almost hysterical with excitement.

Sinclair felt a giggle wriggle and curl in his innards, and he had to control himself not to allow it to burst up and out of his mouth. He could sense Matthew taking over and had to glance down to check his clothing, making sure he wasn't wearing his stalking jeans. "Well, it sort of, umm, could…vaguely… loosely, maybe…" *Stop over-doing it!* "Resemble the person who occasionally comes to the house, remember she never gets out of the car, she picks up my brother."

"Your brother!" There was a choking noise as though the words from the speaker were being strangled.

"Yes, my younger brother, Matthew."

Then there was silence for ten seconds. It took a massive amount of control for the inside giggle not to escalate into a full-blown witch's cackle. He heard the chair scrape back and the good cop run as fast as his legs would carry him to exit the room. When he heard the door slam closed, Sinclair lowered his head and allowed a controlled snigger to slip from his mouth.

Chapter 70

Dan stood alongside Luke waiting for uniformed officers who were to accompany his DC with the apprehending of David Sinclair for questioning. It was nine o'clock in the evening. A previous check had confirmed that the lights were on in Sinclair's house, which verified that the man was almost certainly in, and the journey would not be wasted.

"We're not bothering to pick up the other suspects?"

Dan shook his head. "No, not yet. We'll see what comes out of this. The two girls both picked out Sinclair. I think we should check his alibi. According to Alfie Smith, he definitely saw him with Jason on the night he disappeared. With such a strong lead, I feel, and the boss agrees, we need to absolutely confirm one way or the other that he is our offender before wasting time on those that we only think resemble the guy on the security cameras. Anyway, the other suspects mostly have alibis, so I think we see if we can break Sinclair. He's definitely the current number one suspect."

Luke nodded his agreement. "What did you make of Meena's report on what the two girls said about this lad 'having the gift'?"

"Yeah, I know it seems strange, but we both know Meena's got her head screwed on very firmly. She's not a hysteric, not prone to getting led down the wrong path. She said the weird thing was they both recognised and picked Sinclair out as the guy from the night clubs. Both girls said the same thing about him. Yet none of us even picked him out as a likely. Then using similar words, despite the glasses which obviously alters his appearance somewhat, there was still...what, a presence about him they recognised." Dan paused as he reflected on the girls' recall. "I remember Meena's report. Quote, 'all the madness let out of him'. Emma, obviously the more intelligent one, said, 'like he had an Alter Ego'. I think that's relevant."

Luke frowned, looked at Dan somewhat askance before saying. "Boss, you suggesting he has...like, a split personality?"

Dan shrugged. "Something like that. When he's out stalking, he's one personality. His Alter Ego is probably the complete opposite, a meek and mild choirmaster. OK, we can guess he's not a psychopath in the usual sense, low intelligence etc. I think, well, just a non-expert guess, that when he's the choir master he's just normal, sane, maybe most days his behaviour is stable. When his need arises, his thirst, then the other him emerges, he becomes Nielson, the sociopath. If it's him, everyone who knew him would be shocked. Yeah, maybe you're right, some sort of split personality."

"I don't know if I understand and believe all that psychological bollocks. I think it's a nut cases excuse to do what he does."

Dan grinned at his young DC. "Well, we're not the experts. But what we do know is that when Jason went missing with Sinclair, whether this young Alfie got this so-called gift or not, he's deadly accurate if his description of his accomplice is Van Looy. She definitely is the devil incarnate, black halo round her head or not."

Luke nodded. "Yeah, the lad was certainly right about her. Gifted or not, Meena and Mel reported that when they interviewed the lad it was difficult. The father didn't want him interviewed. Also, the mother, obviously nervous of her husband, agreed they couldn't speak to the lad without her husband being present. Not that we'd suggested the parents shouldn't be present obviously. Meena believes they were both panicking, probably worrying what the lad was going to say.

"It wasn't until Mel explained that if that was the case, the lad would be questioned at the Police Station and then they might have to obtain a warrant to search the house including, and this they emphasised, his garage. He suddenly changed tack and encouraged the lad to tell all he knew."

Dan grinned. "Didn't help the husband though; I understand as soon as the girls left, the lads in blue moved in anyway. The Jag and the Rover hidden in the garage are proving very interesting."

At that moment, a young, fair-haired police officer pushed open the reception door. "Car's outside, sir," she said, smiling shyly and looking in Luke's direction.

"OK, ready." As he followed the police officer, the DC looked over his shoulder and said he'd phone and update Dan as soon as they had apprehended Sinclair and were on the way back to the station.

Dan watched as the car moved away. *Let's hope this is a big leap forward*.

Slowly walking to his office, his brain was already dealing with the next puzzle. What approach they should take when they interviewed Father Francis? Since his interview with Mr O'Leary, he could not work out in his mind where this all fitted together. He knew he should be considering only the facts, and not the weird coincidence that Sinclair was almost certainly a murderer and involved with the evil paedophile Van Looy. Then suddenly they have possibly another paedophile ring in the area if the discovery of the hidden internet site that O'Leary's nephew had uncovered proved correct. Was this all a coincidence?

Did they overlap or was it just a fluke? He had not realised he'd stopped halfway up the stairs during his deliberation until DI Cole's voice filtered into his thoughts.

"You won't solve anything standing there, Blake. Get yourself sat down with a large cup of coffee at your desk and get the Diamond brain of yours working."

Dan grinned as he hurried to his desk. That large cup of coffee sounded very welcome…a good stimulant! Shame he couldn't lace it with a large whisky!

Chapter 71

Yvette Van Looy was worried. She sat in the car far enough away from Sinclair's house to observe any comings and goings, but not obvious should anyone approach the house.

Unaware she was biting her lip as she thought through the events of the last few days, she decided she had a right to be concerned, because obviously something was not right. Not that she was worried that the idiot might be in trouble, it was only how it would affect her that gave her unease.

The last time she had seen him was when they had gone to Pangbourne to 'enjoy' the company of the thick Wendy and her snotty nosed kid, and discovered they'd annoyingly done a runner. She had tried to persuade him that he needed to disappear pretty sharply, but he was adamant that he was safe for the time being. When it was convenient for him to take leave for a few weeks without arousing suspicions, he would disappear.

He'd wanted to stay with her, but she wasn't having that! Now she was wondering if she'd been wise to refuse. At least she could keep an eye on the fool. Having failed to contact him by phone over the last few days, she decided to take the risk and come to his house early in the morning. The lights in the house were on, but he hadn't answered the door. She had crept round the back of the house and peered through the study window. There was a pile of his stamp collection books heaped up, with one book open as though he'd been examining it, but he was nowhere to be seen.

Deciding that it was both easier and safer to keep watch on the property rather than keep visiting, she drove to a local transport café and bought herself a take-away coffee. Settling herself down in the car, she resolved that she'd phone him once more. If there was no reply, she'd observe the house until noon, then knock on the door one more time if necessary. If she still could not contact him, she would think the worst and lay low for a while.

By 3 pm he hadn't answered his phone again, and still hadn't appeared, so she decided to come back later that evening when he was bound to be at home after attending any school and church meetings he probably had during the day.

Arriving promptly at 8.30 she settled down with a drink from the thermos flask she had prepared should it be a long evening. Tipping down the last dregs of her coffee, she almost choked when two police cars appeared around the corner at the top of the road. One stopped at the house before Sinclair's, known as The Old Rectory. Two uniformed officers jumped out from the first car and hurried up the alleyway by the side of Sinclair's house, presumably going to the rear of the property. The second car drew up outside the front gate of his house, and a well-made, blond haired man in a dark suit, presumably a plain-clothes officer, and two more uniformed officers accompanied him up the front path to the front door.

Shite.

Slipping down as far as she could on her seat, but still able to watch the action, Van Looy was thankful she had been as careful as she had been. A feeling of déjà vu swept over her and her mind flew back two years when she had been about to pull into the space in front of her and Gerry Tomas's hideout when a large black car, not unlike the police cars situated before her, had beaten her to it. She had very sensibly driven quickly away, and the prompt action had probably saved her life because Tomas had died that day at the hands of those visitors.

Knowing she should beat a retreat if she was to ensure her safety, curiosity overcame her caution, and she could not resist watching the action. The plain clothed cop knocked repeatedly on the front door, whilst the two uniforms prowled round the front of the house, peering in the downstairs windows. Presumably, the two cops at the back were doing the same. Eventually a third person, built like a modern-day Goliath, whose muscles were obvious even under his uniform, peeled himself from the second car carrying a huge device that Van Looy recognised from seeing cop action on the TV that was used for bashing down doors. It was very effective, and it took only one blow and the door splintered and was open. The four of them tumbled through the opening and disappeared from sight.

Five minutes passed before they came out. There was a discussion on the doorstep and the plain-clothed officer was talking urgently on his mobile. By this time, the uniforms that had gone to the back of the property had now joined their colleagues at the front. After more discussion, all, except one uniform, climbed back into the two cars and drove away, leaving the one police officer guarding the house. The remaining officer did not look happy as the dark grey, pregnant looking clouds that had hung low in the sky most of the day and evening now decided to drop their load. He pulled his hat down over his brow, frowned, and Van Looy guessed that the movement of his lips suggested he was cursing his luck.

Deciding there was no more to be gained by staying; the woman slowly hauled herself into a sitting position, started the engine, slowly drawing away and passing the front of the house. She made a point of not looking in his direction, but watched from the corner of her eyes, and although he glanced briefly at the car, in her rear-view mirror she noticed he looked away the moment the car had passed him.

As she made for her apartment, she thought through her options. Obviously, the cops had not got him in custody, but after their previous discussion when he was adamant that he didn't have to disappear in a hurry, it was evident that wherever he was, it wasn't through his own design. That made things dodgy, and her choices were either that she chanced staying where she was as she was confident no-one except Nielson knew her location, but the drawback was that if they, whoever 'they' were, were also interested in locating her, they could possibly make him spill the beans. The other alternative was that she make a quick skidaddle, and get herself to somewhere safe where her whereabouts was not known to anyone. She nodded at that thought.

Yes, lay low for a few days, see if stupid twit Nielson cum Sinclair re-appears. Then I'll make a permanent decision about future moves.

Going through safe houses in her mind, she discarded all except one.

Yes, that'll do. The police have finished their investigations, and I bet they never discovered the secret room.

She drove home, relieved in one way that she appeared to have rid herself of the man, who, more and more often was proving to be an unreliable and dangerous weight round her neck. She had intended to get rid of him in the near future anyway, so it might as well be sooner rather than later. She smirked, feeling relieved that the decision had been taken out of her hands. Dismissing him from her mind, she decided to celebrate by treating herself to a takeaway curry, and afterwards open a tasty bottle of Rioja.

Chapter 72

"I feel uneasy about this."

Dan turned to look at his DC who was driving the car. "Why? We discussed our approach and you seemed…"

"Yes, uneasy," Meena replied. "What are the facts? OK, we have evidence of an extremely nasty child pornography site that has been set up so only those with knowledge understand how to access it, but I still can't see how that links us into this Father Francis." Dan went to speak, but she hurried on, "We have the strange abduction, or should I say, forced questioning of this Mr O'Leary, and I will agree that whatever information they wanted to get from him was obviously worrying them greatly."

Dan managed to get a word in eventually. "Yes, ok, it must have been disturbing for them to go to such great lengths to hijack him in his own house; keep their identities a secret and then ask him, in his words, *such a load of eejit questions*. Whatever they thought he knew meant that something happened that's dangerous to them or whatever operation they're involved in."

"They obviously thought this phrase that he used, 'Rubies on the Moon', was a phrase that he'd…what… overheard, discovered, and because it was a code or password perhaps coincidently used for their dodgy purposes, they needed to find out how he'd got hold of it."

"Exactly, and so…"

"I know all that. I have no difficulty with that. My unease is about the very loose connection this has to this Father Francis. How exactly are we going to approach this without looking idiots, or eejits as the Irish teacher would say? Except for the fact that he persistently, in O'Leary's opinion, kept asking about it, there is no connection whatsoever to him and this website showing the child pornography. Or none that is currently in our possession."

Dan thought for a moment before replying. "I see where you are coming from. However, I just wish you had been present when I talked to O'Leary and his nephew. He struck me as being a sensible bloke, head screwed very firmly on, and not given to fanciful theories. After he'd gone, I must confess to feeling slightly cautious in terms of what justification we had in pursuing it, but as I've just said, it was O'Leary's level headedness that convinced me we needed to check out this teacher. Secondly, after all the trouble we had breaking up Tomas's paedophile ring four years ago, we know we didn't apprehend all the villains; particularly the leaders of the cells; so just what if, despite all our on-going investigations, they are raising their nasty little heads above the parapet again, and somehow this Francis fellow knows something."

"You mean, the cells are reforming and becoming active. We've had no intelligence whatsoever from the grapevine, or our contacts, albeit they are thin on the ground now."

"Yep, you're right. But I've got this itch, shall we say more professionally, intuition, that something's up and running. We just keep coming back to *paedophile* or in our parlance, nonce, again. I've really considered this, and if it proves to be hot air, then so be it, but at least we didn't ignore an unexplored avenue that might have led us somewhere. How often have we heard that tale? You become so focused on one path, ie, with us, the Van Looy

347

and Nielson inquiry, that we overlooked something else we should have considered, and didn't pursue. OK, today, we might get nowhere, but for the sake of a couple of hours, we can then safely cross it off our list."

Meena stopped at some traffic lights, tapping her fingers on the steering wheel while she considered his words. As the lights changed, and she drew away, she nodded, and said, "Yes, boss, you're right." Turning her head slightly and grinning at him, she added, "Again."

"Let's just hope we're not wasting our time. Especially as Sinclair has disappeared, or at least, not to be found currently." Dan shrugged. "Maybe he got wind of something and scarpered...I dunno... odd though."

"Yes, I was talking to Luke earlier. His sudden disappearance like that, *well weird* as Emma would say." Looking in her driving mirror, and indicating she was moving over to get into the right-hand lane to turn at the next set of traffic lights, she concentrated on this task before continuing. "Luke said it appeared he was in the middle of looking at his stamp collection; lights still on in the house, yet no sign of him."

"An overcoat was hanging on a coat peg in the hall. It wasn't exactly warm weather, so he'd needed a coat."

"Like he left suddenly, unplanned. Maybe Van Looy got tired of him, decided to snatch him and do him in."

Dan laughed. "Probably the only and first decent thing she'd done in her life if that was the case. On the serious side though, if they were in cahoots, she'd have no need to take him."

"Just joking, boss. Still, looks like someone grabbed him, or he bolted quickly, and it appears unplanned. Apparently, he was due to take some piano lessons yesterday afternoon and play the organ at choir practice in the evening."

"Yes, when interviewed, Father Bryan reckons he's extremely reliable and never missed anything like that previously." Dan pointed ahead, adding, "OK, nearly there.

Second on left. Then the entrance is about two hundred yards on the left."

The police officers were silent as Meena negotiated the turn, and then drove to the school entrance. As they turned, they were prevented from driving further by two large, wrought-iron gates.

Pulling up, Meena pointed out a security voice system situated on a brick post at the left-hand side of the gate. "Can you announce us, boss."

Dan alighted from the car and pressed the button at the base of the speaker. Giving it a minute, he was about to ring again, when a metallic sounding, but polite voice asked them who was calling and their purpose.

"I phoned earlier and announced we were coming. I am Detective Sergeant Dan Blake and I am accompanied by a colleague, Detective Constable Meena Mesbah. The head of your establishment, Father Panis Angelicus, is expecting us and agreed we could interview a member of your staff."

There was silence for a few moments before the metallic voice told them that when the gates opened, they were to proceed along the gravel roadway that would eventually swing round to the left in front of the main house, and Father Peter would meet them.

With a squeak and then a groan, the gates swung slowly apart and opened.

As they drove along the driveway, both the police officers admired the stunning setting that comprised of sweeping lawns, and just beyond this a wooded wonder of huge pine, oak and weeping willows and various other foliage came into view.

"Definitely a monied area for rich kids," said Meena. "Daddy must be worth a few quid to send his little darlings to this school."

"You're not kidding."

Meena swung the car round the carriage sweep to the front of a huge, red-bricked Georgian building with steps going up to the front entrance, and white pillars supporting a wide front porch, and as promised, a man in long, black robes came through the front door and hurried down the steps. He was wearing a friendly smile as he stretched out his hand to shake hands with both the officers. If he had not been dressed in the robes of presumably a Jesuit Teacher, neither police officers would have recognised him as such. He was almost as tall as Dan except he was very slim, jet black long hair that curled onto his shoulders and was film star handsome.

"I'm Father Peter. Welcome to St. Stephens Jesuit Academy. Let me take you to see Father Panis Angelicus. He has the coffee pot already bubbling." He rubbed his hands together and shivered. "My word, it's turned cold. No doubt a hot drink will be welcome."

They followed the teacher up the steps and into the house. As they proceeded through a cavernous hallway to the right of a wide wooden staircase that divided the hall, Dan glanced at Meena and raised his eyebrows. The house was stupendous; a dark, gleaming wooden floor complimented the lighter golden colour wood panelling on the walls that rose up to a lofty ceiling. The panelling was covered with portraits, and by the style of their old-fashioned robed clothing, they probably depicted former teachers and pupils.

After a considerable walk through a long winding corridor, they frequently passed more robed teachers at the head of crocodiles of boys of varying ages, all adorned in the same uniform of long black trousers, white shirts, dark green ties and black blazers. The teachers all nodded in a friendly fashion, whilst the children's looks were wide-eyed and curious.

Eventually they arrived at a door that the accompanying Father Peter knocked on in a curiously timid way. Dan had a flash of déjà vu, his mind swept back to his school days when all too frequently he was summoned to the Headmaster for a dire punishment due to some misdemeanour or another. Glancing at Meena, he noticed her wide-eyed look, and wondered if she was having a similar experience. The voice that instructed them to enter, however, sounded a great deal more friendly than his headmaster, a Mr. Towne, and as they entered the room, his smiling face and the aroma of coffee put his mind at rest. Father Peter closed the door quietly behind them and left.

After all the introductions, the Headmaster, himself gowned in the same colour robe, invited them to sit down, and after they had both welcomed the offer of coffee, he placed the cups with a milk jug and sugar bowl on the desk in front of them. Walking around to his seat, he sat down and asked how he could help.

"As I explained on the phone, we have an unusual situation whereby some information has come into our possession that we need to pursue. We have reason to believe that a teacher at this school, Father Francis, may well be able to assist us with our enquiries."

The man stared at Dan for a few moments, no emotion showed on his face. Dan was surprised about his enigmatic expression. In his experience, most people interviewed by the police, unless experienced criminals, usually reveal some sentiment, often shock, perhaps outrage, or even guilt when often totally innocent. Blank was not usual, but before he could ponder further, the man stood up, gulped backed his coffee and said,

"Right, I'll fetch the said person immediately." He hurried from the room.

Meena looked askance at Dan, and shaking her head, said, "Weird, what was that about?"

Dan shrugged. "Don't ask me. I always find these religious types …well…weird, as you said." He drained his cup. "Anyway, not a wasted journey, coffee's good."

They waited in silence, both surveying the room that, similar to the corridor outside, was veneered with dark golden, gleaming imposing wood panels. The only decoration was a large silver crucifix that hung from the right wall, but the overall impression was of grandeur.

"Bit like I imagine the Vatican," muttered Dan. "Maybe not quite so much gold."

"Yes, what's happened to a life of poverty and abstinence?"

Before Dan could answer, the door opened and as they both turned, the head Master appeared with another man, who glanced from Meena to Dan. Father Panis Angelicus had obviously explained to him that he was needed to assist the police with an investigation, and he obviously didn't like that fact the least bit, because both officers witnessed the colour drain from his face until he was the colour of an envelope so cheap that the glue would never have stuck it closed.

Unknown to each other, their thoughts were practically identical.

There stands a frightened and almost certainly a guilty man.

Chapter 73

Yvette left the car at the end of the stony road that eventually led to the Loddon House. She sauntered past the entrance, noting the closed gates, and the fact the place had a deserted look. Observing a few feet of dangling, tatty yellow crime scene tape, the woman was now confident that the gobby Emma had reported her experience here, and the house had been subsequently examined, although the remnants of shabby tape indicated the search was long over. She and Matthew had been thorough in making sure there was nothing left in the house to incriminate them in any way. After previously walking past the next two houses along the lane and noting they were occupied; in both cases lights showing through windows and cars parked in the gardens, she then retraced her steps.

Recalling that Matthew's, aka Sinclair's job, was to keep an eye on the property for some bishop who was on a sabbatical in the United States and he was not due back for another three months. This meant the house had proved useful for their fun and games until the stupid sod had allowed that bitch Emma Bradbury to escape.

The residence had also proved very interesting. The bishop, when showing Sinclair around the house, had conveniently indicated various taps for turning back on the water, the location of fuse boxes and other bits and pieces he wanted checked. Then, very expediently, showed him *'the hidey-hole'*. A previous owner had apparently had a disabled child that he had kept hidden from the world in a corner room he had erected in the extensive loft that covered the whole of the house. Unless you knew of its existence, and had actually been searching for it, you would never have detected its presence. Cleverly built, a casual observer would have thought it was just the end wall of the house. Around the loft floorboards lay the normal junk that tend to be dumped for later use, but rarely is. This rubbish also proved a useful distraction should someone be searching for something in this area.

This hidey-hole would be a perfect place for her to lay low. The fuzz had obviously finished with the place, and the hidden room was perfect. There was electricity, running water, a bed and even a mains toilet and shower in a separate partition at the end of the room. All she had to do was locate the various taps for switching on the water, the switch for reconnecting the electricity, and she'd have a comfortable, safe place to hide until she found out what had happened to Matthew. Not that she cared a jot about his fate, she just wanted to lay low until it was safe for her to re-emerge and move on.

She mused. *What shall I do with the car? I'll check round the back. See if that tumble-down building that's a poor substitute for a garage is unlocked.*

The evening was drawing in, so she needed to get inside before it got too dark. Hurrying past the two houses that she had previously noticed were occupied, she followed the path that went alongside the last house and continued behind the back of all the houses until it came back onto the road where she had parked the car. A small hedge fenced off the back, but at the end was a diamond braced gate that led into the back garden. It was open and swinging loosely on rusty hinges with two securing hinges broken and lying on the ground nearby.

Over the high hedge that separated the properties, she noted that she could only be spotted from one upstair's window on the right-hand side of the neighbouring property. There was no light on, and no-one looking out. Entering the garden, she hurried to the outbuilding that Sinclair had told her doubled as a store and garage when needed. It was not locked. Pulling the two doors back open as far as they would go, she estimated it would enable her to swing the car round and into this building.

Must be my lucky day. So far, so good.

She hesitated for a moment realising that should the cops return they may well locate her car. Remembering the state of the tatty, crime scene tape, she decided she'd take the chance. This hideout was perfect, and even if a nosy copper had to occasionally check the house, knowing how lazy the bastards were, she knew a very quick scan was all that would happen. Anyway, she wasn't staying here long term.

She hurried back round the side of the house and pulled open the wide gates. Even though it was just fading daylight, she knew there was less chance of the car being heard by the neighbours, as almost certainly they would be looking at their televisions or generally busy. At night, although less likely to be seen, the car driving over the gravel pathway would make a hell of a racket, easily heard by the neighbours if lying in their beds with open bedroom windows.

It took just three minutes to retrieve the car and ease it through the gate, round the house and into the garage. She grabbed her three bags, one containing a sleeping bag and blow-up pillow, and dumped them by the kitchen door. Closing the gate, she hurried to the back of the house. From their previous encounters, she had both the front, and back door keys. She knew there was no burglar alarm, but the old fool had had a fire alarm fitted so she would have to sneak out carefully for a cigarette.

Having the forethought to bring milk and tea bags, she was glad the fridge door had been left open so it would not be manky with mould. She placed the two two-pint containers in the door shelf, and then took another ten minutes to locate and reconnect the water and electricity, and another five minutes to pull down the loft ladder and carry her luggage into the loft. Knowing there was a small window at one end, she didn't chance switching on the lights even though it was now getting dark and gloomy. She could switch on the light later when there would be no-one around.

She had come prepared, and the led-light torch easily illuminated her way to the secret room. Unlocking the door, still confident that it was completely hidden near the back of the loft, and impossible to locate unless you knew it was there, she hurried in and slung her bags on to the bed.

This is easy.

Returning to the kitchen, she searched the cupboards for a cup to make herself a badly needed cup of tea. Careful to leave no obvious signs should anyone peer through the kitchen window, after drinking the tea, she washed and wiped the cup before returning it to the cupboard and placed the milk into the fridge.

Realising she had spent enough time in the kitchen, she climbed the ladder, pulling it back into place in the loft. By the time she was back in the hidey hole, her heart was beating hard from the effort and the excitement of her situation. Switching on the light that could not be seen outside the windowless room, she pulled a bottle of Rioja and plastic glass from one of her luggage bags. She relaxed onto an armchair, poured herself a large drink, and after a sip, eased herself back, putting her feet onto a conveniently provided kid's stool.

"Cheers," she said to herself, raising the glass into the air. "Here's to a few weeks peace away from that stupid bastard Nielson."

Chapter 74

Sinclair was tired and bored with the situation. Just deciding that maybe a five-minute doze was in order, he straightened himself up and assumed the wide-eyed, startled look of a deer caught in car headlights when his captives suddenly returned. Three or four sets of footsteps hurried across the floor before the scraping noise of chairs drawn back from the table.

Someone made a harrumphing sound as he cleared his throat.

"Well, David, here we are again." *Definitely good cop*. He cleared his throat again. "My colleagues are very interested in your previous comment."

David assumed a puzzled look, and stuttered, "My previous comment? Mm, sorry, I'm so confused, what did I say?"

"I'll remind you." The voice was gentle, caressing, and persuasive. *Mmm, good cop's sooo sweet*. "I was asking you if you knew the woman in the photo we showed you."

"Yes, but I said I didn't *know* her exactly."

"Yes, David, I know, but then you said, although you hadn't actually seen her face to face, she might resemble someone who arrives in a car to pick up your…um, *brother*."

"Did I? I can't remember. I'm so confused. Probably because I'm so…"

"So…?"

"So…thirsty."

Silence. Then a voice, definitely not good cop, snapped, "Thirsty…oh for God's sake."

"Right, David. Let me remind you again. We showed you a picture of a woman we are anxious to help with our enquiries. You said to me, on looking again at the picture, that although you couldn't be sure, that it may resemble a woman who came to pick up your brother Matthew on occasions."

David considered the statement, keeping up the innocent and slightly puzzled expression. He nodded before mumbling, "Yes. Yes, your right, I remember now. Yvette. Yes, that's her name. Matthew once said, 'Oh that damn Yvette is late again, when he was waiting to be picked up. I remember thinking that was an unusual name."

Again, there were a few moments of silence before some feverish whispering took place.

Good cop again said. "Thank you for that information. Now about your brother…"

"Please," David interrupted. "I'm so thirsty. Is it possible for me to have a cup of tea?"

More whispering. A chair scrapped as someone stood up. David wanted to express a wheedling 'Thank you', using an Uriah Heep type voice whilst twisting and rubbing his hands together, imitating an actor he'd seen playing Uriah's part in a TV adaptation of the David Copperfield book. Taking a deep breath, he metaphorically pinched his leg to make himself behave. The giggling still simmered just below the surface, and he was having a hard time controlling himself.

"OK, drink of tea will be here shortly," said *Good Cop*. He cleared his throat before continuing. "Matthew…um… your brother you say."

"Yes."

"So, Matthew and Yvette are…friends, lovers? What is

the relationship?"

David shrugged. "I'm not sure." He paused dramatically before shaking his head. "No, I wouldn't say they were either. In fact, I don't really think he likes her at all."

"Then why…umm, you say she picks him up in her car. Thus, that would infer they must have some sort of relationship."

"I suppose. I think she's useful to him."

"In what way?"

At that moment David heard a door open, and from the light a cup and saucer appeared and pushed over the table towards him, and his right hand untied. He made a point of leisurely sipping it before he answered. He slowly replaced the cup in the saucer and sat back in his chair, assuming an innocent expression.

"In what way someone asked? Umm, well, she gets him women, I think. He likes women. You know, and other women are good at that sort of thing, recognising the vulnerable ones."

This time he sensed that he could have cut the silence with a knife, it was so thick it reminded him of stirring a liquid until it thickened and hardened. Again, the giggle dangled dangerously just below the surface.

"Gets him women!" This was a different voice that Sinclair had not heard before. "Why would he need her to get him women? What does he do with these women?"

Sinclair looked down, and slowly shrugged. He took a deep breath before he looked up again and stared into the light. "I don't know exactly, but…" He paused dramatically.

"Yes?"

"I didn't think much about their…relationship. But…well…I started reading about these women that are missing." He looked to the side as though considering his words. Glancing back into the light before he continued, he whispered, "He's a troubled soul. We didn't have a happy childhood. Our parents were…cruel. I used to switch off from it, but Matthew was deeply affected."

An impatient voice snapped, "What has this to do with her, this Yvette, getting him women."

"He grew up hating women. I don't understand why, but our Father's cruelty affected him so much. Maybe because he was an emotional, tender man. Anyway, our Mother's cruelty affected him even more. We, Matthew and I, moved here from the Midlands when I got the position of playing the organ and music teacher to various church schools. He'd just lost his job, so he decided to move down here with me. I noticed a change in him; very gradually, but it was there, happening slowly. When he watched the news items about those poor missing women, he'd clap and laugh, and shout that they deserved it. One day I was bringing us coffee into the living room, and the news must once again have been talking about them, and I heard him say. 'Yes, yes, well done...oh, what was her name...oh yes, Yvette. Yvette, you're not much use, but you certainly know how to point out those sad suckers to me'. I froze. I was horrified."

"Did you challenge him?"

Slowly shaking his head, Sinclair said. "It was just last week. I knew I ought to confront him, but he's my brother. I just couldn't believe what I heard."

Looking down into his lap, he whispered, "Yes, I should have done. I guess it wouldn't make any difference to those poor souls."

"But you might have stopped him going after other women."

"Well yes, *if* it was him."

"If! You're just making excuses for him."

Sinclair looked up and nodded slowly. *Ten out of ten for my acting. Wonder if this will get me a Golden Globe Award.* His stomach twirled as though little fairies were dancing around and playing. He hoped the stupid interview would be over soon, or the tittering that he was so magnificently suppressing would burst out of his mouth.

"Thank you, David." *Good cop* said. "That must have been very hard for you to admit. Now it appears that she was useful, but what about her? I can't imagine there wasn't some sort of repayment. What did he have to do for her?"

He put his head on one side, letting the silence dangle like air motes in a light beam. Smelling cigar smoke, he noticed small spinning twirls of smoke rising above the lights, and purposely taking his time to annoy his captors, he hesitated before replying.

"Payment. Yes, I think there was. She's the devil in women's clothing." He looked straight into the light, and although he could not see their faces, he moved his gaze along the line where he calculated they were sitting to give the impression of staring straight into their eyes before he dramatically whispered, "I fear this evil person had a predilection for children; young, innocent children; may God damn her soul."

The giggle was about to burst from his mouth, but he managed to turn it into a sob. He was *so* proud of his efforts!

"I see, that explains a lot of things. She found him vulnerable women for God knows what purpose, and he procured children for her." *Good cop*.

The silence hung in the air again. Sinclair could hear their breathing, sense they were considering his words, deliberating on their meaning.

"Yes, but what I don't understand from your allegations is…" This voice didn't belong to the former two interrogators and Sinclair was sure he had not been quizzed by him previously. He felt uneasy for the first time, there was something about it that made him realise he was not dealing with a fool, but an analytical, very practical person. The man continued, "Children are going missing and that's what we're investigating. You say it's not you that has anything to do with these occurrences. That this is your brother's doing."

Sinclair heard the scrape of a chair and sensed that someone had stood up as he could make out a dark shadow.

An impatient voice snapped, "We need to talk. This is getting ridiculous."

The hood was replaced over Sinclair's head and his free hand was secured again. He heard their footsteps as the men trooped from the room. Until a few minutes ago he had enjoyed the bantering, now it was getting tiresome. He felt the urge for action, but he wasn't in control of his situation, and he didn't like that. He took a deep breath knowing he had to manage this state of affairs without these fools realising he was playing them along. He must not let this set of circumstances deject him, but he knew the moment the opportunity arose, he was going to bash some one round the head and flee.

Chapter 75

Jose looked miserable as she waved goodbye to Emma and Heidi. Climbing onto their bikes, Emma shouted, "Dunno why you've got long gob. At least you'll be in the warm. It's starting to rain."

"Yeah, but I'd rather be wet than missing out on our adventures."

"'Bye, ducky," Heidi called. "Cheer up, we'll be back soon."

Jose watched until the girls were out of sight before she turned back and went indoors. She was very close to tears, but she knew riding for three miles there and back to Coley Park was not sensible or achievable.

Her side still hurt, and the doctor had advised her not to lift anything heavy or do any demanding exercise. That still did not stop her feeling fed up with the situation. Not that she wanted to visit that creepy house again, especially as night was falling. She hoped her friends would be back soon to cheer her up. The constant attention was very appealing.

As the two girls puffed up Castle Hill towards their destination, Heidi's words were decidedly wheezy as she said, "Thank God, the rain's eased off. Just a reminder by the way, we see anything dodgy, we don't do nothing. We head straight back home and phone the cops like you promised."

"Yeah, yeah, don't keep on."

"Well, I know what you're like." Heidi drew a breath before continuing, "Anyway, why the hell are we going back to this creepy place. The cops probably went over it with a fine toothcomb. What do you expect to find?"

"Just got one of me feelings."

"Oh, Christ, no. I can't stand it. What does that mean exactly? Are your knickers warm, so you feel you've wet them?" She tittered as she said it.

"Ha, ha, not funny. Anyway, Jose told us what her mum said. You know that she goes to the same church where that David Sinclair plays the organ. She told Jose that besides being a music teacher at various schools and playing the organ, apparently another of his responsibilities is keeping an eye on church properties when they are vacant. There's apparently one in Pangbourne, one in Caversham and this Loddon house in Coley Park. I started to think about my delightful encounter with Nielson. I bet he uses these places for his own shenanigans."

"We know he used Loddon House, but we don't know about the others. Hang on a sec, let's stop, turn off down here and take a breather before we get to Coley."

The two girls steered onto the path and alighted from their bikes. Both breathed heavily for a few seconds before continuing their conversation. The road, empty of traffic, lined with tall chestnut and oak trees, made it dark and secluded.

"Ooh, bit eerie," said Heidi.

"I dunno. I like the silence. Listen, no sound."

Standing still, they became aware of the hum from the distant motorway.

"Almost silent," Heidi sniggered. "Anyway, you just said that Sinclair, Nielson, whoever, looks after these properties. If they searched Loddon House, they must know who looks after them. They must have gone to the church to question them. D'you reckon they know about the other two properties."

Emma shrugged a 'don't-know'.

"Well, maybe it's worth telling them. After all, there are women still missing. You never know, maybe he buried their bodies in the garden."

"Could be. I'll tell that big copper, what's 'is name. I'll phone in the morning. Come on, let's get going." Emma peered at her watch in the gloom.

"It's nearly eight. Don't want to be round that creepy joint too late. Maybe the ghosties'll be out to play." She rode off, hollering a ghostly cackle as she cycled away.

"Wait for me, you bitch," called Heidi, cycling after her friend; not wanting to be left in the over-hung, leafy, dark road on her own.

Chapter 76

"Do you want me to go or stay?" asked the headmaster after he introduced Father Francis to Dan and Meena.

He left and closed the door quietly after Dan confirmed they wish to interview Father Francis on his own.

"Good day, sir. I'm Detective Sergeant Dan Blake and my colleague is Detective Constable Meena Mesbah." Dan then gave him a smile hoping to put him at his ease, because the white cotton tablecloth colour of the teacher's face had not improved and looked as though he would burst into tears at any second. "What shall I call you, Father Francis or…?"

Dan had never interviewed a Jesuit priest before and had no idea how to address him.

"Francis will do." His voice quavered.

"Right, thank you…umm, Francis, and thank you for agreeing to see us. We are hoping you may be able to help us with a current investigation that we are conducting. We…"

"I don't know anything. I'd like to help but…I just can't…I don't know anything."

His panicked interruption caught Dan and Meena by surprise, especially as Dan had not even given the reason for the interview.

Dan nodded encouragingly and waited. Experience had taught him that if you wait long enough, those people who want to say more would do so. Francis, who had been leaning forward in an anxious pose, leaned back in his chair, and just shook his head. After thirty seconds of silence, he started to nibble his nails.

Again, Dan smiled encouragingly, but as pre-planned, if he did not talk, then Meena should take over. He glanced at Meena and gave a small nod.

"Francis, please don't feel alarmed. You are not under arrest. As my colleague explained, we are conducting an investigation, and it has come to our attention that you may be able to help us with our enquiries." Seeing that he was about to protest again, she hurried on, "So it would be very helpful if you listened to me and then if you can help or give us information that will move us on with our enquiries and be…"

"But I don't know anything," he interrupted again before she finished.

Ignoring his protest and realising that she was not going to get anywhere unless she pushed forward, she continued, "We wondered if you had ever heard this phrase at any time, in any context, of 'Rubies on the Moon."

His subsequent reaction suggested she had asked whether she could cut his throat! His previous pale complexion deteriorated to a sickly khaki, with stark white rings round his eyes and mouth. The police officers glanced at each other; the man looked about to have a heart attack.

"Are you alright, sir? Please, we are only here…"

Before Meena could finish, the priest stood up, took a deep breath, and with wide hysterical eyes, said, "I won't tell you anything unless you promise to protect me; put me in protective custody or whatever it's called." He took another deep gasp, before continuing, "Oh yes, and complete immunity from prosecution." He plonked himself back into his chair, and crossed his arms, the expression now on his face suggesting he was getting himself back under control.

Both officers, although experienced with varying types of interviews and interrogations, were momentarily speechless. Used to hardened criminals who could win an Olympic gold medal should acting become an Olympic sport, and then turn into professional actors at playing the innocent and misunderstood victims, the two officers were flabbergasted by the ease and speed of their progress.

Dan, not wanting to take the moment away from Meena, gave her another nod, eager to find out more before the priest's change of attitude rooted home and he might decide silence was a better option.

"Francis, please relax. I feel we are getting ahead of ourselves. Let us move our conversation forward in steady steps. Shall we focus on my previous question as to whether you have ever heard the phrase, 'Rubies on the Moon?'" Noticing that Francis was about to plunge forward again into a hysterical outburst, she hurried on, "Again I would emphasise that at the moment this is purely a discussion about whether you can help us with our enquiries?"

Francis lowered his eyes to his lap. Dan noticed that he was twisting and squeezing his hands clasped together on the desk in front of him. The man was obviously stressed, and the officer realised he was going to have to change the mood of the moment if they were to progress.

"Francis, would you like a drink of water, cup of tea or coffee? We've just had a drink, but I could manage another cuppa. Do you think that would be possible?"

Meena, instantly understanding the ploy, agreed, and standing up, offered to go and find someone to supply the drink. The change of manoeuvre appeared to work. The look of panic faded from his face, and the host in him took over.

"Yes, just dial zero on Father Panis Angelicus's phone. That takes you through to the kitchen and just explain your needs. I'll have tea."

Meena did just that and the call was answered immediately. "Tea for three in the Headmaster's room please," she said.

Still attempting to cool the situation, Dan asked, "How long have you worked here? It's a remarkable place. As we drove up the drive my colleague and I were very impressed with the beautiful building and grounds."

He had obviously picked on the correct subject to distract the man.

"Yes, it's a wonderful building and grounds. It was left to the school by a very religious and devout man, Sir Humphrey De Vere, in the eighteenth Century. It was his country mansion. I love working here. Often, in the early evening, when I wish to contemplate, I stroll around the grounds. It's so relaxing."

He continued for the next three minutes extolling the virtue of the venue, and Dan was wondering how to interrupt and get him back on track, when thankfully there was a knock on the door. The 'film star' young priest poked his head round the door and asked it was OK for him to bring in the tea tray.

At Meena's nod, he came in and placed the tray on the desk between the priest and the officers.

"I'll pour," offered Meena, also anxious to guide him back to their subject.

They gave the man a minute to relax and sip his tea before starting the questioning again. Dan nodded to Meena.

"That's a good cuppa," said Meena. "Right, Francis, Rubies on the Moon. Can I just ask in what context you heard this phrase? You seem…"

The priest leaned forward, placed his cup back on the tray. He seemed more in control now. Leaning back, he glanced down at his hands now clasped together in his lap like a man praying for forgiveness.

"It all started after the misunderstanding with the lad in Year Ten. Of course, it was all sorted. Father Angelicus is good at that sort of thing. Naturally, when his parents took him away from the school, that helped matters. Although we had to pay to stop them going to the papers. Terrible, but after all, it was just his word against mine." He paused, and still gazing at his lap, it gave Dan and Meena the opportunity to look at each other. Their expressions were mirror images; eyes open wide in surprise. This was not going as they expected, but it was interesting, and they did not intend to stop the flow.

He took a sip of his tea, coughed, and then continued. "Just after that unfortunate incident, I was contacted by a man called Arthur Peach. I understand he is the leader of our local cell."

The word cell instantly alerted and alarmed the two officers, but they both controlled their expressions, and refrained from glancing at each other, although both wanted to. Instead, Dan nodded encouragingly and Meena gave him a reassuring smile.

"By the way, I understand you can't be accused and arrested for thinking about something, but not actually committing an illegal act. Is that correct?"

Dan cleverly avoided any commitment by repeating he was just currently helping with their enquiries and not under arrest. This seemed to assure the priest. He sat back in his chair, took a deep lungful of air, and with his eyes looking into the distance, he explained his connection with the expression, 'Rubies on the Moon'.

His voice and words slid into a Gregorian chant, as though he had been practising it previously. "I was initiated into the cell, just a meeting with the cell leader and his right-hand man. After I gave them some information, they gave me various passwords for, as they put it, an interesting site, on my PC. These passwords that must be used in a certain, strict order or you close the system down and can't get back in. The first and ninth ones being the Rubies password. It led to a site that was disgusting, really obscene child pornography. I may have…well, in some peoples' opinions, unhealthy interest in children, but there's a limit. I was disgusted." He stopped and drained the rest of his drink before he continued. "Unfortunately, by this time, they'd got their hooks into me and started hinting at blackmail if I didn't stick with them. I think because they could see the possibilities of my connection to potential victims, ie, the lads at the school.

"When I heard one of our teachers use the password, I panicked. I thought he knew of my connection. I decided I could do myself some good if I reported the incident. It didn't help. Firstly, I was ordered to kill him would you believe. Then they withdrew that order. I didn't know where I was. I did realise I wasn't a murderer, that's for sure. Anyway, they apparently have meetings at their various houses. I've never yet attended one. I was invited but always managed an excuse, too much school business." He leaned forward putting his elbows on the table, and his head into his hands. Suddenly looking up, he added, "They're having a meeting …umm…tomorrow I believe, at George Hampson's place I think."

After a few seconds had passed, Meena prompted him to continue. "And the name of this teacher who used this phrase?"

"O'Leary. He's not a priest. We do have a couple of teachers who are Catholics but not priests. He lives on campus during term time. Goes to his cottage in Bournemouth during the holidays. Absolutely detestable fellow. Kids think he's wonderful; can't imagine why. Anyway, when he used this phrase, as I said, I panicked. He maintained one of the boys was being stupid and said it during one of his lessons. Ridiculous. Turns out, after I had reported it, it was checked and Arthur now believes this is true, that some boy did say it."

Dan decided that at this point he must interrupt.

"This Arthur Peach, how did he check out Mr O'Leary?"

Francis shrugged. "Not sure. This George Hampson, another cell member, contacted me. Asked if I knew where O'Leary lived. Just told them he had this cottage in

Bournemouth. Goes there in the holidays. Prattles on and on about it. Goes into detail; how he buys his supplies for the week, plays golf twice with his friend, attends mass. Blab la bla. He's the most boring person I've ever met." He suddenly stopped as though something had just occurred to him, then continued. "Umm, maybe they talked to him there. Otherwise, how would they know he didn't know anything about that password. He's just returned from his week off, so no harm…"

He stopped talking and looked at Dan, perhaps suddenly aware he may have said too much. Dan just smiled reassuringly and retrieved his notebook and pen from his jacket inside pocket. Meena did the same.

Flipping open his notebook and clicking the end of his biro, Dan slowly nodded his head, and said, "Thank you Francis, you've been very helpful. A couple of things I'd like to check. Firstly, Arthur Peach and George Hampson. Can you give me their full names and addresses?"

Francis felt his face grow cold and the colour drain from it. He glanced into the glowing dark eyes of the female officer and gulped when he saw her expression. A beautiful, brunette feline who had just been given a huge bowlful of double cream. It was the easiest interview ever! For him, he wasn't so sure.

"Do I need a lawyer?" he asked in a weak voice.

Chapter 77

The girls did not speak as they rode up to the house situated just before Loddon House, but were aware of the noisy crackle made by their bike tyres on the gravelly surface. Pulling up and alighting from their bikes outside this first house, they noticed lights in the downstairs rooms.

"OK, so the ol' folks are home here. Now, let's ride past Loddon and check the houses on the other side," whispered Emma.

"Why're we whispering?" asked Heidi. "Unless they've got Superman hearing, they can't hear us from inside their houses."

"Dunno. Just feel we ought to be extra careful and quiet."

Emma got back on her bike and rode past the high hedge and gate fronting Loddon House. She pointed out the trailing crime scene tape drooping along the ground. As they arrived at the next house, they alighted from their bikes, legs either side of the frames. It was in darkness.

"No-one home."

"You're still whispering, Em."

"So are you." Both girls giggled.

"Back to our objective."

"Emma Bradbury…objective. You're so posh."

"Yep, you're dead right." Emma pushed away, turning

through a small circle until they were back outside Loddon House's gate. Both girls peered round the hedge, but the house was in darkness.

"See," whispered Heidi, before realising what she had done, and continued in her normal voice. "See, wasted journey, black as the night, no mad woman, no crazy rapist cum attacker at home ready to molest us, slit our throats and throw our bodies into the Thames."

"Umm, I dunno. I think we can chance going in the garden and at least peer in some windows."

"Em, face it, the bloody house is empty. Nielson or the ugly taxi driver, if she's in league with that loony Matthew, wouldn't be crackers enough to come back here. OK, the cops might have finished their investigation, but the neighbours must have been questioned and therefore aware it's a …what they call it on the tele…a crime scene. If they saw anyone living here, they'd phone the police as quick as you like."

"Yep, I agree." She shrugged, smiled beguilingly at her friend, and said, "So that means, Honey Bunny Friend, there is nothing wrong, if we're careful, in having a quiet mooch around." Emma lent her bike against the hedge and attempted to open the wrought iron gate by its handle. It did not budge.

"I know it's now dark, dear little Em, but even I can see the bloody great big lock and chain that the police have probably put round the gate to stop nosy parkers wandering round the *crime scene*!"

Emma proceeded to climb up the bars across the gate, swinging her legs over and jumping down into the garden before turning round and saying, with a big grin on her face that made her white teeth gleam in the gloom, "Nothing stops a Bradbury when determined. You coming or not?"

With that, she strode off to the house.

"Shit." Heidi shook her head in frustration, leaned her bike next to her friend's, and followed her over the gate.

Peering towards the house, she was glad Emma was wearing a white rain mac or she would not have been able to see her in the murkiness. At that moment, the rain returned, only as yet a light drizzle, but Heidi swore again as she felt it trickle wormlike down the back of her neck.

The two girls went from window to window along the front of the house, but despite avidly peering into the room, all they could see was the odd blob of light- coloured furniture coverings or their own reflections. The same happened all the way round the house, and even the French windows did not reveal anything suspicious.

"Right, enough's enough, there's no-one home!" whispered Heidi.

"You're whispering now."

"Yeah, but only because I don't want to alert the neighbours. Talking in the road's one thing, in someone's garden's quite another."

"You're right." Emma shook her head in frustration. "S'funny, I just had a feeling…"

"You and your feelings are something else. Warm, wet knickers again. Now let's get the hell out of here before we get soaked to the skin and then get frigging pneumonia."

The girls hurried in a dejected manner to the front gate, Heidi glum because of the rain, Emma due to the lack of success of their venture.

Climbing over the gate, Heidi hurried to her bike, still muttering about the futility of the night's scheme. Emma gave a backward glance at the house, about to sigh with disappointment, when she noticed a momentary spark of light. It went as quickly as it had come.

"Heidi, quick, come and look."

"Em, give it up for God's sake."

"No really, in the roof, that triangle bit under the tiles, I saw a little flash of light."

Heidi, who by this time had the legs bestriding the bike frame, shuffled over. She stared at the house. "Oh yes, I see…absolutely, completely *nothing*. Now let's go home, please."

"But I saw a little light, in the roof area, like someone was shining a little light through a hole."

"No, you didn't." She stretched out her hand towards the house. "There, pitch black. Nothing, zilch, bloody zippo, now…" She looked towards the dark outline of the roof just as Van Looy, using a torch to see the way, had returned and open the door to her hidey-hole that she had vacated a few seconds before. The beam had momentarily hit the small window. Heidi's mouth stayed open mid-sentence, until she gulped out a strangled, "Holy Shite."

Chapter 78

The five men sipped the coffees that George had just made for them. Arthur rubbed his hands together.

"It's really chilly down in your cellar, George. This drink's very welcome."

"Good. Right, what are we going to do about Sinclair? We can't hold him forever."

"Do we believe his story?" Dennis leaned forward as he spoke. "He seemed sincere enough, but…"

"I agree," interrupted John. His voice was almost a whisper. John was a quiet, thoughtful man, not given to speaking a great deal, but when he gave an opinion, his words were always sensible, and well thought through. "He *seems* sincere. Now, either we've been misled about him, and because he was associated with the church schools etc, we've gone down the wrong path. If he truly has a brother that is in league with Van Looy, then we must let him go, and find this brother who looks to be our real target. If the brother is fiction, and Sinclair's just covering his back, we have to prove that too." He glanced around the table. "Don't know about you, but I'm somewhat confused. We've either totally backed up the wrong tree…again… and Sinclair is as innocent as he protests, or he ought to be awarded a medal for his acting abilities, and the brother is a convenient illusion. Either way, we need to sort this out quickly. As

George pointed out, we can't keep him here much longer."

Arthur nodded. "Agreed. Especially if he is innocent."

"This brother. How do we prove his existence, and if he is for real, and is the one who's behind all the disappearances, then how do we find him?" Dennis said.

"The annoying thing is that we don't actually care about these disappearing women. No bodies have been found as far as I know; it's just the connection with Van Looy and the kids being murdered. Queering our pitch and drawing attention to our plans." George considered his words. Turning to Arthur he continued, "This is getting out of hand. First, we interviewed O'Leary. Luckily, there were no repercussions from that. Now we have this Sinclair who may or may not be the person we need to speak to regarding 'queering our pitch' as I've just said."

"I think we're over our head," interrupted John. "Yes, luckily, as you pointed out, there were no repercussions from the O'Leary interview, but we were lucky to get away after being disturbed. We have Sinclair, and we're not sure what to do with him, or if he's telling us the truth. Now if he can prove that this brother exists, and we can track him down, we must let this fellow go. Good God, we're in our sixties and seventies; old men, and we're acting like young American gangsters. It's getting ridiculous."

The silence that hung over the room was painful to their ears, like the ringing deafness experienced after an explosion. Arthur shook his head; his tinnitus was ringing like church bells. He stood up.

"You're right, John. This *is* getting ridiculous. No, not getting…*is* ridiculous. Come George, we give him one more chance. He must tell us where we can find his brother or Van Looy. OK, let's bring him up to the back room, it's too cold in the cellar." He stood up and headed towards the door leading to the stairs that led to the cellar. George and their hired 'heavy' followed, shaking his head with frustration.

A few minutes later, they emerged with Sinclair,

George holding one arm and their 'heavy' firmly holding the other. His wrists were tied, a hood over his head. The heavy guided him to a chair opposite the elderly men, but did not remove the hood until Arthur switched on the lamp so ensuring their faces were once more not discernible.

A look of exasperation painted Sinclair's face as the hood was lifted off, and he surprised them all by snapping, "This is really past a joke. I've been as helpful as I could possibly be. You've kidnapped me, which is a very serious crime, practically scared me to death. I've answered all your questions, *now* what do you want?"

"Mr Sinclair, we are puzzled and need you to clarify a few things. Then we will take you home, unharmed. You claim that your brother was the person involved with Van Looy. You've deduced that she led him to vulnerable women for God knows what purpose, and he obtained children for her."

The silence hung in the air again. Sinclair could hear their breathing, considering his outburst, deliberating on his words.

"I find your explanation somewhat confusing…" This was the questioner, the practical sounding person of whom he had previously been wary. Sinclair felt uneasy again, there was something about this speaker that made him know he was not dealing with a fool. The man continued, "Now, I can understand that she, Van Looy, being a woman herself, may size up and steer him towards vulnerable women, and your brother procure children for her. Is that right?"

Sinclair nodded, still troubled. The man continued, "But why should he be able to kidnap these kids when you're the one, by your own admission, who comes in daily contact with children?"

The question floored Sinclair, and he felt panic sitting in his stomach, scratching like sharp clawed insects. His normal swift answers would not come to his brain, which felt leaden. *God, I just need to kill someone. I need to see my prizes. Oh God, why the hell are they keeping me here?*

The sudden ringing of the doorbell that coursed through the house like a torrent of water and echoed round the corners of the room should have felt like a lifesaver, but for some reason, he was unsure.

He felt the panic in the silence that followed the ringing sound. It hovered in the air, a silent buzzing like the wings of insects. The whispered alarm of his interrogators confirmed his concern.

Straining his ears, he heard *good cop* whisper, "Christ, not again! George, it's your house. You expecting anybody?"

"No, not at this time of night. Sarah and the kids are away. Anyway, they've got their door keys."

When the bell hadn't produced any result, the caller banged on the door. The bell then peeled out again, and this time it had an insistent ring to it.

"You'll have to answer it," whispered Arthur. "They're obviously not going to go away. The lights are on, so they know someone's home. Whoever it is, don't let them in. I know they're not going to come into this back room, but even so, we don't want them in the house at all."

George tiptoed along the L-shaped corridor leading to the front of the house. Pushing open the hall door, he walked to the corner and peered around at the glass-fronted door. The porch light was on and he could make out the shapes of two visitors, men in dark clothing. Glancing at his watch, he frowned in annoyance. He knew immediately who they were; they had come the week before around this time. *Bloody Jehovah's Witnesses. Damn nuisances; can't take no for an answer.*

Hurrying to the door, annoyance buzzing like wasps around his body, he lifted the safety chain, and as he opened the door, preparing to be rude, but when the two callers did not resemble the previous visitors in any way, the words died in his mouth. One was a giant of a man with spiky red hair, and the other a shorter, stocky blond man with wide shoulders with whom you would not want to pick an argument. George felt the bile of apprehension come up into his mouth as often happened when he knew he was in a spot, or rather, in this case, a huge vat of trouble.

"Good evening, sir, I apologise for calling this late." He held up a warrant card, and continued, "I'm Detective Sergeant Dan Blake, and my colleague is Detective Constable Luke Steiner. Are you Mr. George Hampson?"

George nodded, and felt his stomach plunge with apprehension like a lift falling out of control down a lift shaft. The two police officers were unaware of his inward anxiety, but they were conscious, even in the dim light of the late evening, that the colour had drained from his face. Dan's sensed a moment of *déjà vu*. This man's reaction was similar to the recent interview with Father Francis, and he realised immediately that once again he was not wasting his time; and was taking another step in the right direction of solving this investigation.

Dan went on to explain that they believed that George could help them with some enquiries. When George, at a loss for words, failed therefore to make any verbal response, the police officer went on to assure him that they hoped he could assist with an investigation.

George's mind, unable to make a suitable reply, was still blank. Under no circumstances did he want the police to enter his house as all the cell members were present in the back room, and normally their security ensured they never placed themselves in such an exposed position. The fact that they were also holding a kidnapped man in captivity made the situation very precarious. He hoped 'the heavy' had thought to muffle their prisoner; he did not want him yelling out and alerting the visitors.

After a few moments of silence, Dan glanced at Luke and gave a slight nod.

"Sir," Luke prompted. "Apologies again at the lateness

of the hour."

In fact, they had purposely chosen this time, aware that there are certain times when people do not expect this sort of visitation and catching people unawares often paid dividends. "My colleague has explained that we would like to speak to you regarding our enquiries. May we come in and have a conversation out of this inhospitable weather?"

The forecast rain had just arrived, and Luke could feel it had found the space between his overcoat collar and neck, and it was tricking down his back like cold, wriggling little worms and he had to control himself not to shiver loudly.

His words seemed to snap George into life. Shaking his head violently, he said, "No, no, no. It's so late, I can't allow visitors this late. I never normally answer the door after eight. It's so dangerous. You never know who's going to call and attack you in your house. No, no. Call back tomorrow, when it's light, and a sensible time, in the day light."

He stepped back and went to close the door, but his whole demeanour, particularly his ashen face, had confirmed to both Dan and Luke that he had a lot to hide. Luke's quickly outstretched hand stopped the door from closing.

"Perhaps, sir, you would prefer to come to the station if it is not convenient for us to enter your property." Dan's voice was velvet soft, but the lustrous pile coating the words held a hint of menace that even George's hearing, not so sharp as in his youth, detected without effort.

Knowing he should not stop these officers coming into his house if he was 'innocent', he recognised the fact if he asked for a warrant, that would confirm he had something to hide; so he forced himself to smile, and stepped back, opening the door. Praying they had secured Sinclair, unaware of whether this had occurred, he invited them into the house.

Smiling as genuinely as he could manage, he waved his

right hand for the police officers to enter. Holding his left hand behind his back, his fore and middle fingers, crossed tightly for good luck, caused a spiteful arthritic pain to shoot through his palm.

Chapter 79

Emma and Jose were sprawled across the bed. Jose, in order the smoke from her cigarette would be easily dispersed, was nearer the open window despite the wind and rain that had descended with the vengeance of hell's anger across the southern half of the country. Heidi was slumped back on a dark blue, velvet padded chair with her feet resting on the corner of the bed and noisily sucking down the last of her milk shake that Jose's mum was famous for making and selling at the church coffee mornings for charity. If Emma and Heidi begged hard enough, they often had a strawberry flavoured treat themselves.

"So what then?" asked Jose. "You waited over 'alf hour and nuffink happened. Christ, you must've been freezing and scared shitless."

"Umm, delish." The last drop of milk slurped into Heidi's mouth. "Well, bloody freezing that's for sure. The rain started and I just wanted to go home. But you might know, madam…" She thumbed towards Emma, "Mad madam wanted to break in and investigate. I put my foot down with a great thump and said absolutely and definitely no way. Agreed to hang on for another ten minutes and then we skedaddled away as fast as bats from hell."

"Okay, okay, but you must admit you saw something," Emma said, and proceeded to make similar unladylike glugging sounds through her straw as she finished her own milk shake. Shaking the carton to confirm all the drink had been imbibed, she successfully tossed the empty container into a waste bin at the end of the bed. "Yesss, a hit! Anyway, we both saw a light, and that isn't right in an empty house. Someone's in there, I know, and I intend to find out who... or is it whom?"

"If that's what you fink, you gotta tell the police, Em. No use going and looking yourself. We know Matthew what's his name's well dangerous, and what about if he's with that horrible woman you say what drives him about."

"There, see, even Jose who hasn't had a sensible idea in her life is saying the same. If you think there's someone there, and it's either one or both of the terrible twins, we ought to tell the cops." Heidi folded her arms and looked pleased that her argument had also been backed by Jose.

Emma stared into the distance, considering their words. Suddenly standing, she blurted, "Ok, ok, stop nagging. We compromise."

"What's that mean, I've forgot," interrupted Jose.

"We go half and half, sort of," explained Heidi. "Oh, can't think of the right words, you tell her, Em."

"We find the middle ground; co-operate and consider both sides of the argument."

"Oh." Jose's word did not sound convincing, but she did not want to ask for a simpler explanation or they might consider her thick.

"Come on, then, what's this compromise?" Heidi's voice, laced with doubt, and supported by a sceptical expression.

"We phone that nice woman cop. The beautiful Asian one with those dead, long eyelashes. She's really approachable."

"Em, she's not going to be very pleased if we tell her we've been sniffing about that place. For one thing, she told us to leave everything to the police, and in no way go near Loddon House."

"We'll say we were just out for a bike ride…"

"Yeah, like she'd believe that. Going for a bike ride in the rain and dark, and oh… oh yes, what a coincidence, we ended up near Loddon House where we'd specifically been told not to go."

Jose leaned forward to Heidi, offering her a Malteser. "Want one?" As Heidi took a handful, she exclaimed, "Hey, gutty pig. I only meant one. Anyway, I agree with Heidi, even though she's nicked most of me Maltesers. There's no way the cops'll believe that. You reckon I'm well thick, but even I can see that's well stupid."

Emma also took the proffered chocolate, leaned back against the wall, and crossed her arms across her chest, considering their words. Reluctantly nodding, she said, "Yeah, you're probably right." Taking a deep breath, she blew her cheeks out before saying, "What about we make a phone call. Make it an anonymous call. We can say that we were walking past and saw the light. That we knew it was a crime scene and that there shouldn't be anyone living there. Not tell them it was us."

"They're going to ask our names. If we had nothing to hide, why wouldn't we give them our names?"

"Oh God, even after they bollocked us, and even if they believed us, I bet there'd only send round a thick copper in a car in the daylight, who'd take a one quick look at the place, and decide we were imagining things."

"Don't look sulky, Em. You've done all you can. It's up to the cops now."

"Heidi, I just know that place is…I dunno…not evil exactly, I don't believe in all that film nonsense that places can be evil, but that house…well, it is…and definitely hiding something."

"Maybe you've got the gift too," added Jose, tipping her head back to drop the last Malteser into her mouth from the box.

"Gift?"

"You know, like Alfie Smith. Can know things what others don't…sense them sort of."

Emma slipped off the bed, lent backwards, stretching her back, and tipping her head from side to side to loosen her neck muscles.

"Ok, you're right, let's forget it. There was no-one there. I'm dying for a cuppa tea. Come on Jose, where's your hostess manners. No sugar for me."

As Jose groaned, Heidi heaved herself up from the chair. "Come on, I'll give you a hand." As they left the room, Emma heard Heidi ask if there was any more of her mum's cake left.

The girl strolled to the window. She couldn't see out due to the late hour and only her reflection showed in the pane, but she didn't notice it. She was working out her plans for visiting Loddon House, without her nagging friends of course.

Chapter 80

Meena, sitting at a table in an interview room, was perusing the statement that Father Francis had just written. He was sitting on the other side of the table looking relaxed as he sipped a cup of tea.

Glancing up, she said, "Thank you Francis, this is very helpful." Placing the pages in front of her, she leaned forward, putting her elbows on the table and clasping her hands together, she smiled her most disarming smile as she continued. "Just a couple more points that haven't been included that you may well know and would be beneficial to our investigation…"

The priest interrupted, "I assume, being so cooperative, that I am not now or will not in the future be arrested. After all, I have not actually done anything other than give you information. If I was arrested, it would ruin my career you know."

"Francis, you are not under arrest. Currently, you are helping us with our enquiries." She moved on quickly before he noticed she did not mention any 'future situation'. Both she and Dan had earlier discussed his comment referring to the 'misunderstanding with the lad in Year 10.' This deserved further investigation, but not wishing to put him on the defensive, and therefore lose his cooperation, this was for a later discussion. In addition, he had assured her when offered a solicitor that an innocent man did not need such assistance. "Francis, you have very helpfully given us the names of Arthur Peach and George Hampson. How many are in this cell other than these two gentlemen?"

"Oh, lots."

Meena had to control herself not to look too shocked and she could feel a strangled 'Oh' building in her mouth, but she swallowed it and continued. "Lots, does that mean… say ten…fifteen, less, more?"

"As I understand the structure, there's the top rank of the committee or leader's group that organises and decides the next steps for the eager minions and they firmly control them, so they do not step out of line." Realising such personal knowledge might further incriminate him, he backtracked a little. "As I said…umm, as I understand it, but I don't know everything in detail. Then there is a lower level, in which for this local cell there are maybe twenty members. Suppose I'm on this level. At least, that's what I was told and understood. Arthur explained this. They, the head ones, decide on policy, and especially security, particularly as there is a large-scale operation due in the near future."

The horror and disbelief at this statement caused a shockwave to escalate through Meena's body. The police team had barely recovered from the hard work bringing down a nation-wide operation four years ago. This had been a planned campaign by a group of paedophiles controlled by Gerry Tomas and his side kick Yvette Van Looy. Except that Van Looy was still on the run, the police had believed or at least hoped that this was the end of that business. Unsure exactly what Francis knew about the previous failed operation, Meena knew she would have to be careful how she probed his understanding of the previous years, and the current plans to which he had just referred.

"Stepping out of line….by the, uh, minions… would the leading cell members expect this to happen with their security being so tight, and surely the experience of the previous operation would have made them wary?"

"Yes, as much as I understand, on a previous occasion people within the cell, not the leaders, pleased themselves, hence putting their future operation in jeopardy and they had to be disposed of." Before Meena could ask him to expand on this, he answered the query by continuing. "I don't have any more knowledge of this previous operation. All I know is that it was a failure, and I certainly didn't enquire as to how they disposed of the people that stepped out of line. I think the worst though, especially, as I've explained in my statement, when at one point they ordered me to eliminate O'Leary.

"God in his Heaven, I'm no Saint; I'm a priest. OK, albeit not a perfect man by any means, but I'm no gangster." Glancing down, he frowned as thoughts swirled through his brain. He did not elucidate on his plans of getting O'Leary drunk and then pushing his head beneath the bath water, but it had only been an idea and he had not carried it through. He had to keep up the pretence of being a poor misguided man who was blackmailed by the cell leader into doing things abhorrent to him. In his heart of hearts, he knew that cowardice also played a part in his lack of action, and that he had been utterly relieved when told not to continue with the murder. Taking a deep breath, he looked up at Meena and asked, his face a mask of innocence, "So, how can I help you further, and I hope this assistance will stand me in good stead."

"Of course, Francis, and thank you for being so forthcoming." She glanced at her notebook on the table before her, next to his statement, as much as anything to give her a second to recover herself and collect her thoughts. The surprise of another operation 'in the near future' had rattled her, and she knew she must not let him sense this and must stay in control.

Making more notes in her notebook, she looked up and smiled, not realising that this action made him uneasy. Her beauty somehow made him feel vulnerable, as though he was falling into a trap, like the enchanting singing of the half women half bird Sirens that lured unsuspecting and bewitched sailors to their deaths on the rocks, as described in Greek mythology.

Unaware of the effect she was having, Meena continued, using phrases that were an implication but not a firm fact. "If you could help me on three issues that your information has thrown up, I'm sure this data might well help your position. Firstly, do you know who the others are that are members of the top cell, and secondly, and really very important, the details of this approaching operation to which you referred."

"And thirdly?"

"You referred to 'this cell' as though there are others. That's very key. However, one step at a time." Glancing down at her notebook, she continued, "The names of anyone within the cell, particularly the ones in the top layer who are the leaders." When he did not reply, she looked up, smiled encouragingly, raising her eyebrows to emphasise the question.

He shook his head. "No, I don't know their names." He squinted as though thinking, so Meena waited. "Umm, although...umm, I believe Arthur referred to a John once, but never mentioned a surname."

"A name from the next, lower level then?"

"I guess, as I said before, they would have considered me to be in that group, but I never attended any meetings; well, that's if they have meetings, so consequently I never met, or knew anyone else."

Meena nodded and waited, but when no more information was forthcoming on that topic, she said, "The approaching operation to which you referred. Do you have any more details on this?"

"What sort of details?"

"When is it happening, and what exactly is involved?"

Francis shook his head. "When, I don't know exactly,

but I had the feeling it was fairly imminent, and this is why they were so jumpy when I reported that this O'Leary knew about the website."

"OK, but my interpretation about this website was that at a certain, well safeguarded level, it contained pornographic images of children. How does this tie in with this operation?"

"I'm not sure." The priest leaned back in his chair. "Maybe just a taste of what is to come; a titillation perhaps. There was just a hint that some of the children on display were groomed by the leaders, and ready for exploitation. You need to take these men into custody and interrogate them. I was only on the fringe, and as I said previously, when I saw that website, I knew this wasn't for me."

Meena wrote furiously; despite the recorder she was keen to get as much information into written form as soon as possible as she found it useful to mull over later. She could not decide just how innocent the priest really was, whether he was in it up to his neck or that once he realised what was involved with this group, he really did find it abhorrent and regret any connection. The thought that there was some sort of future operation planned was causing sharp-legged spiders to weave their way up her body from their evil web nestling nastily in her stomach. Dan and Luke were currently now going to Arthur and George's addresses, and as soon as possible, she needed to contact them and tell them these people needed to be apprehended and questioned thoroughly.

"Francis, the third point. You referred to this cell; are there other cells?" Once more memories of the operation of four years ago flooded her mind, momentarily drowning out her concentration. Pulling herself together, she focused on the moment. "What do you know about this?"

"Not a lot. There was a vague mention that the previous operation was too large and therefore unwieldy. I understand Arthur's cell is one of three in a compact area. Whether this term compact means Reading town, the county of Berkshire or even the South East, I've no idea. Security is tight, a top priority, and you're only told on a need to know basis. So, I was only told general facts, and no specifics."

"Thank you. I think that's all for the moment." Meena stood up, picking up her notes, and switching off the recording machine after reporting she was leaving the room. As she walked to the door, the uniformed officer opened it for her. She nodded her thanks, but before she passed through the doorway, Francis's words stopped her in her tracks.

"Yes, you do need to interview Arthur and his crew, but I do know they had nothing to do with these children or women that have gone missing over the last few months."

Meena turned, eyes wide open, her mouth open in an 'O' shape. Before she could say a word, he added, "They suspect the curate, David Sinclair."

"How would they know?"

Francis sniggered. "If I tell you this, I shall definitely expect something for my co-operation, and this piece of info." At her nod, he added, "They know a lot about your operation because you have a mole in your organisation, and using his info they're planning to shanghai him...Sinclair that is."

He felt pleased with this blow as he watched the beautiful woman's colour turn from a golden shade to a tinge as grey as a leaden, rainy sky in a bleak November evening.

Feeling sick, she hurried from the room, reaching for her mobile to contact her boss straightaway.

Chapter 81

Dan and Luke entered the elderly man's house into a long passageway decorated with old-fashioned shiny, beige wallpaper, covered in blue flowers. A large golden edged mirror and an old-fashioned coat-stand made the area, although dark, somehow warm and inviting. Both officers noted the several heavy coats hanging on it, suggesting visitors, unless George had an inclination towards an unusual number of outdoor garments.

"Come into the living room," George invited, opening a door on the right side of the hall. Dan noticed several more doors along the hall and wondered if any of them led to a cellar. On ringing the doorbell, he had noted, below ground level, a small window on the left-hand side of the house, protected by an iron grid. He was intrigued and wondered whether the framework was in place to keep intruders out, or a more interesting theory, to keep some one secure inside.

Dan nodded his thanks to George and was just about to walk into the living room, Luke behind him, when he heard a thump coming from somewhere along the hall. Glancing back to Luke, he was about to enquire from George if everything was fine, when a muffled sound echoed from along the passage, and Dan guessed it came from the same source as the thump. It sounded very much like a stifled yelp.

Both officers looked enquiringly at George, unaware their expressions, raised eyebrows, eyes wide open, were identical. At their arrival at the door, his face had paled, and it did not seem possible that his colour could deteriorate further, but they were wrong. His pallor became the worrying, leaden grey of a storm cloud about to deluge on anything beneath it.

When a loud scream followed by the clear words, 'Help me, help," echoed down the hall, George's legs collapsed beneath him, and he fell to the floor, clutching his chest.

"Christ, he's having a heart attack," said Luke, hurrying to his side. Kneeling beside him, he noticed his closed eyes and ragged breathing. Dan, bending down on the man's other side, felt for his pulse and then gently shook him, asking if he could hear them.

Dan stood up. "Right, phone for an ambulance. Stay with him. If he stops breathing, give him mouth to mouth."

Luke winced, looking up to Dan his expression showing distaste for the action. "Must I? I hate that sort of thing. Awful thing to say, but…"

"Jesus, Luke! OK, I'll phone and stay with him, you wuss; you go and investigate that yelling coming from one of those doors. Reckon it comes from a door maybe leading to a cellar, or another room along the passage."

Whilst Dan dialled for an ambulance and police back-up on his mobile, Luke hurried along the hall, opening doors and giving a running commentary on what he saw.

"Broom cupboard; dining room, no-one in there. Kitchen, nothing." He opened the last door on the left and glanced down the dark stairway in front of him. "Aah ha, looks like the cellar." No sooner had the words left his mouth, he yelped in surprise as a man bounded up the last few steps, knocking him over, causing an expletive to come from his mouth.

George was unaware that his companions had hurried to hide back in the cellar when they heard the police officers introducing themselves. The 'heavy' and John, had dragged Sinclair from the back room down to the cellar after the others to keep him silent. Unfortunately, it was a bad move, because their prisoner was younger and fitter than they realised. Consequently, he'd managed to push the heavy down the stairs, managing to shove past John's clutches, pull off his gag and yell as he escaped back up the stairs.

As Luke fell, the man tumbled over him on all fours and crawled down the corridor towards Dan, who by this time, was standing, and staring at the chaos in astonishment.

"Help me, help me. I've been kidnapped." The man jumped to his feet when he spotted the prone George, who appeared still unconscious. "Who's that, is he one of them?"

Dan, phone to his ear, suddenly realised he could hear a voice asking him which service he required. "Ambulance to…Christ, Luke, what's the address?"

As Luke staggered to his feet, he puffed, "22, Darren Close, Caversham."

After giving the address, and the relevant phone number for immediate police back-up, he snapped into the phone, "Yes, this is an emergency. I'm a Police Officer, Detective Sergeant Daniel Blake. There is a man at this address who I believe has had a heart attack, so hurry."

Slipping the phone in to his pocket, he turned to the man, who by this time was attempting to open the front door. Dan eased him back and firmly closed it again.

"Right, sir, what's happening here? I'm Detective Sergeant Blake, and this is my colleague, Detective Constable Steiner. You say you've been kidnapped."

"Yes, damn kidnapped. I'm a man of the church, and him…" he tapped George with his foot, "I believe, is one of the kidnappers. They took me from my house, drugged me."

"You *believe* this gentleman is one of the kidnappers, don't you know?"

"I couldn't see them. They shone a light into my eyes

as they questioned me. One of them left the room when the doorbell rang. They went into a panic. I could hear it in their voices. They put some sort of bandage trapping over my mouth and tried to drag me back to the cellar. In their fright, they hadn't tied my hands too well, and I managed to slip my hand out and pull off the strapping. In the scuffle, I pushed past them and climbed back up the stairs; they're old men, I could tell by their voices."

At that moment, George groaned and opened his eyes.

"One moment, sir." Dan knelt and asked George if he was all right. When the man attempted to sit up, Dan gently restrained him. "Just stay there, sir. I've phoned for an ambulance. Just be patient. Are you in pain?"

"A pain, in my chest." George's voice was gravelly, and obviously had difficulty speaking. "I feel...don't know... really ill."

Again, Dan assured him help was coming. Taking off his overcoat, he covered the man's body."

"I'll get you a cushion for your head. Can you point out your living room?

The man weakly pointed to a door next to the cellar entrance and Dan asked Luke, now standing, to get a cushion to place under the man's head.

In the distance, he could hear sirens. He waited until Luke appeared with the pillow and then saw him disappear through the door to the cellar.

Once sure George was comfortable, Dan stood and opened the door in readiness for the arrival of the ambulance. He turned and asked the person who had fled from the cellar. "Can you tell me your name, sir?"

"David Sinclair. I'm a curate from St Anne's. I need to go. I'm a busy man. I've missed the lessons I'm meant to give. It's disgraceful..."

Dan, whose ears had pricked up on hearing the man's name, interrupted. "You're David Sinclair. You allege this man kidnapped you."

"Yes, and there's other men down in the cellar. I bet they're hiding…I don't think I noticed another way out. They interrogated me for hours. They think I'm involved with some woman, abducting children. They're totally mad, the lot of them."

"And were you?"

"Was I what?"

"Involved with a woman. Abducting children."

"Heaven help us, don't you start! You say you're the police, you should be on my side, helping me."

Dan did not answer. He could hear vehicles drawing up outside and opened the door fully in readiness for the stretcher to get through. Two men with a stretcher walked to the front door, confirming it was the correct address, and asked had someone in the house called an ambulance, a suspected heart attack? Dan nodded them in just as a police car containing two uniformed officers drew up outside the house.

Before Dan could start explaining the situation to the newly arrived constables, he was interrupted by Luke appearing from the cellar door.

"Look what I've got, Boss. A coven of elderly gents. I think we may be needing more transport to escort these persons to the station." Turning to the cellar door, he addressed whoever was coming up the stairs. "Come on up gentlemen. You can explain your interviewing techniques to my boss."

Four men slowly walked through the doorway plus one burly much younger man. "I think this is the heavy," explained Luke. "I bet…"

"Can I go or not?" Sinclair interrupted.

"No, sir." replied Dan, his voice resolute. "I need to question you. We'll need some details from you regarding this allegation."

"Question me. What about, for God sake? I've already explained to this lot." He thumbed at the gaggle of elderly, white haired men gathered outside the cellar door, looking bemused and alarmed. "I've already told this lot, endless times, it's not me you're after, it's my mad brother. He's the one on league with that awful woman, Yvette Van Looy."

Dan and Luke looked at each other. Luke gasped, "What the …?"

Dan almost choked as he spluttered, "Brother!" Had they been chasing the wrong person, their enquiries over the last weeks totally off mark, like an arrow shot to a bull's eye and completely missing the whole target? "Fuck."

His mobile rang. His eyes still wide open with shock, he gasped, "Blake."

"Boss, it's Meena. The George Hampson you've gone to talk to. We need to interview him at the station. Bring him in."

"He's just off to the hospital. Don't worry, there's plenty more people to interview. Be with you shortly." He took a deep breath.

Brother! What brother?

He'd plan to take Lucy Hamilton to the jazz club that evening. As things were, his hot date was shooting away with the speed of a spaceship attempting to fight Earth's gravitational pull and head for the moon. He cursed under his breath again.

Chapter 82

Her mobile rang, and then stopped. Emma groaned. Her head was thumping. She had been to Charlene's 18th birthday party the night before held at the local Working Men's club and had drunk too many vodka and oranges. The last thing she remembered was walking home with Heidi, Jose, Petra, Charlene and various male friends, none of whom were any less happy.

They had been singing at the tops of their voices when a cop car had stopped, and with grins on their faces, the officers had suggested that maybe they should consider the neighbours. After a lot of good-hearted banter, and the cops wishing Charlene happy birthday, they had driven away. The singing had died down as requested, but Emma recalled the endless giggling. After that, everything was a blank. Peering across the room, she noticed her cocktail dress abandoned in the middle of her bedroom; collapsed into a shape of a half-closed concertina, sagging to the left, as though when she'd stepped out from it, it had remained frozen in that shape.

The phone rang again. Forcing open her bleary eyes, she checked the alarm clock.

"Jesus, who'd phone me on a Sunday at 8." She muttered into the mouthpiece, "This had better be worth it."

"Emma. Alfie. I just fort."

"Alfie? What, who…oh yeah, Alfie Smith. You just fort? Who'd you fight with." She heaved herself into a sitting position.

"No, no fight, but I fort a som'ink."

"Oh, you mean, you *thought* of something."

"Yeah, that's what I said."

"OK, so what did you just *fort*?"

"Me and Joey Pritchard, you know, Ginge, and Georgie Dexter goes around the back of the church after choir practice to have a quiet fag."

"Umm huh. Very responsible. Very religious."

"What?"

"Nothing, carry on."

"Behind the church, hidden in the corner is a big tomb, with a great big angel on the top, and if you goes down the steps, there's a door into it."

"You mean the old DeWit crypt. That's years old."

"Yeah, well we hides behind there for the fag 'cos nobody ever comes round there."

"So! Get to the point Alfie, I got a hangover as big as an atom bomb cloud."

What's that, a atom thingy what?"

"Never mind. You're round the back…"

"You said to phone if I fort of som'ink."

"Yep, *hurry* up."

"Well, when we do go around the back, I gets a headache."

"For God's sake. Either don't smoke or take some paracetamols."

"No, I mean one of me special heads. I suddenly realised, it's the crick...tomb."

"Crypt not crick. Anyway, you say it's the tomb, what d'you mean, what's the tomb?"

"It's the tomb what causes the pain. It's evil. It's like that devil woman."

The hangover disappeared. Emma took a gulp of water

from the beaker on the bedside table, her thinking and focus becoming as clear as freshly washed and dried crystal glass."

"You there?"

"Yes, Alfie. Have you ever been inside that crypt… tomb?"

"No, it's locked. We tried. But we're behind there one night. Really late. I know it was late 'cos me dad gave me a clip round the ear 'cos he knows choir practice finishes at half past eight."

He paused. Emma did not know if it was for effect. "Yes, and…"

"Guess who's got a key and went in there?"

Again, silence. Emma knew now it was definitely for effect, but she was, if not one-step ahead of the young boy, side by side with his thinking. "David Sinclair."

The devil woman's side kick.

"Yeah, dead right. I'm there now. Made out I was ill, so I didn't have to go to church. D'you wanna join me? It's locked but we could break in and check out the joint."

"Alfie Smith, your mum lets you watch too many American gangster films. Right, now under no circumstances try to break into that place. We don't want to get in there during the day. Can you get out tonight…early evening I mean?"

"Yeah. Mum'll go to evening service about six. I'll make out I'm still ill, although I don't always have to go in the evening."

"What about your dad?"

"He goes up the pub Sunday in the day, and always falls asleep after tea. I can get out easy."

"Mind you, I don't know how we'll break in, the door looks pretty thick if I remember rightly."

"I'll bring Ginge, he's dead thin, like a snake. There's a little window by the door. Bet he can wiggle in. No trouble."

"Sounds like a plan. I'll see you and snake hips at …"

"Snake who…"

"Never mind, see you at six thirty."

After she had rang off, Emma slid down into her bed. She considered phoning Heidi. "Nope," she answered herself. "she'll only say in a whiney voice, 'Phone the cops'."

She turned over; a smile of a conspirator painted on her lips, and promptly fell asleep for another hour.

Chapter 83

Dan, Meena, Luke were sitting in front of DI Cole's desk, updating him on the situation that had come together as quickly as when the last, mislaid piece of a jigsaw puzzle is found and triumphantly slotted into place.

Cole's face wore its usual dour expression, but the faces of the remaining three were identical and resembled grinning cats that had just discovered a world of mice. After all the months of hard investigation, it seemed as though they were closing in and winning the battle.

Cole shook his head. "So, this is what we have so far." He counted on his fingers. "One, we seem to have four elderly gents in custody, and another one in hospital suffering a suspected heart attack. You allege these men are the top level of a cell planning a similar operation to Operation Hobbledehoy that we successfully closed down, what, four or so years ago." Dan went to reply, but Cole held up his hand. "Second, we have also apprehended the top suspect in the disappearing women and children case."

Again, Dan went to explain, but Cole continued. "However, from what I now understand, Sinclair doesn't resemble in any way the top suspect Matthew Nielson. In fact, he claims we've got it totally wrong, as did the gang of Pensioners now in custody for allegedly kidnapping him, and that the suspect is his dark haired brother who has no

404

limp, and whom we have absolutely no knowledge of his existence, or his whereabouts whatsoever!" Taking a deep breath after his outburst, he leaned back in his chair, crossed his arms, and with a voice laced with sarcasm, said, "Tell me, how's that fucking progress?"

Both Luke and Meena's expressions showed their intimidation, and glanced at Dan to deal with the boss's unexpected outpouring, both separately deciding that *he* was their direct boss, and it was his responsibility, therefore, to explain clearly about their progress.

Taking a deep breath, Dan said, "We're confident that Sinclair and Nielson are one and the same. We have two witnesses who identified him from photographs obtained from security cameras positioned outside night clubs where he patrolled for his victims."

"Two witnesses, *teenage* witnesses, and a boy with a so-called *gift*, picked him out, but both girls admitted there was a resemblance, yet there was something about him that …what were their words if I remember Meena's report: they were 'let all the madness out of him or his counterpart'… very scientific and good evidence…not!"

Dan glanced at his boss, hoping the look that he discharged at him, when it landed, would not actually damage Cole's brain. *Maybe just leave a huge bruise.*

Taking another deep breath to control his annoyance, he continued,

"They both picked him out, using similar phrases that they were sure it was him, but surprised how different he looked. Yes, Sinclair has red hair and a limp, but if he wore a wig for his forays, and maybe a built-up heel, he would, could look …or have, a completely different image."

"And this brother issue?"

"Being checked as we speak. So far, we have no record of him."

"I still don't think we have enough to keep him in custody. If we had the women's bodies it'd help our case, but we haven't so much as a sniff of them. His solicitor is insisting we release him, saying he has suffered enough stress from the kidnapping. Now what progress have we made regarding that? The elderly gents in custody allege he was tied in with Van Looy, but he's denying everything, insisting it was his brother, and we have no proof except some grainy security camera pictures. This whole investigation sounds like it's in total chaos."

Dan nodded at Meena. She was not as brave as Dan in standing up to the indomitable Detective Inspector, but after all their hard work, and the fact they now had Sinclair in custody, including the men that Father Francis claimed were paedophiles, and involved in planning another operation to abduct children, to her it certainly seemed like progress, and had made the team euphoric. Now Cole, dashing their hopes of success to the ground with the intensity of cracking nuts with hard nailed boots, was disappointing to say the least. Unlike her normal cool self, she could feel her temper rising like lava driving up and about to burst forth from a volcano. Feeling her expression harden with annoyance, she controlled herself on noticing Dan's slight warning shake of the head,

"As you know, sir, I have been interviewing Father Francis from St Stephen's Jesuit College." Her voice was controlled but with a grating edge to the words. "He alleges that these five men were the head of a paedophile cell, planning another abduction operation. As you know, Sinclair was going to be brought in for questioning, but he could not be contacted. It appears the coven of elderly gentlemen had already abducted and interrogated him because they also believed that he, Sinclair, aka Nielson, was associating with Van Looy; the two of them hand in hand kidnapping children and the missing women."

"But it's their word, the five men, against Sinclair's, and I say again, we haven't the bodies of these missing women, so…"

Despite Dan's warning look, Meena could feel her temper escalating, the lava beginning to spill over the edge of the volcano! "Well, sir, that may be the case, but what we have going for us is the fact that these men received their information about Sinclair from a mole that we have at the station."

She felt somewhat mollified when DI Cole's mouth dropped open, and his eyes widened in shock and alarm. "So, this *mole* passed on our findings to these men which apparently backed up their suspicions that he, Sinclair, was working hand in hand with Van Looy. As their new operation was imminent, they wanted Sinclair eliminated as he was going to jeopardise it, and they certainly wanted to get their hands on Van Looy. I'm not sure why, and I don't think the priest knew either, because she used to be one of them in the nonces gang. Also, and very worryingly, Father Francis said the cell that they belonged to was just one of three cells involved in this forthcoming operation!"

Cole stared at Meena for a few seconds, his mind obviously whirling with this new information that they had not previously had time to relate to him.

Pressing his lips together, he sniffed, nodded again, and murmured, "A mole you say. This puts a fresh complexion on things in more ways than one." Leaning back in his chair, he said to Meena, "Good work. In fact, good work to all of you. You must understand my position; we must have solid facts and a rock-hard case to put before the CPS. Otherwise, a waste of time and money."

He nodded to Luke. "And what have you got?"

"As you know, Guv, I was with DS Blake when we went to the address of George Hampson to investigate the priest's allegations. We have kept the four men separate and have uniform guarding Hampson who is still in hospital with a suspected heart attack, although the latest info is that it's a mild attack. They are elderly men in their sixties and seventies, and I don't think it will be long before one of them cracks. I can't imagine at their age they'd fancy spending time inside, so if they can buy some good bonus points to help their case, I think they will."

"Who's interrogating them?"

"The three of us, and Mel when needed. I feel confident it won't take long."

DI Cole nodded. "OK." Looking back to Dan, he asked, "And your next steps?"

"Finding the bodies would mean a big step forward. Until we can trace the so-called guilty brother, I agree we have no choice but to let Sinclair go. We will do a line-up and get the girls back in to see if they can pick him out. They picked him out from the photos, but of course in those, his appearance was different." Dan leaned forward and placed his files on Coles' desk. "Guv, the three of us have discussed this and agree that if we let him go, we keep a trace on him, and if he is guilty, and therefore the kidnapper, he may well lead us to the bodies. Then we'll have him."

"OK, but what happens if this brother is not fictitious."

"We've lost nothing. We have let an innocent man go. The brother, Sinclair alleges, lives with him, so we keep a watch on both him and his house. Chances are, he'll turn up sometime, somewhere. If we follow him, and as I said, it might be he leads us to the bodies."

"OK. Sinclair or the brother, Nielson; why the different surnames?"

"We've checked that, and he alleges they have different fathers."

"Sinclair maintains he has nothing to do with these cell members and their future operation. Has that been verified?"

"We are working on that. Presumably, he's a different entity or why would they kidnap him. When one of the five of the white-haired-gang breaks, we'll know for sure."

Cole stood up, collecting his own files from the desktop. "Right. Keep me posted. Just make sure if you let Sinclair go that you don't lose sight of him. I assume you are also thoroughly investigating the mole situation, and the other cells that are operating in the area?"

"Naturally, those two investigations are our top priorities."

Cole grunted a 'Well done, keep up the pace', as he left the room.

"Not exactly overflowing with praise after all our hard work and progress," Meena muttered.

"You must be used to him by now," said Luke as he stood up and stretched his back. "OK, this mole situation. How we going to deal with that?"

"We have to keep that to ourselves. I would have trusted everyone out there with my life, so unless the priest is trying to fool us, all we can do is keep our eyes skinned, and set up security cameras as we discussed. I don't think that's going to show us much, but it's better than nothing. We just watch our tongues." Dan sat back in his chair, and nodded as though considering his words, before he continued.

"We let Sinclair go. We'll have to work out a schedule for watching him, form team pairs; maybe keep that between ourselves because of the mole situation. If he or his 'fictitious brother', and almost certainly a sociopath, is responsible for the disappearances of those women and children, then let's hope he can't resist going to peek at their precious bodies."

"I dunno, I'd think that'll be the last thing he'll do," said Luke.

"Miracles are in the air, I feel it. OK, let's start interviewing the white-haired brigade again, and Inshallah, we get away before the pubs close."

"Right…drinks on you, boss, in the local pub while we sort out the stakeout teams?" said Meena.

"Definitely," grinned Dan. "Just one for me then 'cos I've got a hot date. So, let's get these interviews over first."

Meena was surprised at her reaction to his remark about the hot date. Not so long ago she would have been wounded, but she had no reaction to the words at all. Glancing at Luke, she was pleased when he winked and then grinned at her. She turned away, feeling a blush slowly brushing her cheeks.

Chapter 84

Sinclair wandered around the house, irritated by what he saw. He could tell the police had been here, probably when initially looking for him. He could not remember that they had mentioned actually searching his property, although he recalled something about a search warrant. He shook his head in frustration.

"If they didn't want me to know," he mumbled, "they should've been more careful. The liars made out they broke down the door because my lights were on, and they assumed I was at home but refusing to answer the door. Poppy cock, they enjoyed busting down my door. OK, the lock's mended, but they're going to have to buy me a new, bloody door."

As he meandered, he closed a drawer in his bedside cabinet that they had left a mere centimetre open, but very spottable. The bathroom cabinet that he kept in pristine order was messy. The painkillers were at the back of the bottom shelf instead of at the front, and the indigestion tablets had been replaced on the wrong shelf completely.

Very shabby. Good job you don't work for me.

Slowly working himself through the whole house, he noted the worse mess was in the office. The computer had obviously been moved slightly, revealing a small angle of dust.

They could have dusted for me. He wiped the dust away

with his forefinger.

Even his stamps were out of order. He recalled how he had been enjoying himself when the doorbell rang, and that thug had him whisked away.

Still that's over now. Cops obviously think I'm in the clear. They had nothing to hold me. I've got to go back in tomorrow to make a statement about the incident...should be easy to fool 'em.

Walking to the window, he stared into the gloom, seeing his own reflection more clearly than the view.

The itch arrived. In the usual way, starting at the base of his spine, and like a line of determined bugs, it slithered up, via his stomach, stalking endlessly upwards. Smiling, he waited for it to sneak into his brain, curling and scrambling, looking for the right place. When it found its goal, it caressed, and encouraged until the right thoughts formed, stoking the hunger like coals on a hungry fire.

"*Don't go, Matthew, maybe the cops are trailing you.*"

"*Don't be a wuss, David. They're not interested in me. They were interested in you 'cos you got yourself kidnapped. Now the urge is building. I've told you weeks ago I couldn't go or much longer...without some action.*"

"*What about that girl Wendy with the kid. I thought she was the next one.*"

"*I told you, she scarpered, the little bitch.*"

"*I still think...*"

"*Please, you know I don't take chances. I'll go and get my shoes and hair. My phone for contacting Yvette's there. She's probably wondering where the hell I am. She may have been on the look-out for me for any future clients.*"

"*Why would she bother to do that? You haven't managed to secure any kids for her of late.*"

"*Yes...well we said we'd lay low for a while...but, she's probably as much in the need of a fix as I am.*"

"*OK, you've convinced me. Just be careful in case*

they've got surveillance on you. Slip out the back way, and over the fence. You'd better take a torch, it's dark over those fields."

"You're right. You take such care of me, so caring, little bro. I won't be long. We'll have a nice cup of tea when I return."

"Take care. Don't take any unnecessary chances."
"Bye."
"Bye."

PART 4
BLACK HALO

Chapter 85

It was two days after Alfie's phone call, and Emma was on the way to meet him. She had cancelled the Sunday evening meeting arrangement with him and the skinny ginger kid as her mother's cousin had suddenly died, and although they were not close to him, Emma knew it would be totally inconsiderate to her mum if she swanned out for the evening.

The rain that had plummeted down all day had stopped, but the clouds, dark and heavy, still looked threatening, and as she glanced upwards, she decided the sky was doing a good interpretation of a frown. Her bike had a puncture, so she'd borrowed her sisters, and as it was too big for her, the going was far from easy. By the time she wobbled her way into the graveyard and saw the two lads sitting outside the tomb, night had kicked aside the day and tumbled over the area. Ginge's quiff still stood as proud as the Eiffel tower.

Skidding to an unladylike halt, she glared at the lads who were sitting on two large stones sited either side of the doorway; cigarettes, dangling gangster-like from the corner of their mouths, were glowing in the gloom.

"Put those out, you idiots," she scolded them.

"Warum?" replied Alfie, who had just started to learn German and wanted to demonstrate his multi-lingual skills.

Emma propped the bike against the side of the rough stone-clad walls of the crypt, advancing towards them with a manner menacing enough for Ginge to smartly remove the now dog-end and crush it under foot. Alfie, quivering inside, displayed a brave face.

Emma leaned towards him, face only six inches away, and snarled, "'Cos A, it's bad for you, B, someone may see the glowing ends and wonder what the hell is going on, and C, 'cos I bloody told you to."

Alfie could not think of a smart-alec reply that would make him top dog in this situation, so, lips pursed sulkily, he dropped the dog end and ground it under foot. He could not resist muttering, "S'nearly finished any'ow."

Emma pulled three bags of Maltesers from her mac pocket and tossed one each to the boys. "Right, gang," she said. "How we gonna do this? That little window by the door looks pretty small to me even for Ginge to squeeze his skinny little frame through."

"It'll be easy peasy," said Ginge leaping to his feet and in one movement, as swift as a stripper paid on time-management skills, pulled off his shabby anorak and an equally scruffy tee shirt, both of which had no effect on the solid pompadour hairstyle.

The stone that had supported his fag break was conveniently placed beneath the small window that had one, minute shard of glass sticking up from the bottom of the frame like a shark's fin.

"I don't think we ought to do any more damage," said Emma, "Someone's obviously smashed the glass, but if we don't remove that last piece, it'll rip your skin to shreds." She eased Ginge aside and climbed onto the stone to gain easier access to the window. Tucking her hand into her sleeve, she pushed against the glass shard attempting to remove it. Holding herself steady with the left hand on the door, she tumbled off the stone as the door glided open with the pressure of her hand.

"Jesus H," chortled Alfie, "frigging door was open all the time." Both boys were reduced to holding their sides with laughter at the silly situation.

Emma was about to snap why the hell hadn't they checked but realising she had discovered the lucky situation by chance, she swallowed the words.

"I thought you said it was locked when you phoned me."

"It was."

"Right, laddos, someone's been here. We go in, but be careful," she said, peering cautiously into the darkness, "follow me. Anyone bring a torch?"

"Oh, bugger," said Alfie, "never fort a that."

A bright beam illuminated the tomb. "Good job I've got some brains then."

"You're well clever, Emma," congratulated Ginge, looking admiringly at the pretty girl on whom he was definitely beginning to have a severe crush.

Emma guardedly entered the crypt with the two boys close on her heels. She peered around the gloom but even when her eyes had adjusted, she could not see anything clearly. Despite the open door and the small window, the inside was full of dust, causing all three of them to cough.

Gradually her eyes adjusted to the murk. In the centre of the chamber was a large stone tomb, covered with a heavy looking lid. Around the far side were two further similar sized tombs, whilst along the left side was a smaller one and another made of a dark wood and an identical one on the right.

"Phew," said Alfie, "Wha's that stink?"

"Don't suppose the place has been opened for ages," said Emma. "It's bound to be pretty dusty and musty as well."

"Yeah, but even so, it's 'orrible smelling," added Ginge, holding his nostrils closed as he spoke.

"OK, let's make this quick. Alfie, how's your head?"
"What?"

"You said that while you were having a ciggy here

with your mate, you experienced a terrible headache. Any symptoms?"

"A bit, but nuffink like the other day."

The three wandered around the chamber.

"It's coming from that one," said Ginge, pointing to the coffin in the centre.

"What's coming from where?" asked Emma.

"The stink."

Emma wandered to the coffin, and noticed the lid was not fitted properly, leaving a small open angle where it slanted very slightly towards her. She bent over the opening, Ginge close by, and agreed with him that a pong certainly was emitting from it.

"I would have thought the body would have been put here years ago. This belonged to some posh family that lived in a big manor house demolished ages ago when I was a kid," Emma explained. "You two are too young to remember it."

"Hey, look what I got. Really cool," yelled Alfie from the left corner of the chamber. He shuffled towards them in a large pair of shoes, and a black wig pulled in a lop-sided way over his head and clutching a mobile phone.

"Where the hell did you find those?" said Emma, smirking in unison with Ginge at the comical sight before them.

"Ow, ow, it hurts," yelped Alfie, suddenly holding the side of his head, and bending double as though in pain.

Rushing to his side, Emma put her arm around him, asking how she could help. Ginge turned white, wrapping his arms round himself in distress, mumbling, "Oh dear, what can we do. I've never seen him like this before."

Alfie straightened up, ejected a loud hoot of laughter, and yelled, "Yeah, yeah, yeah. Fooled you both!"

"You little bastard," said Emma, batting him round the head.

"Fucking bastard more like it," muttered Ginge, but he

could not stop himself grinning in relief.

Alfie lifted his right foot, saying in between hiccups of laughter, "Look at this, well weird. This shoes got a big heel while me left heel's flat." He rocked the wig side to side on his head, saying, "And don't I look well sexy in this syrup."

"What? Syrup!"

"Yeah…syrup of figs… wigs…rhyming slang," Ginge explained to Emma. "Did a programme on it on tele last week. Alfie an' me been using it ever since."

The three of them laughed as Alfie performed a lop-sided jig with the uneven shoes, and the wig wobbling on his head and eventually falling over his face, causing Ginge to have hysterics.

"Aah," Alfie moaned, "me head 'urts."

"Don't overdo it, Alfie. It's not funny a second time round."

"I fink he's serious," said Ginge, "He's gone dead white."

"What the fuck d'you think you're doing here with my gear?"

Emma's heart thumped and she had the distinct feeling her stomach had been punched as a man yelled from the door, hands on hips and looking furious. She could only see his outline in the doorway, but she knew who it was. Panic made her eyes adjust quickly. He did not resemble the Matthew Nielson that Emma knew, this person had red-cropped hair and glasses, but unlike the bland photos of him that Emma had checked at the police station, this time the teenager could both see and feel the evil emanating from his expression, his whole being. It swamped the room. Whoever it was, she knew they were in deep shite.

Chapter 86

Luke was checking his emails when his phone rang, and someone asked for DC Steiner.

"Speaking. Who's calling?"

"Sir, it's WPC Maggie Smith. PC Jeff Tanner and I were assigned to watch Sinclair. I think he's scarpered."

"How the hell…?"

"The lights went off about ten minutes ago. We decided it was too early for him to go to bed, yet he hadn't left the house by the front door. Jeff took a look round the side and back. He didn't see anything, but just returning to where I was stationed, he heard a noise; a gate closing maybe, at the bottom of the garden. He hurried back around the house to check, and swears, in the gloom, he saw a figure running over the small field at the back of the garden. He scooted back to tell me, and now he's gone after him, and asked me to knock the door to check whether he was still at home. If there was no answer, I was to report in and ask for back up. I've knocked the door and I'm sure there's no-one there.

"I know the area well. If Sinclair follows the small field to the north, it leads straight into the churchyard where he's the choirmaster. For whatever reason, I think that's where he's headed because on the east there's a wide stream… not crossable on foot. West are farm fields, dug up after the summer crop and now deep in mud after the rain. Can't be sure, but I suspect he must be headed for the cemetery."

"Ok, thanks, Maggie. I'll get a team over there straight away. What are you going to do?"

"I'll report back to Jeff and tell him that I'll drive to the cemetery now and meet up with him and hopefully we spot Sinclair."

"Be careful, Sinclair, if our suspicions are right, is dangerous."

The police officer thanked Luke for the warning and rang off.

Within ten minutes Luke was in a police vehicle with two constables, followed by Dan and Meena driven by a burley police officer, and by the size of his shoulders, Dan was glad they were on the same side.

"I've a bad feeling about this," Dan muttered.

Meena looked sideways at Dan, not sure if he was talking to her. She noticed his perfect profile, and had an urge to say, "I loved you once, you know." Glancing away, she felt suddenly relieved, because although she knew he liked her, it was only as a colleague, and that's how it should be. Her thoughts turned to Luke.

Chapter 87

"Get behind me," Emma ordered the two boys.

Ginge quickly obliged, but Alfie seemed in a daze. Emma grabbed him and pushed him behind her. He staggered and seemed confused as to what was occurring.

"Hold him up, Ginge," she ordered.

"Oh, the strong and forceful Emma Bradbury. How long have I been wanting to find you?" His voice was a snarl, and Emma's stomach lurched painfully.

"What do you want? Who…?" The penny dropped with a big clang, and she suddenly realised who he resembled, and knew they were in big trouble.

"It's Mr Sinclair," whispered Ginge.

"What do you want with us?"

"What do I want? Ooh, lots of things. Just for starters, stabbing my brother in the foot."

"Your brother! What, Matthew Nielson's your brother! He's mad, evil, a total loony, and I know what was on his mind. First date and he thought I was easy pickings."

"Well, all you sluts are easy pickings as you put it so delicately." Emma's eyes, now adjusting to the gloom saw his sneer, and her heart lurched again. He might not have black hair, might not be dressed in a black leather coat, but she recognised that look immediately. Recalling the black wig that was presumably still stuck on Alfie's

424

head, she gasped.

"Your brother! Don't kid me. There's no such person as your loony brother. *You're* the crazy Matthew Nielson. I stabbed *your foot*. You put on a wig and think you're someone else, men's gift to women. Well, you're not, you're a pathetic, murdering nut case."

"You disgusting little slut, you don't know what you're talking about, and you're going to pay for stabbing my brother." He stepped backwards pushing the door closed, and half turned as he did but still keeping his eyes on the three figures frozen with fear as though co-starring in an ice tableau. Sniggering, he slid the bolt across the top of the door. "And when I've finished with you, I'll deal with that little sod who dares to wear the wig and shoes."

Emma's mind was whirling, but the panic, instead of terrorising and freezing her rational thinking, accelerated the fight or flight syndrome swirling in her brain. Realising she must keep him talking in the slim hope that either she could talk him out of attacking them, or an even slimmer hope, that someone might arrive and rescue them in time. Unlikely, but it was all she could hope for.

He clapped his hand, laughed, and with eyes wide open and having a distinctly hysterical look radiating from them, without warning leapt forward and punched Emma in the stomach. Immediately she doubled up, gasping for breath, and feeling sick with the pain. He pushed her away from her position of shielding the two boys, and she tumbled to the floor.

The agony made her nauseous, and she fought not to vomit. Shaking her head to concentrate her thoughts, she was horrified to hear a gurgling sound coming from one of the boys. Forcing up her head to see what was happening, she was aghast to see his hands around Alfie's throat. Even in the gloom, she could see the boy turning purple. Ginge was moaning, frozen to the spot. Forgetting her own pain, she screamed, "Aah, you fucking bastard." He glanced over his shoulder at her and leered. That was his mistake.

Anger roared through her body like a tornado. Desperation and resolve blazed like fire along her limbs filling them with a red-hot strength, and she leapt up onto his back, legs round his waist and used her hands to claw at his eyes. Her false nails were long, acrylic hard, and somewhere in a distant place in her mind, she guessed she was doing her nails irreparable harm, and they'd cost a fortune to have them put on! She didn't care a jot and dug even more viciously as though she possessed the claws of a lion and the two boys were her cubs.

"No-one is killing kids on my fucking watch," she screeched, and twisted her hands to jab even more. She shrieked like a fiend possessed, not realising to Nielson it sounded like a mother lion's roar.

His screams filled the tomb, echoing off the walls, rivalling hers. Letting go of Alfie, who collapsed onto the floor, Sinclair reeled like a whirling dervisher, but even his frenzy could not dislodge her. She tightened her legs around his waist, and though he managed to pull one of her hands away from his face, and squeeze her fingers hard in an attempt to crush her left hand, she then wrapped her right hand round his neck and would not be shifted. In her fury, she did not hear a thumping sound in the distance.

It was not until a woman's voice, urging her to let go, telling her they were safe, that the police were here, and in control of the situation, did the demonic fury abate. Letting go of her prey, she slid away and collapsed into the police officer's arms and sobbed uncontrollably with relief.

Chapter 88

Dan was sitting with Meena around DI Cole's desk, updating him on the capture of David Sinclair. He had written up his report and presented it to the boss, but what the police had witnessed did not sound as good as actually telling the tale, and interspersed with their laughter. Even the strait-laced DI Coles smirked as he explained.

"Guv, you've never seen anything like it. She was wrapped round him like a snake and was attempting to gouge out his eyes, and in her fury, if we hadn't arrived when we did, I'm sure he'd be as blind as a bat, or strangled when she got the arm round his throat. Luckily, Alfie's friend, Ginge, when he heard us knocking, unbolted the door or we'd have never got in. We didn't have a door ram with us." Dan shook his head and laughed again as he recalled the sight that had greeted them. "As I explained in the report, he'd punched Emma, she was doubled up on the floor in agony when she heard a gurgling sound. She realised he was strangling Alfie Smith, and guessed that unless she did something rapidly, he was going to die."

"I think if she hadn't leapt on him, her howling and screeching would deafen him for life," interrupted Meena. "As he couldn't be found anywhere in the churchyard, it seemed we'd lost him until we heard the yelling. When Ginge let us in and we saw what was happening, it took me a good few minutes to make her appreciate we had arrived, and they were safe."

"Me and Meena and the back-up brought them back to the station and got statements from all of them. We left Luke with PCs Jeff Tanner and Maggie Smith to inspect the crypt. As my report states, we found women's bodies hidden in the coffins. It's now a crime scene and SOCOs are having a field day. There's a very fresh body. We've so far accounted for all our local missing women. We're contacting other stations to check if there's a report of a recently missing young woman. Haven't heard anything yet."

"OK. Regarding the site, Chief Superintendent Heath, DCI Jacobs and I are intending to inspect the site once we've finished. Carry on."

"There was also a locked metal box," said Dan. "I couldn't get into it and called in the heavies to break it open once SOCOs had taken their photos and finished their investigations. The contents are horrendous. Sinclair obviously takes souvenirs and stores them in it. Some are body parts, and the stench from those and the bodies is dire. You'll need masks, Sir."

"Ok, so we have enough to arrest him then?" Cole's voice had an ironic ring to it. At Dan's nod, he continued, "And the brother, Matthew?"

"There is no record from Southport of him having a brother. He obviously went out stalking in his black wig, also wearing built up shoe so he didn't have a limp. No wonder when we searched his house, no evidence was found. He kept everything in the crypt."

"You've now arrested him and read him his rights?"

"Yes, already done," said Dan. "He hasn't said a thing, clammed up. When we've finished, I'm back there. There's a black jacket that looks a similar material to the fibres found under *Jason's* nails. That's being examined. We have so much evidence, if he doesn't confess, we've got more than enough to satisfy the CPS. Best thing we did letting him go and tailing him."

"Well done. What's the progress on the White Hair Brigade?"

Dan nodded to Meena to explain. "Singing like canaries, Guv. All of them. At their ages, they're hoping to avoid jail time by being the one to confess, not realising they're all singing."

"And the other cells that the priest referred to? Did you get any information on those?"

"Seventeen people over Berkshire have been arrested so far. The new planned operation is as dead as a dodo."

"Just two more questions. Any sign of Van Looy?"

"She must be holed up. Her face has been on the news and TV, but there are no sightings."

"OK. Any progress on the alleged mole?"

"No, we're pushing on that, and being careful what we say in front of the team. It's really gutting, knowing there's a spy in the camp."

"Anything else I need to know?"

"No. My report is fully detailed and contains all the facts you need to know for the Press Report tomorrow."

At that moment, there was a knock on the door and Luke entered. He nodded to DI Coles and grinned at Dan and Meena.

Coles stood up, collecting his files. He looked at the three police officers opposite him, allowing himself a rare smile, he said, "Well done. Good progress. Sorry I can't join your celebrations in the pub." Putting his hand in his pocket, he handed a bunch of ten-pound notes to Dan. "You three and the rest of the team have a drink on me. No-one drives if they've been drinking."

When Coles exited his room, Luke smirked and muttered under his breath, "No, daddy."

The three stood up in unison and walked to reception. "I've got the dosh, so drinks on me then," said Dan. "First to the bar gets a double."

The sound of an Irish accent caused them all to turn. Behind them stood a grinning Adam Kennedy, hands on his hips. "OK, you three feckin' bastards, what's going down? You look like cats that have just found the cream, double, Cornish at that."

"We're off to the pub," replied Dan. "Celebrating because we've just snared the bastard that's been killing the missing women and kids. A miracle then happened, and the first round is on our beloved DI for a change."

"Fecking' hell, that is definitely a miracle. I was just coming to get you's all. I'm celebrating too."

"Oh yes, what's that all about?" asked Meena.

"Nosey woman. Well, if you must know, I've just got engaged."

"Jesus H, not to the red-head beauty...umm... Danny, the Radio Announcer," said Luke, eyes wide with astonishment, but a smile of delight for his best friend smothering his face.

"Yep. Come on, matey, first rounds on me. Then we spend Coles money and get pissed out of our brains."

The four detectives, all grinning, trooped out of the station heading straight for the nearest pub.

Chapter 89

Meena shook her head in frustration. She looked at her watch and realised although it was almost closing time, she wasn't going to be able to eject her drunken colleagues. They had been talking absolute drivel for the past hour and it was only going to get worse. Now Adam was regaling them with really stupid Irish jokes and his accent was now so slurred by the drink that his words were undecipherable. She knew it didn't matter; the three men were so far gone they'd have laughed if he'd been reciting the alphabet.

She had had enough drink herself, three vodka and diet Pepsis, then a large glass of wine they had insisted on buying her when they had ordered the 'feckin' great beef burgers' that Adam had bought for them to eat an hour or so ago, and she was now planning how to escape unnoticed.

"Just going to the Ladies," she said, recognising they weren't listening and knowing this was the time to escape. Her car was still at the station, so if she could sneak out whilst they were engaged with the nonsense Irish jokes, she could get a taxi home. They still had to get to work on time in the morning, and if they wanted to turn up with hideous hangovers, that was up to them, but she didn't intend to be late or have a killer headache!

She used the toilet, washed her hands, and eased open the cloakroom door that thankfully was around the corner and not in their eyeline. Getting to the entrance, she cursed when she saw the rain coming down like Niagara Fall's younger brother and stopped to slip on her mac. This timing was her undoing when she reflected back on the evening. As she did so, a drunken Luke lurched around the corner and spotted her.

"And where do you think you're going to, my pretty maid? The night's still young," he slurred.

"Not for me," she answered, pushing the door open to make a quick exit.

"Then I'm coming with you."

"Oh no you're not. Go back to Dan and Adam, they'll wonder where you are."

"Nope. They'll guess I escorted you home. Nasty night like this, they'll know a gent like me couldn't possibly let a lady go home unescorted this late at night. They'll be robbers an' thieves and aliens and all sorts out there. We'll get a taxi and get you home."

"You are not under any circumstances sleeping on my sofa."

Despite the drink, the twinkle in Luke's eyes made her heart beat faster. Yes, when she thought back on that incident, that moment, that's when the romance started. Her Muslim parents would have gasped with horror if they knew what happened that night, and Meena had always thought too much drink affected men's performance…how wrong she was!

Chapter 90

"You did what, you crazy cow?" yelled Heidi.

Jose, taking this literally, said, "Yeah, stupid turd went to the tomb with Alfie and Ginge."

"I know she did, dafty, she's just told us. I said what I said 'cos for oners, she'd promised she wouldn't do anything stupid, and twoers, she said she'd always involve either us, or the boys in blue."

"Boys in blue, who's that?" said Jose, whose IQ had not improved since the stabbing.

"The bizzies, the law," explained Emma. Turning back to the frustrated Heidi, she continued. "I didn't think there was any danger. Alfie had phoned and said when he and Ginge went behind the DeWit memorial crypt for a ciggy, he got one of his 'gift' headaches. Thought it worth investigating, although I didn't think there was anything to it. Can you imagine what the police would have thought if I'd phoned and said two lads were smoking in the church yard. They'd have probably put the phone down on me."

"Why didn't you phone me then? You promised you wouldn't start any of your stupid adventures on your own."

"Alright, I'm sorry. Anyway, things worked out ok. The cops have Sinclair. DS Blake wants me to come in again in tomorrow to confirm Sinclair is Nielson. Apparently, there is no record of Matthew Nielson being his brother. Now all we have to do now is find the evil Yvette Van Looy."

"No *now* and no *we* about it," retorted Heidi. "It's up to the cops to find her."

"Yes, just a figure of speech, you know what I mean." Keen to change the subject, she asked Heidi about her new boyfriend, and the conversation drifted away from the topic. That didn't fool Heidi who now intended to watch her friend like a hawk who's spotted his prey running for cover and has no intention of losing it. Jose, whose concentration ability on any topic was severely limited, listened avidly to the boyfriend gossip, the crypt event already forgotten.

It was a Monday morning, and Jose and Heidi, not having college until after lunch, had popped in to hear the gory details. Emma felt mean, but she could not wait for her friends to leave. She was working from home on her design project, and although smiling and nodding at the details of Heidi's first date with the dishy Tommy Taylor, she was finding it hard to concentrate. All she could think about was riding her bike to Loddon House and prowling around the place. She had mentioned it to Meena when she had interviewed her about the incident in the crypt, but the detective assured her a police car had driven past; two constables then walked the grounds, and even been into the house to check the rooms, but there was no sign of anyone having been there.

But Emma sensed in her heart this was not right and nestling deep inside her was an itch that needed to be scratched. She just knew the She-devil in modern clothing was there; could feel it in her very being and had to check just one last time. Promising herself, if she found nothing, she would give up the search, and convince herself that her fixation was an unhealthy obsession.

At midday, her two friends took their leave and rode off to attend their college classes. No sooner had they disappeared round the corner of her road, Emma opened the garage door, put her arms through her backpack straps that she had hung onto the handlebars beforehand, and leaping on her sister's bike, her puncture not yet mended, headed off towards Loddon house.

Although not raining, the sky was heavy and overcast, and as she rode along she noticed the cars were already switching on their lights in the gloom and Emma was glad she was on her sister's bike as it had lights, and her bike did not.

Heading through the alleyways interspersed through her estate, over the Bath Road, and into more 'rat runs', knowledge that all local kids possessed, she shortened the twenty-five-minute journey to fifteen before arriving at the lane leading to the house. Here she slowed, aware she ought to show caution. Leaning her bike against the thick hedge surrounding the property, she peered around the corner. The gate from where she and Heidi had stared and spotted the light was still locked, but that was understandable. If Van Looy was holed up there, she was not going to give the game away by being careless and leaving it ajar.

The wind blew steadily down the stony unmade up road, and Emma shivered. Glad she had thought to bring her anorak, she retrieved it from her backpack and gladly donned it. Decided she would watch for half an hour, and if she had spotted nothing by then, more 'burglary' type action was needed.

Yvette Van Looy surveyed her limited supplies and knew she was going to have to chance it and venture out.

The previous evening, she had risked going to a local corner shop for milk and a paper, but knew she could not chance going to a small shop like that again in case questions were asked, or she was remembered. Tying back her hair in a severe ponytail, and wearing the glasses she used for driving, she was sure she would not be recognised from pictures that had been newsworthy a few weeks ago. Luckily for her, the news media and the public soon grew tired of stories that had not had a recent juicy development, so her face was hopefully ancient and forgotten news.

She had been shocked to see the headlines that a man had been arrested and charged in connection to missing women whose bodies had been recently discovered. His name had not been mentioned, but that meant Sinclair aka Nielson had been caught, and she knew now she had to move on. Although he did not know where she was holed up, the law might put two and two together, and come up with the right math for a change. They would remember that Nielson had used Loddon house, and decide another search was in order. They had been back and searched again, but luckily had not discovered her hidey-hole, but if they returned, they might be more thorough.

Realising time wasn't to be wasted, and the sooner she got a few supplies and moved on, the better. There had been no news regarding her car or its number plate, so she felt confident it was still a usable asset. Deciding that a visit to the supermarket on the edge of Reading was a necessity and safe, because the multi-story car park led straight into the shop so she could drive there, park as close as possible to the entrance, and with the usual disguise, be in and out in twenty minutes. Come nightfall, she would scarper.

She carefully looked through windows on all sides of the house, but no neighbours or nosey parkers were visible. Hurrying down to the kitchen and checking again through the window before unlocking the door, she hurried to the tumble-down garage cum shed hidden behind the small orchard that housed her car.

As she came briefly into view, her fleeting appearance would be visible for only seconds should anyone be watching from the front gate.

Emma, still peering round the hedge, almost choked on the apple from which she had just taken a large bite. She knew immediately who it was, despite the change of appearance.

Grabbing her mobile phone from her pocket, she forced herself not to panic as she scrolled through her list of telephone numbers. Within seconds, she had found DS Blake's number, but no sooner touched the number when she heard a car driving up the lane towards her. She crouched down and pushed herself as far as possible into the hedge, knowing she was still visible, but hopefully now small enough to be out of eyesight for a car driver.

The car drove past and recognising it as the 'taxi' that had driven her to Loddon house on the evening date with Nielson, she jumped to peer round the hedge and read the registration number. Her eyes were good, but the car was already twenty yards away and moving but she managed to read the first four digits.

Suddenly aware of a voice, she realised she had dropped the phone and the voice was coming from there. She snatched it up as she heard the detective's voice. Interrupting him, she said, "DS Blake, it's me, Emma Bradbury. I'm outside Loddon House. I've just seen the taxi driver, Van woman something or other who brought me here that night. She's just driven away in her taxi car, a black Ford. I only got the first part of the registration, it's *AK22* something. I'm going after her. I'm on me bike so I've gotta go. I might catch her if I zip round the lanes and spot her at the main road, find the direction she's going in. Tell your mates to keep an eye open for the car. I'll phone you if I catch her up."

She shut down the phone, not realising she had left a dumb struck detective on the other end with his mouth dropped open in an unmanly fashion.

Chapter 91

Meena glanced up from the desk as she sat writing up a report.

"What's wrong, boss?" she asked, seeing Dan's dazed expression.

"Jesus Christ, you won't believe this. That was Emma Bradbury. She's outside Loddon House and has just seen Van Looy drive away. She's going after her."

"What? Has she got a car?"

"No, she's on her bike. She reckons she can quote, 'zip through the back lanes' and keep up with her."

"Didn't you tell her to leave well alone; leave it to us?"

"I didn't have a chance." Dan stood up and walked to her desk. "Here's the details of the car she gave me. Have it circulated to the patrol cars as soon as possible."

He picked up the coat from the back of his chair and put it on.

"Where are you going, boss?"

"She said she'd phone if she caught up with Van Looy's car. Tell us the direction she's taking. I'm going to phone her from my car and try and persuade the crazy idiot not to follow and get herself into trouble."

"Do you want any assistance?" Meena called to his back.

"No, I'll be in touch. Get that part registration number

and car details out as soon as possible."

With that, he was through the swing doors and gone.

Emma's chest hurt and she had a stitch in her side as she hurtled along the back alleyways, twice having to swerve. The first veer was to avoid a burly young man who shouted words suggesting that her parents had born her out of wedlock. The other incident was, on swinging around a blind corner she almost wiped out two elderly ladies, each carrying two shopping bags. Just touching the outside bag of the woman on the left, and realising she had knocked it from her hand, she felt obliged to skid to a halt, apologise profusely and pick up the groceries strewn over the path.

"So sorry, but lucky no eggs," she said to the old woman as she picked up the shopping bag and tumbled the spilt goods back into it.

Emma did not feel quite so guilty when the woman snatched it back, and said, "Fucking little bitch, you shouldn't be riding like a mad woman down 'ere you know."

Apologising again despite the swearing, Emma leapt on her bike, the brief rest having relieved the aching chest and stitch and rode again like the devil himself was after her. As she zoomed onto the short stretch of road that led to the top of Castle Street where traffic lights directed traffic into or away from Reading, she swerved to a halt. Panting like a longhaired dog on a hot summer's day, she glanced along the road, surveying the long line of traffic waiting for the lights to change. Luckily for Emma, this part of the town was well known for long traffic jams as the lights at this interchange controlled the movement from four directions and was always busy.

Her heart leapt as she spotted a black Ford about five cars from the lights. Pulling up the anorak hood in case the woman spotted her and was alerted, she took out her mobile from her pocket.

The phone only rang three times before Dan answered.

"It's me," she said. "I'm at the top of Castle Hill, at the lights. I can see her car. If you hang on a sec, I can tell you whether she turns left or goes straight over. I'll just…"

"Emma, listen," interrupted Dan. "Stop now. I'll pass on this new information to the patrol cars. This woman is dangerous. Thanks for your help but leave us to do our job."

"Hey, the lights have just changed," Emma said, ignoring his words completely.

"Emma, listen to me. Please leave…"

"She's gone straight across the lights. She's going down Castle Hill. I gotta go and see what she does at the roundabout. I'll phone then."

She did not hear Dan repeat her name. Putting the mobile in her pocket, she pedalled madly on the pavement on the right side of the road, looking frantically for a break in the traffic flow so she would be on the same side as her quarry. Luckily, the downhill incline of the road helped her speed, whereas the traffic was moving sluggishly. Spying a pedestrian crossing about 50 yards ahead, she increased her pedalling, aware she was out of control, but determination made her foolhardy. As she swerved onto the crossing, causing a milk float to screech to a halt and producing a loud clinking of colliding bottles, she ignored the milkman's expletive, aware however that she deserved his anger.

On the other side of the road, she swung round, carefully missing the pedestrians, and was elated when she spotted the car again as it approached the lights and turned left along the town ring road.

Skidding to a halt at the lights, she grabbed her phone from her pocket and once again touched swiped the detective's number. This time he answered after two rings, and before he could utter a word, she explained the progress.

Once more Dan attempted to warn her off, but before he could finish his warning, she interrupted.

"I can see the car again. It's pulled into the right-hand lane, the turning to the multi-story car park that leads up to

Tescos. She's going shopping I bet. If she's been holed up at Loddon for days, bet she's run out of food. I'll see you in the car park or the store."

Ignoring the voice telling her he was only five minutes away and she must go home, she once more tossed the mobile into her pocket, and set out after the prey.

Chapter 92

Dan realised he could do nothing to dissuade the determined teenager. Swinging round the station roundabout towards the bottom road where a left turn would take him towards the multi-storey entrance, he speeded up, but the traffic was also slow moving here. Momentarily he cursed he had not brought a mobile blue light to stick on the top of his car before fathoming that the evil woman would have her eyes and ears peeled for police presence. That might alert her if she heard a siren.

The lights at the bottom of the road changed, and the cars infuriatingly inched forward. As the lights altered back to amber, the car in front slipped through. Normally this last-minute manoeuvre would have irritated Dan, but today was not a day to be picky. Checking no cars were coming from the right, he jumped the lights just as they turned red.

He gritted his teeth with annoyance when the queue of cars from the opposite direction in the centre lane feeding to the multi-storey were slow. This left lane was a subject of constant complaint about the ill-advised position of the carpark, and the store into which it fed. Dan had agreed about the inconvenience, but today, spotting a black Ford which he prayed was Van Looy's, he was glad that the constraints of the council's finances had won the day, and the contentious entrance to the store causing sluggish traffic progress enabled him today to catch up with his target.

Having the right of way, he drove into the car park entrance only three cars behind his quarry. His concentration prevented him from noticing the progress of a foolhardy cyclist weaving in and out of the cars towards him at breakneck speed on the other side of the road.

Yvette Van Looy sighed with relief as she safely entered the car park, deciding that to go to the top level might be the safest option. This floor was three stories above the supermarket, but the top floor had no lift to it, so the shoppers avoided parking there if possible. Plus, she had read in a local paper at one time that the protection balustrades were not considered high enough as there had been two suicide jumpers in the past year. The council advised people to avoid that floor. That was ideal for her needs. What possible interest suicides was to anyone, she couldn't conceive, but if it kept most of the shoppers elsewhere, that was fine with her.

Slowly threading her way up the various levels, she ignored the spaces and continued to the fifth floor. Relieved to see only two cars parked, she drove to the far end, as far away from them as possible.

Emma rode to the barrier, dismounted, and ducking underneath, hurriedly remounted and rode to the lift. Instinctively she knew that this Anti-Christ woman would park where she would have the least chance of being noticed and guessed that would be the controversial top floor. There were four separate lifts available to carry the shoppers to and from the supermarket entrance on the second floor and up to the next two floors. She was forced to wait until there were no shoppers using the lifts, as there was no way she could squeeze in her bike with other passengers. As she exited on the fourth floor, she noticed a navy-blue Honda swinging into the lane leading to the top floor. Butterflies of excitement swirled around her stomach as she leapt on her bike and gave chase, recognising the driver as the huge, red headed giant copper. All her effort went into keeping him in her sights; she was not going to let him have all the pleasure of ensnaring the She Devil who had stabbed her friend.

Dan eased onto the fifth storey. There were just two cars parked this end of the floor, but he saw the black Ford pulling into a space at the far end. He drove slowly towards it, hoping, if the driver was looking, he or she would just think he was deciding where to park. His heart leapt as he saw a woman exit the car. Even from a distance, her hair scraped back into a ponytail and wearing glasses, he recognised her immediately. For endless hours, he had studied the two characters of Nielson and Van Looy caught on the grainy pictures obtained from the security cameras. His eyes narrowed, she only vaguely resembled the woman who had abducted him as a kid as the years hadn't been kind to her, but it was her all right.

Gotcha, you bitch.

He gritted his teeth. His heart pumped so vigorously he could hardly catch his breath, and his chest hurt. It did not matter that he had been waiting for four years to see this person again. Before that, his waiting was even longer, almost twenty long years. The woman who had befriended him in the park all those years ago had been a beauty, long dark hair trailing down her back and a beautiful smile. He had learnt the hard way never to let loveliness deceive him again.

He recalled how she had helped him fly his kite. How she had enticed him into the van, yet the horrors of the following two days, always cloaked in a protective mist to safeguard his mind according to the psychologist, only gave him occasional nightmares now, but that evil event had shaped his life. Now the hour of retribution had arrived, his determination swept aside the mist. He remembered exactly all the details, all the horror, and most of all he recalled that four years ago when she had killed his best friend. Today he would make her pay big-time. He stopped thinking like a cop at that moment. Retribution for his childhood nightmare and his best friend's murder transformed him into a person intent on retaliation. He had been patient and relentless in his pursuit of her, and this day it had come to fruition.

As he stopped the car up a few yards away from where she had parked, and climbed out, she looked up. Although not immediately recognising him, something about his manner shook her to the core. The horror and fear on her face swept pleasure through his body equal to a sexual climax. He had waited so long for her to feel as she did.

Despite the shock, the woman did not intend to submit easily even though the giant of the man before her was a frightening opponent. Taking to her heels, she ran for the balustrade on the back part of the car park floor. Dropping her handbag on the floor, she turned back and using her arms, heaved herself onto the ledge behind the barrier. Dan sauntered towards her.

"There's nowhere to go, Yvette, nowhere to run."

"Fuck off, copper." Just ten yards along was the remains of a fire escape ladder. It had been sealed off to prevent anybody gaining access, and she knew if she got to it, she could slide down using the outside bars.

She drew her legs up onto the top bar and eased herself to a standing position. Like an acrobat, she stretched her arms out sideways to steady herself, and ease along the ledge towards the ladder.

"How quaint, turned into an eagle have we?" Dan smirked at her precarious situation. "Or should I say a vulture."

"Go to hell."

Keeping her eyes on the copper, she continued to edge her way along. Suddenly her foot slipped on pigeon droppings and she wavered as she wobbled, frantically keeping her arms outstretched to keep her upright. She bent her legs, but her unsteadiness grew. Her legs went from under her; she did not fall but slipped down the balustrade on the outside, her hands slithering down the controversial railings that intermittently decorated the wall. Determined, she grasped for the bottom horizontal rung, her knuckles white with effort.

He peered over. "Mm, interesting predicament."

"You're a stupid cop. You won't let me fall. It's not in your psyche, your policeman's soul won't allow it."

He lifted his foot the twelve inches to the rung on which she clung. Grinding his foot onto the fingers of the left hand, he watched with pleasure as the terror spread over her face. She still gripped on. He ground again so hard he heard her fingers break and as the pain and feeling departed, she let go.

"That's for 1994," he snarled.

Swinging out like an ungainly puppet on a broken swing, she desperately gripped on with her remaining hand.

Dan was suddenly aware of Emma.

Steadying herself on one long vertical bar, grasping Dan's arm for support she stepped up onto the concrete which the horizontal iron bars were slotted, her feet positioned either side of Van Looy's desperately clasping fingers.

He was amazed as he watched the girl place her shoe beside the fingers of the woman's last grasping hand, and then she slowly picked up her foot and ground it onto her fingers in the same way as he had. The woman wasn't giving in, and still clung on. Emma changed her tactics and eased the front of her shoe under the desperate woman's fingers, gradually pushing and manoeuvring until the fingertips inevitably slipped away.

"That's for Jose," snarled Emma. "No-one stabs my

mate on my watch, you fucking bitch."

The girl and the detective watched the woman fall; the pleasure enhanced by the impression of it happening in wonderful slow motion. They were on the fifth floor so as she plunged almost elegantly, arms outstretched, disbelief washed her face as she disappeared from their view. They hoped the last thing she saw in this life before she went to hell was their two smiling faces.

Emma turned to Dan. "I've waited a long time for that," she said.

"Not as long as me." He smiled. Holding up his hand, she grinned and returned his high five. "Right, I must close off this floor. This suicide will be investigated. Three suicides leaping from here in the past six months, it's not right. We warned the council the railings weren't high enough."

"Yes, quite right. Three suicides in the last six months you say, terrible."

She returned his smile. "You couldn't give me a lift home, could you? I've borrowed me sister's bike and the saddle's well hard. I've got a really sore bum."

Police sirens echoed up from the road on the other side of the car park.

"Sure, but I've obviously got to deal with this incident. You'll have to make a report."

Emma shrugged. "OK, don't mind, but I didn't see much. Just saw her fling herself off. Guilty conscience maybe?"

"Probably."

The redheaded giant copper and the petite, dark haired teenager made an unusual couple as they walked to his car.

As they ambled to the exit, Luke rushed up to his boss. "Thank God you're safe." Before Dan could reply, he asked. "Where is the bitch?"

"'Fraid we won't have the pleasure of arresting her, she threw herself off the top floor."

He shrugged. "Oh, ok, another suicide. Better phone for an ambulance I suppose."

"No hurry," his boss replied.

Chapter 93

Five Detectives, three Police Sergeants and twelve Police Constables poured into the local pub, all of whom had been involved in cracking the case of the missing women and children and catching the culprits. More officers who had worked behind the scenes were also on their way to the Hanging Man Pub. The landlord, although looking forward to the obvious profits produced by the evening, inwardly groaned as this many coppers meant a very raucous evening, as previous experience had demonstrated.

Dan had also invited Sara and Lucy whom he knew often had a drink here, after their evening yoga class at the local sports hall. Having made two dates with Lucy and then having to phone at the last minute and cancel because of unforeseen events occurring during the investigation, he was hoping this might be a fortuitous time to ply her with his charms and get a third chance. He didn't care if Aliens landed in Reading, nothing was going to stop him chatting her up and getting a firm date in the near future.

Adam Kennedy had invited his new fiancée, Daniella Lewis. Luke and Meena had met her two years ago when they and Adam had been investigating the case of three kidnapped children taken in retribution for the police's success in breaking up a nationwide paedophile operation. Dan had been working elsewhere and had never met her.

The team were pleased with this romantic step. His wife had died five years ago leaving him with two-year-old twins. Life had been harrowing for him, so his police friends were thrilled that life had taken a positive turn.

Luke and Meena's budding romance was still secret but they were both pleased to be there and in each other's company for the evening. Being unsure how their relationship would be viewed at the station, they were playing safe for the time being, deciding it was to remain a clandestine affair, which naturally made it even more exciting.

All the detectives were surprised that their guv had joined them. He was a good boss in many ways but being sociable wasn't top of his skills. They were pleased he had come but knew when the noise rose to a painful level, plus the inevitable jokes, especially Adam's distasteful Irish contributions, DI Cole would quietly slip home.

Dan was three pints down the throat when Sara and Lucy arrived, so he was feeling bold and insisted they had doubles when they both asked for a vodka and diet coke each. Sara could tell immediately what was going on, and as she had been trying to encourage the romance for some time, she didn't protest. Lucy, after years of caution, knew if she didn't demolish the protective wall that she had built around herself to prevent any risky relationship, she was going to end up a lonely and sad soul. She had made a resolution to stop fighting off people, and as she found Dan very attractive, was determined to let the friendship develop, if that's what he wanted. By the big grin all over his good-looking face, tonight was a beginning of that new era.

Sara sidled away, leaving Dan and Lucy on their own. She spied Adam on his way over, so she caught his arm and whispered, "Leave them alone for a few minutes. He's always caught up in an investigation and she's Miss Ultra Cautious. I'm hoping tonight, progress might be made, so give him a few minutes to chat her up." They wandered away, leaving the way clear for Dan to make progress.

Adam took Sara's arm and said, "Come on over to the corner and I'll introduce you to my new missus…well, fiancée as you females like to say."

He introduced the two women and Sara enquired how they had met.

"I work at Radio Star, the Radio station along the Bath Road. Adam came into the station to talk about a young girl who had gone missing, attempting to jog people's memories should they have noticed anything. One thing led to another and here we are today".

Sara noticed Danny's beautiful auburn hair and appreciated how her looks might well have attracted the young police detective.

"Ok, ladies, enough of that female gossip," interrupted Adam. "Sara, you still trying to get the big fella hitched up with Lucy Hamilton cos I assume that's why you dragged me away when I was just gonna buy the big fellah a well-deserved drink?"

His smooth Irish accent caused Sara to smile. "Yes, I confess I am," she replied. "He'd made two dates apparently but the investigation, as usual, got in the way and he couldn't manage either of them. I'm determined tonight he's going to make progress."

"Looks like your wish might come true," murmured Danny. All three glanced across at the couple.

Lucy had been sipping her drink when she watched Sara sidle away, and said to her apparent admirer "Well, that wasn't obvious then, was it."

Dan grinned, shrugged his agreement before saying. "She's been trying to match-make for me these last four years or so. Mind you, I don't think anyone she dragged in particularly liked me, and it didn't matter 'cos I didn't find them attractive either." Leaning forward, he stared into her eyes before saying, "Now you, Miss Lucy Hamilton, are a different kettle of fish, I…"

"No, my name's Polly Ayres." She gulped. "Oh God, that slipped out…"

Dan's pint glass, halfway to his mouth, stopped where it was. His mouth fell open. Lucy could see from his expression that his mind was whirling. She added, "Bit before your police life, so you probably don't remember."

He placed his glass back on the bar. She noticed he had paled.

"Christ, that explains…well, explains a lot."

"In what way?"

He was still staring at her. "Were you…are you in Police Protective Custody?" At her nod, he continued. "In what way…well, for instance, being told out of the blue to stop investigating you by my DI…umm, then your attitude…the big, big defence wall you've constructed round yourself… no-one gets in. When did you stop being Polly Ayres?"

"2001, I was eight."

"Umm, so why the change of mind, or change of tactic?"

"I suddenly realised no-one cared who or where I was. I wasn't the centre of anyone's search. No-one was interested in me anymore and I had to stop the obsessive, bordering on the neurotic position or I'd be on my own for ever. I'm twenty-eight years old and I want to start enjoying my life without carrying this hump of fear on my back."

Dan stared and she began to feel uncomfortable at his penetrating glance.

"You're looking at me like the old days, like a suspicious copper."

Her words seemed to break the spell, and a slight smile crossed his lips. "Good, good," he murmured. "So, what do I call you, Lucy or Polly?"

"I'm used to Lucy and I am Lucy now I guess."

"OK. Dunno if this is the time or place, but while we're on the subject of change…well, fellows don't often notice this kind of things, but…" He paused. "You look different today. What is it?"

"My hair, maybe? I was dark brown, now I'm back to my natural. Sara calls it chestnut."

"How do you females manage to do that?"

"Well, I un-dyed it. This is the real me."

He laughed aloud. "Un-dyed, never heard that word before."

She leaned towards him. "See anything else? The eyes…the colour." When he looked blank, she added, "They're green. The blue colour contact lenses have also gone. What you see is the original Polly, now Lucy, twenty-eight and looking forward to a new life."

"Well, I'm not rushing things, but if we had kids, with my ginger hair, yours being chestnut or whatever, and both having green eyes, we'd have ginger, green eyed kids. "

They both laughed. The banter continued.

"Kids! Now you're joking! Jesus, every date you've ever made with me has never materialised. We're never in a position of any sort to have kids. You know, that means being close in a male, female mating sorta way."

His grin widened. He liked this repartee. Leaning as near to her as he could, he whispered, "I'm trying to leer at you. I think you're talking about sex. I like that sort of talk."

"Good, you've got the gist."

He was just about to kiss her, when someone tapped him on the shoulder.

"Boss, you're never going to believe this."

Turning around, Luke, Meena and Adam were staring at him. A feeling deep in his stomach churned and their pale faces added to his apprehension.

"We've just heard. She's gone," said Luke.

"Who's gone?"

"Van Looy. The she-devil."

"How can she be gone, she's dead? You mean her body's gone from the morgue?"

"Boss, she never got to the morgue. In the ambulance,

one of the guys noticed a faint pulse so they had to take her to the hospital. She's been on a resuscitator although they never expected her to regain consciousness or live with her injuries."

"Why weren't we informed?"

"I don't know, boss," added Meena.

Dan shook his head. "No, no, she can't possibly survive that fall. I don't believe…"

"Unless…" murmured Luke.

"Unless what?"

"We called her the she-devil. Alfie Smith, the gifted kid, saw black halos round her head." He glanced around at her three colleagues, and whispered, "She's not dead because she *is* the devil, and the devil can't be killed."

◆

Printed in Great Britain
by Amazon

45140343R00274